Praise for Michael Moo

"A mythological cycle . . . Highly relevant to the twentieth
century . . . The figure of Elric often resembles many purely
contemporary figureheads from Charles Manson to James Dean."
—*Time Out*

"Elric is back! Herald the event!"
—*Los Angeles Daily News* on *The Fortress of the Pearl*

"[The Elric] novels are totally enthralling."
—*Midwest Book Review*

"Among the most memorable characters in fantasy literature."
—*Science Fiction Chronicle*

"If you are at all interested in fantastic fiction, you must
read Michael Moorcock. He changed the field
single-handedly: He is a giant."
—Tad Williams

"A work of powerful and sustained imagination . . . The vast,
tragic symbols by which Mr. Moorcock continually illuminates
the metaphysical quest of his hero are a measure
of the author's remarkable talents."
—J. G. Ballard, author of *Crash*

"A giant of fantasy."
—*Kirkus Reviews*

"A superb writer."
—*Locus*

DUKE ELRIC

DATE DUE		

DUKE ELRIC

CHRONICLES OF THE
LAST EMPEROR OF MELNIBONÉ

—— VOLUME 4 ——

Michael Moorcock

FULLY ILLUSTRATED BY JUSTIN SWEET

BALLANTINE BOOKS · NEW YORK

A Del Rey Trade Paperback Original

Published in the United States by Del Rey,
an imprint of The Random House Publishing Group,
a division of Random House, Inc., New York.

Del Rey is a registered trademark and the Del Rey colophon
is a trademark of Random House, Inc.

The stories contained in this work originally appeared in
various science fiction magazines and books, as noted on the
following acknowledgments page.

ISBN 978–0–345–49865–6

Printed in the United States of America

www.delreybooks.com

2 4 6 8 9 7 5 3 1

Book design by Julie Schroeder

To my oldest collaborator,
Jim Cawthorn

CONTENTS

Foreword by Michael Chabon.................................. xv

Introduction.. xvii

THE SAILOR ON THE SEAS OF FATE 3

Audiorealms Introduction 5

The Sailor on the Seas of Fate 10

DUKE ELRIC 163

Introduction to Duke Elric................................... 164

Duke Elric.. 165

ASPECTS OF FANTASY (2) 261

THE FLANEUR DES ARCADES DE L'OPERA................. 273

ELRIC: A PERSONALITY AT WAR 323

ORIGINS 329

Early artwork associated with Elric's first appearances
   in magazines and books

FOREWORD

by Michael Chabon

The minor masterpiece at the heart of this volume, *The Sailor on the Seas of Fate,* like almost all of Michael Moorcock's efforts in the subgenre of heroic fantasy, is a complicated work, in the original sense of the term: that is, it *folds together,* with an insight both sophisticated and intuitive, 1) an apparently simple adventure story told in three episodes that are themselves interleaved in puzzling ways; 2) a sharp critique, of adventure stories generally (with their traditional freight of cruelty, wish fulfillment, sexism, and violence), and of the heroic fantasy mode in particular; and 3) a remarkable working out (independently one feels of the work of Joseph Campbell) of the Transcendentalist premise that, as Emerson wrote, "one person wrote all the books." Moorcock took this literary universalism, with its implied corollary that one person *reads* all the books, and in *Sailor* began his career-long demonstration of the logical conclusion that all the books are one book, and all the heroes one hero (or antihero). From here it is only a short step, which the reader of heroic fantasy is eager to make, to the proposition that all readers and all writers are Odysseus, or Kull, or Elric of Melniboné, sharing through the acts of reading and writing a single essential, eternal heroic nature. This nature links us—all we heroes and Moorcocks—across all eras and lands. One might even attempt to chart these interconnections of story, hero, reader, and writer on a single map: Moorcock is such a cartographer. He called his map of our story-shaped world "the Multiverse."

It was Moorcock's insight, and it has been his remarkable artistic accomplishment, not just to complicate all this apparatus and insight and storytelling prowess, packing into one short novel such diverting fare as speculation on ontology and determinism, gory subterranean duels with giant killer baboons, literary criticism (the murmuring soul-vampiric sword Stormbringer offers what is essentially a running commentary on the equivocal nature of heroic swordsmen in fiction), buildings that are really alien beings, and ruminations on the self-similar or endlessly reflective interrelationship of hero, writer, and reader; but to do so with an almost offhanded ease, with a strong, plain, and unaffected English prose style that was nearing its peak in the mid-seventies.

That's part of what I would have liked to tell Michael Moorcock, when I recently had the good fortune to attend the Nebula Awards ceremony, in Austin, Texas, and watch him receive a Grandmaster Award. I would have liked to tell him that when I was fourteen years old I found profound comfort in feeling that I shared in the nature of lost and wandering Elric, isolated but hungering for connection, heroically curious, apparently weak but capable of surprising power, unready and unwilling to sit on the moldering throne of his fathers but having nothing certain to offer in its stead. I would have liked to tell him that his work as a critic, as an editor, and as a writer has made it easier for me and a whole generation of us to roam the "moonbeam roads" of the literary multiverse. But as Mike rose to accept his award all I could do was sit there, next to him—marveling down to the deepest most twisted strands of my literary DNA—and applaud.

INTRODUCTION

During the 1970s I could have asked almost any money I wanted for an Elric book, but I still preferred to write Elric stories for friends who were running anthologies or starting up new magazines. "The Singing Citadel" was written for Sprague de Camp's *Fantastic Swordsmen,* and "The Jade Man's Eyes" was written for my friend, the poet Bill Butler, who ran a funky bookstore in Brighton and a small press that published offbeat writing of all kinds. I had become used, I suppose, to the ethic of the 1960s, when, in many places, altruism was pretty active and if you had a little money, you spread it around. Though I spent comparatively little time in a commune, I still believed in the community.

By 1971, when *The Sleeping Sorceress* came out, Hawkwind, a rather colourful bunch of musical outlaws, were being noticed for having played for nothing outside the famous (or infamous) Isle of Wight Festival. They were also beginning to be heard around Notting Hill/Ladbroke Grove, where I lived, which was then pretty much the nerve centre of British rock and roll and the alternative press. *Oz, IT, Frendz,* and others, including my own *New Worlds,* were all grouped within the same quarter mile and the Mountain Grill, the café where bands habitually met up before boarding a bus to start on a tour, was only two or three shops down from us.

The Grove was more or less the equivalent of the Haight in San Francisco, with a similar history. It was a little dangerous, run-down, famous for its race riots and high percentage of druggies, villains, creative people, and immigrants, with appropriately low rents.... I had lived there since the late 1950s. By 1970, Elric was almost the Grove's main ikon, and Hawkwind's name was borrowed from my Hawkmoon books. The band took inspiration from my work as, I was told, many did, from Deep Purple to Mark Bolan's T Rex. Even Bernie Taupin claimed that reading my stuff inspired the songs he was then writing for Elton John! My friend Bill Harry, who had first published John Lennon in his music paper *Mersey Beat,* brought me and Pink Floyd together. We spent two days visiting early electronic music studios (including Ron Grainer's BBC Radiophonic Workshop, creators of the *Dr. Who* theme) for no reason any of us could work out. There was a sense in the air that we could produce complex, ambitious work that, like *Sgt. Pepper,* would also begin to break down cultural barriers. It was in our blood. I know it was. I came from South London, and half the people you grew up with became musicians, while if you didn't own a copies of Sartre and Camus, you were considered impoverished.

By 1970, then, I was used to a lot of public attention and not especially flattered by most of it. I avoided one notoriously egomaniacal rock star's white Rolls-Royce by mounting the kerb on my bike and making for a pedestrian-only zone as he called after me. I was inclined to avoid musicians I didn't know very well. For various reasons, however, I got on very well with Hawkwind from the beginning. We were natural allies. I wrote material for them like "Sonic Attack," and first performed it with them under the Westway, the stretch of motorway that now crossed the Grove. We perceived a political atmosphere seriously needing new ideas and a Paranoid Authority, increasingly resistant to the public will. I was soon performing with Hawkwind on a fairly regular basis. At that time I didn't write any specific Elric material for the band, but I helped produce an Eternal Champion concept album in *Warrior on the Edge of Time,* a title whose resonance, like *Stormbringer,* was later echoed by other writers' titles. The record was a best seller for the band and remains one of the most popular Hawkwind titles. A little later I would write "Black Blade" for my own band, the Deep Fix. Our first performance was at the Roundhouse during Nik Turner's Bohemian Love-In, which was more proto-punk than late hippy in atmosphere, and it would be recorded in a somewhat different version by my friend Eric Bloom with Blue Öyster Cult.

People who want to get an idea of what we sounded like can obtain the albums on CD, though I still think we did a messy, fussy production on the Deep Fix's *The New World's Fair*! You can hear cleaner versions on *Roller Coaster Holiday.* I'd also recommend the excellent compilation album of Grove bands and performers *Cries from the Midnight Circus.*

The association between Elric and rock music started early, but nobody would begin to do audio versions of the books until this century, when AudioRealms, who have also done Lovecraft and Howard audiobooks, decided to produce unabridged Elric books beginning with *Elric of Melniboné* and finishing with *Stormbringer.* I hope to collect "Black Blade" in a later book. We have, however, included here the original material I recorded for the audio version introducing *The Sailor on the Seas of Fate,* which I rewrote to include two other novellas, using the story to tie the Elric saga into the overall Eternal Champion sequence.

In the late '90s I would begin writing a new kind of Elric story, some of which was set in the historical past, and it seems appropriate to include it here. I decided to break the rule of trying to include material as it originally appeared. It would, we realized, overload future volumes if we saved *Duke Elric,* so we decided to include it here. One episode can't be traced, so John Davey kindly restored it from the published version that ran three parallel stories as *Michael Moorcock's Multiverse,* brought out in 1999 by DC. There have been discussions about creating a complex musical version of the story, but so far nobody has had the time and energy to do so.

Writing was my primary profession, so it would be some while before, with Hawkwind, I would start work on the two-disc concept that first toured and then appeared as *The Chronicle of the Black Sword.* The record is generally available, but I also hope to reprint some of those lyrics in a later volume.

The 1970s were a heady time for my friends and me. We were in our pomp. We wore wild, romantic clothes derived from the Pre-Raphaelites. Artists, too, were rediscovering all the great nineteenth-century romantic painters and illustrators. The first goths were coming into their own; the punks, a whole new shot in the arm for English culture, had turned up. Yet somehow, in spite of a few punks using me as an ikon of their disgust, Elric seemed to move smoothly into the new era. Indeed, through the '70s there were more comics, posters, post-cards, games, and the rest than ever before. The great Michael Whelan covers still adorned the DAW versions of the U.S. Elric books (and others), and Rodney Matthews's images of Elric dominated the U.K. Rock songs continued to be written about him. Readers continued to ask for new stories. I sympathized with anyone who felt they were suffering Elric overkill.

Famously, Conan Doyle became heartily sick of Sherlock Holmes, the character on whom his fortune was founded. He cursed having to write new episodes of the Great Detective's adventures. Many less popular authors have continued to bemoan the burden of successful characters and books, apparently forgetting that they have done something quite remarkable in adding significantly to the world's myths and folk tales.

Interviewers frequently ask if I, too, feel sick of Elric, and I can honestly say that I have never regarded Elric as a burden of any kind. I never saw him as an embarrassingly rich, vulgar relative on whose bounty I live in rather higher style than otherwise. I continue to write about him, if I have an idea that suits him. My only fear is that readers will stop finding the stories as vital as before. I'm heartened by his continued translation, sometimes retranslation, into most European languages, from the Balkans to the Baltic and many other languages, including Hebrew and Japanese. I have never, as far as I recall, won a literary prize for Elric, and Elric is rarely listed when people mention my literary accomplishments. Yet I did my best with him, in the circumstances, and I tried to improve the writing, widen the horizon, develop characters, and fill in backgrounds, histories, and cultures, as well as, in some way, I hope, widen the possibilities of epic fantasy as it was then constituted.

As readers will see, Elric continued to attract first-class illustrators, some of whom I chose to work with and some who were commissioned by publishers. I have admired Justin Sweet since I saw his illustrations for Howard's Solomon Kane stories and was so pleased to find that Betsy Mitchell, my editor at Del Rey, also liked him and was happy to commission him, too. I'm sure readers will enjoy his work as much as I do.

I should again like to mention the work of the series editor, John Davey, and the great help we received from Savoy Books of Manchester, who have preserved much of the archive material reprinted here. No substantial edition of these books could exist without their contributions. Much hard work, not least by Betsy Mitchell and her team at Del Rey, has been done to ensure that these are the fullest editions possible. And then, of course, there's Michael Chabon, a writer of the first class, whose work I have been reading since *The Mysteries of Pittsburgh.* It's an enormous honour to be introduced by a man whose talent is immeasurable and who is doing so much to break down the flimsy but enduring walls between the worlds of literary and popular fiction. Thank you.

Michael Moorcock
The Old Circle Squared
Lost Pines, Texas
March 2008

DUKE ELRIC

THE SAILOR
ON THE SEAS OF FATE

THE SAILOR ON THE SEAS OF FATE

THERE IS A subject discussed frequently by Melniboné's philosophers concerning the number of worlds in the universe and how many universes make up the multiverse. ("Planes" is a more common word they employ, since they do not have the notion of worlds as globes.)

Some believe these can be visited in dreams and reached by the moonbeam roads that run between the worlds. Thus they have developed their sophisticated method of the dream couches, where certain privileged aristocrats lie to dream the dreams of years, centuries, even millennia, in a few hours.

Elric, who had in his youth learned his sorcerous skills on the dream couches of Imrryr, no longer remembered his experience of the moonbeam roads, so the nature of the universe was again a mystery to him, though sometimes a memory would return as a nightmare that would bring him screaming back to wakefulness.

After the events already recorded, Elric determined to explore the lands that surrounded his own, deeming it a matter of common sense to understand the nature of those who, realistically, were planning the destruction of his world and his family with it.

In fact, it is likely the young albino was moved as much by curiosity as moral purpose. Yet who of us at his age is entirely sure of the reason for their actions? Let us accept the reasons he gave and concern ourselves instead with other matters.

Elric had one recurring dream that disturbed his nights. He dreamed he returned to a Melniboné made even stranger and more bizarre under his cousin Yyrkoon's rule. Almost nothing was entirely familiar to him. The great towers of Imrryr were warped and twisted into a troubling architecture that seemed to reflect the mental states of those gone entirely mad. Unnatural beasts prowled the serpentine streets, and gigantic, demonic creatures lolled in the city squares. The palaces had grown huge, to accommodate those newcomers, and Melnibonéans were dwarfed to the size of ants in comparison.

Where Elric's kinfolk had once lived now dwelled creatures of cryptic biology, with carapaces encrusted with carbuncular jewels and organs that throbbed upon the surface of their bodies, with vast, multi-faceted eyes that seemed blind and yet looked into worlds no other could see, with a multitude of arms and legs and other limbs whose function was impossible to guess. Bizarre creatures of Chaos ran through corridors that had become labyrinths, and in the rewrought chambers of the towers Melnibonéans driven mad by their exposure to these new demons feasted on unnatural food and pleasured themselves in even stranger ways. Cries of horror and pain were the perpetual music filling this Melniboné.

In this dream, Elric made his way to the great throne chamber where Yyrkoon, gaunt and crazed, enjoyed intercourse with his demonic allies and lived in a state of perpetual celebration. Clearly he took no delight in Elric's arrival.

"Where is your sister?" demanded the albino. "Where is my betrothed?"

And Yyrkoon at last, reluctantly, sent for her. The woman who came to the throne chamber was only barely recognizable to Elric. She was dressed in heavy clothing encrusted with gold, silver, and platinum. She could barely move, and her eyes were drugged. Little, dwarfish creatures carried her train and crept in and out of her clothing, adjusting this, altering that. When she saw Elric she smiled, and it was a hideous travesty, clear to Elric that she was under an enchantment.

In the dream, Elric led his beloved away from the throne chamber, past ornamental pools where his dragon brothers, the Phoorn, seemed imprisoned. Once, Flamefang, his closest dragon kin, rose from the coruscating liquid and addressed him.

"We are all slaves of Chaos now, dear lord. All slaves of this nightmare." But he promised that when Elric and Cymoril wished to leave he would try to carry them on his back to safety. *"Though this stuff which is not water, it corrodes us in such strange ways."*

Then Elric found himself in a great chamber filled by an enormous bed carved with obscene figures. Cymoril spoke to him in an unfamiliar language. Her lovemaking was that of a stranger. When he did understand her words, he scarcely understood their meaning. Her tongue was thick, as if she had forgotten the High Speech of Melniboné.

"He told me that Arioch had killed you, and eaten your sword."

And when Elric looked up through the canopy of that strange bed, he saw eyes he recognized. They were the mocking, triumphant, sardonic eyes of Arioch himself.

They lay together in that bridal chamber. Some might have considered it ostentatious. Some might have found it terrifying. Elric hardly saw the carvings and the decorations for he was filled with complex premonitions.

"We shall be married, now you are returned to Melniboné," said Cymoril.

And on those words, always, Elric would awake, wondering in panic if he should not return at once to Melniboné, break his word, and reclaim his throne. He feared that his actions had already produced cosmic reverberations of unprecedented significance. But circumstances led him in other directions. Try as he might, he could not find the way home. And eventually he reconciled himself to the fact that his destiny lay elsewhere, that there were things he must do, things he must learn, before he could ever return.

In his wakeful moments, when his sense of reality was restored, he told himself that only by mingling with the people of the Young Kingdoms would he learn what he needed. But as is often the case when the powerful design to learn the secrets of the powerless, his condescension was resented, his company rejected. Like so many before and after him, he discovered what a distance his power put between himself and those he envied.

Envy comprised much of what he felt for people he regarded as less complicated souls, leading simpler lives than his own and carrying less complex burdens. Elric was too young, too self-involved, to realize that only to him were those problems less complex, and that those he envied actually envied him his power, which, from their particular perspective, would if possessed by them entirely simplify and improve their lives.

Beyond the walls of Elric's particular plane, the Lords of the Higher Worlds continued to plot and plan not only Elric's fate but that of his people, their friends and enemies. The machinations of those called "gods" would lead Elric to explore some of the other worlds of the multiverse, falling into the power of legendary Agak and Gagak, encountering the dead Melnibonéan earl Saxif D'Aan, and learning still more of his people's past: Of the mysterious blind captain who steered the ship of fate: And, most important, of the Eternal Champion, of whom he was an avatar.

Other avatars he would meet were called Corum, Erekosë, Hawkmoon, champions whom some knew as the Three Who Are One, before his joining them. Whereupon, naturally enough, they became the Four Who Are One. All these men were bound upon quests of their own. All sought fabled Tanelorn, where it is said the Champion Eternal shall find eternal peace.

They dreamed of Tanelorn. They desired Tanelorn as some men desired women and others desired wealth. They longed for Tanelorn as a place they had lost, perhaps before they were born. As a place that, like Paradise, might not by definition exist at all.

Tanelorn. Some called it the City of Eternal Rest, beloved of those who welcome death. Some, of a simpler and perhaps more cynical disposition, say it is indeed no more than another name for the grave.

But I can tell you that Tanelorn is a powerful dream. It is what causes great heroes and heroines to perform great deeds. It is what raises us above the Lords of the Higher Worlds and makes us, poor mortals that we are, something nobler and more powerful than any who seek to control our destinies.

Dream Tanelorn might be to some of us, but to others it is a reality we have molded from the stuff of imagination and that stands for all

our idealism, all our fine ambitions, all our yearnings, and all our nobler selves. Though we spend many lifetimes seeking Tanelorn, find
her at last we shall. And there, as we are promised, we shall know not
only peace, but wisdom and security.

But the building of that city shall take many great dreams and
much courage, and you can be sure that not a single drop of savagely
spilled blood will taint a single brick or stone of her.

So now begins another tale of the albino.

Forgetting as best he could his cousin Yyrkoon sitting as regent
upon the Ruby Throne of Melniboné, suppressing all thoughts of his
beautiful cousin Cymoril weeping for him and despairing of his ever
returning, Elric went to seek an unknown goal in the worlds of the
Young Kingdoms where Melnibonéans were, at best, disliked.

And it would not be long before he found himself sailing upon the
mysterious seas of fate. What he found upon those seas is the substance
of this story.

THE SAILOR ON THE SEAS OF FATE

(1976)

For Bill Butler, Mike and Tony, and
all at Unicorn Books, Wales

BOOK ONE

SAILING TO THE FUTURE

CHAPTER ONE

IT WAS AS IF the man stood in a vast cavern whose walls and roof were composed of gloomy, unstable colours which would occasionally break and admit rays of light from the moon. That these walls were mere clouds massed above mountains and ocean was hard to believe, for all that the moonlight pierced them, stained them and revealed the black and turbulent sea washing the shore on which the man now stood.

Distant thunder rolled; distant lightning flickered. A thin rain fell. And the clouds were never still. From dusky jet to deadly white they swirled slowly, like the cloaks of men and women engaged in a trance-like and formalistic minuet; the man standing on the shingle of the grim beach was reminded of giants dancing to the music of the faraway storm and felt as one must feel who walks unwittingly into a hall where the gods are at play. He turned his gaze from the clouds to the ocean.

The sea seemed weary. Great waves heaved themselves together with difficulty and collapsed as if in relief, gasping as they struck sharp rocks.

The man pulled his hood closer about his face and he looked over his leathern shoulder more than once as he trudged closer to the sea and let the surf spill upon the toes of his knee-length black boots. He tried to peer into the cavern formed by the clouds but could see only a short distance. There was no way of telling what lay on the other side of the ocean or, indeed, how far the water extended. He put his head on one side, listening carefully, but could hear nothing but the sounds of the sky and the sea. He sighed. For a moment a moonbeam touched him and from the white flesh of his face there glowed two crimson, tormented eyes; then darkness came back. Again the man turned, plainly fearing that the light had revealed him to some enemy. Making as little sound as possible, he headed towards the shelter of the rocks on his left.

Elric was tired. In the city of Ryfel in the land of Pikarayd he had naïvely sought acceptance by offering his services as a mercenary in the army of the governor of that place. For his foolishness he had been imprisoned as a Melnibonéan spy (it was obvious to the governor that Elric could be nothing else) and had but recently escaped with the aid of bribes and some minor sorcery.

The pursuit, however, had been almost immediate. Dogs of great cunning had been employed and the governor himself had led the hunt beyond the borders of Pikarayd and into the lonely, uninhabited shale valleys of a world locally called the Dead Hills, in which little grew or tried to live.

Up the steep sides of small mountains, whose slopes consisted of grey, crumbling slate, which made a clatter to be heard a mile or more away, the white-faced one had ridden. Along dales all but grassless and whose river-bottoms had seen no water for scores of years, through cave-tunnels bare of even a stalactite, over plateaux from which rose cairns of stones erected by a forgotten folk, he had sought to escape his pursuers, and soon it seemed to him that he had left the world he knew for ever, that he had crossed a supernatural frontier and had arrived in one of those bleak places of which he had read in the legends of his people, where once Law and Chaos had fought each other to a stalemate, leaving their battleground empty of life and the possibility of life.

And at last he had ridden his horse so hard that its heart had burst and he had abandoned its corpse and continued on foot, panting to the sea, to this narrow beach, unable to go farther forward and fearing to return lest his enemies should be lying in wait for him.

He would give much for a boat now. It would not be long before the dogs discovered his scent and led their masters to the beach. He shrugged. Best to die here alone, perhaps, slaughtered by those who did not even know his name. His only regret would be that Cymoril would wonder why he had not returned at the end of the year.

He had no food and few of the drugs which had of late sustained his energy. Without renewed energy he could not contemplate working a sorcery which might conjure for him some means of crossing the sea and making, perhaps, for the Isle of the Purple Towns where the people were least unfriendly to Melnibonéans.

It had been months since he had left behind his court and his queen-to-be, letting Yyrkoon sit on the throne of Melniboné until his return. He had thought he might learn more of the human folk of the Young Kingdoms by mixing with them, but they had rejected him either with outright hatred or wary and insincere humility. Nowhere had he found one willing to believe that a Melnibonéan (and they did not know he was the emperor) would willingly throw in his lot with the human beings who had once been in thrall to that cruel and ancient race. And now, as he stood beside a bleak sea feeling trapped and already defeated, he knew himself to be alone in a malevolent universe, bereft of friends and purpose, a useless, sickly anachronism, a fool brought low by his own insufficiencies of character, by his profound inability to believe wholly in the rightness or the wrongness of anything at all. He lacked faith in his race, in his birthright, in gods or men, and above all he lacked faith in himself.

His pace slackened; his hand fell upon the pommel of his black runesword. Stormbringer, seemingly half-sentient, was now his only companion, his only confidant, and it had become his neurotic habit to talk to the sword as another might talk to his horse or as a prisoner might share his thoughts with a cockroach in his cell.

"Well, Stormbringer, shall we walk into the sea and end it now?" His voice was dead, barely a whisper. "At least we shall have the pleasure of thwarting those who follow us."

He made a half-hearted movement toward the sea, but to his fatigued brain it seemed that the sword murmured, stirred against his hip, pulled back. The albino chuckled. "You exist to live and to take lives. Do I exist, then, to die and bring both those I love and hate the mercy of death? Sometimes I think so. A sad pattern, if that should be the pattern. Yet there must be more to all this . . ."

He turned his back upon the sea, peering upward at the monstrous clouds forming and re-forming above his head, letting the light rain fall upon his face, listening to the complex, melancholy music which the sea made as it washed over rocks and shingle and was carried this way and that by conflicting currents. The rain did little to refresh him. He had not slept at all for two nights and had slept hardly at all for several more. He must have ridden for almost a week before his horse collapsed.

At the base of a damp granite crag which rose nearly thirty feet above his head, he found a depression in the ground in which he could squat and be protected from the worst of the wind and the rain. Wrapping his heavy leather cloak tightly about him, he eased himself into the hole and was immediately asleep. Let them find him while he slept. He wanted no warning of his death.

Harsh, grey light struck his eyes as he stirred. He raised his neck, holding back a groan at the stiffness of his muscles, and he opened his eyes. He blinked. It was morning—perhaps even later, for the sun was invisible—and a cold mist covered the beach. Through the mist the darker clouds could still be seen above, increasing the effect of his being inside a huge cavern. Muffled a little, the sea continued to splash and hiss, though it seemed calmer than it had on the previous night, and there were now no sounds of a storm. The air was very cold.

Elric began to stand up, leaning on his sword for support, listening carefully, but there was no sign that his enemies were close by. Doubtless they had given up the chase, perhaps after finding his dead horse.

He reached into his belt pouch and took from it a sliver of smoked bacon and a vial of yellowish liquid. He sipped from the vial, replaced the stopper, and returned the vial to his pouch as he chewed on the meat. He was thirsty. He trudged further up the beach and found a pool of rainwater not too tainted with salt. He drank his fill, staring around him. The mist was fairly thick and if he moved too far from the beach he knew he would become immediately lost. Yet did that matter? He had nowhere to go. Those who had pursued him must have realized that. Without a horse he could not cross back to Pikarayd, the most easterly of the Young Kingdoms. Without a boat he could not venture onto that sea and try to steer a course back to the Isle of the Purple Towns. He recalled no map which showed an eastern sea and he had little idea of how far he had traveled from Pikarayd. He decided that his only hope of surviving was to go north, following the coast in the trust that sooner or later he would come upon a port or a fishing village where he might trade his few remaining belongings for a passage on a boat. Yet that hope was a small one, for his food and his drugs could hardly last more than a day or so.

He took a deep breath to steel himself for the march and then regretted it; the mist cut at his throat and his lungs like a thousand tiny knives. He coughed. He spat upon the shingle.

And he heard something: something other than the moody whisperings of the sea; a regular creaking sound, as of a man walking in stiff leather. His right hand went to his left hip and the sword which rested there. He turned about, peering in every direction for the source of the noise, but the mist distorted it. It could have come from anywhere.

Elric crept back to the rock where he had sheltered. He leaned against it so that no swordsman could take him unawares from behind. He waited.

The creaking came again, but other sounds were added. He heard a clanking; a splash; perhaps a voice, perhaps a footfall on timber; and he guessed that either he was experiencing a hallucination as a side effect of the drug he had just swallowed or he had heard a ship coming towards the beach and dropping its anchor.

He felt relieved and he was tempted to laugh at himself for assuming so readily that this coast must be uninhabited. He had thought that the bleak cliffs stretched for miles—perhaps hundreds of miles—in all directions. The assumption could easily have been the subjective result of his depression, his weariness. It occurred to him that he might as easily have discovered a land not shown on maps, yet with a sophisticated culture of its own: with sailing ships, for instance, and harbours for them. Yet still he did not reveal himself.

Instead he withdrew behind the rock, peering into the mist towards the sea. And at last he discerned a shadow which had not been there the previous night. A black, angular shadow which could only be a ship. He made out the suggestion of ropes, he heard men grunting, he heard the creak and the rasp of a yard as it traveled up a mast. The sail was being furled.

Elric waited at least an hour, expecting the crew of the ship to disembark. They could have no other reason for entering this treacherous bay. But a silence had descended, as if the whole ship slept.

Cautiously Elric emerged from behind the rock and walked down to the edge of the sea. Now he could see the ship a little more clearly. Red sunlight was behind it, thin and watery, diffused by the mist. It was a good-sized ship and fashioned throughout of the same dark wood. Its design was baroque and unfamiliar, with high decks fore and aft and no evidence of rowing ports. This was unusual in a ship either of Melnibonéan or Young Kingdoms design and it tended to prove his theory that he had stumbled upon a civilization for some reason cut off from the rest of the world, just as Elwher and the Unmapped East were cut off by the vast stretches of the Sighing Desert and the Weeping Waste. He saw no movement aboard, heard none of the sounds one might usually expect to hear on a sea-going ship, even if the larger part of the crew was resting. The mist eddied and more of the red light poured through to illuminate the vessel, revealing the large wheels on both the foredeck and the rear-deck, the slender mast with its furled sail, the complicated geometrical carvings of its rails and its figurehead, the great, curving prow which gave the ship its main impression of power and strength and made Elric think it must be a warship rather than a trading vessel. But who was there to fight in such waters as these?

He cast aside his wariness and cupped his hands about his mouth, calling out:

"Hail, the ship!"

The answering silence seemed to him to take on a peculiar hesitancy as if those on board heard him and wondered if they should answer.

"Hail, the ship!"

Then a figure appeared on the port rail and, leaning over, looked casually towards him. The figure had on armour as dark and as strange

as the design of his ship; he had a helmet obscuring most of his face and the main feature that Elric could distinguish was a thick, golden beard and sharp blue eyes.

"Hail, the shore," said the armoured man. His accent was unknown to Elric, his tone was as casual as his manner. Elric thought he smiled. "What do you seek with us?"

"Aid," said Elric. "I am stranded here. My horse is dead. I am lost."

"Lost? Aha!" The man's voice echoed in the mist. "Lost. And you wish to come aboard?"

"I can pay a little. I can give my services in return for a passage, either to your next port of call or to some land close to the Young Kingdoms where maps are available so that I could make my own way thereafter . . ."

"Well," said the other slowly, "there's work for a swordsman."

"I have a sword," said Elric.

"I see it. A good, big battle-blade."

"Then I can come aboard?"

"We must confer first. If you would be good enough to wait awhile . . ."

"Of course," said Elric. He was nonplused by the man's manner, but the prospect of warmth and food on board the ship was cheering. He waited patiently until the blond-bearded warrior came back to the rail.

"Your name, sir?" said the warrior.

"I am Elric of Melniboné."

The warrior seemed to be consulting a parchment, running his finger down a list until he nodded, satisfied, and put the list into his large-buckled belt.

"Well," he said, "there was some point in waiting here, after all. I found it difficult to believe."

"What was the dispute and why did you wait?"

"For you," said the warrior, heaving a rope ladder over the side so that its end fell into the sea. "Will you board now, Elric of Melniboné?"

CHAPTER TWO

Elric was surprised by how shallow the water was and he wondered by what means such a large vessel could come so close to the shore. Shoulder-deep in the sea he reached up to grasp the ebony rungs of the ladder. He had great difficulty heaving himself from the water and was further hampered by the swaying of the ship and the weight of his runesword, but eventually he had clambered awkwardly over the side and stood on the deck with the water running from his clothes to the timbers and his body shivering with cold. He looked about him. Shining, red-tinted mist clung about the ship's dark yards and rigging, white mist spread itself over the roofs and sides of the two large cabins set fore and aft of the mast, and this mist was not of the same character as the mist beyond the ship. Elric, for a moment, had the fanciful notion that the mist traveled permanently wherever the ship traveled. He smiled to himself, putting the dreamlike quality of his experience down to lack of food and sleep. When the ship sailed into sunnier waters he would see it for the relatively ordinary vessel it was.

The blond warrior took Elric's arm. The man was as tall as Elric and massively built. Within his helm he smiled, saying:

"Let us go below."

They went to the cabin forward of the mast and the warrior drew back a sliding door, standing aside to let Elric enter first. Elric ducked his head and went into the warmth of the cabin. A lamp of red-grey glass gleamed, hanging from four silver chains attached to the roof, revealing several more bulky figures, fully dressed in a variety of armours, seated about a square and sturdy sea-table. All faces turned to regard Elric as he came in, followed by the blond warrior who said:

"This is he."

One of the occupants of the cabin, who sat in the farthest corner and whose features were completely hidden by the shadow, nodded. "Aye," he said. "That is he."

"You know me, sir?" said Elric, seating himself at the end of the bench and removing his sodden leather cloak. The warrior nearest him passed him a metal cup of hot wine and Elric accepted it gratefully, sipping at the spiced liquid and marveling at how quickly it dispersed the chill within him.

"In a sense," said the man in the shadows. His voice was sardonic and at the same time had a melancholy ring, and Elric was not offended, for the bitterness in the voice seemed directed more at the owner than at any he addressed.

The blond warrior seated himself opposite Elric. "I am Brut," he said, "once of Lashmar, where my family still holds land, but it is many a year since I have been there."

"From the Young Kingdoms, then?" said Elric.

"Aye. Once."

"This ship journeys nowhere near those nations?" Elric asked.

"I believe it does not," said Brut. "It is not so long, I think, since I myself came aboard. I was seeking Tanelorn, but found this craft, instead."

"Tanelorn?" Elric smiled. "How many must seek that mythical place? Do you know of one called Rackhir, once a Warrior Priest of Phum? We adventured together once. He left to look for Tanelorn."

"I do not know him," said Brut of Lashmar.

"And these waters," said Elric, "do they lie far from the Young Kingdoms?"

"Very far," said the man in the shadows.

"Are you from Elwher, perhaps?" asked Elric. "Or from any other of what we in the West call the Unmapped East?"

"Most of our lands are not on your maps," said the man in the shadows. And he laughed. Again Elric found that he was not offended. And he was not particularly troubled by the mysteries hinted at by the man in the shadows. Soldiers of fortune, as he deemed these men to be, were fond of their private jokes and references; it was usually all that united them save a common willingness to hire their swords to whomever could pay.

Outside the anchor was rattling and the ship rolled. Elric heard the yard being lowered and he heard the smack of the sail as it was unfurled. He wondered how they hoped to leave the bay with so little wind available. He noticed that the faces of the other warriors, where their faces were visible, had taken on a rather set look as the ship began to move. He looked from one grim, haunted face to another and he wondered if his own features bore the same cast.

"For where do we sail?" he asked.

Brut shrugged. "I know only that we had to stop to wait for you, Elric of Melniboné."

"You knew I would be there?"

The man in the shadows stirred and helped himself to more hot wine from the jug set into a hole in the centre of the table. "You are the last one we need," he said. "I was the first taken aboard. So far I have not regretted my decision to make the voyage."

"Your name, sir?" Elric decided he would no longer be at that particular disadvantage.

"Oh, names? Names? I have so many. The one I favour is Erekosë. But I have been called Urlik Skarsol and John Daker and Ilian of Garathorm to my certain knowledge. Some would have me believe that I have been Elric Womanslayer . . ."

"Womanslayer? An unpleasant nickname. Who is this other Elric?"

"That I cannot completely answer," said Erekosë. "But I share a name, it seems, with more than one aboard this ship. I, like Brut, sought Tanelorn and found myself here instead."

"We have that in common," said another. He was a black-skinned warrior, the tallest of the company, his features oddly enhanced by a scar running like an inverted V from his forehead and over both eyes, down his cheeks to his jawbones. "I was in a land called Ghaja-Ki, a most unpleasant, swampy place, filled with perverse and diseased life. I had heard of a city said to exist there and I thought it might be Tanelorn. It was not. And it was inhabited by a blue-skinned, hermaphroditic race who determined to cure me of what they considered my malformations of hue and sexuality. This scar you see was their work. The pain of their operation gave me strength to escape them and I ran naked into the swamps, floundering for many a mile until the swamp became a lake feeding a broad river over which hung black clouds of insects which set upon me hungrily. This ship appeared and I was more than glad to seek its sanctuary. I am Otto Blendker, once a scholar of Brunse, now a hireling sword for my sins."

"This Brunse? Does it lie near Elwher?" said Elric. He had never heard of such a place, nor such an outlandish name, in the Young Kingdoms.

The black man shook his head. "I know naught of Elwher."

"Then the world is a considerably larger place than I imagined," said Elric.

"Indeed it is," said Erekosë. "What would you say if I offered you the theory that the sea on which we sail spans more than one world?"

"I would be inclined to believe you." Elric smiled. "I have studied such theories. More, I have experienced adventures in worlds other than my own."

"It is a relief to hear it," said Erekosë. "Not all on board this ship are willing to accept my theory."

"I come closer to accepting it," said Otto Blendker, "though I find it terrifying."

"It is that," agreed Erekosë. "More terrifying than you can imagine, friend Otto."

Elric leaned across the table and helped himself to a further mug of wine. His clothes were already drying and physically he had a sense of well-being. "I'll be glad to leave this misty shore behind."

"The shore has been left already," said Brut, "but as for the mist, it is ever with us. Mist appears to follow the ship—or else the ship creates the mist wherever it travels. It is rare that we see land at all and when we do see it, as we saw it today, it is usually obscured, like a reflection in a dull and buckled shield."

"We sail on a supernatural sea," said another, holding out a gloved hand for the jug. Elric passed it to him. "In Hasghan, where I come from, we have a legend of a Bewitched Sea. If a mariner finds himself sailing in those waters he may never return and will be lost for eternity."

"Your legend contains at least some truth, I fear, Terndrik of Hasghan," Brut said.

"How many warriors are on board?" Elric asked.

"Sixteen other than the Four," said Erekosë. "Twenty in all. The crew numbers about ten and then there is the captain. You will see him soon, doubtless."

"The Four? Who are they?"

Erekosë laughed. "You and I are two of them. The other two occupy the aft cabin. And if you wish to know *why* we are called the Four, you must ask the captain, though I warn you his answers are rarely satisfying."

Elric realized that he was being pressed slightly to one side. "The ship makes good speed," he said laconically, "considering how poor the wind was."

"Excellent speed," agreed Erekosë. He rose from his corner, a broad-shouldered man with an ageless face bearing the evidence of considerable experience. He was handsome and he had plainly seen much conflict, for both his hands and his face were heavily scarred, though not disfigured. His eyes, though deep-set and dark, seemed of no particular colour and yet were familiar to Elric. He felt that he might have seen those eyes in a dream once.

"Have we met before?" Elric asked him.

"Oh, possibly—or shall meet. What does it matter? Our fates are the same. We share an identical doom. And possibly we share more than that."

"More? I hardly comprehend the first part of your statement."

"Then it is for the best," said Erekosë, inching past his comrades and emerging on the other side of the table. He laid a surprisingly gentle hand on Elric's shoulder. "Come, we must seek audience with the captain. He expressed a wish to see you shortly after you came aboard."

Elric nodded and rose. "This captain—what is his name?"

"He has none he will reveal to us," said Erekosë. Together they emerged onto the deck. The mist was if anything thicker and of the same deathly whiteness, no longer tinted by the sun's rays. It was hard to see to the far ends of the ship and for all that they were evidently moving rapidly, there was no hint of a wind. Yet it was warmer than

Elric might have expected. He followed Erekosë forward to the cabin set under the deck on which one of the ship's twin wheels stood, tended by a tall man in sea-coat and leggings of quilted deerskin who was so still as to resemble a statue. The red-haired steersman did not look around or down as they advanced towards the cabin, but Elric caught a glimpse of his face.

The door seemed built of some kind of smooth metal possessing a sheen almost like the healthy coat of an animal. It was reddish-brown and the most colourful thing Elric had so far seen on the ship. Erekosë knocked softly upon the door. "Captain," he said. "Elric is here."

"Enter," said a voice at once melodious and distant.

The door opened. Rosy light flooded out, half-blinding Elric as he walked in. As his eyes adapted, he could see a very tall, pale-clad man standing upon a richly hued carpet in the middle of the cabin. Elric heard the door close and realized that Erekosë had not accompanied him inside.

"Are you refreshed, Elric?" said the captain.

"I am, sir, thanks to your wine."

The captain's features were no more human than were Elric's. They were at once finer and more powerful than those of the Melnibonéan, yet bore a slight resemblance in that the eyes were inclined to taper, as did the face, toward the chin. The captain's long hair fell to his shoulders in red-gold waves and was kept back from his brow by a circlet of blue jade. His body was clad in buff-coloured tunic and hose and there were sandals of silver and silver-thread laced to his calves. Apart from his clothing, he was twin to the steersman Elric had recently seen.

"Will you have more wine?"

The captain moved towards a chest on the far side of the cabin, near the porthole, which was closed.

"Thank you," said Elric. And now he realized why the eyes had not focused on him. The captain was blind. For all that his movements were deft and assured, it was obvious that he could not see at all. He poured the wine from a silver jug into a silver cup and began to cross towards Elric, holding the cup out before him. Elric stepped forward and accepted it.

"I am grateful for your decision to join us," said the captain. "I am much relieved, sir."

"You are courteous," said Elric, "though I must add that my decision was not difficult to make. I had nowhere else to go."

"I understand that. It is why we put into shore when and where we did. You will find that all your companions were in a similar position before they, too, came aboard."

"You appear to have considerable knowledge of the movements of many men," said Elric. He held the wine untasted in his left hand.

"Many," agreed the captain, "on many worlds. I understand that you are a person of culture, sir, so you will be aware of something of the nature of the sea upon which my ship sails."

"I think so."

"She sails between the worlds, for the most part—between the planes of a variety of aspects of the same world, to be a little more exact." The captain hesitated, turning his blind face away from Elric. "Please know that I do not deliberately mystify you. There are some things I do not understand and other things which I may not completely reveal. It is a trust I have and I hope you feel you can respect it."

"I have no reason as yet to do otherwise," replied the albino. And he took a sip of the wine.

"I find myself with a fine company," said the captain. "I hope that you continue to think it worthwhile honouring my trust when we reach our destination."

"And what is that, Captain?"

"An island indigenous to these waters."

"That must be a rarity."

"Indeed, it is, and once undiscovered, uninhabited by those we must count our enemies. Now that they have found it and realize its power, we are in great danger."

"We? You mean your race or those aboard your ship?"

The captain smiled. "I have no race, save myself. I speak, I suppose, of all humanity."

"These enemies are not human, then?"

"No. They are inextricably involved in human affairs, but this fact has not instilled in them any loyalty to us. I use 'humanity,' of course, in its broader sense, to include yourself and myself."

"I understood," said Elric. "What is this folk called?"

"Many things," said the captain. "Forgive me, but I cannot continue longer now. If you will ready yourself for battle I assure you that I will reveal more to you as soon as the time is right."

Only when Elric stood again outside the reddish-brown door, watching Erekosë advancing up the deck through the mist, did the albino wonder if the captain had charmed him to the point where he had forgotten all common sense. Yet the blind man had impressed him and he had, after all, nothing better to do than to sail on to the island. He shrugged. He could always alter his decision if he discovered that those upon the island were not, in his opinion, enemies.

"Are you more mystified or less, Elric?" said Erekosë, smiling.

"More mystified in some ways, less in others," Elric told him. "And, for some reason, I do not care."

"Then you share the feeling of the whole company," Erekosë told him.

It was only when Erekosë led him to the cabin aft of the mast that Elric realized he had not asked the captain what the significance of the Four might be.

CHAPTER THREE

Save that it faced in the opposite direction, the other cabin resembled the first in almost every detail. Here, too, were seated some dozen men, all experienced soldiers of fortune by their features and their clothing. Two sat together at the centre of the table's starboard side. One was bareheaded, fair and care-worn. The other had features resembling Elric's own and he seemed to be wearing a silver gauntlet on his left hand while the right hand was naked; his armour was delicate and outlandish. He looked up as Elric entered and there was recognition in his single eye (the other was covered by a brocade-work patch).

"Elric of Melniboné!" he exclaimed. "My theories become more meaningful!" He turned to his companion. "See, Hawkmoon, this is the one of whom I spoke."

"You know me, sir?" Elric was nonplused.

"You recognize me, Elric. You must! At the Tower of Voilodion Ghagnasdiak? With Erekosë—though a different Erekosë. I am Corum."

"I know of no such tower, no name which resembles that, and this is the first I have seen of Erekosë. You know me and you know my name, but I do not know you. I find this disconcerting, sir."

"I, too, had never met Prince Corum before he came aboard," said Erekosë, "yet he insists we fought together once. I am inclined to believe him. Time on the different planes does not always run concurrently. Prince Corum might well exist in what we would term the future."

"I had thought to find some relief from such paradoxes here," said Hawkmoon, passing his hand over his face. He smiled bleakly. "But it seems there is none at this present moment in the history of the planes. Everything is in flux and even our identities, it seems, are prone to alter at any moment."

"We were Three," said Corum. "Do you not recall it, Elric? The Three Who Are One?"

Elric shook his head.

Corum shrugged, saying softly to himself, "Well, now we are Four. Did the captain say anything of an island we are supposed to invade?"

"He did," said Elric. "Do you know who these enemies might be?"

"We know no more or less than do you, Elric," said Hawkmoon. "I seek a place called Tanelorn and two children. Perhaps I seek the Runestaff, too. Of that I am not entirely sure."

"We found it once," said Corum. "We three. In the Tower of Voilodion Ghagnasdiak. It was of considerable help to us."

"As it might be to me," Hawkmoon told him. "I served it once. I gave it a great deal."

"We have much in common," Erekosë put in, "as I told you, Elric. Perhaps we share masters in common, too?"

Elric shrugged. "I serve no master but myself."

And he wondered why they all smiled in the same strange way.

Erekosë said quietly, "On such ventures as these one is inclined to forget much, as one forgets a dream."

"This *is* a dream," said Hawkmoon. "Of late I've dreamed many such."

"It is all dreaming, if you like," said Corum. "All existence."

Elric was not interested in such philosophizing. "Dream or reality, the experience amounts to the same, does it not?"

"Quite right," said Erekosë with a wan smile.

They talked on for another hour or two until Corum stretched and yawned and commented that he was feeling sleepy. The others agreed that they were all tired and so they left the cabin and went aft and below where there were bunks for all the warriors. As he stretched himself out in one of the bunks, Elric said to Brut of Lashmar, who had climbed into the bunk above:

"It would help to know when this fight begins."

Brut looked over the edge, down at the prone albino. "I think it will be soon," he said.

Elric stood alone upon the deck, leaning upon the rail and trying to make out the sea, but the sea, like the rest of the world, was hidden by white curling mist. Elric wondered if there were waters flowing under the ship's keel at all. He looked up to where the sail was tight and swollen at the mast, filled with a warm and powerful wind. It was light, but again it was not possible to tell the hour of the day. Puzzled by Corum's comments concerning an earlier meeting, Elric wondered if there had been other dreams in his life such as this might be— dreams he had forgotten completely upon awakening. But the uselessness of such speculation became quickly evident and he turned his attention to more immediate matters, wondering at the origin of the captain and his strange ship sailing on a stranger ocean.

"The captain," said Hawkmoon's voice, and Elric turned to bid good morning to the tall, fair-haired man who bore a strange, regular scar in the centre of his forehead, "has requested that we four visit him in his cabin."

The other two emerged from the mist and together they made their way to the prow, knocking on the reddish-brown door and being at once admitted into the presence of the blind captain, who had four silver wine-cups already poured for them. He gestured them towards the great chest on which the wine stood. "Please help yourselves, my friends."

They did so, standing there with the cups in their hands, four tall, doom-haunted swordsmen, each of a strikingly different cast of features, yet each bearing a certain stamp which marked them as being of a like kind. Elric noticed it, for all that he was one of them, and he tried to recall the details of what Corum had told him on the previous evening.

"We are nearing our destination," said the captain. "It will not be long before we disembark. I do not believe our enemies expect us, yet it will be a hard fight against those two."

"Two?" said Hawkmoon. "Only two?"

"Only two." The captain smiled. "A brother and a sister. Sorcerers from quite another universe than ours. Due to recent disruptions in the fabric of our worlds—of which you know something, Hawkmoon, and you, too, Corum—certain beings have been released who would not otherwise have the power they now possess. And possessing great power, they crave for more—for all the power that there is in our universe. These beings are amoral in a way in which the Lords of Law or Chaos are not. They do not fight for influence upon the Earth, as those gods do; their only wish is to convert the essential energy of our universe to their own uses. I believe they foster some ambition in their particular universe which would be furthered if they could achieve their wish. At present, in spite of conditions highly favourable to them, they have not attained their full strength, but the time is not far off before they do attain it. Agak and Gagak is how they are called in human tongue and they are outside the power of any of our gods, so a more powerful group has been summoned—yourselves. The Champion Eternal in four of his incarnations (and four is the maximum number we can risk without precipitating further unwelcome disruptions among the planes of Earth)—Erekosë, Elric, Corum and Hawkmoon. Each of you will command four others, whose fates are linked with your own and who are great fighters in their own right, though they do not share your destinies in every sense. You may each pick the four with whom you wish to fight. I think you will find it easy enough to decide. We make landfall quite shortly now."

"You will lead us?" Hawkmoon said.

"I cannot. I can only take you to the island and wait for those who survive—if any survive."

Elric frowned. "This fight is not mine, I think."

"It is yours," said the captain soberly. "And it is mine. I would land with you if that were permitted me, but it is not."

"Why so?" asked Corum.

"You will learn that one day. I have not the courage to tell you. I bear you nothing but good will, however. Be assured of that."

Erekosë rubbed his jaw. "Well, since it is my destiny to fight, and since I, like Hawkmoon, continue to seek Tanelorn, and since I gather there is some chance of my fulfilling my ambition if I am successful, I for one agree to go against these two, Agak and Gagak."

Hawkmoon nodded. "I go with Erekosë, for similar reasons."

"And I," said Corum.

"Not long since," said Elric, "I counted myself without comrades. Now I have many. For that reason alone I will fight with them."

"It is perhaps the best of reasons," said Erekosë approvingly.

"There is no reward for this work, save my assurance that your success will save the world much misery," said the captain. "And for you, Elric, there is less reward than the rest may hope for."

"Perhaps not," said Elric.

"As you say." The captain gestured towards the jug of wine. "More wine, my friends?"

They each accepted, while the captain continued, his blind face staring upward at the roof of the cabin.

"Upon this island is a ruin—perhaps it was once a city called Tanelorn—and at the centre of the ruin stands one whole building. It is this building which Agak and his sister use. It is that which you must attack. You will recognize it, I hope, at once."

"And we must slay this pair?" said Erekosë.

"If you can. They have servants who help them. These must be slain, also. Then the building must be fired. This is important." The captain paused. "Fired. It must be destroyed in no other way."

Elric smiled a dry smile. "There are few other ways of destroying buildings, Sir Captain."

The captain returned his smile and made a slight bow of acknowledgment. "Aye, it's so. Nonetheless, it is worth remembering what I have said."

"Do you know what these two look like, these Agak and Gagak?" Corum asked.

"No. It is possible that they resemble creatures of our own worlds; it is possible that they do not. Few have seen them. It is only recently that they have been able to materialize at all."

"And how may they best be overwhelmed?" asked Hawkmoon.

"By courage and ingenuity," said the captain.

"You are not very explicit, sir," said Elric.

"I am as explicit as I can be. Now, my friends, I suggest you rest and prepare your arms."

As they returned to their cabins, Erekosë sighed.

"We are fated," he said. "We have little free will, for all we deceive ourselves otherwise. If we perish or live through this venture, it will not count for much in the overall scheme of things."

"I think you are of a gloomy turn of mind, friend," said Hawkmoon.

The mist snaked through the branches of the mast, writhing in the rigging, flooding the deck. It swirled across the faces of the other three men as Elric looked at them.

"A realistic turn of mind," said Corum.

The mist massed more thickly upon the deck, mantling each man like a shroud. The timbers of the ship creaked and to Elric's ears took on the sound of a raven's croak. It was colder now. In silence they went to their cabins to test the hooks and buckles of their armour, to polish and to sharpen their weapons and to pretend to sleep.

"Oh, I've no liking for sorcery," said Brut of Lashmar, tugging at his golden beard, "for sorcery it was resulted in my shame." Elric had told him all that the captain had said and had asked Brut to be one of the four who fought with him when they landed.

"It is all sorcery here," Otto Blendker said. And he smiled wanly as he gave Elric his hand. "I'll fight beside you, Elric."

His sea-green armour shimmering faintly in the lantern light, another rose, his casque pushed back from his face. It was a face almost as white as Elric's, though the eyes were deep and near-black. "And I," said Hown Serpent-tamer, "though I fear I'm little use on still land."

The last to rise, at Elric's glance, was a warrior who had said little during their earlier conversations. His voice was deep and hesitant. He wore a plain iron battle-cap and the red hair beneath it was braided. At the end of each braid was a small finger-bone which rattled on the shoulders of his byrnie as he moved. This was Ashnar the Lynx, whose eyes were rarely less than fierce. "I lack the eloquence or the breeding of you other gentlemen," said Ashnar. "And I've no familiarity with sorcery or those other things of which you speak, but I'm a good soldier and my joy is in fighting. I'll take your orders, Elric, if you'll have me."

"Willingly," said Elric.

"There is no dispute, it seems," said Erekosë to the remaining four who had elected to join him. "All this is doubtless pre-ordained. Our destinies have been linked from the first."

"Such philosophy can lead to unhealthy fatalism," said Terndrik of Hasghan. "Best believe our fates are our own, even if the evidence denies it."

"You must think as you wish," said Erekosë. "I have led many lives, though all, save one, are remembered but faintly." He shrugged. "Yet I deceive myself, I suppose, in that I work for a time when I shall find this Tanelorn and perhaps be reunited with the one I seek. That ambition is what gives me energy, Terndrik."

Elric smiled. "I fight, I think, because I relish the comradeship of battle. That, in itself, is a melancholy condition in which to find oneself, is it not?"

"Aye." Erekosë glanced at the floor. "Well, we must try to rest now."

CHAPTER FOUR

The outlines of the coast were dim. They waded through white water and white mist, their swords held above their heads. Swords were their only weapons. Each of the Four possessed a blade of unusual size and design, but none bore a sword which occasionally murmured to itself as did Elric's Stormbringer. Glancing back, Elric saw the captain standing at the rail, his blind face turned towards the island, his pale lips moving as if he spoke to himself. Now the water was waist-deep and the sand beneath Elric's feet hardened and became smooth rock. He waded on, wary and ready to carry any attack to those who might be defending the island. But now the mist grew thinner, as if it could gain no hold on the land, and there were no obvious signs of defenders.

Tucked into his belt, each man had a brand, its end wrapped in oiled cloth so that it should not be wet when the time came to light it. Similarly, each was equipped with a handful of smouldering tinder in a little firebox in a pouch attached to his belt, so that the brands could be instantly ignited.

"Only fire will destroy this enemy for ever," the captain had said again as he handed them their brands and their tinderboxes.

As the mist cleared, it revealed a landscape of dense shadows. The shadows spread over red rock and yellow vegetation and they were shadows of all shapes and dimensions, resembling all manner of things. They seemed cast by the huge blood-coloured sun which stood at perpetual noon above the island, but what was disturbing about them was that the shadows themselves seemed without a source, as if the objects they represented were invisible or existed elsewhere than on the island itself. The sky, too, seemed full of these shadows, but whereas those on the island were still, those in the sky sometimes moved, perhaps when the clouds moved. And all the while the red sun poured down its bloody light and touched the twenty men with its unwelcome radiance just as it touched the land.

And at times, as they advanced cautiously inland, a peculiar flickering light sometimes crossed the island so that the outlines of the place became unsteady for a few seconds before returning to focus. Elric suspected his eyes and said nothing until Hown Serpent-tamer, who was having difficulty finding his land-legs, remarked:

"I have rarely been ashore, it's true, but I think the quality of this land is stranger than any other I've known. It shimmers. It distorts."

Several voices agreed with him.

"And whence come all these shadows?" Ashnar the Lynx stared around him in unashamed superstitious awe. "Why cannot we see that which casts them?"

"It could be," Corum said, "that these are shadows cast by objects existing in other dimensions of the Earth. If all dimensions meet here, as has been suggested, that could be a likely explanation." He put his silver hand to his embroidered eye-patch. "This is not the strangest example I have witnessed of such a conjunction."

"Likely?" Otto Blendker snorted. "Pray let none give me an *unlikely* explanation, if you please!"

They pressed on through the shadows and the lurid light until they arrived at the outskirts of the ruins.

These ruins, thought Elric, had something in common with the ramshackle city of Ameeron, which he had visited on his quest for the Black Sword. But they were altogether more vast—more a collection of smaller cities, each one in a radically different architectural style.

"Perhaps this is Tanelorn," said Corum, who had visited the place, "or, rather, all the versions of Tanelorn there have ever been. For Tanelorn exists in many forms, each form depending upon the wishes of those who most desire to find her."

"This is not the Tanelorn I expected to find," said Hawkmoon bitterly.

"Nor I," added Erekosë bleakly.

"Perhaps it is not Tanelorn," said Elric. "Perhaps it is not."

"Or perhaps this is a graveyard," said Corum distantly, frowning with his single eye. "A graveyard containing all the forgotten versions of that strange city."

They began to clamber over the ruins, their arms clattering as they moved, heading for the centre of the place. Elric could tell by the introspective expressions in the faces of many of his companions that they, like him, were wondering if this were not a dream. Why else should they find themselves in this peculiar situation, unquestioningly risking their lives—perhaps their souls—in a fight with which none of them was identified?

Erekosë moved closer to Elric as they marched. "Have you noticed," said he, "that the shadows now represent something?"

Elric nodded. "You can tell from the ruins what some of the buildings looked like when they were whole. The shadows are the shadows of those buildings—the original buildings before they became ruined."

"Just so," said Erekosë. Together, they shuddered.

At last they approached the likely centre of the place and here was a building which was not ruined. It stood in a cleared space, all curves and ribbons of metal and glowing tubes.

"It resembles a machine more than a building," said Hawkmoon.

"And a musical instrument more than a machine," Corum mused.

The party came to a halt, each group of four gathering about its leader. There was no question but that they had arrived at their goal.

Now that Elric looked carefully at the building he could see that it was in fact two buildings—both absolutely identical and joined at various points by curling systems of pipes which might be connecting corridors, though it was difficult to imagine what manner of being could utilize them.

"Two buildings," said Erekosë. "We were not prepared for this. Shall we split up and attack both?"

Instinctively Elric felt that this action would be unwise. He shook his head. "I think we should go together into one, else our strength will be weakened."

"I agree," said Hawkmoon, and the rest nodded.

Thus, there being no cover to speak of, they marched boldly towards the nearest building to a point near the ground where a black opening of irregular proportions could be discerned. Ominously, there was still no sign of defenders. The buildings pulsed and glowed and occasionally whispered, but that was all.

Elric and his party were the first to enter, finding themselves in a damp, warm passage which curved almost immediately to the right. They were followed by the others until all stood in this passage warily glaring ahead, expecting to be attacked. But no attack came.

With Elric at their head, they moved on for some moments before the passage began to tremble violently and sent Hown Serpent-tamer crashing to the floor cursing. As the man in the sea-green armour scrambled up, a voice began to echo along the passage, seemingly coming from a great distance yet nonetheless loud and irritable.

"*Who? Who? Who?*" shrieked the voice.

"*Who? Who? Who invades me?*"

The passage's tremble subsided a little into a constant quivering motion. The voice became a muttering, detached and uncertain.

"*What attacks? What?*"

The twenty men glanced at one another in puzzlement. At length Elric shrugged and led the party on and soon the passage had widened out into a hall whose walls, roof, and floor were damp with sticky fluid and whose air was hard to breathe. And now, somehow passing themselves through the walls of this hall, came the first of the defenders, ugly beasts who must be the servants of that mysterious brother and sister Agak and Gagak.

"*Attack!*" cried the distant voice. "*Destroy this. Destroy it!*"

The beasts were of a primitive sort, mostly gaping mouth and slithering body, but there were many of them oozing towards the twenty men, who quickly formed themselves into the four fighting units and prepared to defend themselves. The creatures made a dreadful slushing sound as they approached and the ridges of bone which served them as teeth clashed as they reared up to snap at Elric and his companions. Elric whirled his sword and it met hardly any resistance as it sliced through several of the things at once. But now the air was thicker than ever and a stench threatened to overwhelm them as fluid drenched the floor.

"Move on through them," Elric instructed, "hacking a path through as you go. Head for yonder opening." He pointed with his left hand.

And so they advanced, cutting back hundreds of the primitive beasts and thus decreasing the breathability of the air.

"The creatures are not hard to fight," gasped Hown Serpent-tamer, "but each one we kill robs us a little of our own chances of life."

Elric was aware of the irony. "Cunningly planned by our enemies, no doubt." He coughed and slashed again at a dozen of the beasts slithering towards him. The things were fearless, but they were stupid, too. They made no attempt at strategy.

Finally Elric reached the next passage, where the air was slightly purer. He sucked gratefully at the sweeter atmosphere and waved his companions on.

Sword-arms rising and falling, they gradually retreated back into the passage, followed by only a few of the beasts. The creatures seemed reluctant to enter the passage and Elric suspected that somewhere within it there must lie a danger which even they feared. There was nothing for it, however, but to press on and he was only grateful that all twenty had survived this initial ordeal.

Gasping, they rested for a moment, leaning against the trembling walls of the passage, listening to the tones of that distant voice, now muffled and indistinct.

"I like not this castle at all," growled Brut of Lashmar, inspecting a rent in his cloak where a creature had seized it. "High sorcery commands it."

"It is only what we knew," Ashnar the Lynx reminded him, and

Ashnar was plainly hard put to control his terror. The finger-bones in his braids kept time with the trembling of the walls and the huge barbarian looked almost pathetic as he steeled himself to go on.

"They are cowards, these sorcerers," Otto Blendker said. "They do not show themselves." He raised his voice. "Is their aspect so loathsome that they are afraid lest we look upon them?" It was a challenge not taken up. As they pushed on through the passages there was no sign either of Agak or his sister Gagak. It became gloomier and brighter in turns. Sometimes the passages narrowed so that it was difficult to squeeze their bodies through, sometimes they widened into what were almost halls. Most of the time they appeared to be climbing higher into the building.

Elric tried to guess the nature of the building's inhabitants. There were no steps in the castle, no artifacts he could recognize. For no particular reason he developed an image of Agak and Gagak as reptilian in form, for reptiles would prefer gently rising passages to steps and doubtless would have little need of conventional furniture. There again it was possible that they could change their shape at will, assuming human form when it suited them. He was becoming impatient to face either one or both of the sorcerers.

Ashnar the Lynx had other reasons—or so he said—for his own lack of patience.

"They said there'd be treasure here," he muttered. "I thought to stake my life against a fair reward, but there's naught here of value." He put a horny hand against the damp material of the wall. "Not even stone or brick. What are these walls made of, Elric?"

Elric shook his head. "That has puzzled me, also, Ashnar."

Then Elric saw large, fierce eyes peering out of the gloom ahead. He heard a rattling noise, a rushing noise, and the eyes grew larger and larger. He saw a red mouth, yellow fangs, orange fur. Then the growling sounded and the beast sprang at him even as he raised Stormbringer to defend himself and shouted a warning to the others. The creature was a baboon, but huge, and there were at least a dozen others following the first. Elric drove his body forward behind his sword, taking the beast in its groin. Claws reached out and dug into his shoulder and waist. He groaned as he felt at least one set of claws draw blood. His arms were trapped and he could not pull Stormbringer free. All he could do was twist the sword in the wound he had already made. With all his might, he turned the hilt. The great ape shouted, its bloodshot eyes blazing, and it bared its yellow fangs as its muzzle shot towards Elric's throat. The teeth closed on his neck, the stinking breath threatened to choke him. Again he twisted the blade. Again the beast yelled in pain.

The fangs were pressing into the metal of Elric's gorget, the only thing saving him from immediate death. He struggled to free at least one arm, twisting the sword for the third time, then tugging it sideways to widen the wound in the groin. The growls and groans of the baboon grew more intense and the teeth tightened their hold on his neck, but now, mingled with the noises of the ape, he began to hear a murmuring and he felt Stormbringer pulse in his hand. He knew that the sword was drawing power from the ape even as the ape sought to destroy him. Some of that power began to flow into his body.

Desperately Elric put all his remaining strength into dragging the sword across the ape's body, slitting its belly wide so that its blood and entrails spilled over him as he was suddenly free and staggering backwards, wrenching the sword out in the same movement. The ape, too, was staggering back, staring down in stupefied awe at its own horrible wound before it fell to the floor of the passage.

Elric turned, ready to give aid to his nearest comrade, and he was in time to see Terndrik of Hasghan die, kicking in the clutches of an even larger ape, his head bitten clean from his shoulders and his red blood gouting.

Elric drove Stormbringer cleanly between the shoulders of Terndrik's slayer, taking the ape in the heart. Beast and human victim fell together. Two others were dead and several bore bad wounds, but the remaining warriors fought on, swords and armour smeared with crimson. The narrow passage stank of ape, of sweat, and of blood. Elric pressed into the fight, chopping at the skull of an ape which grappled with Hown Serpent-tamer, who had lost his sword. Hown darted a look of thanks at Elric as he bent to retrieve his blade and together they

set upon the largest of all the baboons. This creature stood much taller than Elric and had Erekosë pressed against the wall, Erekosë's sword through its shoulder.

From two sides, Hown and Elric stabbed and the baboon snarled and screamed, turning to face the new attackers, Erekosë's blade quivering in its shoulder. It rushed upon them and they stabbed again together, taking the monster in its heart and its lung so that when it roared at them blood vomited from its mouth. It fell to its knees, its eyes dimming, then sank slowly down.

And now there was silence in the passage and death lay all about them.

Terndrik of Hasghan was dead. Two of Corum's party were dead. All of Erekosë's surviving men bore major wounds. One of Hawkmoon's men was dead, but the remaining three were virtually unscathed. Brut of Lashmar's helm was dented, but he was otherwise unwounded and Ashnar the Lynx was disheveled, nothing more. Ashnar had taken two of the baboons during the fight. But now the barbarian's eyes rolled as he leaned, panting, against the wall.

"I begin to suspect this venture of being uneconomical," he said with a half-grin. He rallied himself, stepping over a baboon's corpse to join Elric. "The less time we take over it, the better. What think you, Elric?"

"I would agree." Elric returned his grin. "Come." And he led the way through the passage and into a chamber whose walls gave off a pinkish light. He had not walked far before he felt something catch at his ankle and he stared down in horror to see a long, thin snake winding itself about his leg. It was too late to use his sword; instead he seized the reptile behind its head and dragged it partially free of his leg before hacking the head from the body. The others were now stamping and shouting warnings to each other. The snakes did not appear to be venomous, but there were thousands of them, appearing, it seemed, from out of the floor itself. They were flesh-coloured and had no eyes, more closely resembling earthworms than ordinary reptiles, but they were strong enough.

Hown Serpent-tamer sang a strange song now, with many liquid, hissing notes, and this seemed to have a calming effect upon the creatures. One by one at first and then in increasing numbers, they dropped back to the floor, apparently sleeping. Hown grinned at his success.

Elric said, "Now I understand how you came by your surname."

"I was not sure the song would work on these," Hown told him, "for they are unlike any serpents I have ever seen in the seas of my own world."

They waded on through mounds of sleeping serpents, noticing that the next passage rose sharply. At times they were forced to use their hands to steady themselves as they climbed the peculiar, slippery material of the floor.

It was much hotter in this passage and they were all sweating, pausing several times to rest and mop their brows. The passage seemed to extend upwards for ever, turning occasionally, but never leveling out for more than a few feet. At times it narrowed to little more than a tube through which they had to squirm on their stomachs and at other times the roof disappeared into the gloom over their heads. Elric had long since given up trying to relate their position to what he had seen of the outside of the castle. From time to time small, shapeless creatures rushed towards them in shoals apparently with the intention of attacking them, but these were rarely more than an irritation and were soon all but ignored by the party as it continued its climb.

For a while they had not heard the strange voice which had greeted them upon their entering, but now it began to whisper again, its tones more urgent than before.

"Where? Where? Oh, the pain!"

They paused, trying to locate the source of the voice, but it seemed to come from everywhere at once.

Grim-faced, they continued, plagued by thousands of little creatures which bit at their exposed flesh like so many gnats, yet the creatures were not insects. Elric had seen nothing like them before. They were shapeless, primitive, and all but colourless. They battered at his face as he moved; they were like a wind. Half-blinded, choked, sweating, he felt his strength leaving him. The air was so thick now, so hot, so salty, it was as if he moved through liquid. The others were as badly affected as was he; some were staggering and two men fell, to be helped up again by comrades almost as exhausted. Elric was tempted to strip off his armour, but he knew this would leave more of his flesh to the mercy of the little flying creatures.

Still they climbed and now more of the serpentine things they had seen earlier began to writhe around their feet, hampering them further, for all that Hown sang his sleeping song until he was hoarse.

"We can survive this only a little longer," said Ashnar the Lynx, moving close to Elric. "We shall be in no condition to meet the sorcerer if we ever find him or his sister."

Elric nodded a gloomy head. "My thoughts, too, yet what else may we do, Ashnar?"

"Nothing," said Ashnar in a low voice. "Nothing."

"Where? Where? Where?" The word rustled all about them. Many of the party were becoming openly nervous.

Chapter Five

They had reached the top of the passage. The querulous voice was much louder now, but it quavered more. They saw an archway and beyond the archway a lighted chamber.

"Agak's room, without doubt," said Ashnar, taking a better grip on his sword.

"Possibly," said Elric. He felt detached from his body. Perhaps it was the heat and the exhaustion, or his growing sense of disquiet, but something made him withdraw into himself and hesitate before entering the chamber.

The place was octagonal and each of its eight sloping sides was of a different colour and each colour changed constantly. Occasionally the walls became semi-transparent, revealing a complete view of the ruined city (or collection of cities) far below, and also a view of the twin castle to this one, still connected by tubes and wires.

It was the large pool in the centre of the chamber which attracted most of their attention. It seemed deep and was full of evil-smelling, viscous stuff. It bubbled. Shapes formed in it. Grotesque and strange, beautiful and familiar, the shapes seemed always upon the brink of taking permanent form before falling back into the stuff of the pool. And the voice was still louder and there was no question now that it came from the pool.

"WHAT? WHAT? WHO INVADES?"

Elric forced himself closer to the pool and for a moment saw his own face staring out at him before it melted.

"WHO INVADES? AH! I AM TOO WEAK!"

Elric spoke to the pool. "We are of those you would destroy," he said. "We are those on whom you would feed."

"AH! AGAK! AGAK! I AM SICK! WHERE ARE YOU?"

Ashnar and Brut joined Elric. The faces of the warriors were filled with disgust.

"Agak," growled Ashnar the Lynx, his eyes narrowing. "At last some sign that the sorcerer is here!"

The others had all crowded in, to stand as far away from the pool as possible, but all stared, fascinated by the variety of the shapes forming and disintegrating in the viscous liquid.

"I WEAKEN...MY ENERGY NEEDS TO BE REPLEN-ISHED...WE MUST BEGIN NOW, AGAK...IT TOOK US SO LONG TO REACH THIS PLACE. I THOUGHT I COULD REST. BUT THERE IS DISEASE HERE. IT FILLS MY BODY. AGAK. AWAKEN, AGAK. AWAKEN!"

"Some servant of Agak's, charged with the defense of the chamber?" suggested Hown Serpent-tamer in a small voice.

But Elric continued to stare into the pool as he began, he thought, to realize the truth.

"Will Agak wake?" Brut said. "Will he come?" He glanced nervously around him.

"Agak!" called Ashnar the Lynx. "Coward!"

"Agak!" cried many of the other warriors, brandishing their swords.

But Elric said nothing and he noted, too, that Hawkmoon and

Corum and Erekosë all remained silent. He guessed that they must be filled with the same dawning understanding.

He looked at them. In Erekosë's eyes he saw an agony, a pity both for himself and his comrades.

"We are the Four Who Are One," said Erekosë. His voice shook.

Elric was seized by an alien impulse, an impulse which disgusted and terrified him. "No . . ." He attempted to sheathe Stormbringer, but the sword refused to enter its scabbard.

"*AGAK! QUICKLY!*" said the voice from the pool.

"If we do not do this thing," said Erekosë, "they will eat all our worlds. Nothing will remain."

Elric put his free hand to his head. He swayed upon the edge of that frightful pool. He moaned.

"We must do it, then." Corum's voice was an echo.

"I will not," said Elric. "I am myself."

"And I!" said Hawkmoon.

But Corum Jhaelen Irsei said, "It is the only way for us, for the single thing that we are. Do you not see that? We are the only creatures of our worlds who possess the means of slaying the sorcerers—in the only manner in which they can be slain!"

Elric looked at Corum, at Hawkmoon, at Erekosë, and again he saw something of himself in all of them.

"We are the Four Who Are One," said Erekosë. "Our united strength is greater than the sum. We must come together, brothers. We must conquer here before we can hope to conquer Agak."

"No . . ." Elric moved away, but somehow he found himself standing at a corner of the bubbling, noxious pool from which the voice still murmured and complained, in which shapes still formed, re-formed and faded. And at each of the other three corners stood one of his companions. All had a set, fatalistic look to them.

The warriors who had accompanied the four drew back to the walls. Otto Blendker and Brut of Lashmar stood near the doorway, listening for anything which might come up the passage to the chamber. Ashnar the Lynx fingered the brand at his belt, a look of pure horror on his rugged features.

Elric felt his arm begin to rise, drawn upward by his sword, and he saw that each of his three companions were also lifting their swords. The swords reached out across the pool and their tips met above the exact centre.

Elric yelled as something entered his being. Again he tried to break free, but the power was too strong. Other voices spoke in his head.

"*I understand . . .*" This was Corum's distant murmur. "*It is the only way.*"

"*Oh, no, no . . .*" And this was Hawkmoon, but the words came from Elric's lips.

"*AGAK!*" cried the pool. The stuff became more agitated, more alarmed. "*AGAK! QUICKLY! WAKE!*"

Elric's body began to shake, but his hand kept a firm hold upon the sword. The atoms of his body flew apart and then united again into a single flowing entity which traveled up the blade of the sword towards the apex. And Elric was still Elric, shouting with the terror of it, sighing with the ecstasy of it.

Elric was still Elric when he drew away from the pool and looked upon himself for a single moment, seeing himself wholly joined with his three other selves.

A being hovered over the pool. On each side of its head was a face and each face belonged to one of the companions. Serene and terrible, the eyes did not blink. It had eight arms and the arms were still; it squatted over the pool on eight legs, and its armour and accoutrements were of all colours blending and at the same time separate.

The being clutched a single great sword in all eight hands and both he and the sword glowed with a ghastly golden light.

Then Elric had rejoined this body and had become a different thing—himself and three others and something else which was the sum of that union.

The Four Who Were One reversed its monstrous sword so that the point was directed downward at the frenetically boiling stuff in the pool below. The stuff feared the sword. It mewled.

"*Agak, Agak . . .*"

The being of whom Elric was a part gathered its great strength and began to plunge the sword down.

Shapeless waves appeared on the surface of the pool. Its whole colour changed from sickly yellow to an unhealthy green. *"Agak, I die . . ."*

Inexorably the sword moved down. It touched the surface.

The pool swept back and forth; it tried to ooze over the sides and onto the floor. The sword bit deeper and the Four Who Were One felt new strength flow up the blade. There came a moan; slowly the pool quieted. It became silent. It became still. It became grey.

Then the Four Who Were One descended into the pool to be absorbed.

It could see clearly now. It tested its body. It controlled every limb, every function. It had triumphed; it had revitalized the pool. Through its single octagonal eye it looked in all directions at the same time over the wide ruins of the city; then it focused all its attention upon its twin.

Agak had awakened too late, but he was awakening at last, roused by the dying cries of his sister Gagak, whose body the mortals had first invaded and whose intelligence they had overwhelmed, whose eye they now used and whose powers they would soon attempt to utilize.

Agak did not need to turn his head to look upon the being he still saw as his sister. Like hers, his intelligence was contained within the huge eight-sided eye.

"Did you call me, sister?"

"I spoke your name, that is all, brother." There were enough vestiges of Gagak's life-force in the Four Who Were One for it to imitate her manner of speaking.

"You cried out?"

"A dream." The Four paused and then it spoke again: *"A disease. I dreamed that there was something upon this island which made me unwell."*

"Is that possible? We do not know sufficient about these dimensions or

the creatures inhabiting them. Yet none is as powerful as Agak and Gagak. Fear not, sister. We must begin our work soon."

"It is nothing. Now I am awake."

Agak was puzzled. *"You speak oddly."*

"The dream . . ." answered the creature which had entered Gagak's body and destroyed her.

"We must begin," said Agak. *"The dimensions turn and the time has come. Ah, feel it. It waits for us to take it. So much rich energy. How we shall conquer when we go home!"*

"I feel it," replied the Four, and it did. It felt its whole universe, dimension upon dimension, swirling all about it. Stars and planets and moons through plane upon plane, all full of the energy upon which Agak and Gagak had desired to feed. And there was enough of Gagak still within the Four to make the Four experience a deep, anticipatory hunger which, now that the dimensions attained the right conjunction, would soon be satisfied.

The Four was tempted to join with Agak and feast, though it knew if it did so it would rob its own universe of every shred of energy. Stars would fade, worlds would die. Even the Lords of Law and Chaos would perish, for they were part of the same universe. Yet to possess such power it might be worth committing such a tremendous crime . . . It controlled this desire and gathered itself for its attack before Agak became too wary.

"Shall we feast, sister?"

The Four realized that the ship had brought it to the island at exactly the proper moment. Indeed, they had almost come too late.

"Sister?" Agak was again puzzled. *"What . . . ?"*

The Four knew it must disconnect from Agak. The tubes and wires fell away from his body and were withdrawn into Gagak's.

"What's this?" Agak's strange body trembled for a moment. *"Sister?"*

The Four prepared itself. For all that it had absorbed Gagak's memories and instincts, it was still not confident that it would be able to attack Agak in her chosen form. And since the sorceress had possessed the power to change her form, the Four began to change, groaning greatly, experiencing dreadful pain, drawing all the materials of its stolen being together so that what had appeared to be a building now became pulpy, unformed flesh. And Agak, stunned, looked on.

"Sister? Your sanity . . ."

The building, the creature that was Gagak, threshed, melted, and erupted. It screamed in agony.

It attained its form.

It laughed.

Four faces laughed upon a gigantic head. Eight arms waved in triumph, eight legs began to move. And over that head it waved a single, massive sword.

And it was running.

It ran upon Agak while the alien sorcerer was still in his static form. Its sword was whirling and shards of ghastly golden light fell away from it as it moved, lashing the shadowed landscape. The Four was as large as Agak. And at this moment it was as strong.

But Agak, realizing his danger, began to suck. No longer would this be a pleasurable ritual shared with his sister. He must suck at the energy of this universe if he were to find the strength to defend himself, to gain what he needed to destroy his attacker, the slayer of his sister. Worlds died as Agak sucked.

But not enough. Agak tried cunning.

"This is the centre of your universe. All its dimensions intersect here. Come, you can share the power. My sister is dead. I accept her death. You shall be my partner now. With this power we shall conquer a universe far richer than this!"

"No!" said the Four, still advancing.

"Very well, but be assured of your defeat."

The Four swung its sword. The sword fell upon the faceted eye within which Agak's intelligence-pool bubbled, just as his sister's had once bubbled. But Agak was stronger already and healed himself at once.

Agak's tendrils emerged and lashed at the Four and the Four cut at the tendrils as it sought his body. And Agak sucked more energy to himself. His body, which the mortals had mistaken for a building, began to glow burning scarlet and to radiate an impossible heat.

The sword roared and flared so that black light mingled with the gold and flowed against the scarlet. And all the while the Four could sense its own universe shrinking and dying.

"*Give back, Agak, what you have stolen!*" said the Four.

Planes and angles and curves, wires and tubes, flickered with deep red heat and Agak sighed. The universe whimpered.

"*I am stronger than you,*" said Agak. "*Now.*"

And Agak sucked again.

The Four knew that Agak's attention was diverted for just that short while as he fed. And the Four knew that it, too, must draw energy from its own universe if Agak were to be defeated. So the sword was raised.

The sword was flung back, its blade slicing through tens of thousands of dimensions and drawing their power to it. Then it began to swing back. It swung and black light bellowed from its blade. It swung and Agak became aware of it. His body began to alter. Down towards the sorcerer's great eye, down towards Agak's intelligence-pool swept the black blade.

Agak's many tendrils rose to defend the sorcerer against the sword, but the sword cut through them as if they were not there and it struck the eight-sided chamber which was Agak's eyes and it plunged on down into Agak's intelligence-pool, deep into the stuff of the sorcerer's sensibility, drawing up Agak's energy into itself and thence into its master, the Four Who Were One. And something screamed through the universe and something sent a tremor through the universe. And the universe was dead, even as Agak began to die.

The Four did not dare wait to see if Agak were completely vanquished. It swept the sword out, back through the dimensions, and everywhere the blade touched the energy was restored. The sword rang round and round, round and round, dispersing the energy. And the sword sang its triumph and its glee.

And little shreds of black and golden light whispered away and were reabsorbed.

For a moment the universe had been dead. Now it lived and Agak's energy had been added to it.

Agak lived, too, but he was frozen. He had attempted to change his shape. Now he still half-resembled the building Elric had seen when he first came to the island, but part of him resembled the Four Who Were One—here was part of Corum's face, here a leg, there a fragment of sword-blade—as if Agak had believed, at the end, that the Four could only be defeated if its own form were assumed, just as the Four had assumed Gagak's form.

"*We had waited so long . . .*" Agak sighed and then he was dead.

And the Four sheathed its sword.

Then there came a howling through the ruins of the many cities and a strong wind blustered against the body of the Four so that it was forced to kneel on its eight legs and bow its four-faced head before the gale. Then, gradually, it reassumed the shape of Gagak, the sorceress, and then it lay within Gagak's stagnating intelligence-pool and then it rose over it, hovered for a moment, withdrew its sword from the pool. The four beings fled apart and Elric and Hawkmoon and Erekosë and Corum stood with sword-blades touching over the centre of the dead brain.

The four men sheathed their swords. They stared for a second into each other's eyes and all saw terror and awe there. Elric turned away.

He could find neither thoughts nor emotions in him which would relate to what had happened. There were no words he could use. He stood looking dumbly at Ashnar the Lynx and he wondered why Ashnar giggled and chewed at his beard and scraped at the flesh of his own face with his fingernails, his sword forgotten upon the floor of the grey chamber.

"*Now I have flesh again. Now I have flesh,*" Ashnar kept saying.

Elric wondered why Hown Serpent-tamer lay curled in a ball at Ashnar's feet, and why when Brut of Lashmar emerged from the passage he fell down and lay stretched upon the floor, stirring a little and moaning as if in disturbed slumber. Otto Blendker came into the chamber. His sword was in its scabbard. His eyes were tight shut and he hugged at himself, shivering.

Elric thought to himself: *I must forget all this or sanity will disappear for ever.*

He went to Brut and helped the blond warrior to his feet. "What did you see?"

"More than I deserved, for all my sins. We were trapped—trapped in that skull . . ." Then Brut began to weep as a small child might weep and Elric took the tall warrior in his own arms and stroked his head and could not find words or sounds with which to comfort him.

"We must go," said Erekosë. His eyes were glazed. He staggered as he walked.

Thus, dragging those who had fainted, leading those who had gone mad, leaving those who had died behind, they fled through the dead passages of Gagak's body, no longer plagued by the things she had created in her attempt to rid that body of those she had experienced as an invading disease. The passages and chambers were cold and brittle and the men were glad when they stood outside and saw the ruins, the sourceless shadows, the red, static sun.

Otto Blendker was the only one of the warriors who seemed to retain his sanity through the ordeal, when they had been absorbed, unknowingly, into the body of the Four Who Were One. He dragged his brand from his belt and he took out his tinder and ignited it. Soon the brand was flaming and the others lighted theirs from his. Elric trudged to where Agak's remains still lay and he shuddered as he recognized in a monstrous stone face part of his own features. He felt that the stuff could not possibly burn, but it did. Behind him Gagak's body blazed, too. They were swiftly consumed and pillars of growling fire jutted into the sky, sending up a smoke of white and crimson which for a little while obscured the red disc of the sun.

The men watched the corpses burn.

"I wonder," said Corum, "if the captain knew why he sent us here?"

"Or if he suspected what would happen?" said Hawkmoon. Hawkmoon's tone was near to resentful.

"Only we—only that being—could battle Agak and Gagak in anything resembling their own terms," said Erekosë. "Other means would not have been successful, no other creature could have the particular qualities, the enormous power needed to slay such strange sorcerers."

"So it seems," said Elric, and he would talk no more of it.

"Hopefully," said Corum, "you will forget this experience as you forgot—or will forget—the other."

Elric offered him a hard stare. "Hopefully, brother," he said.

Erekosë's chuckle was ironic. "Who could recall that?" And he, too, said no more.

Ashnar the Lynx, who had ceased his gigglings as he watched the fire, shrieked suddenly and broke away from the main party. He ran towards the flickering column and then veered away, disappearing among the ruins and the shadows.

Otto Blendker gave Elric a questioning stare, but Elric shook his head. "Why follow him? What can we do for him?" He looked down at Hown Serpent-tamer. He had particularly liked the man in the sea-green armour. He shrugged.

When they moved on, they left the curled body of Hown Serpent-tamer where it lay, helping only Brut of Lashmar across the rubble and down to the shore.

Soon they saw the white mist ahead and knew they neared the sea, though the ship was not in sight.

At the edge of the mist both Hawkmoon and Erekosë paused.

"I will not rejoin the ship," said Hawkmoon. "I feel I've served my passage now. If I can find Tanelorn, this, I suspect, is where I must look."

"My own feelings." Erekosë nodded his head.

Elric looked at Corum. Corum smiled. "I have already found Tanelorn. I go back to the ship in the hope that soon it will deposit me upon a more familiar shore."

"That is my hope," said Elric. His arm still supported Brut of Lashmar.

Brut whispered, "What was it? What happened to us?"

Elric increased his grip upon the warrior's shoulder. "Nothing," he said.

Then, as Elric tried to lead Brut into the mist, the blond warrior stepped back, breaking free. "I will stay," he said. He moved away from Elric. "I am sorry."

Elric was puzzled. "Brut?"

"I am sorry," Brut said again. "I fear you. I fear that ship."

Elric made to follow the warrior, but Corum put a hard silver hand upon his shoulder. "Comrade, let us be gone from this place." His smile was bleak. "It is what is back there that I fear more than the ship."

They stared over the ruins. In the distance they could see the remains of the fire and there were two shadows there now, the shadows of Gagak and Agak as they had first appeared to them.

Elric drew a cold breath of air. "With that I agree," he told Corum.

Otto Blendker was the only warrior who chose to return to the ship with them. "If that is Tanelorn, it is not, after all, the place I sought," he said.

Soon they were waist-deep in the water. They saw again the outlines of the Dark Ship; they saw the captain leaning on the rail, his arm raised as if in salute to someone or something upon the island.

"Captain," called Corum, "we come aboard."

"You are welcome," said the captain. "Yes, you are welcome." The blind face turned towards them as Elric reached out for the rope ladder. "Would you care to sail for a while into the silent places, the restful places?"

"I think so," said Elric. He paused, halfway up the ladder, and he touched his head. "I have many wounds."

He reached the rail and with his own cool hands the captain helped him over. "They will heal, Elric."

Elric moved closer to the mast. He leaned against it and watched the silent crew as they unfurled the sail. Corum and Otto Blendker came aboard. Elric listened to the sharp sound of the anchor as it was drawn up. The ship swayed a little.

Otto Blendker looked at Elric, then at the captain, then he turned and went into his cabin, saying nothing at all as he closed the door.

The sail filled, the ship began to move. The captain reached out and found Elric's arm. He took Corum's arm, too, and led them towards his cabin. "The wine," he said. "It will heal all the wounds."

At the door of the captain's cabin Elric paused. "And does the wine have other properties?" he asked. "Does it cloud a man's reason? Was it that which made me accept your commission, Captain?"

The captain shrugged. "What is reason?"

The ship was gathering speed. The white mist was thicker and a cold wind blew at the rags of cloth and metal Elric wore. He sniffed, thinking for a moment that he smelled smoke upon that wind.

He put his two hands to his face and touched his flesh. His face was cold. He let his hands fall to his sides and he followed the captain into the warmth of the cabin.

The captain poured wine into silver cups from his silver jug. He stretched out a hand to offer a cup to Elric and to Corum. They drank.

A little later the captain said, "How do you feel?"

Elric said, "I feel nothing."

And that night he dreamed only of shadows and in the morning he could not understand his dream at all.

BOOK TWO

SAILING TO THE PRESENT

CHAPTER ONE

HIS BONE-WHITE, long-fingered hand upon a carved demon's head in black-brown hardwood (one of the few such decorations to be found anywhere about the vessel), the tall man stood alone in the ship's fo'c'sle and stared through large, slanting crimson eyes at the mist into which they moved with a speed and sureness to make any mortal mariner marvel and become incredulous.

There were sounds in the distance, incongruous with the sounds of even this nameless, timeless sea: thin sounds, agonized and terrible, for all that they remained remote—yet the ship followed them, as if drawn by them; they grew louder—pain and despair were there, but terror was predominant.

Elric had heard such sounds echoing from his cousin Yyrkoon's sardonically named "Pleasure Chambers" in the days before he had fled the responsibilities of ruling all that remained of the old Melnibonéan Empire. These were the voices of men whose very souls were under siege; men to whom death meant not mere extinction, but a continuation of existence, forever in thrall to some cruel and supernatural master. He had heard men cry so when his salvation and his nemesis, his great black battle-blade Stormbringer, drank their souls.

He did not savour the sound: he hated it, turned his back away from the source and was about to descend the ladder to the main deck when he realized that Otto Blendker had come up behind him. Now that Corum had been borne off by friends with chariots which could ride upon the surface of the water, Blendker was the last of those comrades to have fought at Elric's side against the two alien sorcerers Gagak and Agak.

Blendker's black, scarred face was troubled. The ex-scholar, turned hireling sword, covered his ears with his huge palms.

"Ach! By the Twelve Symbols of Reason, Elric, who makes that din? It's as though we sail close to the shores of hell itself!"

Prince Elric of Melniboné shrugged. "I'd be prepared to forgo an answer and leave my curiosity unsatisfied, Master Blendker, if only our ship would change course. As it is, we sail closer and closer to the source."

Blendker grunted his agreement. "I've no wish to encounter whatever it is that causes those poor fellows to scream so! Perhaps we should inform the captain."

"You think he does not know where his own ship sails?" Elric's smile had little humour.

The tall black man rubbed at the inverted V-shaped scar which ran from his forehead to his jawbones. "I wonder if he plans to put us into battle again."

"I'll not fight another for him." Elric's hand moved from the carved rail to the pommel of his runesword. "I have business of my own to attend to, once I'm back on real land."

A wind came from nowhere. There was a sudden rent in the mist. Now Elric could see that the ship sailed through rust-coloured water. Peculiar lights gleamed in that water, just below the surface. There was an impression of creatures moving ponderously in the depths of the ocean and, for a moment, Elric thought he glimpsed a white, bloated face not dissimilar to his own—a Melnibonéan face. Impulsively he whirled, back to the rail, looking past Blendker as he strove to control the nausea in his throat.

For the first time since he had come aboard the Dark Ship he was able clearly to see the length of the vessel. Here were the two great wheels, one beside him on the foredeck, one at the far end of the ship on the rear-deck, tended now as always by the steersman, the captain's sighted twin. There was the great mast bearing the taut black sail, and fore and aft of this, the two deck cabins, one of which was entirely empty (its occupants having been killed during their last landfall) and one of which was occupied only by himself and Blendker. Elric's gaze was drawn back to the steersman and not for the first time the albino wondered how much influence the captain's twin had over the course of the Dark Ship. The man seemed tireless, rarely, to Elric's knowledge, going below to his quarters, which occupied the stern deck as the captain's occupied the foredeck. Once or twice Elric or Blendker had tried to involve the steersman in conversation, but he appeared to be as dumb as his brother was blind.

The cryptographic, geometrical carvings covering all the ship's wood and most of its metal, from sternpost to figurehead, were picked out by the shreds of pale mist still clinging to them (and again Elric wondered if the ship actually generated the mist normally surrounding it) and, as he watched, the designs slowly turned to pale pink fire as the light from that red star, which forever followed them, permeated the overhead cloud.

A noise from below. The captain, his long red-gold hair drifting in a breeze which Elric could not feel, emerged from his cabin. The captain's circlet of blue jade, worn like a diadem, had turned to something of a violet shade in the pink light, and his buff-coloured hose and tunic reflected the hue—even the silver sandals with their silver lacing glittered with the rosy tint.

Again Elric looked upon that mysterious blind face, as unhuman, in the accepted sense, as his own, and puzzled upon the origin of the one who would allow himself to be called nothing but "Captain."

As if at the captain's summons, the mist drew itself about the ship again, as a woman might draw a froth of furs about her body. The red star's light faded, but the distant screams continued.

Did the captain notice the screams now for the first time, or was this a pantomime of surprise? His blind head tilted, a hand went to his ear. He murmured in a tone of satisfaction, "Aha!" The head lifted. "Elric?"

"Here," said the albino. "Above you."

"We are almost there, Elric."

The apparently fragile hand found the rail of the companionway. The captain began to climb.

Elric faced him at the top of the ladder. "If it's a battle . . ."

The captain's smile was enigmatic, bitter. "It was a fight—or shall be one."

" . . . we'll have no part of it," concluded the albino firmly.

"It is not one of the battles in which my ship is directly involved," the blind man reassured him. "Those whom you can hear are the vanquished—lost in some future which I think you will experience close to the end of your present incarnation."

Elric waved a dismissive hand. "I'll be glad, Captain, if you would cease such vapid mystification. I'm weary of it."

"I'm sorry it offends you. I answer literally, according to my instincts."

The captain, going past Elric and Otto Blendker so that he could stand at the rail, seemed to be apologizing. He said nothing for a while, but listened to the disturbing and confused babble from the mist. Then he nodded, apparently satisfied.

"We'll sight land shortly. If you would disembark and seek your own world, I should advise you to do so now. This is the closest we shall ever come again to your plane."

Elric let his anger show. He cursed, invoking Arioch's name, and put a hand upon the blind man's shoulder. "What? You cannot return me directly to my own plane?"

"It is too late." The captain's dismay was apparently genuine. "The ship sails on. We near the end of our long voyage."

"But how shall I find my world? I have no sorcery great enough to move me between the spheres! And demonic assistance is denied me here."

"There is one gateway to your world," the captain told him. "That is why I suggest you disembark. Elsewhere there is none at all. Your sphere and this one intersect directly."

"But you say this lies in my future."

"Be sure—you will return to your own time. Here you are timeless. It is why your memory is so poor. It is why you remember so little of what befalls you. Seek for the gateway—it is crimson and it emerges from the sea off the coast of the island."

"Which island?"

"The one we approach."

Elric hesitated. "And where shall you go, when I have landed?"

"To Tanelorn," said the captain. "There is something I must do there. My brother and I must complete our destiny. We carry cargo as well as men. Many will try to stop us now, for they fear our cargo. We might perish, but yet we must do all we can to reach Tanelorn."

"Was that not, then, Tanelorn, where we fought Agak and Gagak?"

"That was nothing more than a broken dream of Tanelorn, Elric."

The Melnibonéan knew that he would receive no more information from the captain.

"You offer me a poor choice—to sail with you into danger and never see my own world again, or to risk landing on yonder island inhabited, by the sound of it, by the damned and those which prey upon the damned!"

The captain's blind eyes moved in Elric's direction. "I know," he said softly. "But it is the best I can offer you, nonetheless."

The screams, the imploring, terrified shouts, were closer now, but there were fewer of them. Glancing over the side, Elric thought he saw a pair of armoured hands rising from the water; there was foam, red-flecked and noxious, and there was yellowish scum in which pieces of frightful flotsam drifted; there were broken timbers, scraps of canvas, tatters of flags and clothing, fragments of weapons and, increasingly, there were floating corpses.

"But where was the battle?" Blendker whispered, fascinated and horrified by the sight.

"Not on this plane," the captain told him. "You see only the wreckage which has drifted over from one world to another."

"Then it was a supernatural battle?"

The captain smiled again. "I am not omniscient. But, yes, I believe there were supernatural agencies involved. The warriors of half a world fought in the sea-battle—to decide the fate of the multiverse. It is—or will be—one of the decisive battles to determine the fate of Mankind, to fix Man's destiny for the coming Cycle."

"Who were the participants?" asked Elric, voicing the question in spite of his resolve. "What were the issues as they understood them?"

"You will know in time, I think." The captain's head faced the sea again.

Blendker sniffed the air. "Ach! It's foul!"

Elric, too, found the odour increasingly unpleasant. Here and there now the water was lighted by guttering fires which revealed the faces of the drowning, some of whom still managed to cling to pieces of blackened driftwood. Not all the faces were human, though they had the appearance of having once been human; things with the snouts of pigs and of bulls raised twisted hands to the Dark Ship and grunted plaintively for succour, but the captain ignored them and the steersman held his course.

Fires spluttered and water hissed; smoke mingled with the mist. Elric had his sleeve over his mouth and nose and was glad that the smoke and mist between them helped obscure the sights, for as the wreckage grew thicker not a few of the corpses he saw reminded him more of reptiles than of men, their pale, lizard bellies spilling something other than blood.

"If that is my future," Elric told the captain, "I've a mind to remain on board, after all."

"You have a duty, as have I," said the captain quietly. "The future must be served, as much as the past and the present."

Elric shook his head. "I fled the duties of an empire because I sought freedom," the albino told him. "And freedom I must have."

"No," murmured the captain. "There is no such thing. Not yet. Not for us. We must go through much more before we can even begin to guess what freedom is. The price for the knowledge alone is probably higher than any you would care to pay at this stage of your life. Indeed, life itself is often the price."

"I also sought release from metaphysics when I left Melniboné," said Elric. "I'll get the rest of my gear and take the land that's offered. With luck this Crimson Gate will be quickly found and I'll be back among dangers and torments which will, at least, be familiar."

"It is the only decision you could have made." The captain's blind head turned towards Blendker. "And you, Otto Blendker? What shall you do?"

"Elric's world is not mine and I like not the sound of those screams. What can you promise me, sir, if I sail on with you?"

"Nothing but a good death." There was regret in the captain's voice.

"Death is the promise we're all born with, sir. A good death is better than a poor one. I'll sail on with you."

"As you like. I think you're wise." The captain sighed. "I'll say farewell to you, then, Elric of Melniboné. You fought well in my service and I thank you."

"Fought for what?" Elric asked.

"Oh, call it Mankind. Call it Fate. Call it a dream or an ideal, if you wish."

"Shall I never have a clearer answer?"

"Not from me. I do not think there is one."

"You allow a man little faith." Elric began to descend the companionway.

"There are two kinds of faith, Elric. Like freedom, there is a kind which is easily kept but proves not worth the keeping, and there is a kind which is hard-won. I agree, I offer little of the former."

Elric strode towards his cabin. He laughed, feeling genuine affection for the blind man at that moment. "I thought I had a penchant for such ambiguities, but I have met my match in you, Captain."

He noticed that the steersman had left his place at the wheel and was swinging out a boat on its davits, preparatory to lowering it.

"Is that for me?"

The steersman nodded.

Elric ducked into his cabin. He was leaving the ship with nothing but that which he had brought aboard, only his clothing and his armour were in a poorer state of repair than they had been, and his mind was in a considerably greater state of confusion.

Without hesitation he gathered up his things, drawing his heavy cloak about him, pulling on his gauntlets, fastening buckles and thongs, then he left the cabin and returned to the deck. The captain was pointing through the mist at the dark outlines of a coast. "Can you see land, Elric?"

"I can."

"You must go quickly, then."

"Willingly."

Elric swung himself over the rail and into the boat. The boat struck the side of the ship several times, so that the hull boomed like the beating of some huge funeral drum. Otherwise there was silence now upon the misty waters and no sign of wreckage.

Blendker saluted him. "I wish you luck, comrade."

"You, too, Master Blendker."

The boat began to sink towards the flat surface of the sea, the pulleys of the davits creaking. Elric clung to the rope, letting go as the boat hit the water. He stumbled and sat down heavily upon the seat, releasing the ropes so that the boat drifted at once away from the Dark Ship. He got out the oars and fitted them into their rowlocks.

As he pulled towards the shore he heard the captain's voice calling to him, but the words were muffled by the mist and he would never know, now, if the blind man's last communication had been a warning or merely some formal pleasantry. He did not care. The boat moved smoothly through the water; the mist began to thin, but so, too, did the light fade.

Suddenly he was under a twilight sky, the sun already gone and stars appearing. Before he had reached the shore it was already completely dark, with the moon not yet risen, and it was with difficulty that he beached the boat on what seemed flat rocks, and stumbled inland until he judged himself safe enough from any inrushing tide.

Then, with a sigh, he lay down, thinking just to order his thoughts before moving on; but, almost instantly, he was asleep.

CHAPTER TWO

Elric dreamed.

He dreamed not merely of the end of his world but of the end of an entire cycle in the history of the cosmos. He dreamed that he was not only Elric of Melniboné but that he was other men, too—men who were pledged to some numinous cause which even they could not describe. And he dreamed that he had dreamed of the Dark Ship and Tanelorn and Agak and Gagak while he lay exhausted upon a beach somewhere beyond the borders of Pikarayd; and when he woke up he was smiling sardonically, congratulating himself for the possession of a grandiose imagination. But he could not clear his head entirely of the impression left by that dream.

This shore was not the same, so plainly something had befallen him—perhaps he had been drugged by slavers, then later abandoned when they found him not what they expected . . . But, no, the explanation would not do. If he could discover his whereabouts, he might also recall the true facts.

It was dawn, for certain. He sat up and looked about him.

He was sprawled upon a dark, sea-washed limestone pavement, cracked in a hundred places, the cracks so deep that the small streams of foaming salt water rushing through these many narrow channels made raucous what would otherwise have been a very still morning.

Elric climbed to his feet, using his scabbarded runesword to steady himself. His bone-white lids closed for a moment over his crimson eyes as he sought, again, to recollect the events which had brought him here.

He recalled his flight from Pikarayd, his panic, his falling into a coma of hopelessness, his dreams. And, because he was evidently neither dead nor a prisoner, he could at least conclude that his pursuers had, after all, given up the chase, for if they had found him they would have killed him.

Opening his eyes and casting about him, he marked the peculiar blue quality of the light, doubtless a trick of the sun behind the grey clouds, which made the landscape ghastly and gave the sea a dull, metallic look.

The limestone terraces which rose from the sea and stretched above him shone intermittently, like polished lead. On an impulse he held his hand to the light and inspected it. The normally lustreless white of his skin was now tinged with a faint, bluish luminosity. He found it pleasing and smiled as a child might smile, in innocent wonder.

He had expected to be tired, but he now realized that he felt unusually refreshed, as if he had slept long after a good meal, and, deciding not to question the fact of this fortunate (and unlikely) gift, he determined to climb the cliffs in the hope that he might get some idea of his bearings before he decided which direction he would take.

Limestone could be a little treacherous, but it made easy climbing, for there was almost always somewhere that one terrace met another.

He climbed carefully and steadily, finding many footholds, and seemed to gain considerable height quite quickly, yet it was noon before he had reached the top and found himself standing at the edge of a broad, rocky plateau which fell away sharply to form a close horizon. Beyond the plateau was only the sky. Save for sparse, brownish grass, little grew here and there were no signs at all of human habitation. It was now, for the first time, that Elric realized the absence of any form of wildlife. Not a single seabird flew in the air, not an insect crept through the grass. Instead, there was an enormous silence hanging over the brown plain.

Elric was still remarkably untired, so he decided to make the best use he could of his energy and reach the edge of the plateau in the hope that, from there, he would sight a town or a village. He pressed on, feeling no lack of food and water, and his stride was singularly energetic, still; but he had misjudged his distance and the sun had begun to set well before his journey to the edge was completed. The sky on all sides turned a deep, velvety blue and the few clouds that there were in it were also tinged blue, and now, for the first time, Elric realized that the sun itself was not its normal shade, that it burned blackish purple, and he wondered again if he still dreamed.

The ground began to rise sharply and it was with some effort that he walked, but before the light had completely faded he was on the steep flank of a hill, descending towards a wide valley which, though bereft of trees, contained a river which wound through rocks and russet turf and bracken.

After a short rest, Elric decided to press on, although night had fallen, and see if he could reach the river where he might at least drink and, possibly, in the morning find fish to eat.

Again, no moon appeared to aid his progress and he walked for two or three hours in a darkness which was almost total, stumbling occasionally into large rocks, until the ground leveled and he felt sure he had reached the floor of the valley.

He had developed a strong thirst by now and was feeling somewhat hungry, but decided that it might be best to wait until morning before seeking the river when, rounding a particularly tall rock, he saw, with some astonishment, the light of a campfire.

Hopefully this would be the fire of a company of merchants, a trading caravan on its way to some civilized country which would allow him to travel with it, perhaps in return for his services as a mercenary swordsman (it would not be the first time, since he had left Melniboné, that he had earned his bread in such a way).

Yet Elric's old instincts did not desert him; he approached the fire cautiously and let no-one see him. Beneath an overhang of rock, made shadowy by the flame's light, he stood and observed the group of fifteen or sixteen men who sat or lay close to the fire, playing some kind of game involving dice and slivers of numbered ivory.

Gold, bronze and silver gleamed in the firelight as the men staked large sums on the fall of a die and the turn of a slip of ivory.

Elric guessed that, if they had not been so intent on their game, these men must certainly have detected his approach, for they were not, after all, merchants. By the evidence, they were warriors, wearing scarred leather and dented metal, their weapons ready to hand, yet they belonged to no army—unless it be an army of bandits—for they were of all races and, oddly, seemed to be from various periods in the history of the Young Kingdoms.

It was as if they had looted some scholar's collection of relics. An axeman of the later Lormyrian Republic, which had come to an end some two hundred years ago, lay with his shoulder rubbing the elbow of a Chalalite bowman, from a period roughly contemporary with Elric's own. Close to the Chalalite sat a short Ilmioran infantryman of a century past. Next to him was a Filkharian in the barbaric dress of that nation's earliest times. Tarkeshites, Shazaarians, Vilmirians all mingled and the only thing they had in common, by the look of them, was a villainous, hungry cast to their features.

In other circumstances Elric might have skirted this encampment and moved on, but he was so glad to find human beings of any sort that he ignored the disturbing incongruities of the group; yet he remained content to watch them.

One of the men, less unwholesome than the others, was a bulky, black-bearded, bald-headed sea-warrior clad in the casual leathers and silks of the people of the Purple Towns. It was when this man produced a large gold Melnibonéan wheel—a coin not minted, as most coins, but carved by craftsmen to a design both ancient and intricate—that Elric's caution was fully conquered by his curiosity.

Very few of those coins existed in Melniboné and none, that Elric had heard of, outside; for the coins were not used for trade with the Young Kingdoms. They were prized, even by the nobility of Melniboné.

It seemed to Elric that the bald-headed man could only have acquired the coin from another Melnibonéan traveler—and Elric knew of no other Melnibonéans who shared his penchant for exploration. His wariness dismissed, he stepped into the circle.

If he had not been completely obsessed by the thought of the Melnibonéan wheel he might have taken some satisfaction in the sudden scuffle to arms which resulted. Within seconds, the majority of the men were on their feet, their weapons drawn.

For a moment, the gold wheel was forgotten. His hand upon his runesword's pommel, he presented the other in a placatory gesture.

"Forgive the interruption, gentlemen. I am but one tired fellow

soldier who seeks to join you. I would beg some information and purchase some food, if you have it to spare."

On foot, the warriors had an even more ruffianly appearance.
They grinned among themselves, entertained by Elric's courtesy but
not impressed by it.

One, in the feathered helmet of a Pan Tangian sea-chief, with features to match—swarthy, sinister—pushed his head forward on its
long neck and said banteringly:

"We've company enough, white-face. And few here are overfond
of the man-demons of Melniboné. You must be rich."

Elric recalled the animosity with which Melnibonéans were regarded in the Young Kingdoms, particularly by those from Pan Tang
who envied the Dragon Isle her power and her wisdom and, of late,
had begun crudely to imitate Melniboné.

Increasingly on his guard, he said evenly, "I have a little money."

"Then we'll take it, demon." The Pan Tangian presented a dirty
palm just below Elric's nose as he growled, "Give it over and be on your
way."

Elric's smile was polite and fastidious, as if he had been told a poor
joke.

The Pan Tangian evidently thought the joke better than did
Elric, for he laughed heartily and looked to his nearest fellows for approval.

Coarse laughter infected the night and only the bald-headed,
black-bearded man did not join in the jest, but took a step or two back,
while all the others pressed forward.

The Pan Tangian's face was close to Elric's own; his breath was
foul and Elric saw that his beard and hair were alive with lice, yet he
kept his head, replying in the same equable tone:

"Give me some decent food, a flask of water—some wine, if you
have it—and I'll gladly give you the money I have."

The laughter rose and fell again as Elric continued:

"But if you would take my money and leave me with naught—
then I must defend myself. I have a good sword."

The Pan Tangian strove to imitate Elric's irony. "But you will note, Sir Demon, that we outnumber you. Considerably."

Softly the albino spoke: "I've noticed that fact, but I'm not disturbed by it," and he had drawn the black blade even as he finished speaking, for they had come at him with a rush.

And the Pan Tangian was the first to die, sliced through the side, his vertebrae sheared, and Stormbringer, having taken its first soul, began to sing.

A Chalalite died next, leaping with stabbing javelin poised, on the point of the runesword, and Stormbringer murmured with pleasure.

But it was not until it had sliced the head clean off a Filkharian pike-master that the sword began to croon and come fully to life, black fire flickering up and down its length, its strange runes glowing.

Now the warriors knew they battled sorcery and became more cautious, yet they scarcely paused in their attack, and Elric, thrusting and parrying, hacking and slicing, needed all of the fresh, dark energy the sword passed on to him.

Lance, sword, axe and dirk were blocked, wounds were given and received, but the dead had not yet outnumbered the living when Elric found himself with his back against the rock and nigh a dozen sharp weapons seeking his vitals.

It was at this point, when Elric had become somewhat less than confident that he could best so many, that the bald-headed warrior, axe in one gloved hand, sword in the other, came swiftly into the firelight and set upon those of his fellows closest to him.

"I thank you, sir!" Elric was able to shout, during the short respite this sudden turn produced. His morale improved, he resumed the attack.

The Lormyrian was cloven from hip to thigh as he dodged a feint; a Filkharian, who should have been dead four hundred years before, fell with the blood bubbling from lips and nostrils, and the corpses began to pile one upon the other. Still Stormbringer sang its sinister battle-song and still the runesword passed its power to its master so that with every death Elric found strength to slay more of the soldiers.

Those who remained now began to express their regret for their hasty attack. Where oaths and threats had issued from their mouths, now came plaintive petitions for mercy and those who had laughed with such bold braggadocio now wept like young girls, but Elric, full of his old battle-joy, spared none.

Meanwhile the man from the Purple Towns, unaided by sorcery, put axe and sword to good work and dealt with three more of his one-time comrades, exulting in his work as if he had nursed a taste for it for some time.

"Yoi! But this is worthwhile slaughter!" cried the black-bearded one.

And then that busy butchery was suddenly done and Elric realized that none was left save himself and his new ally, who stood leaning on his axe, panting and grinning like a hound at the kill, replacing a steel skull-cap upon his pate from where it had fallen during the fight, and wiping a bloody sleeve over the sweat glistening on his brow, and saying, in a deep, good-humoured tone:

"Well now, it is we who are wealthy, of a sudden."

Elric sheathed a Stormbringer still reluctant to return to its scabbard. "You desire their gold. Is that why you aided me?"

The black-bearded soldier laughed. "I owed them a debt and had been biding my time, waiting to pay. These rascals are all that were left of a pirate crew which slew everyone aboard my own ship when we wandered into strange waters—they would have slain me had I not told them I wished to join them. Now I am revenged. Not that I am above taking the gold, since much of it belongs to me and my dead brothers. It will go to their wives and their children when I return to the Purple Towns."

"How did you convince them not to kill you, too?" Elric sought among the ruins of the fire for something to eat. He found some cheese and began to chew upon it.

"They had no captain or navigator, it seemed. None were real sailors at all, but coast-huggers, based upon this island. They were stranded here, you see, and had taken to piracy as a last resort, but were too terrified to risk the open sea. Besides, after the fight, they had no ship. We had managed to sink that as we fought. We sailed mine to this shore, but provisions were already low and they had no stomach for setting sail without full holds, so I pretended that I knew this coast (may the gods take my soul if I ever see it again after this business) and offered to lead them inland to a village they might loot. They had heard of no such village, but believed me when I said it lay in a hidden valley. That way I prolonged my life while I waited for the opportunity to be revenged upon them. It was a foolish hope, I know. Yet—" grinning—"as it happened, it was well-founded after all! Eh?"

The black-bearded man glanced a little warily at Elric, uncertain of what the albino might say, hoping, however, for comradeship, though it was well known how haughty Melnibonéans were. Elric could tell that all these thoughts went through his new acquaintance's mind; he had seen many others make similar calculations. So he smiled openly and slapped the man on the shoulder.

"You saved my life, also, my friend. We are both fortunate."

The man sighed in relief and slung his axe upon his back. "Aye—lucky's the word. But shall our luck hold, I wonder?"

"You do not know the island at all?"

"Nor the waters, either. How we came to them I'll never guess. Enchanted waters, though, without question. You've seen the colour of the sun?"

"I have."

"Well—" the seaman bent to remove a pendant from around the Pan Tangian's throat—"you'd know more about enchantments and sorceries than I. How came you here, Sir Melnibonéan?"

"I know not. I fled from some who hunted me. I came to a shore and could flee no further. Then I dreamed a great deal. When next I awoke I was on the shore again, but of this island."

"Spirits of some sort—maybe friendly to you—took you to safety, away from your enemies."

"That's just possible," Elric agreed, "for we have many allies among the elementals. I am called Elric and I am self-exiled from Melniboné. I travel because I believe I have something to learn from the folk of the Young Kingdoms. I have no power, save what you see . . ."

The black-bearded man's eyes narrowed in appraisal as he pointed at himself with his thumb. "I'm Smiorgan Baldhead, once a sea-lord of the Purple Towns. I commanded a fleet of merchantmen. Perhaps I still do. I shall not know until I return—if I ever do return."

"Then let us pool our knowledge and our resources, Smiorgan Baldhead, and make plans to leave this island as soon as we can."

Elric walked back to where he saw traces of the abandoned game, trampled into the mud and the blood. From among the dice and the ivory slips, the silver and the bronze coins, he found the gold Melnibonéan wheel. He picked it up and held it in his outstretched palm. The wheel almost covered the whole palm. In the old days, it had been the currency of kings.

"This was yours, friend?" he asked Smiorgan.

Smiorgan Baldhead looked up from where he was still searching the Pan Tangian for his stolen possessions. He nodded.

"Aye. Would you keep it as part of your share?"

Elric shrugged. "I'd rather know whence it came. Who gave it you?"

"It was not stolen. It's Melnibonéan, then?"

"Yes."

"I guessed it."

"From whom did you obtain it?"

Smiorgan straightened up, having completed his search. He scratched at a slight wound on his forearm. "It was used to buy passage on our ship—before we were lost—before the raiders attacked us."

"Passage? By a Melnibonéan?"

"Maybe," said Smiorgan. He seemed reluctant to speculate.

"Was he a warrior?"

Smiorgan smiled in his beard. "No. It was a woman gave that to me."

"How came she to take passage?"

Smiorgan began to pick up the rest of the money. "It's a long tale and, in part, a familiar one to most merchant sailors. We were seeking new markets for our goods and had equipped a good-sized fleet, which I commanded as the largest shareholder." He seated himself casually upon the big corpse of the Chalalite and began to count the money. "Would you hear the tale or do I bore you already?"

"I'd be glad to listen."

Reaching behind him, Smiorgan pulled a wine-flask from the belt of the corpse and offered it to Elric, who accepted it and drank sparingly of a wine which was unusually good.

Smiorgan took the flask when Elric had finished. "That's part of our cargo," he said. "We were proud of it. A good vintage, eh?"

"Excellent. So you set off from the Purple Towns?"

"Aye. Going towards the Unmapped East. We sailed for a couple of weeks, sighting some of the bleakest coasts I have ever seen, and then we saw no land at all for another week. That was when we entered a stretch of water we came to call the Roaring Rocks—like the Serpent's Teeth off Shazaar's coast, but much greater in expanse, and larger, too. Huge volcanic cliffs which rose from the sea on every side and around which the waters heaved and boiled and howled with a fierceness I've rarely experienced. Well, in short, the fleet was dispersed and at least four ships were lost on those rocks. At last we were able to escape those waters and found ourselves becalmed and alone. We searched for our sister ships for a while and then decided to give ourselves another week before turning for home, for we had no liking to go back into the Roaring Rocks again. Low on provisions, we sighted land at last—grassy cliffs and hospitable beaches and, inland, some signs of cultivation, so we knew we had found civilization again. We put into a small fishing port and satisfied the natives—who spoke no tongue used in the Young Kingdoms—that we were friendly. And that was when the woman approached us."

"The Melnibonéan woman?"

"If Melnibonéan she was. She was a fine-looking woman, I'll say that. We were short of provisions, as I told you, and short of any means of purchasing them, for the fishermen desired little of what we had to trade. Having given up our original quest, we were content to head westward again."

"The woman?"

"She wished to buy passage to the Young Kingdoms—and was content to go with us as far as Menii, our home port. For her passage she gave us two of those wheels. One was used to buy provisions in the town—Graghin, I think it was called—and after making repairs we set off again."

"You never reached the Purple Towns?"

"There were more storms—strange storms. Our instruments were useless, our lodestones were of no help to us at all. We became even more completely lost than before. Some of my men argued that we had gone beyond our own world altogether. Some blamed the woman, saying she was a sorceress who had no intention of going to Menii. But I believed her. Night fell and seemed to last for ever until we sailed into a calm dawn beneath a blue sun. My men were close to panic—and it takes much to make my men panic—when we sighted the island. As we headed for it those pirates attacked us in a ship which belonged to history—it should have been on the bottom of the ocean, not on the surface. I've seen pictures of such craft in murals on a temple wall in Tarkesh. In ramming us, she stove in half her port side and was sinking even when they swarmed aboard. They were desperate, savage men, Elric—half-starved and blood-hungry. We were weary after our voyage, but fought well. During the fighting the woman disappeared, killed herself, maybe, when she saw the stamp of our conquerors. After a long fight only myself and one other, who died soon after, were left. That was when I became cunning and decided to wait for revenge."

"The woman had a name?"

"None she would give. I have thought the matter over and suspect that, after all, we were used by her. Perhaps she did not seek Menii and the Young Kingdoms. Perhaps it was this world she sought, and, by sorcery, led us here."

"This world? You think it different from our own?"

"If only because of the sun's strange colour. Do you not think so, too? You, with your Melnibonéan knowledge of such things, must believe it."

"I have dreamed of such things," Elric admitted, but he would say no more.

"Most of the pirates thought as I—they were from all the ages of the Young Kingdoms. That much I discovered. Some were from the earliest years of the era, some from our own time—and some were from the future. Adventurers, most of them, who, at some stage in their lives, sought a legendary land of great riches which lay on the other side of an ancient gateway, rising from the middle of the ocean; but they found themselves trapped here, unable to sail back through this mysterious gate. Others had been involved in sea-fights, thought themselves drowned and woken up on the shores of the island. Many, I suppose, had once had reasonable virtues, but there is little to support life on the island and they had become wolves, living off one another or any ship unfortunate enough to pass, inadvertently, through this gate of theirs."

Elric recalled part of his dream. "Did any call it the 'Crimson Gate'?"

"Several did, aye."

"And yet the theory is unlikely, if you'll forgive my skepticism," Elric said. "As one who has passed through the Shade Gate to Ameeron . . ."

"You know of other worlds, then?"

"I've never heard of this one. And I am versed in such matters. That is why I doubt the reasoning. And yet, there was the dream . . ."

"Dream?"

"Oh, it was nothing. I am used to such dreams and give them no significance."

"The theory cannot seem surprising to a Melnibonéan, Elric!" Smiorgan grinned again. "It's I who should be skeptical, not you."

And Elric replied, half to himself: "Perhaps I fear the implications more." He lifted his head, and with the shaft of a broken spear, began to poke at the fire. "Certain ancient sorcerers of Melniboné proposed that an infinite number of worlds co-exist with our own. Indeed, my dreams, of late, have hinted as much!" He forced himself to smile. "But I cannot afford to believe such things. Thus, I reject them."

"Wait for the dawn," said Smiorgan Baldhead. "The colour of the sun shall prove the theory."

"Perhaps it will prove only that we both dream," said Elric. The smell of death was strong in his nostrils. He pushed aside those corpses nearest to the fire and settled himself to sleep.

Smiorgan Baldhead had begun to sing a strong yet lilting song in his own dialect, which Elric could scarcely follow.

"Do you sing of your victory over your enemies?" the albino asked.

Smiorgan paused for a moment, half-amused. "No, Sir Elric, I sing to keep the shades at bay. After all, these fellows' ghosts must still be lurking nearby, in the dark, so little time has passed since they died."

"Fear not," Elric told him. "Their souls are already eaten."

But Smiorgan sang on, and his voice was louder, his song more intense, than ever it had been before.

Just before he fell asleep, Elric thought he heard a horse whinny, and he meant to ask Smiorgan if any of the pirates had been mounted, but he fell asleep before he could do so.

CHAPTER THREE

Recalling little of his voyage on the Dark Ship, Elric would never know how he came to reach the world in which he now found himself. In later years he would recall most of these experiences as dreams, and indeed they seemed dreamlike even as they occurred.

He slept uneasily, and in the morning the clouds were heavier, shining with that strange, leaden light, though the sun itself was obscured. Smiorgan Baldhead of the Purple Towns was pointing upward, already on his feet, speaking with quiet triumph:

"Will that evidence suffice to convince you, Elric of Melniboné?"

"I am convinced of a quality about the light—possibly about this terrain—which makes the sun appear blue," Elric replied. He glanced with distaste around him at the carnage. The corpses made a wretched sight and he was filled with a nebulous misery that was neither remorse nor pity.

Smiorgan's sigh was sardonic. "Well, Sir Skeptic, we had best retrace my steps and seek my ship. What say you?"

"I agree," the albino told him.

"How far had you marched from the coast when you found us?"

Elric told him.

Smiorgan smiled. "You arrived in the nick of time, then. I should have been most embarrassed by today if the sea had been reached and I could show my pirate friends no village! I shall not forget this favour you have done me, Elric. I am a count of the Purple Towns and have much influence. If there is any service I can perform for you when we return, you must let me know."

"I thank you," Elric said gravely. "But first we must discover a means of escape."

Smiorgan had gathered up a satchel of food, some water and some wine. Elric had no stomach to make his breakfast among the dead, so he slung the satchel over his shoulder. "I'm ready," he said.

Smiorgan was satisfied. "Come—we go this way."

Elric began to follow the sea-lord over the dry, crunching turf. The steep sides of the valley loomed over them, tinged with a peculiar and unpleasant greenish hue, the result of the brown foliage being stained by the blue light from above. When they reached the river, which was narrow and ran rapidly through boulders giving easy means of crossing, they rested and ate. Both men were stiff from the previous night's fighting; both were glad to wash the dried blood and mud from their bodies in the water.

Refreshed, the pair climbed over the boulders and left the river behind, ascending the slopes, speaking little so that their breath was saved for the exertion. It was noon by the time they reached the top of the valley and observed a plain not unlike the one which Elric had first crossed. Elric now had a fair idea of the island's geography: it resembled the top of a mountain, with an indentation near the centre which was the valley. Again he became sharply aware of the absence of any wildlife and remarked on this to Count Smiorgan, who agreed that he

had seen
nothing—
no bird, fish nor beast
since he had arrived.

"It's a barren little
world, friend Elric, and a
misfortune for a mariner to be
wrecked upon its shores."

They moved on, until the sea could be observed meeting the horizon in the far distance.

It was Elric who first heard the sound behind them, recognizing the steady thump of the hoofs of a galloping horse, but when he looked back over his shoulder he could see no sign of a rider, nor anywhere that a rider could hide. He guessed that, in his tiredness, his ears were betraying him. It had been thunder that he had heard.

Smiorgan strode implacably onward, though he, too, must have heard the sound.

Again it came. Again, Elric turned. Again he saw nothing.

"Smiorgan? Did you hear a rider?"

Smiorgan continued to walk without looking back. "I heard," he grunted.

"You have heard it before?"

"Many times since I arrived. The pirates heard it, too, and some believed it their nemesis—an Angel of Death seeking them out for retribution."

"You don't know the source?"

Smiorgan paused, then stopped, and when he turned his face was grim. "Once or twice I have caught a glimpse of a horse, I think. A tall horse—white—richly dressed—but with no man upon his back. Ignore it, Elric, as I do. We have larger mysteries with which to occupy our minds!"

"You are afraid of it, Smiorgan?"

He accepted this. "Aye. I confess it. But neither fear nor speculation will rid us of it. Come!"

Elric was bound to see the sense of Smiorgan's statement and he accepted it; yet when the sound came again, about an hour later, he could not resist turning. Then he thought he glimpsed the outline of a large stallion, caparisoned for riding, but that might have been nothing more than an idea Smiorgan had put in his mind.

The day grew colder and in the air was a peculiar, bitter odour. Elric remarked on the smell to Count Smiorgan and learned that this, too, was familiar.

"The smell comes and goes, but it is usually here in some strength."

"Like sulphur," said Elric.

Count Smiorgan's laugh had much irony in it, as if Elric made reference to some private joke of Smiorgan's own. "Oh, aye! Sulphur right enough!"

The drumming of hoofs grew louder behind them as they neared the coast and at last Elric, and Smiorgan too, turned around again, to look.

And now a horse could be seen plainly—riderless, but saddled and bridled, its dark eyes intelligent, its beautiful white head held proudly.

"Are you still convinced of the absence of sorcery here, Sir Elric?" Count Smiorgan asked with some satisfaction. "The horse was invisible. Now it is visible." He shrugged the battle-axe on his shoulder into a better position. "Either that, or it moves from one world to another with ease, so that all we mainly hear are its hoofbeats."

"If so," said Elric sardonically, eyeing the stallion, "it might bear us back to our own world."

"You admit, then, that we are marooned in some limbo?"

"Very well, yes. I admit the possibility."

"Have you no sorcery to trap the horse?"

"Sorcery does not come so easily to me, for I have no great liking for it," the albino told him.

As they spoke, they approached the horse, but it would let them get no closer. It snorted and moved backwards, keeping the same distance between them and itself.

At last, Elric said, "We waste time, Count Smiorgan. Let's get to your ship with speed and forget blue suns and enchanted horses as quickly as we may. Once aboard the ship I can doubtless help you with a little incantation or two, for we'll need aid of some sort if we're to sail a large ship by ourselves."

They marched on, but the horse continued to follow them. They came to the edge of the cliffs, standing high above a narrow, rocky bay in which a battered ship lay at anchor. The ship had the high, fine lines of a Purple Towns merchantman, but its decks were piled with shreds of torn canvas, pieces of broken rope, shards of timber, torn-open bales of cloth, smashed wine-jars, and all manner of other refuse, while in several places her rails were smashed and two or three of her yards had splintered. It was evident that she had been through both storms and sea-fights and it was a wonder that she still floated.

"We'll have to tidy her up as best we can, using only the mains'l for motion," mused Smiorgan. "Hopefully we can salvage enough food to last us . . ."

"Look!" Elric pointed, sure that he had seen someone in the shadows near the afterdeck. "Did the pirates leave any of their company behind?"

"None."

"Did you see anyone on the ship, just then?"

"My eyes play filthy tricks on my mind," Smiorgan told him. "It is this damned blue light. There is a rat or two aboard, that's all. And that's what you saw."

"Possibly." Elric looked back. The horse appeared to be unaware of them as it cropped the brown grass. "Well, let's finish the journey."

They scrambled down the steeply sloping cliff-face and were soon on the shore, wading through the shallows for the ship, clambering up the slippery ropes which still hung over the sides and, at last, setting their feet with some relief upon the deck.

"I feel more secure already," said Smiorgan. "This ship was my home for so long!" He searched through the scattered cargo until he found an unbroken wine-jar, carved off the seal and handed it to Elric. Elric lifted the heavy jar and let a little of the good wine flow into his mouth. As Count Smiorgan began to drink Elric was sure he saw another movement near the afterdeck, and he moved closer.

Now he was certain that he heard strained, rapid breathing—like the breathing of one who sought to stifle his need for air rather than be detected. They were slight sounds, but the albino's ears, unlike his eyes, were sharp. His hand ready to draw his sword, he stalked towards the source of the sound, Smiorgan now behind him.

She emerged from her hiding place before he reached her. Her hair hung in heavy, dirty coils about her pale face; her shoulders were slumped and her soft arms hung limply at her sides, and her dress was stained and ripped.

As Elric approached, she fell on her knees before him. "Take my life," she said humbly, "but I beg you—do not take me back to Saxif D'Aan, though I know you must be his servant or his kinsman."

"It's she!" cried Smiorgan in astonishment. "It's our passenger. She must have been in hiding all this time."

Elric stepped forward, lifting up the girl's chin so that he could study her face. There was a Melnibonéan cast about her features, but she was, to his mind, of the Young Kingdoms; she lacked the pride of a Melnibonéan woman, too. "What name was that you used, girl?" he asked kindly. "Did you speak of Saxif D'Aan? Earl Saxif D'Aan of Melniboné?"

"I did, my lord."

"Do not fear me as his servant," Elric told her. "And as for being a kinsman, I suppose you could call me that, on my mother's side—or rather my great-grandmother's side. He was an ancestor. He must have been dead for two centuries, at least!"

"No," she said. "He lives, my lord."

"On this island?"

"This island is not his home, but it is in this plane that he exists. I sought to escape him through the Crimson Gate. I fled through the gate in a skiff, reached the town where you found me, Count Smiorgan, but he drew me back once I was aboard your ship. He drew me back and the ship with me. For that, I have remorse—and for what befell your crew. Now I know he seeks me. I can feel his presence growing nearer."

"Is he invisible?" Smiorgan asked suddenly. "Does he ride a white horse?"

She gasped. "You see! He *is* near! Why else should the horse appear on this island?"

"He rides it?" Elric asked.

"No, no! He fears the horse almost as much as I fear him. The horse pursues him!"

Elric produced the Melnibonéan gold wheel from his purse. "Did you take this from Earl Saxif D'Aan?"

"I did."

The albino frowned.

"Who is this man, Elric?" Count Smiorgan asked. "You describe him as an ancestor—yet he lives in this world. What do you know of him?"

Elric weighed the large gold wheel in his hand before replacing it in his pouch. "He was something of a legend in Melniboné. His story is part of our literature. He was a great sorcerer—one of the greatest—and he fell in love. It's rare enough for Melnibonéans to fall in love, as others understand the emotion, but rarer for one to have such feelings for a girl who was not even of our own race. She was half-Melnibonéan, so I heard, but from a land which was, in those days, a

Melnibonéan possession, a western province close to Dharijor. She was bought by him in a batch of slaves he planned to use for some sorcerous experiment, but he singled her out, saving her from whatever fate it was the others suffered. He lavished his attention upon her, giving her everything. For her, he abandoned his practices, retired to live quietly away from Imrryr, and I think she showed him a certain affection, though she did not seem to love him. There was another, you see, called Carolak, as I recall, and also half-Melnibonéan, who had become a mercenary in Shazaar and risen in the favour of the Shazaarian court. She had been pledged to this Carolak before her abduction . . ."

"She loved him?" Count Smiorgan asked.

"She was pledged to marry him, but let me finish my story . . ." Elric continued: "Well, at length Carolak, now a man of some substance, second only to the king in Shazaar, heard of her fate and swore to rescue her. He came with raiders to Melniboné's shores and, aided by sorcery, sought out Saxif D'Aan's palace. That done, he sought the girl, finding her at last in the apartments Saxif D'Aan had set aside for her use. He told her that he had come to claim her as his bride, to rescue her from persecution. Oddly, the girl resisted, suggesting that she had been too long a slave in the Melnibonéan harem to re-adapt to the life of a princess in the Shazaarian court. Carolak scoffed at this and seized her. He managed to escape the castle and had the girl over the saddle of his horse and was about to rejoin his men on the coast when Saxif D'Aan detected them. Carolak, I think, was slain, or else a spell was put on him, but Saxif D'Aan, in his terrible jealousy and certain that the girl had planned the escape with a lover, ordered her to die upon the Wheel of Chaos—a machine rather like that coin in design. Her limbs were broken slowly and Saxif D'Aan sat and watched, through long days, while she died. Her skin was peeled from her flesh, and Earl Saxif D'Aan observed every detail of her punishment. Soon it was evident that the drugs and sorcery used to sustain her life were failing and Saxif D'Aan ordered her taken from the Wheel of Chaos and laid upon a couch. 'Well,' he said, 'you have been punished for betraying me and I am glad. Now you may die.' And he saw that her lips, blood-caked and frightful, were moving, and he bent to hear her words."

"Those words? Revenge? An oath?" asked Smiorgan.

"Her last gesture was an attempt to embrace him. And the words were those she had never uttered to him before, much as he had hoped that she would. Then she died."

Smiorgan rubbed at his beard. "Gods! What then? What did your ancestor do?"

"He knew remorse."

"Of course!"

"Not so, for a Melnibonéan. Remorse is a rare emotion with us. Few have ever experienced it. Torn by guilt, Earl Saxif D'Aan left Melniboné, never to return. It was assumed that he had died in some remote land, trying to make amends for what he had done to the only creature he had ever loved. But now, it seems, he sought the Crimson Gate, perhaps thinking it an opening into hell."

"But why should he plague me!" the girl cried. "I am not she! My name is Vassliss. I am a merchant's daughter, from Jharkor. I was voyaging to visit my uncle in Vilmir when our ship was wrecked. A few of us escaped in an open boat. More storms seized us. I was flung from the boat and was drowning when"—she shuddered—"when *his* galley found me. I was grateful, then . . ."

"What happened?" Elric pushed the matted hair away from her face and offered her some of their wine. She drank gratefully.

"He took me to his palace and told me that he would marry me, that I should be his empress for ever and rule beside him. But I was frightened. There was such pain in him—and such cruelty, too. I thought he must devour me, destroy me. Soon after my capture, I took the money and the boat and fled for the gateway, which he had told me about . . ."

"You could find this gateway for us?" Elric asked.

"I think so. I have some knowledge of seamanship, learned from my father. But what would be the use, sir? He would find us again and drag us back. And he must be very near, even now."

"I have a little sorcery myself," Elric assured her, "and will pit it against Saxif D'Aan's, if I must." He turned to Count Smiorgan. "Can we get a sail aloft quickly?"

"Fairly quickly."

"Then let's hurry, Count Smiorgan Baldhead. I might have the means of getting us through this Crimson Gate and free from any further involvement in the dealings of the dead!"

CHAPTER FOUR

While Count Smiorgan and Vassliss of Jharkor watched, Elric lowered himself to the deck, panting and pale. His first attempt to work sorcery in this world had failed and had exhausted him.

"I am further convinced," he told Smiorgan, "that we are in another plane of existence, for I should have worked my incantations with less effort."

"You have failed."

Elric rose with some difficulty. "I shall try again."

He turned his white face skyward; he closed his eyes; he stretched out his arms and his body tensed as he began the incantation again, his voice growing louder and louder, higher and higher, so that it resembled the shrieking of a gale.

He forgot where he was; he forgot his own identity; he forgot those who were with him as his whole mind concentrated upon the Summoning. He sent his call out beyond the confines of the world, into that strange plane where the elementals dwelled—where the powerful creatures of the air could still be found—the *sylphs* of the breeze, and the *sharnahs,* who lived in the storms, and the most powerful of all, the *h'Haarshanns,* creatures of the whirlwind.

And now at last some of them began to come at his summons, ready to serve him as, by virtue of an ancient pact, the elementals had served his forefathers. And slowly the sail of the ship began to fill, and the timbers creaked, and Smiorgan raised the anchor, and the ship was sailing away from the island, through the rocky gap of the harbour, and out into the open sea, still beneath a strange blue sun.

Soon a huge wave was forming around them, lifting up the ship and carrying it across the ocean, so that Count Smiorgan and the girl marveled at the speed of their progress, while Elric, his crimson eyes open now, but blank and unseeing, continued to croon to his unseen allies.

Thus the ship progressed across the waters of the sea, and at last the island was out of sight and the girl, checking their position against the position of the sun, was able to give Count Smiorgan sufficient information for him to steer a course.

As soon as he could, Count Smiorgan went up to Elric, who straddled the deck, still as stiff-limbed as before, and shook him.

"Elric! You will kill yourself with this effort. We need your friends no longer!"

At once the wind dropped and the wave dispersed and Elric, gasping, fell to the deck.

"It is harder here," he said. "It is so much harder here. It is as if I have to call across far greater gulfs than any I have known before."

And then Elric slept.

He lay in a warm bunk in a cool cabin. Through the porthole filtered diffused blue light. He sniffed. He caught the odour of hot food, and turning his head, saw that Vassliss stood there, a bowl of broth in her hands. "I was able to cook this," she said. "It will improve your health. As far as I can tell, we are nearing the Crimson Gate. The seas are always rough around the gate, so you will need your strength."

Elric thanked her pleasantly and began to eat the broth as she watched him.

"You are very like Saxif D'Aan," she said. "Yet harder in a way—and gentler, too. He is so remote. I know why that girl could never tell him that she loved him."

Elric smiled. "Oh, it's nothing more than a folk-tale, probably, the story I told you. This Saxif D'Aan could be another person altogether—or an impostor, even, who has taken his name—or a sorcerer.

Some sorcerers take the names of other sorcerers, for they think it gives them more power."

There came a cry from above, but Elric could not make out the words.

The girl's expression became alarmed. Without a word to Elric, she hurried from the cabin.

Elric, rising unsteadily, followed her up the companionway.

Count Smiorgan Baldhead was at the wheel of his ship and he was pointing towards the horizon behind them. "What do you make of that, Elric?"

Elric peered at the horizon but could see nothing. Often his eyes were weak, as now. But the girl said in a voice of quiet despair:

"It is a golden sail."

"You recognize it?" Elric asked her.

"Oh, indeed I do. It is the galleon of Earl Saxif D'Aan. He has found us. Perhaps he was lying in wait along our route, knowing we must come this way."

"How far are we from the gate?"

"I am not sure."

At that moment, there came a terrible noise from below, as if something sought to stave in the timbers of the ship.

"It's in the forward hatches!" cried Smiorgan. "See what it is, friend Elric! But take care, man!"

Cautiously Elric prised back one of the hatch covers and peered into the murky fastness of the hold. The noise of stamping and thumping continued on, and as his eyes adjusted to the light, he saw the source.

The white horse was there. It whinnied as it saw him, almost in greeting.

"How did it come aboard?" Elric asked. "I saw nothing. I heard nothing."

The girl was almost as white as Elric. She sank to her knees beside the hatch, burying her face in her arms.

"He has us! He has us!"

"There is still a chance we can reach the Crimson Gate in time,"

Elric reassured her. "And once in my own world, why, I can work much stronger sorcery to protect us."

"No," she sobbed, "it is too late. Why else would the white horse be here? He knows that Saxif D'Aan must soon board us."

"He'll have to fight us before he shall have you," Elric promised her.

"You have not seen his men. Cut-throats all. Desperate and wolfish! They'll show you no mercy. You would be best advised to hand me over to Saxif D'Aan at once and save yourselves. You'll gain nothing from trying to protect me. But I'd ask you a favour."

"What's that?"

"Find me a small knife to carry, that I may kill myself as soon as I know you two are safe."

Elric laughed, dragging her to her feet. "I'll have no such melodramatics from you, lass! We stand together. Perhaps we can bargain with Saxif D'Aan."

"What have you to barter?"

"Very little. But he is not aware of that."

"He can read your thoughts, seemingly. He has great powers!"

"I am Elric of Melniboné. I am said to possess a certain facility in the sorcerous arts, myself."

"But you are not as single-minded as Saxif D'Aan," she said simply. "Only one thing obsesses him—the need to make me his consort."

"Many girls would be flattered by the attention—glad to be an empress with a Melnibonéan emperor for a husband." Elric was sardonic.

She ignored his tone. "That is why I fear him so," she said in a murmur. "If I lost my determination for a moment, I could love him. I should be destroyed! It is what *she* must have known!"

Chapter Five

The gleaming galleon, sails and sides all gilded so that it seemed the sun itself pursued them, moved rapidly upon them while the girl and Count Smiorgan watched aghast and Elric desperately attempted to recall his elemental allies, without success.

Through the pale blue light the golden ship sailed relentlessly in their wake. Its proportions were monstrous, its sense of power vast, its gigantic prow sending up huge, foamy waves on both sides as it sped silently towards them.

With the look of a man preparing himself to meet death, Count Smiorgan Baldhead of the Purple Towns unslung his battle-axe and loosened his sword in its scabbard, setting his little metal cap upon his bald pate. The girl made no sound, no movement at all, but she wept.

Elric shook his head and his long, milk-white hair formed a halo around his face for a moment. His moody crimson eyes began to focus on the world around him. He recognized the ship; it was of a pattern with the golden battle-barges of Melniboné—doubtless the ship in which Earl Saxif D'Aan had fled his homeland, searching for the Crimson Gate. Now Elric was convinced that this must be that same Saxif D'Aan and he knew less fear than did his companions, but considerably greater curiosity. Indeed, it was almost with nostalgia that he noted the ball of fire, like a natural comet, glowing with green light, come hissing and spluttering towards them, flung by the ship's forward catapult. He half expected to see a great dragon wheeling in the sky overhead, for it was with dragons and gilded battle-craft like these that Melniboné had once conquered the world.

The fireball fell into the sea a few inches from their bow and was evidently placed there deliberately, as a warning.

"Don't stop!" cried Vassliss. "Let the flames slay us! It will be better!"

Smiorgan was looking upward. "We have no choice. Look! He has banished the wind, it seems."

They were becalmed. Elric smiled a grim smile. He knew now

what the folk of the Young Kingdoms must have felt when his ancestors had used these identical tactics against them.

"Elric?" Smiorgan turned to the albino. "Are these your people? That ship's Melnibonéan without question!"

"So are the methods," Elric told him. "I am of the blood royal of Melniboné. I could be emperor, even now, if I chose to claim my throne. There is some small chance that Earl Saxif D'Aan, though an ancestor, will recognize me and, therefore, recognize my authority. We are a conservative people, the folk of the Dragon Isle."

The girl spoke through dry lips, hopelessly: "He recognizes only the authority of the Lords of Chaos, who give him aid."

"All Melnibonéans recognize that authority," Elric told her with a certain humour.

From the forward hatch, the sound of the stallion's stamping and snorting increased.

"We're besieged by enchantments!" Count Smiorgan's normally ruddy features had paled. "Have you none of your own, Prince Elric, you can use to counter them?"

"None, it seems."

The golden ship loomed over them. Elric saw that the rails, high overhead, were crowded not with Imrryrian warriors but with cutthroats equally as desperate as those he had fought on the island, and, apparently, drawn from the same variety of historical periods and nations. The galleon's long sweeps scraped the sides of the smaller vessel as they folded, like the legs of some water insect, to enable the grappling irons to be flung out. Iron claws bit into the timbers of the little ship and the brigandly crowd overhead cheered, grinning at them, menacing them with their weapons.

The girl began to run to the seaward side of the ship, but Elric caught her by the arm.

"Do not stop me, I beg you!" she cried. "Rather, jump with me and drown!"

"You think that death will save you from Saxif D'Aan?" Elric said. "If he has the power you say, death will only bring you more firmly into his grasp!"

"Oh!" The girl shuddered and then, as a voice called down to them from one of the tall decks of the gilded ship, she gave a moan and fainted into Elric's arms, so that, weakened as he was by his spell-working, it was all that he could do to stop himself falling with her to the deck.

The voice rose over the coarse shouts and guffaws of the crew. It was pure, lilting and sardonic. It was the voice of a Melnibonéan, though it spoke the common tongue of the Young Kingdoms, a corruption, in itself, of the speech of the Bright Empire.

"May I have the captain's permission to come aboard?"

Count Smiorgan growled back: "You have us firm, sir! Don't try to disguise an act of piracy with a polite speech!"

"I take it I have your permission, then." The unseen speaker's tone remained exactly the same.

Elric watched as part of the rail was drawn back to allow a gangplank, studded with golden nails to give firmer footing, to be lowered from the galleon's deck to theirs.

A tall figure appeared at the top of the gangplank. He had the fine features of a Melnibonéan nobleman, was thin, proud in his bearing, clad in voluminous robes of cloth-of-gold, an elaborate helmet in gold and ebony upon his long auburn locks. He had grey-blue eyes, pale, slightly flushed skin, and he carried, so far as Elric could see, no weapons of any kind.

With considerable dignity, Earl Saxif D'Aan began to descend, his rascals at his back. The contrast between this beautiful intellectual and those he commanded was remarkable. Where he walked with straight back, elegant and noble, they slouched, filthy, degenerate, unintelligent, grinning with pleasure at their easy victory. Not a man among them showed any sign of human dignity; each was overdressed in tattered and unclean finery, each had at least three weapons upon his person, and there was much evidence of looted jewelry, of nose-rings, earrings, bangles, necklaces, toe- and finger-rings, pendants, cloak-pins and the like.

"Gods!" murmured Smiorgan. "I've rarely seen such a collection of

scum, and I thought I'd encountered most kinds in my voyages. How can such a man bear to be in their company?"

"Perhaps it suits his sense of irony," Elric suggested.

Earl Saxif D'Aan reached their deck and stood looking up at them to where they still positioned themselves, on the poop deck. He gave a slight bow. His features were controlled and only his eyes suggested something of the intensity of emotion dwelling within him, particularly as they fell upon the girl in Elric's arms.

"I am Earl Saxif D'Aan of Melniboné, now of the Islands beyond the Crimson Gate. You have something with you which is mine. I would claim it from you."

"You mean the Lady Vassliss of Jharkor?" Elric said, his voice as steady as Saxif D'Aan's.

Saxif D'Aan seemed to note Elric for the first time. A slight frown crossed his brow and was quickly dismissed. "She is mine," he said. "You may be assured that she will come to no harm at my hands."

Elric, seeking some advantage, knew that he risked much when he next spoke, in the High Tongue of Melniboné, used between those of the blood royal. "Knowledge of your history does not reassure me, Saxif D'Aan."

Almost imperceptibly, the golden man stiffened and fire flared in his grey-blue eyes. "Who are you, to speak the Tongue of Kings? Who are you, who claims knowledge of my past?"

"I am Elric, son of Sadric, and I am the four-hundred-and-twenty-eighth emperor of the folk of R'lin K'ren A'a, who landed upon the Dragon Isle ten thousand years ago. I am Elric, your emperor, Earl Saxif D'Aan, and I demand your fealty." And Elric held up his right hand, upon which still gleamed a ring set with a single Actorios stone, the Ring of Kings.

Earl Saxif D'Aan now had firm control of himself again. He gave no sign that he was impressed. "Your sovereignty does not extend beyond your own world, noble emperor, though I greet you as a fellow monarch." He spread his arms so that his long sleeves rustled. "This world is mine. All that exists beneath the blue sun do I rule. You trespass, therefore, in my domain. I have every right to do as I please."

"Pirate pomp," muttered Count Smiorgan, who had understood nothing of the conversation but had gathered something of what passed by the tone. "Pirate braggadocio. What does he say, Elric?"

"He convinces me that he is not, in your sense, a pirate, Count Smiorgan. He claims that he is ruler of this plane. Since there is apparently no other, we must accept his claim."

"Gods! Then let him behave like a monarch and let us sail safely out of his waters!"

"We may—if we give him the girl."

Count Smiorgan shook his head. "I'll not do that. She's my passenger, in my charge. I must die rather than do that. It is the code of the sea-lords of the Purple Towns."

"You are famous for your adherence to that code," Elric said. "As for myself, I have taken this girl into my protection and, as hereditary emperor of Melniboné, I cannot allow myself to be browbeaten."

They had conversed in a murmur, but, somehow, Earl Saxif D'Aan had heard them.

"I must let you know," he said evenly, in the common tongue, "that the girl is mine. You steal her from me. Is that the action of an emperor?"

"She is not a slave," Elric said, "but the daughter of a free merchant in Jharkor. You have no rights upon her."

Earl Saxif D'Aan said, "Then I cannot open the Crimson Gate for you. You must remain in my world for ever."

"You have closed the gate? Is it possible?"

"To me."

"Do you know that the girl would rather die than be captured by you, Earl Saxif D'Aan? Does it give you pleasure to instill such fear?"

The golden man looked directly into Elric's eyes as if he made some cryptic challenge. "The gift of pain has ever been a favourite gift among our folk, has it not? Yet it is another gift I offer her. She calls herself Vassliss of Jharkor, but she does not know herself. I know her. She is Gratyesha, Princess of Fwem-Omeyo, and I would make her my bride."

"How can it be that she does not know her own name?"

"She is reincarnated—soul and flesh are identical—that is how I know. And I have waited, Emperor of Melniboné, for many scores of years for her. Now I shall not be cheated of her."

"As you cheated yourself, two centuries past, in Melniboné?"

"You risk much with your directness of language, brother monarch!" There was a hint of a warning in Saxif D'Aan's tone, a warning much fiercer than any implied by the words.

"Well"—Elric shrugged—"you have more power than we do. My sorcery works poorly in your world. Your ruffians outnumber us. It should not be difficult for you to take her from us."

"You must give her to me. Then you may go free, back to your own world and your own time."

Elric smiled. "There is sorcery here. She is no reincarnation. You'd bring your lost love's spirit from the netherworld to inhabit this girl's body. Am I not right? That is why she must be given freely, or your sorcery will rebound upon you—or might—and you would not take the risk."

Earl Saxif D'Aan turned his head away so that Elric might not see his eyes. "She is the girl," he said, in the High Tongue. "I know that she is. I mean her soul no harm. I would merely give it back its memory."

"Then it is stalemate," said Elric.

"Have you no loyalty to a brother of the royal blood?" Saxif D'Aan murmured, still refusing to look at Elric.

"You claimed no such loyalty, as I recall, Earl Saxif D'Aan. If you accept me as your emperor, then you must accept my decisions. I keep the girl in my custody. Or you must take her by force."

"I am too proud."

"Such pride shall ever destroy love," said Elric, almost in sympathy. "What now, King of Limbo? What shall you do with us?"

Earl Saxif D'Aan lifted his noble head, about to reply, when from the hold the stamping and the snorting began again. His eyes widened. He looked questioningly at Elric, and there was something close to terror in his face.

"What's that? What have you in the hold?"

"A mount, my lord, that is all," said Elric equably.

"A horse? An ordinary horse?"

"A white one. A stallion, with bridle and saddle. It has no rider."

At once Saxif D'Aan's voice rose as he shouted orders for his men. "Take those three aboard our ship. This one shall be sunk directly. Hurry! Hurry!"

Elric and Smiorgan shook off the hands which sought to seize them and they moved towards the gangplank, carrying the girl between them, while Smiorgan muttered, "At least we are not slain, Elric. But what becomes of us now?"

Elric shook his head. "We must hope that we can continue to use Earl Saxif D'Aan's pride against him, to our advantage, though the gods alone know how we shall resolve the dilemma."

Earl Saxif D'Aan was already hurrying up the gangplank ahead of them.

"Quickly," he shouted. "Raise the plank!"

They stood upon the decks of the golden battle-barge and watched as the gangplank was drawn up, the length of rail replaced.

"Bring up the catapults," Saxif D'Aan commanded. "Use lead. Sink that vessel at once!"

The noise from the forward hold increased. The horse's voice echoed over ships and water. Hoofs smashed at timber and then, suddenly, it came crashing through the hatch-covers, scrambling for purchase on the deck with its front hoofs, and then standing there, pawing at the planks, its neck arching, its nostrils dilating, and its eyes glaring, as if ready to do battle.

Now Saxif D'Aan made no attempt to hide the terror on his face. His voice rose to a scream as he threatened his rascals with every sort of horror if they did not obey him with utmost speed. The catapults were dragged up and huge globes of lead were lobbed onto the decks of Smiorgan's ship, smashing through the planks like arrows through parchment so that almost immediately the ship began to sink.

"Cut the grappling hooks!" cried Saxif D'Aan, wrenching a blade from the hand of one of his men and sawing at the nearest rope. "Cast loose—quickly!"

Even as Smiorgan's ship groaned and roared like a drowning beast, the ropes were cut. The ship keeled over at once, and the horse disappeared.

"Turn about!" shouted Saxif D'Aan. "Back to Fhaligarn and swiftly, or your souls shall feed my fiercest demons!"

There came a peculiar, high-pitched neighing from the foaming water, as Smiorgan's ship, stern uppermost, gasped and was swallowed. Elric caught a glimpse of the white stallion, swimming strongly.

"Go below!" Saxif D'Aan ordered, indicating a hatchway. "The horse can smell the girl and thus is doubly difficult to lose."

"Why do you fear it?" Elric asked. "It is only a horse. It cannot harm you."

Saxif D'Aan uttered a laugh of profound bitterness. "Can it not, brother monarch? Can it not?"

As they carried the girl below, Elric was frowning, remembering a little more of the legend of Saxif D'Aan, of the girl he had punished so cruelly, and of her lover, Prince Carolak. The last he heard of Saxif D'Aan was the sorcerer crying:

"More sail! More sail!"

And then the hatches had closed behind them and they found themselves in an opulent Melnibonéan day-cabin, full of rich hangings, precious metal, decorations of exquisite beauty and, to Count Smiorgan, disturbing decadence. But it was Elric, as he lowered the girl to a couch, who noticed the smell.

"Augh! It's the smell of a tomb—of damp and mould. Yet nothing rots. It is passing peculiar, friend Smiorgan, is it not?"

"I scarcely noticed, Elric." Smiorgan's voice was hollow. "But I would agree with you on one thing. We are entombed. I doubt we'll live to escape this world now."

Chapter Six

An hour had passed since they had been forced aboard. The doors had been locked behind them, and it seemed Saxif D'Aan was too preoccupied with escaping the white stallion to bother with them. Peering through the lattice of a porthole, Elric could look back to where their ship had been sunk. They were many leagues distant already; yet he still thought, from time to time, that he saw the head and shoulders of the stallion above the waves.

Vassliss had recovered and sat pale and shivering upon the couch.

"What more do you know of that horse?" Elric asked her. "It would be helpful to me if you could recall anything you have heard."

She shook her head. "Saxif D'Aan spoke little of it, but I gather he fears the rider more than he does the horse."

"Ah!" Elric frowned. "I suspected it! Have you ever seen the rider?"

"Never. I think that Saxif D'Aan has never seen him, either. I think he believes himself doomed if that rider should ever sit upon the white stallion."

Elric smiled to himself.

"Why do you ask so much about the horse?" Smiorgan wished to know.

Elric shook his head. "I have an instinct, that is all. Half a memory. But I'll say nothing and think as little as I may, for there is no doubt Saxif D'Aan, as Vassliss suggests, has some power of reading the mind."

They heard a footfall above, descending to their doors.

A bolt was drawn and Saxif D'Aan, his composure fully restored, stood in the opening, his hands in his golden sleeves.

"You will forgive, I hope, the peremptory way in which I sent you here. There was danger which had to be averted at all costs. As a result, my manners were not all that they should have been."

"Danger to us?" Elric asked. "Or to you, Earl Saxif D'Aan?"

"In the circumstances, to all of us, I assure you."

"Who rides the horse?" Smiorgan asked bluntly. "And why do you fear him?"

Earl Saxif D'Aan was master of himself again, so there was no sign of a reaction. "That is very much my private concern," he said softly. "Will you dine with me now?"

The girl made a noise in her throat and Earl Saxif D'Aan turned piercing eyes upon her. "Gratyesha, you will want to cleanse yourself and make yourself beautiful again. I will see that facilities are placed at your disposal."

"I am not Gratyesha," she said. "I am Vassliss, the merchant's daughter."

"You will remember," he said. "In time, you will remember." There was such certainty, such obsessive power, in his voice that even Elric experienced a frisson of awe. "The things will be brought to you, and you may use this cabin as your own until we return to my palace on Fhaligarn. My lords . . ." He indicated that they should leave.

Elric said, "I'll not leave her, Saxif D'Aan. She is too afraid."

"She fears only the truth, brother."

"She fears you and your madness."

Saxif D'Aan shrugged insouciantly. "I shall leave first, then. If you would accompany me, my lords . . ." He strode from the cabin and they followed.

Elric said, over his shoulder, "Vassliss, you may depend upon my protection." And he closed the cabin doors behind him.

Earl Saxif D'Aan was standing upon the deck, exposing his noble face to the spray which was flung up by the ship as it moved with supernatural speed through the sea.

"You called me mad, Prince Elric? Yet you must be versed in sorcery, yourself."

"Of course. I am of the blood royal. I am reckoned knowledgable in my own world."

"But here? How well does your sorcery work?"

"Poorly, I'll admit. The spaces between the planes seem greater."

"Exactly. But I have bridged them. I have had time to learn how to bridge them."

"You are saying that you are more powerful than am I?"

"It is a fact, is it not?"

"It is. But I did not think we were about to indulge in sorcerous battles, Earl Saxif D'Aan."

"Of course. Yet, if you were to think of besting me by sorcery, you would think twice, eh?"

"I should be foolish to contemplate such a thing at all. It could cost me my soul. My life, at least."

"True. You are a realist, I see."

"I suppose so."

"Then we can progress on simpler lines, to settle the dispute between us."

"You propose a duel?" Elric was surprised.

Earl Saxif D'Aan's laughter was light. "Of course not—against your sword? That has power in all worlds, though the magnitude varies."

"I'm glad that you are aware of that," Elric said significantly.

"Besides," added Earl Saxif D'Aan, his golden robes rustling as he moved a little nearer to the rail, "you would not kill me—for only I have the means of your escaping this world."

"Perhaps we'd elect to remain," said Elric.

"Then you would be my subjects. But, no—you would not like it here. I am self-exiled. I could not return to my own world now, even if I wished to do so. It has cost me much, my knowledge. But I would found a dynasty here, beneath the blue sun. I must have my wife, Prince Elric. I must have Gratyesha."

"Her name is Vassliss," said Elric obstinately.

"She thinks it is."

"Then it is. I have sworn to protect her, as has Count Smiorgan. Protect her we shall. You will have to kill us all."

"Exactly," said Earl Saxif D'Aan with the air of a man who has been coaching a poor student towards the correct answer to a problem. "Exactly. I shall have to kill you all. You leave me with little alternative, Prince Elric."

"Would that benefit you?"

"It would. It would put a certain powerful demon at my service for a few hours."

"We should resist."

"I have many men. I do not value them. Eventually, they would overwhelm you. Would they not?"

Elric remained silent.

"My men would be aided by sorcery," added Saxif D'Aan. "Some would die, but not too many, I think."

Elric was looking beyond Saxif D'Aan, staring out to sea. He was sure that the horse still followed. He was sure that Saxif D'Aan knew, also.

"And if we gave up the girl?"

"I should open the Crimson Gate for you. You would be honoured guests. I should see that you were borne safely through, even taken safely to some hospitable land in your own world, for even if you passed through the gate there would be danger. The storms."

Elric appeared to deliberate.

"You have only a little time to make your decision, Prince Elric. I had hoped to reach my palace, Fhaligarn, by now. I shall not allow you very much longer. Come, make your decision. You know I speak the truth."

"You know that I can work some sorcery in your world, do you not?"

"You summoned a few friendly elementals to your aid, I know. But at what cost? Would you challenge me directly?"

"It would be unwise of me," said Elric.

Smiorgan was tugging at his sleeve. "Stop this useless talk. He knows that we have given our word to the girl and that we *must* fight him!"

Earl Saxif D'Aan sighed. There seemed to be genuine sorrow in his voice. "If you are determined to lose your lives . . ." he began.

"I should like to know why you set such importance upon the speed with which we make up our minds," Elric said. "Why cannot we wait until we reach Fhaligarn?"

Earl Saxif D'Aan's expression was calculating, and again he looked full into Elric's crimson eyes. "I think you know," he said, almost inaudibly.

But Elric shook his head. "I think you give me too much credit for intelligence."

"Perhaps."

Elric knew that Saxif D'Aan was attempting to read his thoughts; he deliberately blanked his mind, and suspected that he sensed frustration in the sorcerer's demeanour.

And then the albino had sprung at his kinsman, his hand chopping at Saxif D'Aan's throat. The earl was taken completely off guard. He tried to call out, but his vocal cords were numbed. Another blow, and he fell to the deck, senseless.

"Quickly, Smiorgan," Elric shouted, and he had leaped into the rigging, climbing swiftly upward to the top yards. Smiorgan, bewildered, followed, and Elric had drawn his sword, even as he reached the crow's nest, driving upward through the rail so that the lookout was taken in the groin scarcely before he realized it.

Next, Elric was hacking at the ropes holding the mainsail to the yard. Already a number of Saxif D'Aan's ruffians were climbing after them.

The heavy golden sail came loose, falling to envelop the pirates and take several of them down with it.

Elric climbed into the crow's nest and pitched the dead man over the rail in the wake of his comrades. Then he had raised his sword over his head, holding it in his two hands, his eyes blank again, his head raised to the blue sun, and Smiorgan, clinging to the mast below, shuddered as he heard a peculiar crooning come from the albino's throat.

More of the cut-throats were ascending, and Smiorgan hacked at the rigging, having the satisfaction of seeing half a score go flying down to break their bones on the deck below, or be swallowed by the waves.

Earl Saxif D'Aan was beginning to recover, but he was still stunned.

"Fool!" he was crying. "Fool!" But it was not possible to tell if he referred to Elric or to himself.

Elric's voice became a wail, rhythmical and chilling, as he chanted his incantation, and the strength from the man he had killed flowed into him and sustained him. His crimson eyes seemed to flicker with fires of another, nameless colour, and his whole body shook as the strange runes shaped themselves in a throat which had never been made to speak such sounds.

His voice became a vibrant groan as the incantation continued, and Smiorgan, watching as more of the crew made efforts to climb the mainmast, felt an unearthly coldness creep through him.

Earl Saxif D'Aan screamed from below:

"You would not dare!"

The sorcerer began to make passes in the air, his own incantation tumbling from his lips, and Smiorgan gasped as a creature made of smoke took shape only a few feet below him. The creature smacked its lips and grinned and stretched a paw, which became flesh even as it moved, towards Smiorgan. He hacked at the paw with his sword, whimpering.

"Elric!" cried Count Smiorgan, clambering higher so that he grasped the rail of the crow's nest. "Elric! He sends demons against us now!"

But Elric ignored him. His whole mind was in another world, a darker, bleaker world even than this one. Through grey mists, he saw a figure, and he cried a name. "Come!" he called in the ancient tongue of his ancestors. "Come!"

Count Smiorgan cursed as the demon became increasingly substantial. Red fangs clashed and green eyes glared at him. A claw stroked his boot and no matter how much he struck with his sword, the demon did not appear to notice the blows.

There was no room for Smiorgan in the crow's nest, but he stood on the outer rim, shouting with terror, desperate for aid. Still Elric continued to chant.

"Elric! I am doomed!"

The demon's paw grasped Smiorgan by his ankle.

"Elric!"

Thunder rolled out at sea; a bolt of lightning appeared for a second and then was gone. From nowhere there came the sound of a horse's hoofs pounding, and a human voice shouting in triumph.

Elric sank back against the rail, opening his eyes in time to see Smiorgan being dragged slowly downward. With the last of his strength he flung himself forward, leaning far out to stab downwards with Stormbringer. The runesword sank cleanly into the demon's right eye. It roared, letting go of Smiorgan, striking at the blade which drew its energy from it, and as that energy passed into the blade and thence to Elric, the albino grinned a frightful grin so that, for a second, Smiorgan became more frightened of his friend than he had been of the demon. The demon began to dematerialize, its only means of escape from the sword which drank its life-force, but more of Saxif D'Aan's rogues were behind it, and their blades rattled as they sought the pair.

Elric swung himself back over the rail, balanced precariously on the yard as he slashed at their attackers, yelling the old battle-cries of his people. Smiorgan could do little but watch. He noted that Saxif D'Aan was no longer on deck and he shouted urgently to Elric:

"Elric! Saxif D'Aan. He seeks out the girl."

Elric now took the attack to the pirates, and they were more than anxious to avoid the moaning runesword, some even leaping into the sea rather than encounter it. Swiftly the two leaped from yard to yard until they were again upon the deck.

"What does he fear? Why does he not use more sorcery?" panted Count Smiorgan, as they ran towards the cabin.

"I have summoned the one who rides the horse," Elric told him. "I had so little time—and I could tell you nothing of it, knowing that Saxif D'Aan would read my intention in your mind, if he could not in mine!"

The cabin doors were firmly secured from the inside. Elric began to hack at them with the black sword.

But the doors resisted as they should not have resisted. "Sealed by sorcery and I've no means of unsealing it," said the albino.

"Will he kill her?"

"I don't know. He might try to take her into some other plane. We must—"

Hoofs clattered on the deck and the white stallion reared behind them, only now it had a rider, clad in bright purple-and-yellow armour. He was bareheaded and youthful, though there were several old scars upon his face. His hair was thick and curly and blond and his eyes were a deep blue.

He drew tightly upon his reins, steadying the horse. He looked piercingly at Elric. "Was it you, Melnibonéan, who opened the pathway for me?"

"It was."

"Then I thank you, though I cannot repay you."

"You have repaid me," Elric told him, then drew Smiorgan aside as the rider leaned forward and spurred his horse directly at the closed doors, smashing through as though they were rotted cotton.

There came a terrible cry from within and then Earl Saxif D'Aan, hampered by his complicated robes of gold, rushed from the cabin, seizing a sword from the hand of the nearest corpse, darting Elric a look not so much of hatred but of bewildered agony as he turned to face the blond rider.

The rider had dismounted now and came from the cabin, one arm around the shivering girl, Vassliss, one hand upon the reins of his horse, and he said, sorrowfully:

"You did me a great wrong, Earl Saxif D'Aan, but you did Gratyesha an infinitely more terrible one. Now you must pay."

Saxif D'Aan paused, drawing a deep breath, and when he looked up again, his eyes were steady, his dignity had returned.

"Must I pay in full?" he said.

"In full."

"It is all I deserve," said Saxif D'Aan. "I escaped my doom for many years, but I could not escape the knowledge of my crime. She loved me, you know. Not you."

"She loved us both, I think. But the love she gave you was her entire soul and I should not want that from any woman."

"You would be the loser, then."

"You never knew how much she loved you."

"Only—only afterwards . . ."

"I pity you, Earl Saxif D'Aan." The young man gave the reins of his horse to the girl, and he drew his sword. "We are strange rivals, are we not?"

"You have been all these years in limbo, where I banished you—in that garden on Melniboné?"

"All these years. Only my horse could follow you. The horse of Tendric, my father, also of Melniboné, and also a sorcerer."

"If I had known that, then, I'd have slain you cleanly and sent the horse to limbo."

"Jealousy weakened you, Earl Saxif D'Aan. But now we fight as we should have fought then—man to man, with steel, for the hand of the one who loves us both. It is more than you deserve."

"Much more," agreed the sorcerer. And he brought up his sword to lunge at the young man who, Smiorgan guessed, could only be Prince Carolak himself.

The fight was predetermined. Saxif D'Aan knew that, if Carolak did not. Saxif D'Aan's skill in arms was up to the standard of any Melnibonéan nobleman, but it could not match the skill of a professional soldier, who had fought for his life time after time.

Back and forth across the deck, while Saxif D'Aan's rascals looked on in open-mouthed astonishment, the rivals fought a duel which should have been fought and resolved two centuries before, while the girl they both plainly thought was the reincarnation of Gratyesha watched them with as much concern as might her original have watched when Saxif D'Aan first encountered Prince Carolak in the gardens of his palace, so long ago.

Saxif D'Aan fought well, and Carolak fought nobly, for on many occasions he avoided an obvious advantage, but at length Saxif D'Aan threw away his sword, crying: "Enough. I'll give you your vengeance, Prince Carolak. I'll let you take the girl. But you'll not give me your damned mercy—you'll not take my pride."

And Carolak nodded, stepped forward, and struck straight for Saxif D'Aan's heart.

The blade entered clean and Earl Saxif D'Aan should have died, but he did not. He crawled along the deck until he reached the base of the mast, and he rested his back against it, while the blood pumped from the wounded heart. And he smiled.

"It appears," he said faintly, "that I cannot die, so long have I sustained my life by sorcery. I am no longer a man."

He did not seem pleased by this thought, but Prince Carolak, stepping forward and leaning over him, reassured him. "You will die," he promised, "soon."

"What will you do with her—with Gratyesha?"

"Her name is Vassliss," said Count Smiorgan insistently. "She is a merchant's daughter, from Jharkor."

"She must make up her own mind," Carolak said, ignoring Smiorgan.

Earl Saxif D'Aan turned glazed eyes on Elric. "I must thank you," he said. "You brought me the one who could bring me peace, though I feared him."

"Is that why, I wonder, your sorcery was so weak against me?" Elric said. "Because you wished Carolak to come and release you from your guilt?"

"Possibly, Elric. You are wiser in some matters, it seems, than am I."

"What of the Crimson Gate?" Smiorgan growled. "Can that be opened? Have you still the power, Earl Saxif D'Aan?"

"I think so." From the folds of his bloodstained garments of gold, the sorcerer produced a large crystal which shone with the deep colours of a ruby. "This will not only lead you to the gate, it will enable you to pass through, only I must warn you . . ." Saxif D'Aan began to cough. "The ship"—he gasped, "the ship—like my body—has been sustained by means of sorcery—therefore . . ." His head slumped forward. He raised it with a huge effort and stared beyond them at the girl who still held the reins of the white stallion. "Farewell, Gratyesha, Princess of Fwem-Omeyo. I loved you." The eyes remained fixed upon her, but they were dead eyes now.

Carolak turned back to look at the girl. "How do you call yourself, Gratyesha?"

"They call me Vassliss," she told him. She smiled up into his youthful, battle-scarred face. "That is what they call me, Prince Carolak."

"You know who I am?"

"I know you now."

"Will you come with me, Gratyesha? Will you be my bride, at last, in the strange new lands I have found, beyond the world?"

"I will come," she said.

He helped her up into the saddle of his white stallion and climbed so that he sat behind her. He bowed to Elric of Melniboné. "I thank you again, Sir Sorcerer, though I never thought to be helped by one of the royal blood of Melniboné."

Elric's expression was not without humour. "In Melniboné," he said, "I'm told it's tainted blood."

"Tainted with mercy, perhaps."

"Perhaps."

Prince Carolak saluted them. "I hope you find peace, Prince Elric, as I have found it."

"I fear my peace will more resemble that which Saxif D'Aan found," Elric said grimly. "Nonetheless, I thank you for your good words, Prince Carolak."

Then Carolak, laughing, had ridden his horse for the rail, leaped it, and vanished.

There was a silence upon the ship. The remaining ruffians looked uncertainly from one to the other. Elric addressed them:

"Know you this—I have the key to the Crimson Gate—and only I have the knowledge to use it. Help me sail the ship, and you'll have freedom from this world! What say you?"

"Give us our orders, captain," said a toothless individual, and he cackled with mirth. "It's the best offer we've had in a hundred years or more!"

CHAPTER SEVEN

It was Smiorgan who first saw the Crimson Gate. He held the great red gem in his hand and pointed ahead.

"There! There, Elric! Saxif D'Aan has not betrayed us!"

The sea had begun to heave with huge, turbulent waves, and with the mainsail still tangled upon the deck, it was all that the crew could do to control the ship, but the chance of escape from the world of the blue sun made them work with every ounce of energy and, slowly, the golden battle-barge neared the towering crimson pillars.

The pillars rose from the grey, roaring water, casting a peculiar light upon the crests of the waves. They appeared to have little substance, and yet stood firm against the battering of the tons of water lashing around them.

"Let us hope they are wider apart than they look," said Elric. "It would be a hard enough task steering through them in calm waters, let alone this kind of sea."

"I'd best take the wheel, I think," said Count Smiorgan, handing Elric the gem, and he strode back up the tilting deck, climbing to the covered wheelhouse and relieving the frightened man who stood there.

There was nothing Elric could do but watch as Smiorgan turned the huge vessel into the waves, riding the tops as best he could, but sometimes descending with a rush which made Elric's heart rise to his mouth. All around them, then, the cliffs of water threatened, but the ship was taking another wave before the main force of water could crash onto her decks. For all this, Elric was quickly soaked through and, though sense told him he would be best below, he clung to the rail, watching as Smiorgan steered the ship with uncanny sureness towards the Crimson Gate.

And then the deck was flooded with red light and Elric was half blinded. Grey water flew everywhere; there came a dreadful scraping sound, then a snapping as oars broke against the pillars. The ship shuddered and began to turn, sideways to the wind, but Smiorgan forced her around and suddenly the quality of the light changed subtly, though the sea remained as turbulent as ever and Elric knew, deep within him, that overhead, beyond the heavy clouds, a yellow sun was burning again.

But now there came a creaking and a crashing from within the bowels of the battle-barge. The smell of mould, which Elric had noted earlier, became stronger, almost overpowering.

Smiorgan came hurrying back, having handed over the wheel. His face was pale again. "She's breaking up, Elric," he called out, over the noise of the wind and the waves. He staggered as a huge wall of water struck the ship and snatched away several planks from the deck. "She's falling apart, man!"

"Saxif D'Aan tried to warn us of this!" Elric shouted back. "As he was kept alive by sorcery, so was his ship. She was old before he sailed her to that world. While there, the sorcery which sustained her remained strong—but on this plane it has no power at all. Look!" And he pulled at a piece of the rail, crumbling the rotten wood with his fingers. "We must find a length of timber which is still good."

At that moment a yard came crashing from the mast and struck the deck, bouncing, then rolling towards them.

Elric crawled up the sloping deck until he could grasp the spar and test it. "This one's still good. Use your belt or whatever else you can and tie yourself to it!"

The wind wailed through the disintegrating rigging of the ship; the sea smashed at the sides, driving great holes below the waterline.

The ruffians who had crewed her were in a state of complete panic, some trying to unship small boats which crumbled even as they swung them out, others lying flat against the rotted decks and praying to whatever gods they still worshipped.

Elric strapped himself to the broken yard as firmly as he could and Smiorgan followed his example. The next wave to hit the ship full on

lifted them with it, cleanly over what remained of the rail and into the chilling, shouting waters of that terrible sea.

Elric kept his mouth tight shut against the water and reflected on the irony of his situation. It seemed that, having escaped so much, he was to die a very ordinary death, by drowning.

It was not long before his senses left him and he gave himself up to the swirling and somehow friendly waters of the ocean.

He awoke, struggling.

There were hands upon him. He strove to fight them off, but he was too weak. Someone laughed, a rough, good-humoured sound.

The water no longer roared and crashed around him. The wind no longer howled. Instead there was a gentler movement. He heard waves lapping against timber. He was aboard another ship.

He opened his eyes, blinking in warm, yellow sunlight. Red-cheeked Vilmirian sailors grinned down at him. "You're a lucky man—if man you be!" said one.

"My friend?" Elric sought for Smiorgan.

"He was in better shape than were you. He's down in Duke Avan's cabin now."

"Duke Avan?" Elric knew the name, but in his dazed condition could remember nothing to help him place the man. "You saved us?"

"Aye. We found you both drifting, tied to a broken yard carved with the strangest designs I've ever seen. A Melnibonéan craft, was she?"

"Yes, but rather old."

They helped him to his feet. They had stripped him of his clothes and wrapped him in woolen blankets. The sun was already drying his hair. He was very weak. He said:

"My sword?"

"Duke Avan has it, below."

"Tell him to be careful of it."

"We're sure he will."

"This way," said another. "The duke awaits you."

BOOK THREE

SAILING TO THE PAST

CHAPTER ONE

ELRIC SAT BACK in the comfortable, well-padded chair and accepted the wine-cup handed him by his host. While Smiorgan ate his fill of the hot food provided for them, Elric and Duke Avan appraised one another.

Duke Avan was a man of about forty, with a square, handsome face. He was dressed in a gilded silver breastplate, over which was arranged a white cloak. His britches, tucked into black knee-length boots, were of cream-coloured doeskin. On a small sea-table at his elbow rested his helmet crested with scarlet feathers.

"I am honoured, sir, to have you as my guest," said Duke Avan. "I know you to be Elric of Melniboné. I have been seeking you for several months, ever since news came to me that you had left your homeland (and your power) behind and were wandering, as it were, incognito in the Young Kingdoms."

"You know much, sir."

"I, too, am a traveler by choice. I almost caught up with you in Pikarayd, but I gather there was some sort of trouble there. You left quickly and then I lost your trail altogether. I was about to give up looking for your aid when, by the greatest of good fortune, I found you floating in the water!" Duke Avan laughed.

"You have the advantage of me," said Elric, smiling. "You raise many questions."

"He's Avan Astran of Old Hrolmar," grunted Count Smiorgan from the other side of a huge ham bone. "He's well known as an adventurer—explorer—trader. His reputation's the best. We can trust him, Elric."

"I recall the name now," Elric told the duke. "But why should you seek my aid?"

The smell of the food from the table had at last impinged and Elric got up. "Would you mind if I ate something while you explained, Duke Avan?"

"Eat your fill, Prince Elric. I am honoured to have you as a guest."

"You have saved my life, sir. I have never had it saved so courteously!"

Duke Avan smiled. "I have never before had the pleasure of, let us say, catching so courteous a fish. If I were a superstitious man, Prince Elric, I should guess that some other force threw us together in this way."

"I prefer to think of it as coincidence," said the albino, beginning to eat. "Now, sir, tell me how I can aid you."

"I shall not hold you to any bargain, merely because I have been lucky enough to save your life," said Duke Avan Astran. "Please bear that in mind."

"I shall, sir."

Duke Avan stroked the feathers of his helmet. "I have explored most of the world, as Count Smiorgan rightly says. I have been to your own Melniboné and I have even ventured east, to Elwher and the Unmapped East. I have been to Myyrrhn, where the Winged Folk live. I have traveled as far as World's Edge and hope one day to go beyond. But I have never crossed the Boiling Sea and I know only a small stretch of coast along the Western Continent—the continent that has no name. Have you been there, Elric, in your travels?"

The albino shook his head. "I seek experience of other cultures, other civilizations—that is why I travel. There has been nothing, so far, to take me there. The continent is inhabited only by savages, is it not?"

"So we are told."

"You have other intelligence?"

"You know that there is some evidence," said Duke Avan in a deliberate tone, "that your own ancestors came originally from that mainland?"

"Evidence?" Elric pretended lack of interest. "A few legends, that is all."

"One of those legends speaks of a city older than dreaming Imrryr. A city that still exists in the deep jungles of the West."

Elric recalled his conversation with Earl Saxif D'Aan, and he smiled to himself. "You mean R'lin K'ren A'a?"

"Aye. A strange name." Duke Avan Astran leaned forward, his eyes alight with delighted curiosity. "You pronounce it more fluently than could I. You speak the secret tongue, the High Tongue, the Speech of Kings . . ."

"Of course."

"You are forbidden to teach it to any but your own children, are you not?"

"You appear conversant with the customs of Melniboné, Duke Avan," Elric said, his lids falling so that they half covered his eyes. He leaned back in his seat as he bit into a piece of fresh bread with relish. "Do you know what the words mean?"

"I have been told that they mean simply 'Where the High Ones Meet' in the ancient speech of Melniboné," Duke Avan Astran told him.

Elric inclined his head. "That is so. Doubtless only a small town, in reality. Where local chiefs gathered, perhaps once a year, to discuss the price of grain."

"You believe that, Prince Elric?"

Elric inspected a covered dish. He helped himself to veal in a rich, sweet sauce. "No," he said.

"You believe, then, that there was an ancient civilization even before your own, from which your own culture sprang? You believe that R'lin K'ren A'a is still there, somewhere in the jungles of the West?"

Elric waited until he had swallowed. He shook his head.

"No," he said. "I believe that it does not exist at all."

"You are not curious about your ancestors?"

"Should I be?"

"They were said to be different in character from those who founded Melniboné. Gentler . . ." Duke Avan Astran looked deep into Elric's face.

Elric laughed. "You are an intelligent man, Duke Avan of Old Hrolmar. You are a perceptive man. Oh, and indeed you are a cunning man, sir!"

Duke Avan grinned at the compliment. "And you know much more of the legends than you are admitting, if I am not mistaken."

"Possibly." Elric sighed as the food warmed him. "We are known as a secretive people, we of Melniboné."

"Yet," said Duke Avan, "you seem untypical. Who else would desert an empire to travel in lands where his very race was hated?"

"An emperor rules better, Duke Avan Astran, if he has close knowledge of the world in which he rules."

"Melniboné rules the Young Kingdoms no longer."

"Her power is still great. But that, anyway, was not what I meant. I am of the opinion that the Young Kingdoms offer something which Melniboné has lost."

"Vitality?"

"Perhaps."

"Humanity!" grunted Count Smiorgan Baldhead. "That is what your race has lost, Prince Elric. I say nothing of you—but look at Earl Saxif D'Aan. How can one so wise be such a simpleton? He lost everything—pride, love, power—because he had no humanity. And what humanity he had—why, it destroyed him."

"Some say it will destroy me," said Elric, "but perhaps 'humanity' is, indeed, what I seek to bring to Melniboné, Count Smiorgan."

"Then you will destroy your kingdom!" said Smiorgan bluntly. "It is too late to save Melniboné."

"Perhaps I can help you find what you seek, Prince Elric," said Duke Avan Astran quietly. "Perhaps there is time to save Melniboné, if you feel such a mighty nation is in danger."

"From within," said Elric. "But I speak too freely."

"For a Melnibonéan, that is true."

"How did you come to hear of this city?" Elric wished to know. "No other man I have met in the Young Kingdoms has heard of R'lin K'ren A'a."

"It is marked on a map I have."

Deliberately, Elric chewed his meat and swallowed it. "The map is doubtless a forgery."

"Perhaps. Do you recall anything else of the legend of R'lin K'ren A'a?"

"There is the story of the Creature Doomed to Live." Elric pushed the food aside and poured wine for himself. "The city is said to have received its name because the Lords of the Higher Worlds once met there to decide the rules of the Cosmic Struggle. They were overheard by the one inhabitant of the city who had not flown when they came. When they discovered him, they doomed him to remain alive for ever, carrying the frightful knowledge in his head . . ."

"I have heard that story, too. But the one that interests me is that the inhabitants of R'lin K'ren A'a never returned to their city. Instead they struck northwards and crossed the sea. Some reached an island we now call Sorcerer's Isle while others went further—blown by a great storm—and came at length to a large island inhabited by dragons whose venom caused all it touched to burn . . . to Melniboné, in fact."

"And you wish to test the truth of that story. Your interest is that of a scholar?"

Duke Avan laughed. "Partly. But my main interest in R'lin K'ren A'a is more materialistic. For your ancestors left a great treasure behind them when they fled their city. Particularly they abandoned an image of Arioch, the Lord of Chaos—a monstrous image, carved in jade, whose eyes were two huge, identical gems of a kind unknown anywhere else in all the lands of the Earth. Jewels from another plane of existence. Jewels which could reveal all the secrets of the Higher Worlds, of the past and the future, of the myriad planes of the cosmos . . ."

"All cultures have similar legends. Wishful thinking, Duke Avan, that is all . . ."

"But the Melnibonéans had a culture unlike any others. The Melnibonéans are not true men, as you well know. Their powers are superior, their knowledge far greater . . ."

"It was once thus," Elric said. "But that great power and knowledge is not mine. I have only a fragment of it . . ."

"I did not seek you in Bakshaan and later in Jadmar because I believed you could verify what I have heard. I did not cross the sea to Filkhar, then to Argimiliar and at last to Pikarayd because I thought you would instantly confirm all that I have spoken of—I sought you because I think you the only man who would wish to accompany me on a voyage which would give us the truth or falsehood to these legends once and for all."

Elric tilted his head and drained his wine-cup.

"Cannot you do that for yourself? Why should you desire my company on the expedition? From what I have heard of you, Duke Avan, you are not one who needs support in his venturings . . ."

Duke Avan laughed. "I went alone to Elwher when my men deserted me in the Weeping Waste. It is not in my nature to know physical fear. But I have survived my travels this long because I have shown proper foresight and caution before setting off. Now it seems I must face dangers I cannot anticipate—sorcery, perhaps. It struck me, therefore, that I needed an ally who had some experience of fighting sorcery. And since I would have no truck with the ordinary kind of wizard such as Pan Tang spawns, you were my only choice. You seek knowledge, Prince Elric, just as I do. Indeed, it could be said that if it had not been for your yearning for knowledge, your cousin would never have attempted to usurp the Ruby Throne of Melniboné . . ."

"Enough of that," Elric said bitterly. "Let's talk of this expedition. Where is the map?"

"You will accompany me?"

"Show me the map."

Duke Avan drew a scroll from his pouch. "Here it is."

"Where did you find it?"

"On Melniboné."

"You have been there recently?" Elric felt anger rise in him.

Duke Avan raised a hand. "I went there with a group of traders and I gave much for a particular casket which had been sealed, it seemed, for an eternity. Within that casket was this map." He spread out the scroll on the table. Elric recognized the style and the script—the old High Speech of Melniboné. It was a map of part of the Western Continent—more than he had ever seen on any other map. It showed a great river winding into the interior for a hundred miles or more. The river appeared to flow through a jungle and then divide into two rivers which later rejoined. The "island" of land thus formed had a black circle marked on it. Against this circle, in the involved writing of ancient Melniboné, was the name R'lin K'ren A'a. Elric inspected the scroll carefully. It did not seem to be a forgery.

"Is this all you found?" he asked.

"The scroll was sealed and this was embedded in the seal," Duke Avan said, handing something to Elric.

Elric held the object in his palm. It was a tiny ruby of a red so deep as to seem black at first, but when he turned it into the light he saw an image at the centre of the ruby and he recognized that image. He frowned, then he said, "I will agree to your proposal, Duke Avan. Will you let me keep this?"

"Do you know what it is?"

"No. But I should like to find out. There is a memory somewhere in my head . . ."

"Very well, take it. I will keep the map."

"When did you have it in mind to set off?"

Duke Avan's smile was sardonic. "We are already sailing around the southern coast to the Boiling Sea."

"There are few who have returned from that ocean," Elric murmured bitterly. He glanced across the table and saw that Smiorgan was imploring with his eyes for Elric not to have any part of Duke Avan's scheme. Elric smiled at his friend. "The adventure is to my taste."

Miserably, Smiorgan shrugged. "It seems it will be a little longer before I return to the Purple Towns."

Chapter Two

The coast of Lormyr had disappeared in warm mist and Duke Avan Astran's schooner dipped its graceful prow towards the West and the Boiling Sea.

The Vilmirian crew of the schooner were used to a less demanding climate and more casual work than this and they went about their tasks, it seemed to Elric, with something of an aggrieved air.

Standing beside Elric on the ship's poop deck, Count Smiorgan Baldhead wiped sweat from his pate and growled: "Vilmirians are a lazy lot, Prince Elric. Duke Avan needs real sailors for a voyage of this kind. I could have picked him a crew, given the chance . . ."

Elric smiled. "Neither of us was given the chance, Count Smiorgan. It was a *fait accompli.* He's a clever man, Duke Astran."

"It is not a cleverness I entirely respect, for he offered us no real choice. A free man is a better companion than a slave, says the old aphorism."

"Why did you not disembark when you had the chance, then, Count Smiorgan?"

"Because of the promise of treasure," said the black-bearded man frankly. "I would return with honour to the Purple Towns. Forget you not that I commanded the fleet that was lost . . ."

Elric understood.

"My motives are straightforward," said Smiorgan. "Yours are much more complicated. You seem to desire danger as other men desire love-making or drinking—as if in danger you find forgetfulness."

"Is that not true of many professional soldiers?"

"You are not a mere professional soldier, Elric. That you know as well as I."

"Yet few of the dangers I have faced have helped me forget," Elric pointed out. "Rather they have strengthened the reminder of what I am—of the dilemma I face. My own instincts war against the traditions of my race." Elric drew a deep, melancholy breath. "I go where danger is because I think that an answer might lie there—some reason for all this tragedy and paradox. Yet I know I shall never find it."

"But it is why you sail to R'lin K'ren A'a, eh? You hope that your remote ancestors had the answer you need?"

"R'lin K'ren A'a is a myth. Even should the map prove genuine what shall we find but a few ruins? Imrryr has stood for ten thousand years and she was built at least two centuries after my people settled on Melniboné. Time will have taken R'lin K'ren A'a away."

"And this statue, this Jade Man, Avan spoke of?"

"If the statue ever existed, it could have been looted at any time in the past hundred centuries."

"And the Creature Doomed to Live?"

"A myth."

"But you hope, do you not, that it is all as Duke Avan says . . . ?" Count Smiorgan put a hand on Elric's arm. "Do you not?"

Elric stared ahead, into the writhing steam which rose from the sea. He shook his head.

"No, Count Smiorgan. I *fear* that it is all as Duke Avan says."

The wind blew whimsically and the schooner's passage was slow as the heat grew greater and the crew sweated still more and murmured fearfully. And upon each face, now, was a stricken look.

Only Duke Avan seemed to retain his confidence. He called to them all to take heart; he told them that they should all be rich soon; and he gave orders for the oars to be unshipped, for the wind could no longer be trusted. They grumbled at this, stripping off their shirts to reveal skins as red as cooked lobsters. Duke Avan made a joke of that. But the Vilmirians no longer laughed at his jokes as they had done in the milder seas of their home waters.

Around the ship the sea bubbled and roared, and they navigated by their few instruments, for the steam obscured everything.

Once a green thing erupted from the sea and glared at them before disappearing.

They ate and slept little and Elric rarely left the poop deck. Count Smiorgan bore the heat silently and Duke Avan, seemingly oblivious to any discomfort, went cheerfully about the ship, calling encouragement to his men.

Count Smiorgan was fascinated by the waters. He had heard of them, but never crossed them. "These are only the outer reaches of this sea, Elric," he said in some wonder. "Think what it must be like at the middle."

Elric grinned. "I would rather not. As it is, I fear I'll be boiled to death before another day has passed."

Passing by, Duke Avan heard him and clapped him on the shoulder. "Nonsense, Prince Elric! The steam is good for you! There is nothing healthier!" Seemingly with pleasure, Duke Avan stretched his limbs. "It cleans all the poisons from the system."

Count Smiorgan offered him a glowering look and Duke Avan laughed. "Be of better cheer, Count Smiorgan. According to my charts—such as they are—a couple of days will see us nearing the coasts of the Western Continent."

"The thought fails to raise my spirits very greatly," said Count Smiorgan, but he smiled, infected by Avan's good humour.

*   *   *

But shortly thereafter the sea grew slowly less frenetic and the steam began to disperse until the heat became more tolerable.

At last they emerged into a calm ocean beneath a shimmering blue sky in which hung a red-gold sun.

But three of the Vilmirian crew had died to cross the Boiling Sea, and four more had a sickness in them which made them cough a great deal, and shiver, and cry out in the night.

For a while they were becalmed, but at last a soft wind began to blow and fill the schooner's sails and soon they had sighted their first land—a little yellow island where they found fruit and a spring of fresh water. Here, too, they buried the three men who had succumbed to the sickness of the Boiling Sea, for the Vilmirians had refused to have them buried in the ocean on the grounds that the bodies would be "stewed like meat in a pot."

While the schooner lay at anchor, just off the island, Duke Avan called Elric to his cabin and showed him, for a second time, that ancient map.

Pale golden sunlight filtered through the cabin's ports and fell upon the old parchment, beaten from the skin of a beast long since extinct, as Elric and Duke Avan Astran of Old Hrolmar bent over it.

"See," Duke Avan said, pointing. "This island's marked. The map's scale seems reasonably accurate. Another three days and we shall be at the mouth of the river."

Elric nodded. "But it would be wise to rest here for a while until our strength is fully restored and the morale of the crew is raised higher. There are reasons, after all, why men have avoided the jungles of the West over the centuries."

"Certainly there are savages there—some say they are not even human—but I'm confident we can deal with those dangers. I have much experience of strange territories, Prince Elric."

"But you said yourself you feared other dangers."

"True. Very well, we'll do as you suggest."

*   *   *

On the fourth day a strong wind began to blow from the east and they raised anchor. The schooner leaped over the waves under only half her canvas and the crew saw this as a good omen.

"They are mindless fools," Smiorgan said as they stood clinging to the rigging in the prow. "The time will come when they will wish they were suffering the cleaner hardships of the Boiling Sea. This journey, Elric, could benefit none of us, even if the riches of R'lin K'ren A'a are still there."

But Elric did not answer. He was lost in strange thoughts, un-usual thoughts for him, for he was remembering his childhood and his father who had been the last true ruler of the Bright Empire—proud, insouciant, cruel. His father had expected him—perhaps be-cause of his strange albinism—to restore the glories of Melniboné. Instead Elric threatened to destroy what was left of that glory. Like himself, his father had had no real place in this new age of the Young Kingdoms, but had refused to acknowledge it. This journey to the Western Continent, to the land of his ancestors, had a peculiar at-traction for him. Here no new nations had emerged. The continent had, as far as he knew, remained the same since R'lin K'ren A'a had been abandoned. The jungles would be the jungles his folk had known, the land would be the land that had given birth to his pecu-liar race, moulded the character of its people with their sombre plea-sures, their melancholy arts and their dark delights. Had his ancestors felt this agony of knowledge, this impotence in the face of the understanding that existence had no point, no purpose, no hope? Was this why they had built their civilization in that particular pat-tern, why they had disdained the more placid, spiritual values of mankind's philosophers? He knew that many of the intellectuals of the Young Kingdoms pitied the powerful folk of Melniboné as mad. But if they had been mad and if they had imposed a madness upon the world that had lasted a hundred centuries, what had made them so? Perhaps the secret did lie in R'lin K'ren A'a—not in any tangible form but in the ambiance created by the dark jungles and the deep, old rivers. Perhaps here, at last, he would be able to feel at one with himself.

He ran his fingers through his milk-white hair and there was a kind of innocent anguish in his crimson eyes. He might be the last of his kind and yet he was unlike his kind. Smiorgan had been wrong. Elric knew that everything that existed had its opposite. In danger he might find peace. And yet, of course, in peace there was danger. Being an imperfect creature in an imperfect world, he would always know paradox. And that was why in paradox there was always a kind of truth. That was why philosophers and soothsayers flourished. In a perfect world there would be no place for them. In an imperfect world the mysteries were always without solution and that was why there was always a great choice of solutions.

It was on the morning of the third day that the coast was sighted and the schooner steered her way through the sandbanks of the great delta and anchored, at last, at the mouth of the dark and nameless river.

CHAPTER THREE

Evening came and the sun began to set over the black outlines of the massive trees. A rich, ancient smell came from the jungle and through the twilight echoed the cries of strange birds and beasts. Elric was impatient to begin the quest up the river. Sleep—never welcome—was now impossible to achieve. He stood unmoving on the deck, his eyes hardly blinking, his brain barely active, as if expecting something to happen to him. The rays of the sun stained his face and threw black shadows over the deck and then it was dark and still under the moon and the stars. He wanted the jungle to absorb him. He wanted to be one with the trees and the shrubs and the creeping beasts. He wanted thought to disappear. He drew the heavily scented air into his lungs as if that alone would make him become what at that moment he desired to be. The drone of insects became a murmuring voice that called him into the heart of the old, old forest. And yet he could not move—could not answer. And at length Count Smiorgan came up on deck and touched his shoulder and said something and passively he went below to his bunk and wrapped himself in his cloak and lay there, still listening to the voice of the jungle.

Even Duke Avan seemed more introspective than usual when they upped anchor the next morning and began to row against the sluggish current. There were few gaps in the foliage above their heads and they had the impression that they were entering a huge, gloomy tunnel, leaving the sunlight behind with the sea. Bright plants twined among the vines that hung from the leafy canopy and caught in the ship's masts as they moved. Ratlike animals with long arms swung through the branches and peered at them with bright, knowing eyes. The river turned and the sea was no longer in sight. Shafts of sunlight filtered down to the deck and the light had a greenish tinge to it. Elric became more alert than he had ever been since he agreed to accompany Duke Avan. He took a keen interest in every detail of the jungle and the black river over which moved schools of insects like agitated clouds of mist and in which blossoms drifted like drops of blood in ink. Everywhere were rustlings, sudden squawks, barks and wet noises made by fish or river animals as they hunted the prey disturbed by the ship's oars which cut into the great clumps of weed and sent the things that hid there scurrying. The others began to complain of insect bites, but Elric was not troubled by them, perhaps because no insect could desire his deficient blood.

Duke Avan passed him on the deck. The Vilmirian slapped at his forehead. "You seem more cheerful, Prince Elric."

Elric smiled absently. "Perhaps I am."

"I must admit I personally find all this a bit oppressive. I'll be glad when we reach the city."

"You are still convinced you'll find it?"

"I'll be convinced otherwise when I've explored every inch of the island we're bound for."

So absorbed had he become in the atmosphere of the jungle that

Elric was hardly aware of the ship or his companions. The ship beat very slowly up the river, moving at little more than walking speed.

A few days passed, but Elric scarcely noticed, for the jungle did not change—and then the river widened and the canopy parted and the wide, hot sky was suddenly full of huge birds crowding upwards as the ship disturbed them. All but Elric were pleased to be under the open sky again and spirits rose. Elric went below.

The attack on the ship came almost immediately. There was a whistling noise and a scream and a sailor writhed and fell over clutching at a grey, thin semi-circle of something which had buried itself in his stomach. An upper yard came crashing to the deck, bringing sail and rigging with it. A headless body took four paces towards the poop deck before collapsing, the blood pumping from the obscene hole that was its neck. And everywhere was the thin whistling noise. Elric heard the sounds from below and came back instantly, buckling on his sword. The first face he saw was Smiorgan's. The bald-pated man looked perturbed as he crouched against a rail on the starboard side. Elric had the impression of grey blurs whistling past, slashing into flesh and rigging, wood and canvas. Some fell to the deck and he saw that they were thin discs of crystalline rock, about a foot in diameter. They were being hurled from both banks of the river and there was no protection against them.

He tried to see who was throwing the discs and glimpsed something moving in the trees along the right bank. Then the discs ceased suddenly and there was a pause before some of the sailors dashed across the deck to seek better cover. Duke Avan suddenly appeared in the stern. He had unsheathed his sword.

"Get below. Get your bucklers and any armour you can find. Bring bows. Arm yourselves, men, or you're finished."

And as he spoke their attackers broke from the trees and began to wade into the water. No more discs came and it seemed likely they had exhausted their supply.

"By Chardros!" Avan gasped. "Are these real creatures or some sorcerer's conjurings?"

The things were essentially reptilian but with feathery crests and neck wattles, though their faces were almost human. Their forelegs were like the arms and hands of men, but their hindlegs were incredibly long and storklike. Balanced on these legs, their bodies towered over the water. They carried great clubs in which slits had been cut and doubtless these were what they used to hurl the crystalline discs. Staring at their faces, Elric was horrified. In some subtle way they reminded him of the characteristic faces of his own folk—the folk of Melniboné. Were these creatures his cousins? Or were they a species from which his people had evolved? He stopped asking the questions as an intense hatred for the creatures filled him. They were obscene: sight of them brought bile into his throat. Without thinking, he drew Stormbringer from its sheath.

The Black Sword began to howl and the familiar black radiance spilled from it. The runes carved into its blade pulsed a vivid scarlet which turned slowly to a deep purple and then to black once more.

The creatures were wading through the water on their stiltlike legs and they paused when they saw the sword, glancing at one another. And they were not the only ones unnerved by the sight, for Duke Avan and his men paled, too.

"Gods!" Avan yelled. "I know not which I prefer the look of— those who attack us or that which defends us!"

"Stay well away from that sword," Smiorgan warned. "It has the habit of killing more than its master chooses."

And now the reptilian savages were upon them, clutching at the ship's rails as the armed sailors rushed back on deck to meet the attack.

Clubs came at Elric from all sides, but Stormbringer shrieked and parried each blow. He held the sword in both hands, whirling it this way and that, ploughing great gashes in the scaly bodies.

The creatures hissed and opened red mouths in agony and rage while their thick, black blood sank into the waters of the river. Although from the legs upward they were only slightly larger than a tall, well-built man, they had more vitality than any human and the deepest cuts hardly seemed to affect them, even when administered by Stormbringer. Elric was astonished at this resistance to the sword's power.

Often a nick was enough for the sword to draw a man's soul from him. These things seemed immune. Perhaps they had no souls . . .

He fought on, his hatred giving him strength.

But elsewhere on the ship the sailors were being routed. Rails were torn off and the great clubs crushed planks and brought down more rigging. The savages were intent on destroying the ship as well as the crew. And there was little doubt, now, that they would be successful.

Avan shouted to Elric. "By the names of all the gods, Prince Elric, can you not summon some further sorcery? We are doomed else!"

Elric knew Avan spoke truth. All around him the ship was being gradually pulled apart by the hissing reptilian creatures. Most of them had sustained horrible wounds from the defenders, but only one or two had collapsed. Elric began to suspect that they did, in fact, fight supernatural enemies.

He backed away and sought shelter beneath a half-crushed doorway as he tried to concentrate on a method of calling upon supernatural aid.

He was panting with exhaustion and he clung to a beam as the ship rocked back and forth in the water. He fought to clear his head.

And then the incantation came to him. He was not sure if it was appropriate, but it was the only one he could recall. His ancestors had made pacts, thousands of years before, with all the elementals who controlled the animal world. In the past he had summoned help from various of these spirits but never from the one he now sought to call. From his mouth began to issue the ancient, beautiful and convoluted words of Melniboné's High Speech.

"King with Wings! Lord of all that work and are not seen, upon whose labours all else depends! Nnuuurrrr'c'c of the Insect Folk, I summon thee!"

Save for the motion of the ship, Elric ceased to be aware of all else happening around him. The sounds of the fight dimmed and were heard no more as he sent his voice out beyond his plane of the Earth into another—the plane dominated by King Nnuuurrrr'c'c of the Insects, paramount lord of his people.

In his ears now Elric heard a buzzing and gradually the buzzing formed itself in words.

"Who art thou, mortal? What right hast thee to summon me?"

"I am Elric, ruler of Melniboné. My ancestors aided thee, Nnuuur-rrr'c'c."

"Aye—but long ago."

"And it is long ago that they last called on thee for thine aid!"

"True. What aid dost thou now require, Elric of Melniboné?"

"Look upon my plane. Thou wilt see that I am in danger. Canst thou abolish this danger, friend of the Insects?"

Now a filmy shape formed and could be seen as if through several layers of cloudy silk. Elric tried to keep his eyes upon it, but it kept leaving his field of vision and then returning for a few moments. He knew that he looked into another plane of the Earth.

"Canst thou help me, Nnuuurrrr'c'c?"

"Hast thou no patron of thine own species? Some Lord of Chaos who can aid thee?"

"My patron is Arioch and he is a temperamental demon at best. These days he aids me little."

"Then I must send thee allies, mortal. But call upon me no more when this is done."

"I shall not summon thee again, Nnuuurrrr'c'c."

The layers of film disappeared and with them the shape.

The noise of the battle crashed once again on Elric's consciousness and he heard with sharper clarity than before the screams of the sailors and the hissing of the reptilian savages and when he looked out from his shelter he saw that at least half the crew were dead.

As he came on deck Smiorgan ran up. "I thought you slain, Elric! What became of you?" He was plainly relieved to see his friend still lived.

"I sought aid from another plane—but it does not seem to have materialized."

"I'm thinking we're doomed and had best try to swim downstream away from here and seek a hiding place in the jungle," Smiorgan said.

"What of Duke Avan? Is he dead?"

"He lives. But those creatures are all but impervious to our weapons. This ship will sink ere long." Smiorgan lurched as the deck tilted and he reached out to grab a trailing rope, letting his long sword dangle by its wrist-thong. "They are not attacking the stern at present. We can slip into the water there . . ."

"I made a bargain with Duke Avan," Elric reminded the islander. "I cannot desert him."

"Then we'll all perish!"

"What's that?" Elric bent his head, listening intently.

"I hear nothing."

It was a whine which deepened in tone until it became a drone. Now Smiorgan heard it also and looked about him, seeking the source of the sound. And suddenly he gasped, pointing upward. "Is that the aid you sought?"

There was a vast cloud of them, black against the blue of the sky. Every so often the sun would flash on a dazzling colour—a rich blue, green, or red. They came spiraling down towards the ship and now both sides fell silent, staring skyward.

The flying things were like huge dragonflies and the brightness and richness of their colouring was breathtaking. It was their wings which made the droning sound which now began to increase in loudness and heighten in pitch as the huge insects sped nearer.

Realizing that they were the object of the attack the reptile men stumbled backwards on their long legs, trying to reach the shore before the gigantic insects were upon them.

But it was too late for flight.

The dragonflies settled on the savages. Soon nothing could be seen of the bodies. The hissing increased and sounded almost pitiful as the insects bore their victims down to the surface and then inflicted on them whatever terrible death it was. Perhaps they stung with their tails—it was not possible for the watchers to see.

Sometimes a storklike leg would emerge from the water and thrash in the air for a moment. But soon, just as the reptiles were covered by the insect bodies, so were their cries drowned by the strange and blood-chilling humming that arose on all sides.

A sweating Duke Avan, sword still in hand, ran up the deck. "Is this your doing, Prince Elric?"

Elric looked on with satisfaction, but the others were plainly disgusted. "It was," he said.

"Then I thank you for your aid. This ship is holed in a dozen places and is letting in water at a terrible rate. It's a wonder we have not yet sunk. I've given orders to begin rowing and I hope we make it to the island in time." He pointed upstream. "There, you can just see it."

"What if there are more of those savages there?" Smiorgan asked.

Avan smiled grimly, indicating the further shore. "Look." On their peculiar legs a dozen or more of the reptiles were fleeing into the jungle, having witnessed the fate of their comrades. "They'll be reluctant to attack us again, I think."

Now the huge dragonflies were rising into the air again and Avan turned away as he glimpsed what they had left behind. "By the gods, you work fierce sorcery, Prince Elric! Ugh!"

Elric smiled and shrugged. "It is effective, Duke Avan." He sheathed his runesword. It seemed reluctant to enter the scabbard and it moaned as if in resentment.

Smiorgan glanced at it. "That blade looks as if it will want to feast soon, Elric, whether you desire it or not."

"Doubtless it will find something to feed on in the forest," said the albino. He stepped over a piece of broken mast and went below.

Count Smiorgan Baldhead looked at the new scum on the surface of the water and he shuddered.

CHAPTER FOUR

The wrecked schooner was almost awash when the crew clambered overboard with lines and began the task of dragging it up the mud that formed the banks of the island. Before them was a wall of foliage that seemed impenetrable. Smiorgan followed Elric, lowering himself into the shallows. They began to wade ashore.

As they left the water and set foot on the hard, baked earth, Smiorgan stared at the forest. No wind moved the trees and a peculiar silence had descended. No birds called from the trees, no insects buzzed, there were none of the barks and cries of animals they had heard on their journey upriver.

"Those supernatural friends of yours seem to have frightened more than the savages away," the black-bearded man murmured. "This place seems lifeless."

Elric nodded. "It is strange."

Duke Avan joined them. He had discarded his finery—ruined in the fight, anyway—and now wore a padded leather jerkin and doeskin breeches. His sword was at his side. "We'll have to leave most of our men behind with the ship," he said regretfully. "They'll make what repairs they can while we press on to find R'lin K'ren A'a." He tugged his light cloak about him. "Is it my imagination, or is there an odd atmosphere?"

"We have already remarked on it," Smiorgan said. "Life seems to have fled the island."

Duke Avan grinned. "If all we face is as timid, we have nothing further to fear. I must admit, Prince Elric, that had I wished you harm and then seen you conjure those monsters from thin air, I'd think twice about getting too close to you! Thank you, by the way, for what you did. We should have perished by now if it had not been for you."

"It was for my aid that you asked me to accompany you," Elric said wearily. "Let's eat and rest and then continue with our expedition."

A shadow passed over Duke Avan's face then. Something in Elric's manner had disturbed him.

Entering the jungle was no easy matter. Armed with axes the six members of the crew (all that could be spared) began to hack at the undergrowth. And still the unnatural silence prevailed . . .

By nightfall they were less than half a mile into the forest and completely exhausted. The forest was so thick that there was barely room to pitch their tent. The only light in the camp came from the small, sputtering fire outside the tent. The crewmen slept where they could in the open.

Elric could not sleep, but now it was not the jungle which kept him awake. He was puzzled by the silence, for he was sure that it was not their presence which had driven all life away. There was not a single small rodent, bird or insect anywhere to be seen. There were no traces of animal life. The island had been deserted by all but vegetation for a long while—perhaps for centuries or tens of centuries. He remembered another part of the old legend of R'lin K'ren A'a. It had been said that when the gods came to meet there not only the citizens fled, but also all the wildlife. Nothing had dared see the High Lords or listen to their conversation. Elric shivered, turning his white head this way and that on the rolled cloak that supported it, his crimson eyes tortured. If there were dangers on this island, they would be subtler dangers than those they had faced on the river.

The noise of their passage through the forest was the only sound to be heard on the island as they forced their way on the next morning.

With lodestone in one hand and map in the other, Duke Avan Astran sought to guide them, directing his men where to cut their path.

But the going became even slower and it was obvious that no creatures had come this way for many ages.

By the fourth day they had reached a natural clearing of flat volcanic rock and found a spring there. Gratefully they made camp. Elric began to wash his face in the cool water when he heard a yell behind him. He sprang up. One of the crewmen was reaching for an arrow and fitting it to his bow.

"What is it?" Duke Avan called.

"I saw something, my lord!"

"Nonsense, there are no—"

"Look!" The man drew back the string and let fly into the upper terraces of the forest. Something did seem to stir then and Elric thought he saw a flash of grey among the trees.

"Did you see what kind of creature it was?" Smiorgan asked the man.

"No, master. I feared at first it was those reptiles again."

"They're too frightened to follow us onto this island," Duke Avan reassured him.

"I hope you're right," Smiorgan said nervously.

"Then what could it have been?" Elric wondered.

"I—I thought it was a man, master," the crewman stuttered.

Elric stared thoughtfully into the trees. "A man?"

Smiorgan asked, "You were hoping for this, Elric?"

"I am not sure . . ."

Duke Avan shrugged. "More likely the shadow of a cloud passing over the trees. According to my calculations we should have reached the city by now."

"You think, after all, that it does not exist?" Elric said.

"I am beginning not to care, Prince Elric." The duke leaned against the bole of a huge tree, brushing aside a vine which touched his face. "Still there's naught else to do. The ship won't be ready to sail yet." He looked up into the branches. "I did not think I should miss those damned insects that plagued us on our way here . . ."

The crewman who had shot the arrow suddenly shouted again. "There! I saw him! It is a man!"

While the others stared but failed to discern anything Duke Avan continued to lean against the tree. "You saw nothing. There is nothing here to see."

Elric turned towards him. "Give me the map and the lodestone, Duke Avan. I have a feeling I can find the way."

The Vilmirian shrugged, an expression of doubt on his square, handsome face. He handed the things over to Elric.

They rested the night and in the morning they continued, with Elric leading the way.

And at noon they broke out of the forest and saw the ruins of R'lin K'ren A'a.

CHAPTER FIVE

Nothing grew among the ruins of the city. The streets were broken and the walls of the houses had fallen, but there were no weeds flowering in the cracks and it seemed that the city had but recently been brought down by an earthquake. Only one thing still stood intact, towering over the ruins. It was a gigantic statue of white, grey and green jade—the statue of a naked youth with a face of almost feminine beauty that turned sightless eyes towards the north.

"The eyes!" Duke Avan Astran said. "They're gone!"

The others said nothing as they stared at the statue and the ruins surrounding it. The area was relatively small and the buildings had had little decoration. The inhabitants seemed to have been a simple, well-to-do folk—totally unlike the Melnibonéans of the Bright Empire. Elric could not believe that the people of R'lin K'ren A'a had been his ancestors. They had been too sane.

"The statue's already been looted," Duke Avan continued. "Our damned journey's been in vain!"

Elric laughed. "Did you really think you would be able to prise the Jade Man's eyes from their sockets, my lord?"

The statue was as tall as any tower of the Dreaming City and the head alone must have been the size of a reasonably large building. Duke Avan pursed his lips and refused to listen to Elric's mocking voice. "We may yet find the journey worth our while," he said. "There were other treasures in R'lin K'ren A'a. Come . . ."

He led the way into the city.

Very few of the buildings were even partially standing, but they were nonetheless fascinating if only for the peculiar nature of their building materials, which were of a kind the travelers had never seen before.

The colours were many, but faded by time—soft reds and yellows and blues—and they flowed together to make almost infinite combinations.

Elric reached out to touch one wall and was surprised at the cool feel of the smooth material. It was neither stone nor wood nor metal. Perhaps it had been brought here from another plane?

He tried to visualize the city as it had been before it was deserted. The streets had been wide, there had been no surrounding wall, the houses had been low and built around large courtyards. If this was, indeed, the original home of his people, what had happened to change them from the peaceful citizens of R'lin K'ren A'a to the insane builders of Imrryr's bizarre and dreaming towers? Elric had thought he might find a solution to a mystery here, but instead he had found another mystery. It was his fate, he thought, shrugging to himself.

And then the first crystal disc hummed past his head and smashed against a collapsing wall.

The next disc split the skull of a crewman and a third nicked Smiorgan's ear before they had thrown themselves flat amongst the rubble.

"They're vengeful, those creatures," Avan said with a hard smile. "They'll risk much to pay us back for their comrades' deaths!"

Terror was on the face of each surviving crewman and fear had begun to creep into Avan's eyes.

More discs clattered nearby, but it was plain that the party was temporarily out of sight of the reptiles. Smiorgan coughed as white dust rose from the rubble and caught in his throat.

"You'd best summon those monstrous allies of yours again, Elric."

Elric shook his head. "I cannot. My ally said he would not serve me a second time." He looked to his left where the four walls of a small house still stood. There seemed to be no door, only a window.

"Then call something," Count Smiorgan said urgently. "Anything."

"I am not sure . . ."

Then Elric rolled over and sprang for the shelter, flinging himself through the window to land on a pile of masonry that grazed his hands and knees.

He staggered upright. In the distance he could see the huge blind statue of the god dominating the city. This was said to be an image of Arioch—though it resembled no image of Arioch Elric remembered. Did that image protect R'lin K'ren A'a—or did it threaten it? Someone screamed. He glanced through the opening and saw that a disc had chopped through a man's forearm.

He drew Stormbringer and raised it, facing the jade statue.

"Arioch!" he cried. "Arioch—aid me!"

Black light burst from the blade and it began to sing, as if joining in Elric's incantation.

"Arioch!"

Would the demon come? Often the patron of the kings of Melniboné refused to materialize, claiming that more urgent business called him—business concerning the eternal struggle between Law and Chaos.

"Arioch!"

Sword and man were now wreathed in a palpitating black mist and Elric's white face was flung back, seeming to writhe as the mist writhed.

"Arioch! I beg thee to aid me! It is Elric who calls thee!"

And then a voice reached his ears. It was a soft, purring, reasonable voice. It was a tender voice.

"Elric, I am fondest of thee. I love thee more than any other mortal—but aid thee I cannot—not yet."

Elric cried desperately: "Then we are doomed to perish here!"

"Thou canst escape this danger. Flee alone into the forest. Leave the others while thou hast time. Thou hast a destiny to fulfill elsewhere and elsewhen . . ."

"I will not desert them."

"Thou art foolish, sweet Elric."

"Arioch—since Melniboné's founding thou hast aided her kings. Aid her last king this day!"

"I cannot dissipate my energies. A great struggle looms. And it would cost me much to return to R'lin K'ren A'a. Flee now. Thou shalt be saved. Only the others will die."

And then the Duke of Hell had gone. Elric sensed the passing of his presence. He frowned, fingering his belt pouch, trying to recall something he had once heard. Slowly, he resheathed the reluctant sword. Then there was a thump and Smiorgan stood panting before him.

"Well, is aid on the way?"

"I fear not." Elric shook his head in despair. "Once again Arioch refuses me. Once again he speaks of a greater destiny—a need to conserve his strength."

"Your ancestors could have picked a more tractable demon as their patron. Our reptilian friends are closing in. Look . . ." Smiorgan pointed to the outskirts of the city. A band of about a dozen stilt-legged creatures were advancing, their huge clubs at the ready.

There was a scuffling noise from the rubble on the other side of the wall and Avan appeared, leading his men through the opening. He was cursing.

"No extra aid is coming, I fear," Elric told him.

The Vilmirian smiled grimly. "Then the monsters out there knew more than did we!"

"It seems so."

"We'll have to try to hide from them," Smiorgan said without much conviction. "We'd not survive a fight."

The little party left the ruined house and began to inch its way through what cover it could find, moving gradually nearer to the centre of the city and the statue of the Jade Man.

A sharp hiss from behind them told them that the reptile warriors had sighted them again and another Vilmirian fell with a crystal disc protruding from his back. They broke into a panicky run.

Ahead now was a red building of several storeys which still had its roof.

"In there!" Duke Avan shouted.

With some relief they dashed unhesitatingly up worn steps and through a series of dusty passages until they paused to catch their breath in a great, gloomy hall.

The hall was completely empty and a little light filtered through cracks in the wall.

"This place has lasted better than the others," Duke Avan said. "I wonder what its function was. A fortress, perhaps."

"They seem not to have been a warlike race," Smiorgan pointed out. "I suspect the building had some other function."

The three surviving crewmen were looking fearfully about them. They looked as if they would have preferred to have faced the reptile warriors outside.

Elric began to cross the floor and then paused as he saw something painted on the far wall.

Smiorgan saw it too. "What's that, friend Elric?"

Elric recognized the symbols as the written High Speech of old Melniboné, but it was subtly different and it took him a short time to decipher its meaning.

"Know you what it says, Elric?" Duke Avan murmured, joining them.

"Aye—but it's cryptic enough. It says: 'If thou hast come to slay me, then thou art welcome. If thou hast come without the means to awaken the Jade Man, then begone . . .' "

"Is it addressed to us, I wonder," Avan mused, "or has it been there for a long while?"

Elric shrugged. "It could have been inscribed at any time during the past ten thousand years . . ."

Smiorgan walked up to the wall and reached out to touch it. "I would say it was fairly recent," he said. "The paint still being wet."

Elric frowned. "Then there are inhabitants here still. Why do they not reveal themselves?"

"Could those reptiles out there be the denizens of R'lin K'ren A'a?" Avan said. "There is nothing in the legends that says they were humans who fled this place . . ."

Elric's face clouded and he was about to make an angry reply when Smiorgan interrupted.

"Perhaps there is just one inhabitant. Is that what you are thinking, Elric? The Creature Doomed to Live? Those sentiments could be his . . ."

Elric put his hands to his face and made no reply.

"Come," Avan said. "We've no time to debate on legends." He strode across the floor and entered another doorway, beginning to descend steps. As he reached the bottom they heard him gasp.

The others joined him and saw that he stood on the threshold of another hall. But this one was ankle-deep in fragments of stuff that had been thin leaves of a metallic material which had the flexibility of parchment. Around the walls were thousands of small holes, rank upon rank, each with a character painted over it.

"What is it?" Smiorgan asked.

Elric stooped and picked up one of the fragments. This had half a Melnibonéan character engraved on it. There had even been an attempt to obliterate this.

"It was a library," he said softly. "The library of my ancestors. Someone has tried to destroy it. These scrolls must have been virtually indestructible, yet a great deal of effort has gone into making them indecipherable." He kicked at the fragments. "Plainly our friend—or friends—is a consistent hater of learning."

"Plainly," Avan said bitterly. "Oh, the *value* of those scrolls to the scholar! All destroyed!"

Elric shrugged. "To limbo with the scholar—their value to me was quite considerable!"

Smiorgan put a hand on his friend's arm and Elric shrugged it off. "I had hoped . . ."

Smiorgan cocked his bald head. "Those reptiles have followed us into the building, by the sound of it."

They heard the distant sound of strange footsteps in the passages behind them.

The little band of men moved as silently as they could through the ruined scrolls and crossed the hall until they entered another corridor which led sharply upward.

Then, suddenly, daylight was visible.

Elric peered ahead. "The corridor has collapsed ahead of us and is blocked, by the look of it. The roof has caved in and we may be able to escape through the hole."

They clambered upward over the fallen stones, glancing warily behind them for signs of their pursuers.

At last they emerged in the central square of the city. On the far sides of this square were placed the feet of the great statue, which now towered high above their heads.

Directly before them were two peculiar constructions which, unlike the rest of the buildings, were completely whole. They were domed and faceted and were made of some glasslike substance which diffracted the rays of the sun.

From below they heard the reptile men advancing down the corridor.

"We'll seek shelter in the nearest of those domes," Elric said. He broke into a trot, leading the way.

The others followed him through the irregularly shaped opening at the base of the dome.

Once inside, however, they hesitated, shielding their eyes and blinking heavily as they tried to discern their way.

"It's like a maze of mirrors!" Smiorgan gasped. "By the gods, I've never seen a better. Was that its function, I wonder."

Corridors seemed to go off in all directions—yet they might be nothing more than reflections of the passage they were in. Cautiously Elric began to continue further into the maze, the five others following him.

"This smells of sorcery to me," Smiorgan muttered as they advanced. "Have we been forced into a trap, I wonder."

Elric drew his sword. It murmured softly—almost querulously.

Everything shifted suddenly and the shapes of his companions grew dim.

"Smiorgan! Duke Avan!"

He heard voices murmuring, but they were not the voices of his friends.

"Count Smiorgan!"

But then the burly sea-lord faded away altogether and Elric was alone.

Chapter Six

He turned and a wall of red brilliance struck his eyes and blinded him.

He called out and his voice was turned into a dismal wail which mocked him.

He tried to move, but he could not tell whether he remained in the same spot or walked a dozen miles.

Now there was someone standing a few yards away, seemingly obscured by a screen of multicoloured transparent gems. He stepped forward and made to dash away the screen, but it vanished and he stopped suddenly.

He looked on a face of infinite sorrow.

And the face was his own face, save that the man's colouring was normal and his hair was black.

"What are you?" Elric said thickly.

"I have had many names. One is Erekosë. I have been many men. Perhaps I am all men."

"But you are like me!"

"I am you."

"No!"

The phantom's eyes held tears as it stared in pity at Elric.

"Do not weep for me!" Elric roared. "I need no sympathy from you!"

"Perhaps I weep for myself, for I know our fate."

"And what is that?"

"You would not understand."

"Tell me."

"Ask your gods."

Elric raised his sword. Fiercely he said, "No—I'll have my answer from you!"

And the phantom faded away.

Elric shivered. Now the corridor was populated by a thousand such phantoms. Each murmured a different name. Each wore different clothes. But each had his face, if not his colouring.

"Begone!" he screamed. "Oh, gods, what is this place?"

And at his command they disappeared.

"Elric?"

The albino whirled, sword ready. But it was Duke Avan Astran of Old Hrolmar. He touched his own face with trembling fingers, but said levelly, "I must tell you that I believe I am losing my sanity, Prince Elric . . ."

"What have you seen?"

"Many things. I cannot describe them."

"Where are Smiorgan and the others?"

"Doubtless each went his separate way, as we did."

Elric raised Stormbringer and brought the blade crashing against a crystal wall. The Black Sword moaned, but the wall merely changed its position.

But through a gap now Elric saw ordinary daylight. "Come, Duke Avan—there is escape!"

Avan, dazed, followed him and they stepped out of the crystal and found themselves in the central square of R'lin K'ren A'a.

But there were noises. Carts and chariots moved about the square. Stalls were erected on one side. People moved peacefully about. And the Jade Man did not dominate the sky above the city. Here, there was no Jade Man at all.

Elric looked at the faces. They were the eldritch features of the folk of Melniboné. Yet these had a different cast to them which he could not at first define. Then he recognized what they had. It was tranquility. He reached out his hand to touch one of the people.

"Tell me, friend, what year . . . ?"

But the man did not hear him. He walked by.

Elric tried to stop several of the passers-by, but not one could see or hear him.

"How did they lose this peace?" Duke Avan asked wonderingly. "How did they become like you, Prince Elric?"

Elric almost snarled as he turned sharply to face the Vilmirian. "Be silent!"

Duke Avan shrugged. "Perhaps this is merely an illusion."

"Perhaps," Elric said sadly, "But I am sure this is how they lived—until the coming of the High Ones."

"You blame the gods, then?"

"I blame the despair that the gods brought."

Duke Avan nodded gravely. "I understand."

He turned back towards the great crystal and then stood listening. "Do you hear that voice, Prince Elric? What is it saying?"

Elric heard the voice. It seemed to be coming from the crystal. It was speaking the old tongue of Melniboné, but with a strange accent. "This way," it said. "This way."

Elric paused. "I have no liking to return there."

Avan said, "What choice have we?"

They stepped together through the entrance.

Again they were in the maze that could be one corridor or many and the voice was clearer. "Take two paces to your right," it instructed.

Avan glanced at Elric. "What was that?"

Elric told him.

"Shall we obey?" Avan asked.

"Aye." There was resignation in the albino's voice.

They took two paces to their right.

"Now four to your left," said the voice.

They took four paces to their left.

"Now one forward."

They emerged into the ruined square of R'lin K'ren A'a.

Smiorgan and one Vilmirian crewman stood there.

"Where are the others?" Avan demanded.

"Ask him," Smiorgan said wearily, gesturing with the sword in his right hand.

They stared at the man who was either an albino or a leper. He was completely naked and he bore a distinct likeness to Elric. At first Elric thought this was another phantom, but then he saw that there were also several differences in their faces. There was something sticking from the man's side, just above the third rib. With a shock, Elric recognized it as the broken shaft of a Vilmirian arrow.

The naked man nodded. "Aye—the arrow found its mark. But it could not slay me, for I am J'osui C'reln Reyr . . ."

"You believe yourself to be the Creature Doomed to Live," Elric murmured.

"I am he." The man gave a bitter smile. "Do you think I try to deceive you?"

Elric glanced at the arrow shaft and then shook his head.

"You are ten thousand years old?" Avan stared at him.

"What does he say?" asked J'osui C'reln Reyr of Elric. Elric translated.

"Is that all it has been?" The man sighed. Then he looked intently at Elric. "You are of my race?"

"It seems so."

"Of what family?"

"Of the royal line."

"Then you have come at last. I, too, am of that line."

"I believe you."

"I notice that the Olab seek you."

"The Olab?"

"Those primitives with the clubs."

"Aye. We encountered them on our journey upriver."

"I will lead you to safety. Come."

Elric allowed J'osui C'reln Reyr to take them across the square to where part of a tottering wall still stood. The man then lifted a flagstone and showed them steps leading down into darkness. They followed him, descending cautiously as he caused the flagstone to lower itself above their heads. And then they found themselves in a room lit by crude oil lamps. Save for a bed of dried grasses the room was empty.

"You live sparely," Elric said.

"I have need for nothing else. My head is sufficiently furnished . . ."

"Where do the Olab come from?" Elric asked.

"They are but recently arrived in these parts. Scarcely a thousand years ago—or perhaps half that time—they came from further upriver after some quarrel with another tribe. They do not usually come to the island. You must have killed many of them for them to wish you such harm."

"We killed many."

J'osui C'reln Reyr gestured at the others who were staring at him in some discomfort. "And these? Primitives, also, eh? They are not of our folk."

"There are few of our folk left."

"What does he say?" Duke Avan asked.

"He says that those reptile warriors are called the Olab," Elric told him.

"And was it these Olab who stole the Jade Man's eyes?"

When Elric translated the question the Creature Doomed to Live was astonished. "Did you not know, then?"

"Know what?"

"Why, you have been *in* the Jade Man's eyes! Those great crystals in which you wandered—that is what they are!"

Chapter Seven

When Elric offered this information to Duke Avan, the Vilmirian burst into laughter. He flung his head back and roared with mirth while the others looked gloomily on. The cloud that had fallen across his features of late suddenly cleared and he became again the man whom Elric had first met.

Smiorgan was the next to smile and even Elric acknowledged the irony of what had happened to them.

"Those crystals fell from his face like tears soon after the High Ones departed," continued J'osui C'reln Reyr.

"So the High Ones did come here."

"Aye—the Jade Man brought the message and all the folk departed, having made their bargain with him."

"The Jade Man was not built by your people?"

"The Jade Man is Duke Arioch of Hell. He strode from the forest one day and stood in the square and told the people what was to come about—that our city lay at the centre of some particular configuration and that it was only there that the Lords of the Higher Worlds could meet."

"And the bargain?"

"In return for their city, our royal line might in the future increase their power with Arioch as their patron. He would give them great knowledge and the means to build a new city elsewhere."

"And they accepted this bargain without question?"

"There was little choice, kinsman."

Elric lowered his eyes to regard the dusty floor. "And thus they were corrupted," he murmured.

"Only I refused to accept the pact; I did not wish to leave this city and I mistrusted Arioch. When all others set off down the river, I remained here—where we are now—and I heard the Lords of the Higher Worlds arrive and I heard them speak, laying down the rules under which Law and Chaos would fight thereafter. When they had gone, I emerged. But Arioch—the Jade Man—was still here. He looked down on me through his crystal eyes and he cursed me. When that was done the crystals fell and landed where you now see them. Arioch's spirit departed, but his jade image was left behind."

"And you still retain all memory of what transpired between the Lords of Law and Chaos?"

"That is my doom."

"Perhaps your fate was less harsh than that which befell those who left," Elric said quietly. "I am the last inheritor of that particular doom . . ."

J'osui C'reln Reyr looked puzzled and then he stared into Elric's eyes and an expression of pity crossed his face. "I had not thought there was a worse fate—but now I believe there might be . . ."

Elric said urgently, "Ease my soul, at least. I must know what passed between the High Lords in those days. I must understand the nature of my existence—as you, at least, understand yours. Tell me, I beg you!"

J'osui C'reln Reyr frowned and he stared deeply into Elric's eyes. "Do you not know all my story, then?"

"Is there more?"

"I can only *remember* what passed between the High Lords—but when I try to tell my knowledge aloud or try to write it down, I cannot . . ."

Elric grasped the man's shoulder. "You must try! You must try!"

"I know that I cannot."

Seeing the torture in Elric's face, Smiorgan came up to him. "What is it, Elric?"

Elric's hand clutched his head. "Our journey has been useless." Unconsciously he used the old Melnibonéan tongue.

"It need not be," said J'osui C'reln Reyr. "For me, at least." He paused. "Tell me, how did you find this city? Was there a map?"

Elric produced the map. "This one."

"Aye, that is the one. Many centuries ago I put it into a casket which I placed in a small trunk. I launched the trunk into the river, hoping that it would follow my people and they would know what it was."

"The casket was found in Melniboné, but no-one had bothered to open it," Elric explained. "That will give you an idea of what happened to the folk who left here . . ."

The strange man nodded gravely. "And was there still a seal upon the map?"

"There was. I have it."

"An image of one of the manifestations of Arioch, embedded in a small ruby?"

"Aye. I thought I recognized the image, but I could not place it."

"The Image in the Gem," murmured J'osui C'reln Reyr. "As I prayed, it has returned—borne by one of the royal line!"

"What is its significance?"

Smiorgan interrupted. "Will this fellow help us to escape, Elric? We are becoming somewhat impatient . . ."

"Wait," the albino said. "I will tell you everything later."

"The Image in the Gem could be the instrument of my release," said the Creature Doomed to Live. "If he who possesses it is of the royal line, then he can command the Jade Man."

"But why did you not use it?"

"Because of the curse that was put on me. I had the power to command, but not to summon the demon. It was a joke, I understand, of the High Lords."

Elric saw bitter sadness in the eyes of J'osui C'reln Reyr. He looked at the white, naked flesh and the white hair and the body that was neither old nor young, at the shaft of the arrow sticking out above the third rib on the left side.

"What must I do?" he asked.

"You must summon Arioch and then you must command him to enter his body again and recover his eyes so that he may see to walk away from R'lin K'ren A'a."

"And when he walks away?"

"The curse goes with him."

Elric was thoughtful. If he did summon Arioch—who was plainly reluctant to come—and then commanded him to do something he did not wish to do, he stood the chance of making an enemy of that powerful, if unpredictable entity. Yet they were trapped here by the Olab warriors, with no means of escaping them. If the Jade Man walked, the Olab would almost certainly flee and there would be time to get back to the ship and reach the sea. He explained everything to his companions. Both Smiorgan and Avan looked dubious and the remaining Vilmirian crewman looked positively terrified.

"I must do it," Elric decided, "for the sake of this man. I must call Arioch and lift the doom that is on R'lin K'ren A'a."

"And bring a greater doom to us!" Duke Avan said, putting his hand automatically upon his sword-hilt. "No. I think we should take our chances with the Olab. Leave this man—he is mad—he raves. Let's be on our way."

"Go if you choose," Elric said. "But I will stay with the Creature Doomed to Live."

"Then you will stay here for ever. You cannot believe his story!"

"But I do believe it."

"You must come with us. Your sword will help. Without it, the Olab will certainly destroy us."

"You saw that Stormbringer has little effect against the Olab."

"And yet it has some. Do not desert me, Elric!"

"I am not deserting you. I must summon Arioch. That summoning will be to your benefit, if not to mine."

"I am unconvinced."

"It was my sorcery you wanted on this venture. Now you shall have my sorcery."

Avan backed away. He seemed to fear something more than the Olab, more than the Summoning. He seemed to read a threat in Elric's face of which even Elric was unaware.

"We must go outside," said J'osui C'reln Reyr. "We must stand beneath the Jade Man."

"And when this is done," Elric asked suddenly, "how will we leave R'lin K'ren A'a?"

"There is a boat. It has no provisions, but much of the city's treasure is on it. It lies at the west end of the island."

"That is some comfort," Elric said. "And you could not use it yourself?"

"I could not leave."

"Is that part of the curse?"

"Aye—the curse of my timidity."

"Timidity has kept you here ten thousand years?"

"Aye . . ."

They left the chamber and went out into the square. Night had fallen and a huge moon was in the sky. From where Elric stood it seemed to frame the Jade Man's sightless head like a halo. It was completely silent. Elric took the Image in the Gem from his pouch and held it between the forefinger and thumb of his left hand. With his right he drew Stormbringer. Avan, Smiorgan and the Vilmirian crewman fell back.

He stared up at the huge jade legs, the genitals, the torso, the arms, the head, and he raised his sword in both hands and screamed:

"ARIOCH!"

Stormbringer's voice almost drowned his. It pulled in his hands; it threatened to leave his grasp altogether as it howled.

"ARIOCH!"

All the watchers saw now was the throbbing, radiant sword, the white face and hands of the albino and his crimson eyes glaring through the blackness.

"ARIOCH!"

And then a voice which was not Arioch's came to Elric's ears and it seemed that the sword itself spoke.

"Elric—Arioch must have blood and souls. Blood and souls, my lord . . ."

"No. These are my friends and the Olab cannot be harmed by Stormbringer. Arioch must come without the blood, without the souls."

"Only those can summon him for certain!" said a voice, more clearly now. It was sardonic and it seemed to come from behind him. He turned, but there was nothing there.

He saw Duke Avan's nervous face, and as his eyes fixed on the Vilmirian's countenance, the sword swung around, twisting against Elric's grip, and plunging towards the duke.

"No!" cried Elric. "Stop!"

But Stormbringer would not stop until it had plunged deep into Duke Avan's heart and quenched its thirst. The crewman stood transfixed as he watched his master die.

Duke Avan writhed. "Elric! What treachery do you . . . ?" He screamed. "Ah, no!"

He jerked. "Please . . ."

He quivered. "My soul . . ."

He died.

Elric withdrew the sword and cut the crewman down as he ran to his master's aid. The action had been without thought.

"Now Arioch has his blood and his souls," he said coldly. "Let Arioch come!"

Smiorgan and the Creature Doomed to Live had retreated, staring at the possessed Elric in horror. The albino's face was cruel.

"LET ARIOCH COME!"

"I am here, Elric."

Elric whirled and saw that something stood in the shadow of the statue's legs—a shadow within a shadow.

"Arioch—thou must return to this manifestation and make it leave R'lin K'ren A'a forever."

"I do not choose to, Elric."

"Then I must command thee, Duke Arioch."

"Command? Only he who possesses the Image in the Gem may command Arioch—and then only once."

"I have the Image in the Gem." Elric held up the tiny object. "See."

The shadow within a shadow swirled for a moment as if in anger.

"If I obey your command, you will set in motion a chain of events which you might not desire," Arioch said, speaking suddenly in Low Melnibonéan as if to give extra gravity to his words.

"Then let it be. I command you to enter the Jade Man and pick up its eyes so that it might walk again. Then I command you to leave here and take the curse of the High Ones with you."

Arioch replied, "When the Jade Man ceases to guard the place where the High Ones meet, then the great struggle of the Upper Worlds begins on this plane."

"I command thee, Arioch. Go into the Jade Man!"

"You are an obstinate creature, Elric."

"Go!" Elric raised Stormbringer. It seemed to sing in monstrous glee and it seemed at that moment to be more powerful than Arioch himself, more powerful than all the Lords of the Higher Worlds.

The ground shook. Fire suddenly blazed around the form of the great statue. The shadow within a shadow disappeared.

And the Jade Man stooped.

Its great bulk bent over Elric and its hands reached past him and it groped for the two crystals that lay on the ground. Then it found them and took one in each hand, straightening its back.

Elric stumbled towards the far corner of the square where Smiorgan and J'osui C'reln Reyr already crouched in terror.

A fierce light now blazed from the Jade Man's eyes and the jade lips parted.

"*It is done, Elric!*" said a huge voice.

J'osui C'reln Reyr began to sob.

"Then go, Arioch."

"I go. The curse is lifted from R'lin K'ren A'a and from J'osui C'reln Reyr—but a greater curse now lies upon your whole plane."

"What is this, Arioch? Explain yourself!" Elric cried.

"Soon you will have your explanation. Farewell!"

The enormous legs of jade moved suddenly and in a single step had cleared the ruins and had begun to crash through the jungle. In a moment the Jade Man had disappeared.

Then the Creature Doomed to Live laughed. It was a strange joy that he voiced. Smiorgan blocked his ears.

"And now!" shouted J'osui C'reln Reyr. "Now your blade must take my life. I can die at last!"

Elric passed his hand across his face. He had hardly been aware of any of the recent events. "No," he said in a dazed tone. "I cannot . . ."

And Stormbringer flew from his hand—flew to the body of the Creature Doomed to Live and buried itself in its chest.

And as he died, J'osui C'reln Reyr laughed. He fell to the ground and his lips moved. A whisper came from them. Elric stepped nearer to hear.

"The sword has my knowledge now. My burden has left me."

The eyes closed.

J'osui C'reln Reyr's ten-thousand-year life-span had ended.

Weakly, Elric withdrew Stormbringer and sheathed it. He stared down at the body of the Creature Doomed to Live and then he looked up, questioningly, at Smiorgan.

The burly sea-lord turned away.

The sun began to rise. Grey dawn came. Elric watched the corpse of J'osui C'reln Reyr turn to powder that was stirred by the wind and mixed with the dust of the ruins. He walked back across the square to where Duke Avan's twisted body lay and he fell to his knees beside it.

"You were warned, Duke Avan Astran of Old Hrolmar, that ill befell those who linked their fortunes with Elric of Melniboné. But you thought otherwise. Now you know." With a sigh he got to his feet.

Smiorgan stood beside him. The sun was now touching the taller parts of the ruins. Smiorgan reached out and gripped his friend's shoulder.

"The Olab have vanished. I think they've had their fill of sorcery."

"Another man has been destroyed by me, Smiorgan. Am I forever to be tied to this cursed sword? I must discover a way to rid myself of it or my heavy conscience will bear me down so that I cannot rise at all."

Smiorgan cleared his throat, but was otherwise silent.

"I will lay Duke Avan to rest," Elric said. "You go back to where we left the ship and tell the men that we come."

Smiorgan began to stride across the square towards the east.

Elric tenderly picked up the body of Duke Avan and went towards the opposite side of the square, to the underground room where the Creature Doomed to Live had lived out his life for ten thousand years.

It seemed so unreal to Elric now, but he knew that it had not been a dream, for the Jade Man had gone. His tracks could be seen through the jungle. Whole clumps of trees had been flattened.

He reached the place and descended the stairs and laid Duke Avan down on the bed of dried grasses. Then he took the duke's dagger and, for want of anything else, dipped it in the duke's blood and wrote on the wall above the corpse:

This was Duke Avan Astran of Old Hrolmar. He explored the world and brought much knowledge and treasure back to Vilmir, his land. He dreamed and became lost in the dream of another and so died. He enriched the Young Kingdoms—and thus encouraged another dream. He died so that the Creature Doomed to Live might die, as he desired . . .

Elric paused. Then he threw down the dagger. He could not justify his own feelings of guilt by composing a high-sounding epitaph for the man he had slain.

He stood there, breathing heavily, then once again picked up the dagger.

He died because Elric of Melniboné desired a peace and a knowledge he could never find. He died by the Black Sword.

*   *   *

Outside in the middle of the square, at noon, still lay the lonely body of the last Vilmirian crewman. Nobody had known his name. Nobody felt grief for him or tried to compose an epitaph for him. The dead Vilmirian had died for no high purpose, followed no fabulous dream. Even in death his body would fulfill no function. On this island there was no carrion-eater to feed. In the dust of the city there was no earth to fertilize.

Elric came back into the square and saw the body. For a moment, to Elric, it symbolized everything that had transpired here and would transpire later.

"There is no purpose," he murmured.

Perhaps his remote ancestors had, after all, realized that, but had not cared. It had taken the Jade Man to make them care and then go mad in their anguish. The knowledge had caused them to close their minds to much.

"Elric!"

It was Smiorgan returning. Elric looked up.

"I met the only survivor on the trail. Before he died he told me the Olab had dealt with the crew and the ship before they came after us. They're all slain. The boat is destroyed."

Elric remembered something the Creature Doomed to Live had told him. "There is a boat," he said. "It lies at the west end of the island."

It took them the rest of the day and all of that night to discover where J'osui C'reln Reyr had hidden his boat. They pulled it down to the water in the diffused light of the morning and they inspected it.

"It's a sturdy boat," said Count Smiorgan approvingly. "By the look of it, it's made of that same strange material we saw in the library of R'lin K'ren A'a." He climbed in and searched through the lockers.

Elric was staring back at the city, thinking of a man who might have become his friend, just as Count Smiorgan had become his friend. He had no friends, save Cymoril, in Melniboné. He sighed.

Smiorgan had opened several lockers and was grinning at what he saw there. "Pray the gods I return safe to the Purple Towns—we have what I sought! Look, Elric! Treasure! We have benefited from this venture, after all!"

"Aye . . ." Elric's mind was on other things. He forced himself to think of more practical matters. "But the jewels will not feed us, Count Smiorgan," he said. "It will be a long journey home."

"Home?" Count Smiorgan straightened his great back, a bunch of necklaces in either fist. "Melniboné?"

"The Young Kingdoms. You offered to guest me in your house, as I recall."

"For the rest of your life, if you wish. You saved my life, friend Elric—now you have helped me save my honour."

"These past events have not disturbed you? You saw what my blade can do—to friends as well as enemies."

"We do not brood, we of the Purple Towns," said Count Smiorgan seriously. "And we are not fickle in our friendships. You know an anguish, Prince Elric, that I'll never feel—never understand—but I have already given you my trust. Why should I take it away again? That is not how we are taught to behave in the Purple Towns." Count Smiorgan brushed at his black beard and he winked. "I saw some cases of provisions among the wreckage of Avan's schooner. We'll sail around the island and pick them up."

Elric tried to shake the black mood from himself, but it was hard, for he had slain a man who had trusted him, and Smiorgan's talk of trust only made the guilt heavier.

Together they launched the boat into the weed-thick water and Elric looked back once more at the silent forest and a shiver passed through him. He thought of all the hopes he had entertained on the journey upriver and he cursed himself for a fool.

He tried to think back, to work out how he had come to be in this place, but too much of the past was confused with those singularly graphic dreams to which he was prone. Had Saxif D'Aan and the world of the blue sun been real? Even now, it faded. Was this place real? There was something dreamlike about it. It seemed to him he had sailed on many fateful seas since he had fled from Pikarayd. Now the promise of the peace of the Purple Towns was very dear to him.

Soon the time must come when he must return to Cymoril and the Dreaming City, to decide if he was ready to take up the responsibilities of the Bright Empire of Melniboné, but until that moment he would guest with his new friend, Smiorgan, and learn the ways of the simpler, more direct folk of Menii.

As they raised the sail and began to move with the current, Elric said to Smiorgan suddenly, "You trust me, then, Count Smiorgan?"

The sea-lord was a little surprised by the directness of the question. He fingered his beard. "Aye," he said at length, "as a man. But we live in cynical times, Prince Elric. Even the gods have lost their innocence, have they not?"

Elric was puzzled. "Do you think that I shall ever betray you— as—as I betrayed Avan, back there?"

Smiorgan shook his head. "It's not in my nature to speculate upon such matters. You are loyal, Prince Elric. You feign cynicism, yet I think I've rarely met a man so much in need of a little real cynicism." He smiled. "Your sword betrayed you, did it not?"

"To serve me, I suppose."

"Aye. There's the irony of it. Man may trust man, Prince Elric, but perhaps we'll never have a truly sane world until men learn to trust mankind. That would mean the death of magic, I think."

And it seemed to Elric, then, that his runesword trembled at his side, and moaned very faintly, as if it were disturbed by Count Smiorgan's words.

DUKE ELRIC

DUKE ELRIC

a graphic novel
drawn by John Ridgway
(1997)

What follows is the script for "Duke Elric," a graphic story drawn by John Ridgway, which together with two other tales ("Moonbeams and Roses", drawn by Walter Simonson and "The Metatemporal Detective" drawn by Mark Reeve) formed the graphic novel Michael Moorcock's Multiverse, *originally serialized across twelve comic issues in 1997–98.*

This script was never intended for textual publication but was written solely for the artists and letterer to work from. Some reformatting has had to take place, therefore, in order for it to have more narrative cohesion.

Also, it was not possible to locate the original script for part five, so dialogue for that has been taken directly from the comic issue and descriptions similar to those in the other eleven parts have been added for what is going on around it.

The final part overlaps with Simonson's "Moonbeams and Roses," and was mainly drawn by him. It therefore takes a rather marked stylistic shift, incorporating (or referring to) some characters and events that might not have appeared in the rest of "Duke Elric."

PART ONE

EXILE FROM ALBION

A THOUSAND YEARS ago. The disastrous reign of Ethelred the Unready. England's bravest warrior is suddenly exiled—expelled as an atheist sorcerer accused of unnatural relations with his own sister. Most at court agree, however, it's Duke Elric's realistic and aggressive policy to the invading Danes which set his devious king against him—confiscating Elric's rich western lands, stripping him of honours and leaving him with only his ancestral title—**Duke of the Middlemarch . . .**

With bitter cynicism Elric Sadricson glances briefly back at the land his people loved and served for millennia. Ahead lies a Europe still struggling from centuries of brutal ignorance . . .

It's raining. On board a beautiful Saxon ship, the rich figurehead prominently featured, Duke Elric, the long-haired albino son of an ancient line who some say is a changeling or even a halfling, turns brooding, intelligent crimson eyes towards Frankland across the sea. Elric himself is a picture of the tenth-century Anglo-Saxon dandy from the shine of his circlet to the jeweled hilt of his sword and the softness of his doeskin boots. But, for all his almost feminine beauty, he has the stance, muscles and responses of a man of action. For years he has commanded English legions against the Danes. They say his ancestors fought against the Romans and the Saxons before bringing their own power-ful western fiefdom into King Alfred's kingdom. Their ancient castle on Michael's Mount has been in their family since the time of the Picts.

ELRIC: "Let the Danes conquer England. The squabbling English de-serve to lose her. As for me—this 'exile' permits me to pursue a

long-postponed quest . . . I'll not be diverted again. I've loyalty only to myself!"

Elric rides away from the run-down Roman/Gaulish quay where the ship has berthed. The predominantly wooden town's only a few rows deep. Beyond it are fields and beyond that dense woods. It is raining and windy and Elric's heavy woolen cloak is whipped about him. He's an object of curiosity to the rabble of Franks, Gauls and down-at-heel Normans who hang around the port.

The weather's still foul. Elric is riding through deep Dark Age woods and comes to a clearing with a rocky, moated mound in the centre of it. On this is built a Romanesque fortified monastery. The monastery of St. Obyn. A monk spots him and rings the monastery's horrible bell.

The interior of the monastery. Massive stones. A great stone cross, clearly centuries old and of Celtic origin, is propped against the wall. There are books and vellums here and there, as well as a writing stand. Brother Constant, a wise and kindly monk in his early thirties, holds a great iron key in his hand. Elric reaches for it impatiently. He and the monk are old friends. The monk is concerned for Elric's soul as well as his body.

CONSTANT: "You said you'd never need the sword again. My potions were enough to sustain you . . ."

ELRIC: "I was wrong, old friend. Your strongest potion would be too weak for the task ahead. It must be the sword—"

Deep in the bowels of the monastery, the monk opens a door. There on the wall, sending out a strange black radiance, is a sheathed Stormbringer, the runecarved black blade of legend. Behind the sword is a round shield. It appears to bear a Celtic cross, but this cross is in fact the eight-arrowed symbol of Chaos, intricately worked into the Celtic patterns. Hanging by a thong is an ancient war-horn, also Celtic in origin.

CONSTANT: "Locked here centuries since, when Charlemagne sought aid against the Saracen and you refused."

ELRIC: "He asked too much of me. I could accept his god, but would not reject my own. My people have more direct experience of the supernatural in all its various manifestations . . . Besides, I had no cause against the Moor."

Elric takes down the scabbarded sword and weighs it in his hands. He feels very ambiguously towards the thing.

Elric has the Chaos Shield on his back, the war-horn slung at his side and the Black Sword behind his saddle. He leans from his saddle to kiss his old friend's hand.

ELRIC: "Farewell,
friend. I go
to seek the
Silverskin . . ."

*Brother Constant watches
his friend ride away into the
woods.*

CONSTANT: "Then I pray all the
harder for your tortured
soul . . ."

Later . . .

*For a moment the rain has let up
and the sun breaks through thick
cloud showing Elric riding
through a narrow valley with
steeply wooded sides. He is clearly
sick and having a hard time staying
in his saddle. He has been spotted
by a rabble of Franks led by a
couple of shiftless Norman cap-
tains who have camped with their
crude wagon in a clearing high above
him.*

FIRST NORMAN: "Look how he slumps in
the saddle. That weakling has no right
to be traveling our dangerous world
untaxed . . ."

SECOND NORMAN: "We'll give him a sharp lesson in good old-fashioned
Norman common sense!"

*It's now obvious that Elric is aware of the armed men behind him and is
smiling a little to himself. He murmurs:*

ELRIC: "At last!"

Eight armed men attack in a nasty, overwhelming ambush—
      —and Elric grins like a wolf—
      —he almost licks his lips—
      —for here is his sustenance volunteering to him . . .
*and now the runecarved black blade is in his hands, the scarlet runes flicker-
ing up and down its black iron—*
*and the bloodletting is swift, ghastly, and horrifying to those of Elric's at-
tackers who realize that their souls are being sucked from them to feed the
albino and his own dark gods . . .*

ELRIC: *"Arioch! Arioch! Blood and souls for my lord Arioch!"*

SECOND NORMAN: "My soul! Not my soul!"

ELRIC (*grins at the dying man*): "Like you, my friend, I live on whatever
      passing prey comes my way . . ."

*He pants like a wolf, his crimson eyes glutted with stolen lifestuff, as, dis-
mounted, he leads his horse away from the corpses, up-hill towards the
camp, where a column of smoke reveals the dead Normans' fire.*

Elric comes upon the Normans' camp—cooking fires, a decrepit wagon.

He hears a voice from within the wagon—"Mmmmfffffff!"

*When he looks in the wagon, piled with miscellaneous junk, he sees two
bundled figures, bound and gagged—a heavy, muscular man in middle
years and a slender woman.*

Elric hauls the two out of the wagon. The woman is veiled—her veil having become part of her gag. He ungags the man first. The man is a handsome Jewish soldier-scholar in rich silks and wearing a breastplate. He has many flesh-wounds and has clearly been fighting.

The man himself deals with the woman's bonds while Elric watches.

MAN: "I thank you, stranger. I am Isaak D'Israeli and this is my daughter Rebecca. You'll get a handsome ransom for us, be sure of that . . ."

ELRIC: "I've neither time nor desire to ransom you, sir. You're free. How did you become prisoners of that Norman scum?"

Isaak rummages in the wagon and gets out his own bits of armour and weaponry as well as a hooded cloak for his daughter. He continues his conversation with Elric.

ISAAK: "They kidnapped her. Arrogantly I thought I could take on fourteen of them . . ."

ELRIC: "So you only killed six?"

ISAAK (*smiling*): "Five. One had meanwhile died of the pox. I tire too readily, these days. My old bones aren't what they were . . ."

Checking his property, Isaak opens a small chest of books and scrolled manuscripts in a variety of languages—Greek, Hebrew, Arabic but not the despised Latin which most Arab scholars found crude and useless.

ELRIC: "You're a scholar as well as a soldier?"

ISAAK: "I am whatever an intelligent man must be in these uncertain times. We are not so different, I think."

Rebecca is shy. She prefers to stay in the wagon, sorting out their stuff

*from the Norman booty. Elric picks up one of Isaak's books and opens it
to read.*

ELRIC: "A man who loves wisdom."

ISAAK: "Among other things."

Elric is frowning, trying not to seem too eager as he asks a question of Isaak:

ELRIC: "Then you'll have heard of a creature called 'The Silverskin'?"

ISAAK: "*Ah*—that old story!"

Elric almost glares.

ELRIC: "Fresh enough to me. Where does he live, this glinting king?"

ISAAK: "It's no more than misty legend. There are only vague stories—
confusing contradictions."

Elric urgently interrogates Isaak.

ELRIC: "Tell me what you know!"

Isaak is a bit taken aback. Elric presses him.

ISAAK: "No more than is written in the great Book of Tales."

ELRIC: "What's that?"

*Isaak speaks of a book. We see it—a wonderful, jeweled Arabian book. The
towers and domes of Cordova.*

ISAAK: "I saw it once in the library of the Caliph in Cordova. It contains
a wealth of stories—some true and some invented. A traveler

claimed to describe the court of 'King Silverskin'—but I had no time to read the tale . . ."

ELRIC: "In Cordova, you say? How would I find that city?"

They are seated drinking heated wine served by the mysterious Rebecca. Isaak is not too certain about what he's committing himself to—

ISAAK: "I have business there. We were on our way to Cordova when this happened."

ELRIC: "Good. We'll travel together. Safety in numbers."

Isaak is sardonic. Elric is surprised.

ISAAK: "Is anyone safe from that infamous sword of yours, Duke Elric?"

ELRIC: "You know me?"

Isaak turns away frowning.

ISAAK: "Well enough. I know you owe no allegiance to the teachings of our holy book."

ELRIC: "My religion's a little older than yours. It inclines neither towards charity nor humility . . ."

The three have reached the shores of a tranquil lake. Rebecca is in the wagon and Isaak drives it. They lead spare horses. Elric is on his own horse, reining in as he stares in astonishment at the wonderful border city of Al-Zaman', fortress against the Infidel. For these are in the great expansive years of the Chamberlain Hajib Muhammed, lover of Aurora, Oum-Hisham, mother of the young Caliph in whose name Muhammed, a great law-maker, scholar and warrior, ruled the whole of the Moorish Empire from the Pyrenees to the Atlas and beyond. Silk flags fly over the minarets and domes, the crenelated walls. It is a city from an Arabian Nights *fantasy.*

ISAAK: "Be prepared, Duke Elric. The politics of the border regions can be unstable."

A great raft, poled by an ancient, but familiar figure (could it be Jack Karaquazian, from Walter Simonson's Moonbeams and Roses?) *in a loincloth and turban, comes towards them across the water.*

ISAAK: "I think, too, you'll find the Moors rather better-educated than the English—and much less easily deceived . . ."

PART TWO

A BARGAIN IN CARPETS

A LMORAVID SPAIN, 1000 AD. Curious for news of Christendom the Kayed of Al-Zaman' extended Moorish chivalry's finest hospitality—his guests must have only the best . . . And for this, using Greek as their common language, they were glad to pay with tales of the barbarian West . . .

Evening. Mostly interior. A great kiosk, partly open to the soft, starry night. This is real, but it's also full-strength Arabian Nights, Thief of Baghdad, *over-the-top orientalist fantasy—mountains of cushions (but no 'beautiful slave girls'—just mostly Teutonic male slaves) in which lounge, eating Moorish-style with only the right hand, Elric, Isaak—and their host, the Kayed of Al-Zaman', a distinguished, middle-aged intellectual with a greying beard. Outside there are fountains, cedars and poplars, distant minarets, the works . . .*

KAYED: "I'm an old veteran tired of war and fired only by learning. That's why they gave me this distant post. I am intelligent enough to sense danger to our empire, indolent enough to want no more power than I have now. I read how well the Duke of Normandy organizes his peasants."

ELRIC: "But fails to educate them, it seems . . ."

Mid-shot of the Kayed, amused.

KAYED: "You understand economics as well as I do. While our great conquests continue and we hold the Northern Christians in vassalage it is in our interest to encourage education. But should we defend against more savage enemies, we should need a different kind of peasantry . . . less questioning, less individual . . ."

ISAAK: "You Moors have so much more time to spend on theory. Tell me—how are things in Cordova?"

A shot through the columns of the kiosk. It's a magical night.

KAYED: "I heard the capital was quiet. The Regent Al-Mansur, may he be blessed by Allah, is returning triumphant against the Christian dukes. This makes him indulgent in turn to our own Jews and Christians. You should be safe enough. Do you visit friends or go to trade?"

Mid-shot of Elric.

ELRIC: "For my own part I seek knowledge of a creature called 'The Silverskin' . . ."

KAYED: "Our library is one of the three finest in the world. Thousands of volumes—some even in *your* rough tongue, Duke Elric! If the information exists, you'll find it there."

ISAAK: "My business in Cordova is more prosaic. I have money waiting. I left rather hastily several years ago, when the regent's mood was not so temperate."

The Kayed is reassuring. A lute player now entertains them. Isaak's attitude is somewhat frosty.

KAYED: "I'll give you safe conducts and introductions. Presumably you'll be seeking a rich husband for your daughter?"

ISAAK: "My daughter, sir, is already betrothed."

Kayed points towards distant hills—

KAYED: "There are two roads to Cordova. Take the longest. It has no
bandits. The forest route is dangerous."

*Exterior. Day. Isaak, Elric and Rebecca are back on the road to Cordova.
The city behind them in the far distance, they come to a fork in the road . . .*

ISAAK: "The Kayed warned against the forest road."

ELRIC: "Take the safe road—I'll join you later . . ."

*Exterior. Day. Elric rides along down a rocky-sided path through the deep
forest. He is smiling privately and murmuring to himself—*

ELRIC: "I think I smell predators . . ."

*There follows a mélange—four turbaned bandits come rushing down off
the rocks to attack Elric who draws Stormbringer—and disposes of them all
in a rapid and familiar (if largely unseen) fashion . . .*

*Exterior. Day. The safe road to Cordova. Elric joins his companions on it.
He looks more content—even well-fed.*

*Exterior. Day. The three approach their goal. The wonderful outlines of
Cordova are off in the distance. Isaak points excitedly:*

ISAAK: "Cordova at last!"

*Exterior. Day. The city of Cordova. This is a city with street-lighting (brass
oil-lamps), paved roads, baths, running water, schools, libraries and a tradition of tolerance. A dense, busy population, bartering, chatting, running,*

*scheming. Carts, donkeys, camels, dogcarts, oxen, etc., crowd the gates and
the three companions ride through . . .*

ISAAK: "Let's separate. We'll complete our business and meet back here
as soon as possible."

ELRIC: "I'll see you at sunset."

*Interior. Day. Elric is in the great library, surrounded by vellum books and
scrolls. A kindly, bespectacled librarian has helped him find the books he
needs. He's inspecting a scroll.*

LIBRARIAN: "There are a few references. I suspect the legend is fairly
recent."

ELRIC: "But all the tales say Silverskin's realm lies at the heart of
Africa."

Interior. Day. Elric hands a scroll back to the librarian.

ELRIC: "How do I begin to look for him?"

LIBRARIAN: "The continent is measureless. Some believe it to be of infinite size. You must go there. It is all you can do."

*Exterior. Close to sunset. Elric is in a contemplative mood as he walks
through the bazaar towards the Bab Maghrib, the Gate of the West. He's in
the street of the carpet sellers. They all vie for his attention. In the distance,
Isaak spots him.*

SELLER: "These carpets are woven by the delicate fingers of six-year-old
girls. Look at the quality! Hang it on your wall. Put it on your
floor. Impress your neighbours with your taste and wealth."

Something about the seller makes Elric pause and turn towards him.

The seller has jade-green eyes, an ironic manner . . .

SELLER: "*Er . . .* I know I have a carpet exactly to your taste, sir . . ."

The seller turns towards his piled stock behind him reaching his hand towards a certain carpet whose patterns will be significant to us later . . .

SELLER: "Even a—magic carpet?"

Elric shows open skepticism at this.

ELRIC: "Magic? Now what magic can a carpet work?"

Isaak joins him at the stall. He can't believe Elric seems to be falling for the man's scam . . .

ISAAK: "You're falling for the oldest line in Arabia!"

ELRIC: "How much?"

SELLER: "For such a carpet I must ask a thousand dirham."

ELRIC: "But it is only worth a ten to me . . ."

And so the long bargaining began . . .

Night. Cordova. The Bazaar. Isaak is even more disbelieving as darkness settles in, the street lights are lit, the activities of the evening begin, and still Elric bargains . . .

ISAAK: "It's the ugliest carpet I've ever seen! At least look at something with a bit of elegance to it . . ."

ELRIC: "I've taken pity on it. Twenty—and five for your inventive story . . ."

SELLER: "If I sell for less than a hundred my children will starve."

ELRIC: "Then fly them on the carpet to where there is food!"

At last a bargain is struck. Money changes hands and everyone seems satisfied. Elric has the carpet over his shoulder. Isaak looks thoroughly disgusted.

SELLER: "You have a great bargain, sir."

ELRIC: "Time will tell, my friend. Thanks."

ISAAK: "Magic carpet? *Bah!* It's the work of a crazed spider!"

At the caravanserai where they would spend the night . . .

It's an opulent caravanserai (a place where travelers can be under cover, water their beasts, cook their food and so on) with all mod. cons. Ostlers care for the beasts and there are women who cook. Elric, Isaak and Rebecca purchase plates of "tajin" (stew named after the pot it's cooked in) with kus-kus from one of these stalls. Elric still has the carpet over his shoulder.

ISAAK: "I took you for a man of sophistication! Then you behave like a
    foolish tourist! That carpet is trash!"

ELRIC (*smiling*): "It's worth all I own."

In a quiet corner of the caravanserai, where red-gold firelight casts deep shadows, Elric opens up the carpet and, with an ornamental brass lamp in his hand, shows Isaak what they actually have. The markings incorporate the eight arrows of Chaos, but more as geographical markings in this case. Everything radiates out from a centre and there are words woven into the fabric, in a language that is neither Arabic nor Latin, nor Greek. The carpet incorporates in its central circular panel a complicated (for the eleventh century) map. Around the edge are rather crude zodiacal signs, perhaps im-

itated from Persian work. Isaak's eyes widen as he begins to understand what Elric has bought . . . Even Rebecca shows interest.

ISAAK: "A map! But the language is gibberish!"

ELRIC: "Not to me. This could lead us to King Silverskin."

As usual with maps of the day, Jerusalem lay at the centre . . .

A better look at the map. Where we'll be going will be towards the rich and independent kingdoms of Timbuktu, Ghana (not the same Ghana) and perhaps Mali before we reach our city even further into the African hinterland. The language is a corrupted form of Melnibonéan, with Anglo-Saxon additions. Elric points at the place they seek.

Elric: "T'aan-al-Oorn, City of the Silverskin—and, legend says, source of all Africa's treasure, the richest city in the world."

Isaak looks at Elric with a new admiration. Rebecca's interest in the albino also increases. Elric glances down as he replies to Isaak.

ISAAK: "So it's *treasure* you seek!"

ELRIC: "You could call it that."

Isaak embraces Elric, kissing him. Elric's a little sardonic.

ISAAK: "God has been good to us—we thought you a demon, but you reveal yourself as an angel!"

ELRIC: "You're a prudent man, Sir Isaak. Why not reserve your judgment of me until we find the Silverskin?"

Cordova's luxuries behind them, they came eventually to one of the ancient Pillars of Hercules, the great rock of Jebel-al-Tarik, where a

Moor could stand and see his mother country with the naked eye. Here, less water separated Africa from Europe than England from France . . . Here, they would easily find a ship . . .

Gibraltar. A bustling international seaport with ships from China and India, as well as most of the contemporary Mediterranean and Atlantic ports. Orientals rub shoulders with burly Vikings and fastidious Greeks. Normans. Englishmen. Gaels. Celts. Egyptians. Franks. The whole vital flux is here.

Elric, Isaak and Rebecca, most of their belongings carried by porters (not the carpet, which Elric has over his shoulder), move towards one of the ships at the dock. It's a sturdy, lateen-rigged trading dhow. Sitting on a pile of bales is a huge, rather Falstaffian figure (Mustapha-ben-Barca). He's clearly Germanic in origin, but he wears the faded, torn silks and remains of a decorative armour of one of the old "Slav" guards, with whose help the old Caliph reconquered vast areas. He's certainly no longer in first youth and enjoys a beer or two. Indeed, he has a stone beaker in his hand at that moment. He greets the three:

MUSTAPHA-BEN-BARCA: "Passengers for Ceuta?"

ISAAK: "When do you leave?"

MUSTAPHA: "On the next tide."

ELRIC: "What's your price?"

MUSTAPHA: "Whatever's fair to you—I need any cargo I can get . . ."

The old dhow is at sea. Isaak and Rebecca go below while Captain Mustapha talks to Elric:

MUSTAPHA: "Those port charges are scandalous! I couldn't pay for another hour! We're being taxed to fight the regent's wars! In my day we fought for what we could loot. We were proper soldiers. Where are you headed, friend? Mecca?"

ELRIC: "I seek one called the Silverskin. Have you heard of him?"

Mustapha has paled and gone very pensive, biting his lower lip as he looks across the water, avoiding Elric's eye . . . Elric is alert to this—

MUSTAPHA: "*Oh,* yes. I've heard of him."

ELRIC: "What do you know?"

Mustapha's eyes are filled with remembered dread.

MUSTAPHA: "Nothing I've the courage to repeat."

And then, as the sun set, the captain found urgent work to do. The albino was left alone—

Mustapha in the background issuing orders to his hands. Elric, outlined against the setting sun, stares forward over the water.

—to contemplate a dangerous and improbable future . . .

PART THREE

STAGES ON LIFE'S WAY

*B*ound for Africa. Out of the dawn—Isaak, Mustapha and Elric have
their backs to us maybe. They're all in the prow looking to the east
where the sun's coming up like thunder framing the deeper scarlet sail of a
magnificent ship. On her triangular sail is emblazoned the eight-arrowed
sign of Chaos in vivid yellow and black but the most remarkable thing about
the vessel (which has a score of rows of oars pushing her rapidly in their direction, with the wind behind the sail) is that she has two prows—rearing in
two directions—dragon-heads in a style which could be Persian . . .

ISAAK: "The same blazon's on your shield. Do you follow the same
cause?"

ELRIC: "I fear so."

MUSTAPHA: "Two prows! See! By Allah, I know her! She's the *Either/Or*
out of Las Cascadas! 'Tis the Barbary Rose! We've no chance at all
against her hand-picked cutthroats . . ."

We get a closer view of the wonderful Barbary Rose (the Rose from Moonbeams and Roses) *whose beautiful face is calm as the sea she sails on and
her Berber robes, including her great, loose turban, are pink, russet and
green, giving an impression of petals. They swathe her as she keeps her arm
on the ship's tiller, her other hand on her strange sword Swift Thorn, scabbarded beneath her robes, as she sails relentlessly towards her prey. Inset (we
don't really have to see the two men clearly):*

ISAAK: "A woman pirate?"

MUSTAPHA: "An afrit! There's none more ruthless on the five seas!"

Pirates come alongside. The foul crew which serves the beautiful woman who now stands amidships directing them, her sword free in her hand, looks to her with some surprise, for she does not order them to attack. Instead, she and Elric look eye into eye and remember more than one shared secret. There is an odd sort of stillness to the scene, as if for the moment all were frozen.

For a moment, as the pirates came alongside, there was a pause. The Rose's crew awaited her call to attack—

But the Rose was suddenly staring into a thousand memories . . .

Mustapha looks baffled. He's ready to die, even though he has his old scimitar in his hand. They look from Elric to the Rose.

MUSTAPHA: "Why don't they kill us?"

ISAAK: "Something between those two."

Holding up her hand to restrain her crew from following, the Rose steps aboard and moves towards Elric.

ROSE: "Good morning, Duke Elric! So you kept your promise to follow me?"

ELRIC: "Delayed a few years, I fear, lady."

ROSE: "All the better for the waiting, sir."

The Rose extends an hospitable hand to all. She's inviting Elric and his ship to her stronghold of Las Cascadas. And Elric is accepting. But Mustapha confides privately to Isaak that he's suspicious of her motives.

ROSE: "You'll be my guests at Las Cascadas."

MUSTAPHA: "We have no choice. But be wary of this clever thief—she's all deception!"

Las Cascadas. Base this on the early Craig Russell (First Comics) cliffs of Melniboné. Add a deep, good harbour, also very steep and occupied by dwellings of all kinds. The inhabitants lounge over balconies festooned with foliage, looking with some interest at the Either/Or. *As she sails gracefully into her home-port with a prize in tow.*

Standing beside the Rose, Elric asks her a question.

ELRIC: "Tell me, Rose. Have you ever heard of a creature called 'The Silverskin'?"

ROSE: "Never . . ."

But her face is to us and she's frowning slightly. She's clearly lying.

The Rose's hospitality was lavish. Then—

Mustapha, Elric, Isaak and Rebecca are enjoying the savage luxury of the Rose's wonderful court. A fantastic palace. All kinds of trained animals. All sorts of grotesques here and there in nooks and crannies.

MUSTAPHA: "So this is the notorious inner realm of the demon queen!"

ROSE: "It offers some of the simpler comforts . . ."

A feast, primarily North African in foods—lots of beans and pulses—but elaborately prepared. As they are close to finishing their meal, a newcomer draws their attention to the entrance. The entrance frames Sidi Oratio Kwyll' (Captain Horace Quelch from Moonbeams and Roses) *with a leopard on a leash in one hand and a string over his shoulder attached to*

some glamorous slaves. Clearly Christian, however. Quelch is rather aston-
ished by the company.

SIDI ORATIO KWYLL': "Here we are again, Rose, home from the—*eh?*"

ROSE: "Guests, Oratio."

Sidi Oratio Kwyll', the infamous "Christian Corsair," far from his native Wales.

Almost goadingly Isaak points at the slaves and Kwyll' responds somewhat
flustered.

ISAAK: "Could those be *Christian* slaves?"

KWYLL': "Indeed they are—and soon to be free. But first we must con-
    fess 'em . . . and finding a priest in these parts is a little hard . . ."

Elric raises a hand. He has no liking for Kwyll', though he knows him.

KWYLL': "Greetings, Duke Elric. Your king still owes me treasure!"

ELRIC: "My king no longer, sidi. Besides, you betrayed us. Fled south
    with Danish gold."

KWYLL': "Well, 'tis a turning world, sir."

Later that night . . .

Elric, Mustapha, Isaak and Rebecca make urgent preparations to leave the
Rose's palace.

ELRIC: "The Rose is dangerous, but with Kwyll' she's doubly so. Let's
    leave while we still can . . ."

ISAAK: "How do you know them?"

ELRIC: "King Ethelred, my foolish liege, hired them as mercenaries to fight the Danes . . ."

In the moonlight, they make their cautious way through twisting, narrow, steep streets, leading radically downwards to the harbour where their ship can be seen.

ISAAK: "Our sailors! They're still aboard! We're in luck . . ."

ELRIC: "Approach warily. They could plan a trap."

A couple of Rose's guards sleep nearby as the four go up the gangplank and into the ship.

ISAAK: "Arrogant fools!"

ELRIC: "We'll sail at once. When the moon sets they'll never find us . . ."

MUSTAPHA (*sniffs*): "Bit of a storm brewing. Better than staying here, though."

They are sailing into pitchy darkness, but Mustapha is exulting. The others are also elated, as are the hands in the rigging, going about their jobs.

MUSTAPHA: "Think of the tale! I must be the only captain in the Middle Sea to meet the Rose and live!"

Down in their cabin, which they share, Elric and Isaak check that their goods are still all there. Elric's sword, shield and horn are there. Isaak's various bags. But Isaak looks up, puzzled.

ELRIC: "Nothing touched, it seems!"

ISAAK: "Where's the carpet?"

Elric and Isaak have searched the whole cabin. The carpet is gone.

ELRIC: "Stolen! That was what she sought!"

ISAAK: "Our map? She has our map? But why? And how did she know?"

Close-up of Elric and Isaak as the moon finally sinks on the horizon. Everything becomes silvery, especially Elric . . .

ELRIC: "I'd guess that pair, like me, seeks the Silverskin."

ISAAK: "And have a better chance than we do of finding it!"

Close-up of Elric staring moodily into an uncertain future.

ELRIC: "Perhaps."

Mustapha shouts from above:

MUSTAPHA: "Get the hatches battened! There's a storm to larb'rd and she's coming up fast!"

PART FOUR

SOUL IN THE IRON

Mediterranean. Thursday, 26th June, 1000 AD.

*E*lric, *Isaak, Rebecca and Mustapha the Goth are tiny figures aboard their ship as crashing waves descend on them, lightning rends the midnight black and we get a full-strength* sturm und drang. *Ah, Pathetic Mortals so weak before the Mighty Power of Nature.*

Elric on deck realizes his peril and turns to dash towards his cabin.

ELRIC: "Stormbringer!"

Elric fails to reach his sword, shield, etc.

A single great wave descends on the ship and smashes it! All know they are doomed.

And they're in the water, sinking fast in all directions.

Elric begins to drown—in his head he calls a name:

As Elric drowned he called an alien name—

ELRIC: *"Stra-aaa-aaa-sha-a-a-a-"*

Once it might have invoked a demigod—now it summons only a million memories . . .

As Elric sinks he is surrounded by all his memories—bizarre landscapes and peoples, bizarre beasts and battles—(if you have any Russell or Gilbert Elric comics those might refresh your memory.)

The panorama of a somewhat over-active life swims before him.

Elric fades . . .

ELRIC (*thinks*): "*All that was familiar is gone for ever—all that was vivid has faded—it's best I finish like this . . .*"

Next thing he knows Elric is waking up on the beach. Rebecca appears to have given him the kiss of life. She is fastening back her heavy veil. Isaak is there with a potion in a goblet.

ISAAK: "Everything's gone except—by God's grace—my wisdom! My books and medicines were washed ashore."

ELRIC: "The sword . . ."

Isaak is not entirely unhappy that the runesword does mumble nearby.

ISAAK: "On the bottom, I fear, with everything—and everyone—else."

Elric is reconciled to his doom.

ELRIC: "Then I'm doomed."

Isaak cheerful and trying to cheer Elric up—

ISAAK: "Believe me, you'll feel better if you drink this."

As Elric reluctantly drinks, Isaak speaks but is interrupted by a yell from up the beach where they see a mounted Mustapha the Goth.

ISAAK: "Our main dilemma is that we're completely lost—"

MUSTAPHA: "By Allah! My prayers are answered! The infidels live!"

And Mustapha has companions—a bunch of heavily armed and armoured Berber warriors, magnificent in their barbaric silver and mother-of-pearl. These handsome, aquiline Berbers have no Arab blood to speak of. Their pale skins are darkened by the sun. These are members of one of the huge tribes making up the Fatimid alliance. Their long spears and small round shields on their backs, they look down arrogantly on the companions. Mustapha indicates them as he speaks to his new pals—

MUSTAPHA: "These are the friends I feared dead! Victims, like me, of Almoravid oppression . . ."

One of the riders takes Rebecca on his saddle and another takes Isaak's box. With some difficulty Elric rises. He almost falls—

—but Mustapha, seeing something wrong, kindly leans to offer him an arm—

MUSTAPHA: "Almost dead, eh? Come on, Your Dukeship. You can ride with me."

As they ride in the wake of the rest of the party, Mustapha winks at Elric and tells him what's happening:

MUSTAPHA: "They're Fatimids—claim descent from the Prophet, may Allah bless His name, through His daughter Fatima—"

Mustapha deliberately drops back a little.

MUSTAPHA: "They hate the monkish Almoravids who now rule Spain."

MUSTAPHA (*grins*): "Any enemy of theirs is a friend of the Fatimids!"

Elric is already growing weaker. He's almost asleep in Mustapha's saddle. Mustapha is now riding beside Isaak:

MUSTAPHA: "He's blank. As if he left his soul in that sword he lost."

Isaak has crested the hill a little ahead—he's impressed at what he sees below.

ISAAK: "Great Moses! Who would have guessed it? An Arab army on the march!"

They are riding over the sand-dunes down on to the rach—the stoney semi-desert, dotted with the odd scrubby bush on which goats graze. There are herds of goats and sheep attached to the tent city of a semi-nomadic Berber clan. Standards fly here and there, designating the various families of the clan. The tents are elaborate and magnificent, as old as many houses. They are woven of the heavy black wool and decorated with vivid designs—many of them representational, for the Berbers have adopted their own form of Islam which is dissimilar to the Arab.

Around the tent city a low earthworks has been raised, mostly to keep in the herds, but also for defense.

It appears that Mustapha has been a little over-confident about their auto-matic friendship, however—

The Sharif—a glowering hawk-nosed patriarch who looks as if he could personally hold the Khyber Pass—signs for the box to be placed at his feet—and shows a more than fatherly interest in the veiled Rebecca.

SHARIF: "Kill the leper and the old man and bring the girl to my tent."

MUSTAPHA: "But we are friends . . ."

The chest is now open and the Sharif looks at it disdainfully.

SHARIF: "Friends bring better presents than a few books nobody can
     read!"

MUSTAPHA: "It is written that you shall not draw the blood of guests!"

SHARIF: "True . . ."

*Last panel has Elric and Co. staked out in the sand—but from the Sharif's
tent where the Sharif and Rebecca are shown in silhouette, the Sharif is
backing off from Rebecca whose veil has dropped to one side and he's
screaming with terror and outrage.*

SHARIF (*in silhouette*): "*Eeh! Eeh!* Take it away! Take it away!"

Dawn . . .

*The Taureq attack. These magnificent blue-veiled Caucasians, with glaring
blue and green eyes, blue skin (from the dye in their costumes) and tattooed
foreheads and cheeks, with spears and bows thudding everywhere in the
Berber camp, charge down on the tents, their magnificent pure-blood horses
hardly seeming to touch the ground.*

*They are led by a gigantic black man. He looks a bit like Jimi Hendrix (and
very like Sam Oakenhurst from* Moonbeams and Roses) *but you can't tell
what his whole face is because it, too, is loosely veiled—the veil threatening
to rip off as he leads his warriors in a savage and canny attack—descending
on the camp on four sides. This is Lo-bin-Gha, the Desert Wind, the most
feared Taureq chief of all time, whose own story is a strange one. He is from
the far south of the continent.*

LO-BIN-GHA: "Faster, my children! For God—and victory!"

Isaak looks up from where Rebecca is staked beside him, swathed in a heavy winter djelaba, as if to keep her entirely from sight. Elric looks somewhat further gone.

ISAAK: "Are we saved?"

It was Lo-bin-Gha—the Desert Wind—

Now the Taureq are mopping up, killing the wounded, the old and the sick. Seeing to the herds, sorting boys and girls, men and women, to sell as slaves. The Sharif's tent has been trampled. He lies in the ruins looking as if he died horribly—but rigor mortis has set in fast, it seems. Mustapha, too, is dead with a lance through his head.

The magnificent leader of the Taureq rides up to the three staked people and issues an order to his men—

ISAAK (*tries to speak civilly to him*): "Good morning, sire. Now at least we can resume our conversation—"

Lo-bin-Gha doesn't even look at him.

LO-BIN-GHA: "Kill the leper and the old man and put the girl with the others."

PART FIVE

MASK OF THE LIONESS

The Western Sahara. 9th August, 1000 AD. Captured by the Desert Wind . . .

*E*lric, Isaak and the dead Mustapha are still staked out in the sand. *Lo-bin-Gha, mounted, has ordered his men to kill the two left alive. Rebecca, who has been freed, runs to the open chest and grabs from it one of Isaak's books, carrying it towards LBG and offering it to him.*

ISAAK (*pleading*): "Great lord! Surely you don't forget the owner of those books?"

LBG (*inset*): "What? Books?"

ISAAK: "We fought together, my lord!"

Flashback to LBG and Isaak riding at the head of a great army.

ISAAK (*inset of the two men in friendly debate over books*): " . . . as fiercely as we argued on philosophy!"

LBG: "Isaak! My old comrade! Forgive me! I am one man in war and another in peace . . ."

LBG (*to one of his puzzled-looking men*): "Release them!"

Once freed, Isaak helps the still-weakened Elric to rise.

LBG: "You'll be my guests. We camp at the Romi city, yonder."

Outside LBG's tent, pitched in a square of the Romi city. Elric lies on a stretcher, being tended to by Rebecca.

ELRIC: "We all seek the City of the Silverskin . . ."

ISAAK: " . . . said to lie somewhere near the Interior."

LBG: "I have heard the tale. That city's not far from my own land . . ."

Flashback to two tall, native-dressed African men walking near an idyllic-looking, riverside tribal village.

LBG (*inset*): "I was taken from it as a child . . . and I yearn to return . . ."

LBG: "What if we were to combine forces?"

ISAAK: "It would greatly improve our chances!"

ELRIC: "But our map is stolen . . ."

ISAAK (*pulling a scroll from beneath an outer garment*): "I took the precaution of making a rough copy."

LBG (*taking the scroll, unrolling and examining it*): "Yes! This directs us to Tan-al-Oorn, lost city of the Silverskin—and beyond it is the land of King Solomon. The land of gold. My land."

ISAAK: "Then it's agreed?"

LBG: "I'll prepare at once. We leave in the morning!"

That night—

Isaak sits consulting old books beside Elric, still prone on his stretcher.

ISAAK: "These herbals and grimoires are bound to provide some cure for your affliction, friend Elric."

ELRIC: "I fear you're optimistic, Isaak. Without my sword—I'm useless . . ."

ISAAK: "You have a poor opinion of yourself."

ELRIC: "Maybe . . ."

ISAAK (*rising to leave*): "Sleep well, friend."

Later—

Elric awoke suddenly . . .

He is being carried away from the camp, still on his stretcher, by a group of strange creatures. They are pallid, grey-skinned, slightly simian-looking, with large, black eyes; skinny, hairless, and dressed only in small, tight loincloths.

ELRIC: "What? Who are you?"

Next morning . . .

Isaak, LBG and Rebecca discover Elric's absence. Rebecca crouches down, examining possible tracks leading away from their camp.

ISAAK: "But how could he have vanished?"

LBG: "A hungry lion, maybe? Even jackals will attack a feeble man . . ."

LBG (*head bowed*): "He's dead. We must press on."

Meanwhile, far underground . . .

Elric is still being carried, through corridors and caves half man-made, half natural. Seeming to know where they are going, as if it is home to them, the troglodytes begin chanting, ignoring Elric's pleas . . .

ELRIC: "Deeper and deeper! Where do you take me?"

TROGLODYTES: *"Silvery-silvery-silvery-skin silvery-silvery-silvery-sweet . . ."*

The intermittent man-made sections of the tunnels give way finally to a vast, natural cavern, hung with stalactites. In the shadows ahead of Elric and his abductors can be seen other creatures, standing in front of what appears to be a cage containing yet another, larger beast.

SMALL TROG: *"Now we trade!"*

FIRST LARGE TROG: *"More blood! Less bone!"*

SECOND LARGE TROG: *"Good bone bad blood!"*

Elric knew they were bargaining with his life—but why?

The larger trogs are revealed; just as pale and simian as the smaller ones but broad-shouldered, muscular, fierce-looking, with bigger heads covered in matted hair.

They were reaching agreement . . .

The large trogs move to take possession of Elric's stretcher, sending the smaller ones over towards the still-obscured cage.

LARGE TROG: *"The marrow is all we need . . ."*

Elric tries to resist, but is too weak. Suddenly from one side of the cave there comes a great roaring—

"GRRRARRRRG!"

A giant lioness is revealed, standing, confronting the trogs; she is not rearing on hind legs but standing as a human would. Trogs of all sizes, and Elric, are startled by this new arrival, but the trogs are plainly terrified, cowering. The smaller ones struggle with the door of the cage, attempting to release the creature therein.

The door opens and a huge, green, reptilian beast leaps forth out of it, towards the lioness which drops to all fours, adopting a more leonine posture, ferocious, ready to pounce. The reptile lets rip a series of piercing screeches . . .

"SHMEE SHMEE SHMEE!"

The two giant creatures—lioness and reptile—do battle, until finally the lioness pins her foe to the floor of the cave, tearing at its exposed throat with her fangs.

She pounces again, landing amongst and scattering in all directions the retreating trogs.

Slowly, stealthily, she approaches Elric who can do nothing to ward her off. Her great maw opens wide, revealing sharp teeth ready to tear him asunder.

But instead she picks him up gently in her mouth, as she might a lion cub, and runs, carrying him back the way he was brought down through the catacombs.

ELRIC: "Who are you? Why do you help me?"

Once again, the albino lost consciousness . . .

It is night. The lioness, still carrying Elric, runs on through the desert. From atop a dune, they descend, approaching a group of unguarded tents. As she places Elric on the sand outside one of the tents, he awakes.

ELRIC: "Who?"

Perhaps he passes out again, perhaps he does not, but the next Elric knows is that a veiled woman leans over him, offering him liquid from a goblet. Her eyes, all that he can see of her, are large and dark.

WOMAN: "Drink this. You'll be stronger."

ELRIC: "Who are you?"

The woman turns her head away before answering.

REBECCA: "I am the daughter of Isaak D'Israeli. Who else would I be?"

ELRIC: "Time alone will tell, perhaps?"

PART SIX

KNIGHT OF THE FAITH

The Western Sahara. 12th August, 1000 AD.

*E*lric, Isaak, Rebecca and LBG are now deep in the desert, beneath blistering sun, etc. Endless dunes, many strangely shaped. Wagons abandoned, Isaak and Rebecca ride camels. Isaak consults his crude, copied map. They are paused, to check their direction. Elric holds up a lodestone and points in the opposite direction to the direction it points.

ISAAK: "I suppose it's possible I miscopied the original map . . ."

ELRIC: "The lodestone tells us south is yonder."

LBG: "I'll ride ahead and look for landmarks."

LBG comes tearing back. He's seen something. He alerts the others, who've made camp and are brewing up.

LBG: "A small force—Ouled Naf', by their squalid camp—over there— a dry oasis. They'll have seen your fire."

ISAAK: "They'll attack?"

LBG: "It depends how desperate they are. We should prepare for the worst."

Elric accepts a potion which Rebecca makes him drink. There is a dark intelligence in her eyes, which meet his directly.

REBECCA: "You'll need this soon . . ."

ELRIC: "Are you an oracle, madam, as well as all else?"

But Rebecca chose not to answer.

That evening, invigorated by Rebecca's brew, Elric felt the urge to see the Bedouin camp for himself . . .

Sun sets magnificently across the desert, semi-silhouetting the camp of a bunch of degenerate Bedouin men, whose only women are slaves, even more bedraggled and downtrodden than themselves. They are armed with long spears and shields, some curved swords and daggers. They have only a few horses, camels, mules and donkeys, a few very thin sheep.

ELRIC (*thinks*): "The rejected of every tribe. Not one without several crimes on his conscience . . . but cowards . . . no great danger to us . . ."

Then . . .

Elric is about to return to his camp when he sees two figures riding in from the left. These are a cut above the degenerate Bedouin and they know it. Half-seen, they are the outlines of the Rose and Oratio Kwyll', the Welsh privateer, mounted on magnificent Arab stallions.

ELRIC (*thinks*): "?"

The albino recognizes the newcomers and is cynically amused . . . It's a haughty Rose and a scowling Quelch (Rose and Kwyll'), lording it over the cowed Bedouin.

ELRIC (*thinks*): "The Barbary Rose and her unsavoury ally Oratio Kwyll', the Welsh privateer . . . come to steal what little we have left!"

Elric is back at camp in conference with his fellow travelers.

ELRIC: "Those two could make an effective force out of that rabble."

LBG: "Do they know we're here?"

ELRIC: "Probably."

ISAAK: "But what are *they* doing this deep into the Sahara?"

Isaak smiles rather wryly as he listens to Elric's reply. The albino is contemptuous.

ELRIC: "There's not much doubt—they seek the lost gold of King Solomon, as you do. And perhaps they, too, think the Silverskin can show them the way . . ."

Isaak looks at Elric in some surprise.

ISAAK: "You know so much about us!"

ELRIC: "My people cared more for experience than profit . . . You humans will always mistake the symbol for the thing itself . . . Relatives of mine have seen whole universes made of gold. Worth how many dinarae?"

LBG looks somewhat sardonically over at Elric. Elric replies with gloomy self-mockery.

LBG: "You are quick to recognize vice and virtue, eh, Duke Elric? Is that not for God to judge?"

ELRIC: "I judge nothing but the vice within myself, dear prince."

LBG is in whispered conference with his friends as they extinguish the fire.

LBG: "We can't readily beat them. Flight's the best . . ."

But even as they make to leave, a small ball of Greek Fire hurtles upwards into the night, illuminating all—it's been shot on an adapted crossbow by Oratio Kwyll'—and our companions are horribly exposed . . .

KWYLL': "Modern science—so spectacular in antique climes!"

ISAAK: "Byzantine Sunshine, we used to call that horrible stuff!"

LBG: "Greek Fire. And we're surrounded!"

The Rose urged the rabble on—

The Rose appears on a magnificent black stallion, whose hoofs lash at the air. Whose eyes blaze almost as brightly as hers. She sports a great scimitar whose handle is shaped like a rose and whose blade is engraved with roses. A small silver shield on her arm. She has never looked more beautiful and never fiercer as she directs her Bedouin rabble against the four companions who now stand back to back, anticipating the worst. Rebecca whispers so that only Elric can hear—

REBECCA: "There's no lioness to help us now, Duke Elric . . ."

They are entirely surrounded by spear-wielding Bedouin who make an increasingly tight circle. Isaak raises his eyes heavenwards.

ISAAK: "God of Abraham, accept my soul!"

Isaak lowers his eyes and speaks to himself—

ISAAK: "And spare, Lord, I beg thee, my suffering child."

Grinning at LBG, Isaak lifts his own sword. He prepares for his last fight.

Elric leans on a staff, a common sword in his hand which he's barely able to raise.

ISAAK: "Let our deaths be good and theirs what they deserve!"

LBG is the only one to be slightly wounded by a spear which he drags from his side and—

—breaks contemptuously. Other spears land all around them. Isaak is astonished at their continuing to live—

ISAAK: "A miracle! We live!"

LBG: "A miracle they hit me. They are naught but dog-butchers with no stomach or training for battle!"

ELRIC: "But numbers enough to extinguish us, I think!"

LBG wryly admits to this—

LBG: "Aye."

Brightening—

LBG: "But who knows what fortune Allah plans for us?"

What indeed?

A distance away a newcomer watches the scene. Elric & Co. are seriously outnumbered. He is the camel-mounted Taureq knight, Tarak-al-Tan-al-Oorn. Mounted on a magnificent albino camel, swathed in subtle shades of indigo, with a shield full of delicate inlays and every sword and dagger on him a work of art, his long spears on his back. Every inch of his camel's harness and saddle is to the same level of workmanship. He's a dandy of the desert. He also carries the Chaos Shield on his back, a wrapped sword across his pommel. In particular he bears an uncanny resemblance to Jack Karaquazian (see the Simonson pages of JK).

We have no idea of his involvement with any of the other characters or why he has Elric's shield. You can make this an excuse to give the Taureq his full finery—just a gorgeous picture of a desert knight.

PART SEVEN

THE ART OF IGNORANCE

F ROM AFAR, Rose and Kwyll' directed the Ouled Naf's attack on
Elric and his friends . . .

*Elric, Isaak, LBG have withstood the first attack of the Ouled Naf' and are
dealing with another as Rose & Kwyll' continue to direct from a distance. It
looks as if they're done for when—*

*Main picture—Tarak-al-Tan-al-Oorn, the Taureq knight, mounted on his
magnificent white camel, comes galloping down on the attackers, his scimitar whirling—*

Tarak scythes his way through the attackers, spreading concern—

Together Our Trio and Tarak send the remaining attackers packing—

Elric turns to thank the Taureq knight—

ELRIC: "Thanks, stranger, we—"

*Tarak gallops past Elric, flinging down the Chaos Shield and the Black
Sword as he goes—*

TARAK: "If you want the horn, find it in the Valley of the Phoorn—"

We see Tarak galloping off in one direction—Rose and Kwyll' in another.

TARAK: "Ride south for ten days!"

Elric is mystified as he picks up his sword and shield and inspects them. Rebecca shows an interest in the weapons. The others look to the disappearing Rose and Kwyll', scratching their heads.

ELRIC: "How did he come by these?"

REBECCA: "He seems a good, if mysterious friend."

LBG: "Scampered off!"

ISAAK: "We'll see them again, no doubt."

The four are regrouping, tidying their goods and equipment, seeing to their damaged tents, packing what they can onto their horses. Isaak checks his map—

ISAAK: "Did I copy this right? I don't quite know if we go due south or south-east . . ."

ELRIC: "Due south."

LBG is amused, looking up from his pack—

LBG: "The return of your weapons has restored your judgment, eh?"

ELRIC: "So it seems."

South Sahara. August, 1000 AD. Nine days later . . .

Elric & Co. are close to dying of desert exposure. They lead gaunt horses over the burning sand, their eyes staring almost sightlessly ahead as they tramp on.

LBG: "There's not a drop of water for a thousand miles . . ."

ISAAK: "Your instincts aren't what they were, my friend—death grows
      close now . . ."

*Isaak looks with melancholy humour at the sword Elric carries behind
him . . .*

ISAAK: "At least for those of us who do not have the means of living off
      their companions . . ."

*Elric turns his gaunt head, an anguished predator, and glares at Isaak with
blazing red eyes, but he says nothing.*

The tenth day . . .

*They are all but crawling. The tongues of the horses are swollen and lolling.
LBG points to a rise in the far background where two mounted figures
pause in their pursuit . . .*

LBG: "The Rose and her shifty consort. Jackals expecting our end . . ."

ELRIC: "I'm hoping they'll move in soon to finish us off—we could use
      their energy . . ."

But the Rose and Kwyll' were too wily to risk coming close to Stormbringer when all they had to do was wait . . .

Then, on the evening of the eleventh day—

*Our heroes have reached a rise, almost a bluff, and are looking south as the
sun begins to set over a narrow valley—of which we can only see the opening—they are looking at a sight we can't see—a sight so astonishing that all
are entranced by it—we might even see the edge of one of the pyramids
they're looking at (because in the next episode we'll see it is a valley entirely
consisting of pyramids, most of which are the size of the Great Pyramid of
Giza, arranged in orderly ranks for as far as the eye can see—an impossible*

building project—but these pyramids, although otherwise identical to that at Giza, have strangely wrought "crowns" at their peaks—bizarre metalwork whose function isn't immediately evident)—Elric looks somewhat relieved that he's arrived at last.

LBG: *"Impossible!"*

ISAAK: "It is the legendary *Valley of the Phoorn.* Even *I* doubted its existence!"

ELRIC: "It's just as I remember it . . ."

PART EIGHT

SLEEP AND DREAMING

September 3rd, 1000 AD. South Central Sahara.

ELRIC AND HIS companions had come at last to the legendary Valley of the Phoorn . . .

Our travelers can now see the first of the great pyramids, each as huge as the Great Pyramid of Giza and topped by the peculiar "crown." The object of this page and the next two is to show the extraordinary scale of the pyramids. Already the riders are dwarfed—and they are nowhere near the first pyramid.

REBECCA: "The capital of the great Phoorn lords who were banished from Egypt ten thousand years ago . . ."

ISAAK: "And built their empire when the Sahara was green . . ."

ELRIC: "And knew the real purpose of the pyramids . . ."

The pyramids stretch as far as the eye can see. It's crucial to get the sense of scale. Most are of roughly the same gigantic size, but there are a few smaller ones set beside the larger ones, as at Giza. Each one is topped by the remains (in different states of decay) of the metal-and-leather "crowns." They march in orderly ranks the length and breadth of the long, shallow valley. In comparison, the figures of our protagonists in the foreground are tiny. Perhaps a suggestion of the huge skeletons and remains we'll see later.

ISAAK: "Holy Abraham! What is it? A titan's necropolis?"

ELRIC: "Not a necropolis, Sir Isaak. At least not originally—but you might call it a dormitory."

LBG: "Our legends speak of the Phoorn as witch-folk, shape-changers who consorted with snakes and crocodiles. All feared them, but none ever saw their capital . . ."

ELRIC: "Their capital, Qu'of, perished in a single catastrophic moment. It took far longer for the inhabitants of this place to die . . . My folk and the Phoorn share common blood."

The companions ride closer to the pyramids now. They are totally dwarfed by the nearest structures. Suggestion of dragon skulls and bones buried in the surrounding sand. Elric tells a little more of the story of the Phoorn. Isaak marvels.

ISAAK: "Hard to believe these structures were made by men!"

ELRIC: "If you call the Phoorn 'men.' They built these pyramids with their own hands—to honour the folk with whom they shared their power . . . And who were also called the Phoorn . . . A fruitful symbiosis while Qu'of ruled the lushest part of the continent . . ."

Elric continues talking as they ride past a huge reptilian ribcage.

ELRIC: "But her farmers took too much and gave back too little, until— almost in an instant—the earth turned to dust—forests, fields and orchards became an endless waste of sand . . . which covered everything except this valley—leaving the ancient Phoorn without help, foraging further and further for food . . . and slowly falling into a sleep of centuries . . . and from sleep into death . . ."

ISAAK: "No doubt these are their monuments. Do any still live?"

ELRIC: "I doubt it . . ."

LBG: "The gods be thanked. Theirs was an evil empire maintained by unnatural sorcery and foul alliances with the underworld . . ."

Inset of Elric raising a sardonic eyebrow.

ELRIC: "Indeed?"

Suddenly, to Elric's astonishment, the faintest whiff of sulphur . . .

Alerted by the smell of sulphur, Elric looks up.

A great dragon skull could be in the foreground here as they ride under the shadow of a pyramid from near the top of which will come the voice of the unseen dragon who rests on the pyramids—they are dragon "beds" or "thrones"—using the "crown" for their long jaws and unfolding their wings down the sides of the pyramid. Elric is half-turning at the sound of a voice, perhaps the faintest drift of vapour, from above and is looking upward to the top of the pyramid for the source. There is a softness, a pleasure to Elric's surprise. Their horses now show some agitation. Lo-bin-Gha looks distinctly unhappy with the situation.

ELRIC: "Is that you, old friend . . . ?"

A hint of the dragon—perhaps a pyramid "throne" seen past Elric's head . . .

VOICE: "*I have waited, master. I have waited ten thousand years, and now at last you have come!*"

PART NINE

IMPROBABLE MEETINGS

Deep Sahara. September, 1000 AD. A ten-thousand-year reunion . . .

*T*he face of a dragon who is at least thirty thousand years old and has been waiting in this same place for ten thousand . . . (see sketch) This is Flamefang, Elric's own dragon-bondmate from the stories, and he is huge—Elric's about the size of a hamster in comparison. These are what the pyramid thrones were made for and it is on one of these that Flamefang now wakes, bleary and ancient, grey-muzzled, mild-eyed and with massive, but broken and worn away, teeth. (It's important he should be very geriatric-looking.) A little sulphur smoke escapes his wrinkled nostrils and yet a little life sparks in him as he speaks to his old bondmate Elric. Elric reaches a tiny hand to stroke the great snout. There is enormous affection between the two.

ELRIC: "∇⊇ξψ!! ⇓◊◊⇓⇒⊕ℑ!!! ψ⇓⊇ξ! . . . *Flamefang!* My old dragon-brother! *You still live!*"

FLAMEFANG: "⇓⇒⊕ . . . *Long enough to serve you, brother, one last time . . .*"

Unlike the others, who are merely astonished, LBG reacts with horror and disgust.

LBG: "*Foul sorcery!* Kill the creature while it's weak!"

Elric rounds furiously on LBG, his hand moving to his sword-hilt—

ELRIC: "Watch your tongue, my lord! You speak of my blood brother."

LBG is mad with fear and anger. Isaak tries to control him and calm him.

LBG: "Then maybe we should kill you both!"

ISAAK: "Silence, old friend. You don't know what you're saying . . ."

But LBG raves on, careless of Elric's narrowing eyes . . .

LBG: *"This is foulness from the dawn of time! This is the afterbirth of cre-ation! Kill it, Elric—or I shall kill it!"*

ELRIC: "Take charge of yourself, my lord—*or suffer the conse-quences . . .*"

ISAAK: "Listen to him, old friend! *Listen to him!*"

. . . But the Desert Wind's blood recognized its ancient enemy—and would not be quieted . . .

LBG takes a sword and draws back his arm to aim a blow at the huge ailing beast.

LBG: "The thing's an obscenity! I'll do the deed if you will not!"

ELRIC: *"Mortal fool!* No man threatens my brother—"

Elric draws Stormbringer, his eyes beginning to blaze—

ELRIC: *"—and keeps his soul!"*

Isaak shouts out—

ISAAK: "Please, Elric! Spare him. He doesn't understand—"

Elric and LBG clash, sword to sword.

LBG: "*Demon*! You'll die with that hellspawn!"

LBG's eyes widen in horrified realization as Elric's sword enters his body—

LBG: "*Ooohhh! N-o-o-o. My s-s-s-o-u-l . . .*"

We pull back to see the sword's glowing black blade, the writhing red runes, as LBG's soul is devoured.

And Elric's face—demonic as he feeds off LBG's soul—

ELRIC: "Thanks, friend, for your lifestuff. It will revive my brother . . ."

LBG: "*—please—n-o-o-o . . .*"

Elric, sword still unsheathed, turns away from LBG towards Flamefang. Isaak kneels beside the Desert Wind, his friend, holding him tenderly and staring with horror at Elric who is already moving towards the dragon, his attention on his vast reptilian brother.

ISAAK: "Now he'll not see his homeland . . ."

ELRIC: "We were no threat to him. Here, brother, I bring you food . . ."

Flamefang's strangely forked tongue wraps itself around the blade . . . black light courses from metal to flesh . . . red fire writhes . . .

. . . and a fresh light begins to dawn in his ancient, almost lifeless eyes . . .

Only Rebecca continues to look on.

Her father turns away in distress and horror.

ISAAK: *"Oh, great Abraham! How I wish I had never witnessed such an abomination . . ."*

Isaak is weeping as he closes his old friend's still-shrieking eyes.

Rebecca's own strange eyes are shining almost with hero-worship . . .

ISAAK: "I'd heard all the tales, Elric. Yet still I could not believe you a demon . . ."

REBECCA: "Demon, Father? *He's much more powerful than that . . .*"

Elric and the dragon seem linked in symbiotic semi-trance. A small flame flickers in the great beast's eyes.

FLAMEFANG: "ꙄꙄꙄ₵ƎⱯⱭⱭ≡⊨!♥! . . . *But my senses are still so dim, brother. I need my old* skeffla'a. *Did you bring it?*"

ELRIC: "Stolen. But there's still hope . . ."

Close-up of grim-faced albino.

ELRIC: "The thieves are nearby. They believe themselves safe from my vengeance . . . But I have an ally out there."

Watching from far away are the Rose and Kwyll'. They are just behind some dunes, but we can see the crests of the pyramids.

Watching them is Tarak-al-Tan-al-Oorn, the mysterious Taureq on his white camel.

Still distressed, Isaak rounds on Elric—

ISAAK: "What? Did you lead us here, simply as sacrifice to your blade's insatiable lust for souls?"

Close-up of Elric's face. It's suddenly racked with conflicting pain. An appalling ambiguity.

ELRIC: "I sincerely hope not . . ."

PART TEN

INEVITABLE CONJUNCTIONS

Valley of the Phoorn. Central Sahara, Tuesday, 1st October, AD 1000. Elric is reunited with his blood brother, Flamefang, last surviving member of a race once bonded with Elric's folk . . .

*I*saak, *avoiding looking at the corpse of his friend, places a hand on a gigantic bone. Elric's attention is on whatever we can see of Flamefang. Rebecca is also staring hard at the dragon.*

ISAAK: "Our Book tells us there were giants in those days."

REBECCA: "But as usual, people wouldn't see them . . ."

ELRIC: "Isn't it how you humans always deal with unwelcome realities?"

ISAAK: "Existence is what we make of it, my lord."

FLAMEFANG: "*The* skeffla'a, *brother—I can only help you if I have it . . .*"

Inset—Elric reassures his dragon brother (Let's have vast dragon and the figures absolutely tiny.)

ELRIC: "Soon, brother, soon . . ."

And nearby . . .

We see Jack/Tarak in a small picture riding down on unseen foes—his camel is racing, his shield is on his arm and his spears are in his hands . . .

Isaak is disgusted. He is making moves to leave the scene. He's had enough. But Rebecca stops him. Meanwhile Elric looks towards where the unseen Tarak is now approaching.

ELRIC: "Any moment now . . ."

ISAAK: "This sorcery is too complex for an ordinary scholar like myself. It's time to leave, I think . . ."

REBECCA: "Stay! A great weaving of destinies is taking place . . . You're safer here . . ."

Isaak looks up—following Elric's eye . . .

ISAAK: "What? Another stranger? Too much for me. I promised to bring you here, daughter. Now it's time to wander on alone . . ."

This stranger had brought gifts of sorts . . .

Tarak-al-Tan-al-Oorn arrives with the Rose and Kwyll' trussed up as his prisoners. They stumble along ahead of him while Tarak pokes them with a spear tip. They are glowering, thoroughly fed up. Around Quelch/Kwyll's shoulders is the carpet we first saw in episode two and which they stole from Elric on the ship. The newcomer is absolutely clearly Jack Karaquazian. There's a faint smile on his face as he raises his hand in greeting.

TARAK: "I believe my prisoners want to return some stolen property . . ."

KWYLL': "Damn you, Jack. You're going too far."

ROSE: "Jack never knew what 'too far' meant . . ."

Tarak presents the captives to Elric—a gift. He looks directly at Elric, ignoring Rose & Kwyll'.

ROSE: "Playing for Law now, are we, Jack?"

KWYLL': "You're behaving melodramatically, Jack. Ease up on the bonds a little, eh?"

TARAK: "I give them to you, brother, to do with as you choose."

ELRIC: "I'm eternally grateful . . ."

Elric turns, displaying the carpet, once again in his possession, to the enfeebled dragon.

ELRIC: "See, dear brother! We have the *skeffla'a!*"

The dragon brightens a little.

FLAMEFANG: *"At last . . ."*

Tarak is already riding away—followed by Isaak on his camel—watched by Rebecca.

ISAAK: "Wait, sir. I'll travel with you . . ."

REBECCA: "Farewell, Father. May your soul find ease!"

Elric suddenly realizes! He calls after Tarak who has almost disappeared behind a dune . . .

ELRIC: "The horn! You said it was here?"

TARAK: *"Look within!"*

He's gone.

Taking the stolen carpet, Elric climbed with familiar ease . . .

Elric carries the "magic carpet" as he scales the dragon—Kwyll' on the ground looks baffled.

KWYLL': "The carpet! What's he doing with it?"

REBECCA: "What it was always designed to do . . ."

. . . until he stood at a certain spot on the monster's back . . .

Elric now begins to unroll the carpet. He stands on the dragon's back. It is a huge, broad back and is almost a landscape of its own, very irregular, but at the centre near the beginning of his neck is a large, smooth area, almost like a great burn, deep in his scaly skin. This area is large enough to accommodate the carpet and the carpet will be just large enough to take Elric, Rebecca, Rose and Kwyll' when the dragon eventually takes off.

FLAMEFANG: "*Ah, brother, I feel its strength already . . . It is my own lost skeffla'a . . . My senses return—all my powers . . .*"

Rose and the others watch in astonishment as the energy from the carpet spills and ripples—the "chart" is veins, blending with the dragon's own central nervous system . . .

ROSE: "I've heard of this. It's a membrane—marries with the creature's central nervous system so it can migrate between the planes. A psychic as well as a physical navigation system . . . There's more. I can't recall . . ."

KWYLL': "Quite enough for me, thanks, Rose . . ."

Pulsing, glowing, the carpet merges with the dragon . . .

. . . until the whole area of the beast's back is alive with strange light and the onlookers stagger back from the radiance . . .

. . . mystic crackles spread from Elric's hands to the dragon's rearing neck . . . They are communicating—the force is like reins, allowing Elric to guide the dragon . . .

ELRIC: "Now, Flamefang! Now, brother!"

The dragon rears up and something pours from its mouth—not fire exactly, but a kind of black radiance, similar to the sword's—and it's directed at the pyramid. Again Kwyll' and the others are forced back by the terrible power . . .

ELRIC: *"Now!"*

The dragon directed the full force of its strange power upon the pyramid . . .

The dragon's strange breath actually destroys the pyramid in a single violent eruption—Elric's face is demonic as he directs his brother . . .

The dust and smoke clears away from the pyramid site . . .

. . . to reveal the Horn of Fate, seated on a miniature version of the same pyramid we have just destroyed. Kwyll' is almost beside himself with rage and dismay—

KWYLL': "That horn! All this for a *horn?*"

Dismounted from the dragon, Elric stretches his hand towards the horn—

ELRIC: "This is the horn which brought me here two centuries ago . . . This is the horn which will now take me home . . . *To the palace of the Silverskin!*"

PART ELEVEN

FOUCAULT'S PIT

The lost Valley of the Phoorn. South-west Sahara, October, AD 1000. Meetings, resolutions—and the burden of a prophecy . . .

*E**lric has dismounted from the dragon and reaches for the Horn of Fate, now revealed.*

ELRIC: "For two centuries I have carried my weird within me—once I fought for this horn—at the last moment I lost the courage to sound it—but now, at long last, I fulfill my destiny—"

ELRIC: "—to herald in the night!"

Elric puts the horn to his lips.

ELRIC: "Three blasts to change the multiverse . . . The first will free us from this world . . ."

Elric blows the horn . . .

BAAAAAAAAAAAAA—OOOOOOOOOOOOOM—
BAAAAAAAAAAAAA . . . aaar-ooom-baaaaa . . . aa-oom-daa-doo-a-
oo-aa-oo . . .

The others cover their ears in agony . . . The sound passes to the next page . . .

A spread across two pages—Everyone's back on Flamefang who is poised to take off—as the whole of the valley begins to collapse in on itself—forming a vast pit into which sand pours like water—A great cosmic event—the stars begin to form new patterns overhead.

Elric is triumphant. Demonic, even . . .

(Fading horn): OOOOOooooooooooo—ooooooooo—ooooommmmmmm

ELRIC: *"Free at last!"*

KWYLL'/QUELCH: "Free for *what?*"

ROSE: "To change the nature of reality, maybe? Ride with the tide, Horatio—this deal's bigger than both of us . . ."

With a great crack of his monstrous tail, Flamefang dives first skyward, then turns to dive rapidly downwards so everyone has to hang on very tight—down into the vast pit . . . down into organic darkness—down towards the Grey Fees—Elric is full of wild excitement—Stormbringer seems to give them both a kind of black radiance . . .

ELRIC: "Down, Flamefang, down! Down to confront our yearning sin! Down to redeem King *Silverskin!*"

Elric raises Stormbringer high as they fly through the Grey Fees (see Walter's version)—this strange limbo of organic rock and petrified life—

—from which great grey shadowy figures—far larger than themselves or the dragon—threaten them—these giants are actually exactly the same creatures as the trogs who carried Elric off earlier . . . The trogs could be drawn normal size and the dragon with figures aboard could be very small . . . We're demonstrating discrepancies of scale.

ELRIC: "Here they come!"

QUELCH: "*Giants!* Impossible!"

ROSE: "You know nothing's impossible in the Grey Fees, Horace ... Time and scale's meaningless here ..."

A vast hand stretches towards the seemingly tiny dragon and the figures on it ... Quelch is drawing his sword ...

QUELCH: "*Oops!* Looks like we're the trolls' *plat du jour*."

But Rebecca (Colinda Dovero from Moonbeams and Roses) *is tearing off her veil . . . Her eyes are catlike, beginning to stir with a strange fire . . .*

Rebecca's face is revealed at last—a snarling lioness—possibly with a hint of a leper's 'lion-mask'—bone-white—underneath, basically the same character as Colinda Dovero.

LIONESS: *"GRRRRR!"*

The trogs are terrified of her, as they were earlier—and as they are whenever they see any kind of cat—whatever size—she's lioness size to Elric—tiny to the trogs.

The trogs retreat from her in terror—

LIONESS: *"Aarrrraaaarrrr!* Degenerate creatures! Begone! For I am *Sekhmet.* I am *Niphur.* And I am *Bast!* All three can destroy you!"

They leave the trogs behind—though the cat's still poised on the dragon's back with the others—and the dragon begins to head upwards again—

ROSE: "The only living thing those monsters fear . . ."

The trog-giants half-grab at the disappearing dragon overhead but they're also covering their faces. They really fear Sekhmet. As would I in their circumstances . . . Elric glances back in wild glee—calling out to the dragon— as they head for glimmering water overhead—

ELRIC: "Up, Flamefang! Up, brother! Destiny beckons! Fate must be fulfilled!"

—and burst upwards through the surface of the lake in a great spout of water and lake-debris—out of Loch Auchy—with Castle Auchy (from Moonbeams and Roses) *clearly visible . . .*

Small panel: The four "passengers" disembark by the stone jetty of Castle Auchy.

ROSE: "This looks familiar."

ELRIC: "Pray to your most powerful gods that we're in time."

Elric reaches out to say farewell to Flamefang—

ELRIC: "Farewell, friend. You were a thousand times more virtuous than I . . ."

—who affectionately wraps his strange tongue around the albino's body, almost in a gentle gesture—its eyes sad—

FLAMEFANG: "Adieu, *little brother. Our work together is finally over . . . But your last task will be the hardest . . .*"

Flamefang turned for home—

Flamefang is beginning to re-submerge. The humans stand on the jetty wishing him farewell.

His tail flicks once above the waves—

And Elric draws his sword—advancing towards the door—the great snarling lioness at his side but slightly ahead—leading them inside. Elric still grasps the horn in readiness. Rose and Quelch hang back a little warier of the lioness and the sword than the door.

ELRIC: "Now to confront King *Silverskin* . . ."

MOONBEAMS AND ROSES
(drawn by Walter Simonson)

PART TWELVE

CONCLUSION—THE HARMONIES OF CHAOS

Warming up for the final game. Elric faces the Silverskin . . .

*E*lric hesitates before the portal, a little further in.

The portal is murmuring, excreting silvery mist.

PORTAL: "Ah, it is too long, no room in my tortured mind for further
memories . . .
We are, all of us, guilty—
all of us—
Those Jews, those gypsies . . .
Armenians . . .
Moslems . . .
Slavs . . .
slaves . . .
I can't—I can't—There is only the abyss, only the darkness,
only the Cold.
We fade, we fade . . . The agony of it . . . It is cold, so cold on
the edge of time . . ."

*Elric's baffled—speaks to Moonglum [who in Part Eleven of Moonbeams
and Roses is found by Elric outside the Silverskin's castle] . . .*

ELRIC: "I don't believe I've summoned Chaos—The horn's song has
called me to something I fear far worse—The one we sometimes
name 'The Other'—not my *self,* exactly, but my *selves* . . ."

ELRIC: "This is the confrontation I turned from once—I am sworn not to turn from it twice . . . Watch for me, friend Moonglum. Chance is—you alone will live to tell this tale."

He steps through. Maybe his back's to us.

We still don't see the Silverskin.

ELRIC: "Greetings—King Silverskin . . ."

SILVERSKIN: "At last, Elric. At last you are home . . . Have you brought us the comfort of the grave?"

ELRIC: "I fear, sire, I bear more of life's demands. At best brief rest—but not the oblivion you crave."

A fresh face at the Terminal Café . . .

"Taffy" Quelch walks into the Café with a box under his arm, waving to familiar faces both at the tables and in the audience.

TAFFY: "Don't mind me, pards . . . I just dropped in to watch the game."

Taffy finds himself a seat by making some of the machinoix move along a bit . . . The machinoix are in holiday mood, perfectly agreeable . . .

TAFFY: "Thanks, pards. Any chance of a cup of tea?"

A machinoix offers him a dark, gleaming icepop on a stick and a large paper cup which has written on the side "Poincaré's Solution Xtra-Strong"—

MACHINOIX: "Plasma-pop?"

Taffy raises a graceful hand to refuse the offer . . .

TAFFY: "Kind of you, lad. I'll wait for the Darjeeling."

He looks back at the tier behind—

TAFFY: "Anybody know the score?"

At the main table Jack Karaquazian, Michael Moorcock, Walter Simonson & Colinda Dovero are playing intensely. Jack in particular is absorbed.

We see the Original Insect within the table.

WALTER: "We can save Sam here . . ."

MM: "Let the poor bastard go."

COLINDA: "Save him—or play on?—Make your move, sir."

JACK: "Put on some speed—watch over me . . . no time for senti- ment . . ."

Now—out of the table—comes the schooner, piloted by the Rose. The machinoix are spectacularly delighted and so is Quelch.

MACHINOIX: "The Rose!"
   "Our girl is racing for the touchdown!"

QUELCH: "What a pilot! She made it! Now our side has a chance!"

Spammer Gain's progress is suddenly stopped—she's achieved maxi- mum mass and is perfectly balanced between being and non- being . . . She's reached Oblivion Dock . . .

This picture could make a virtue of compression, if you liked, so we could give the next panel maximum space . . .

SPAMMER: "Ah, this density, this constipated meaning...I can no longer move. I'll never see my fishlings again...Past fades. There's no future. And the present is a universe of pain..."

Kaprikorn Schultz, who sought to slay her with his trickery, is himself no more than an entropic echo...

KAPRIKORN: "We need no metaphysics
        To sanction what we do
        Or to muffle us in comfort
        From what we did not do...

        "Again the multiverse defeats me
        And turns me to dissipate smoke
        So it's goodbye
        To bagpipe music
        As the bell begins her stroke"

...and the Rose discovers the Original Insect already threatening the Grey Fees...

The Rose steers her schooner to the Grey Fees where the Chaos Engineers are already embattled. Noble deaths as the Straight Arrows tear everything up. But the Chaos Engineers retaliate with every musical force they can muster ... Buggerly Otherly, MaMa Singh, Father Fry and one or two others are left—Corporal Pork and Raider Miles are killed by Yanni and Schubert respectively ...

ROSE: "Howdy, pards. Looks like you're losing ..."

MAMA: "*Rose!* I knew you'd come. Pearl Peru's imprisoned and Spammer's lost to Oblivion Dock!"

BUGGERLY: "Every moment we lose more of our best to Law's sententious appetites. Sweet Rose! By heck, I'm glad to see thee!"

*The Original Insect—her pathway cleared for her by the Straight Arrows which now swarm around and ahead of her like those little fish that swarm with sharks—is eating up the Second Ether, this time in the persons of the Chaos Engineers. Everything behind her is a total void, an absolute **absence**... Speed Camus' plane is in trouble. All this on a giant display by Captain Otherly as she shows Rose the problem. Rose still has the helmeted head of Prince Gaynor the Damned* [wrested from his body in Part Eleven of *Moonbeams and Roses*].

BUGGERLY: "We've tried everything—Mozart Squadron's gone, Rotten Wing's down, you name them ... Not a riff, not a symphony pierced that thing's appalling armour."

MAMA: "We've lost Wagner and Siouxsie Command. Joy Division's holding. Bartók, Reich, Zappa, Garcia, Debussy, Townshend, Ravel, Grainger and Kingsize Taylor Squadrons—all down—We have one Graham Parker side holding the whole 596th single-handed."

FATHER FRY: "Hendrix Wing drowned in some unthinkable mixture of Elton John and Puccini. T'most hideous death I've ever witnessed. Even Zoot Money couldn't save 'em."

BUGGERLY: "The best we've thrown against the Insect and *still* it munches its way to our extinction and its own ... What hope have we, Rose? Bloody thing's **tone deaf!!!** Spammer's our Grail! Save her for us, Rose!"

ROSE: "Don't worry, Captain. I'm sure she'll turn up ..."

At the Terminal Café, there was no time for talk—

Are we engaged with the table or are we engaged with it! Everything's happening—cards consulted, tossed in, stakes piled high—while the winds of limbo continue to blow. While down there deep in the table we see Elric passing through the portal, sharp and tiny, while all around him rise up what could be demons, every one of them himself. The audience leans forward. All attention is on that tiny figure.

—only for song . . .

Inset of our z-band (or just singer): "Skin of silver,
    Skin so thin
    Bones to dust
    Blood to rust
    The stigma of eternal sin."

SINGER (*continues*): "Who to lose
    Who to win
    Who can save
    Poor Silverskin?"

The scene in the table has changed. Now we see the Rose, Buggerly Otherly, a bit of the advancing Insect.

Rose, Buggerly, Insect . . .

BUGGERLY: "We've seven squadrons left! Goodman's, Van Zant's and Costello's are holding Havercall Brian Eno Quadrant. But how long can sophisticated song-writing resist all that noisy greed? Wi'out tha help, lass, we're t'Insect's last supper . . . !"

Head swings to follow her—?

Rose walks towards her plane (see issue 1). Everyone's gearing up for battle. They're astonished to see her leaving.

ROSE: "Sorry, Cap. I have to be in Biloxi. I'd hate to miss the Saturday night game."

MAMA: "All this waiting—and now you fail us, our Rose?"

FATHER FRY (*triumphant*): "I'm right—those time gamblers serve only their own cause . . . She's betrayed the trust you invested . . . and doomed us all to the Grand Consumer."

Plane takes off into the Second Ether. Buggerly grimly continues preparations.

BUGGERLY: "Aye, so it seems.
          But our minds are sharp
          Our wits are keen—
          We'll make the moves
          Wi'out our queen."

Private moment with Buggerly:

BUGGERLY: "Poor lass.
          I guess we all have our cracking points . . .
          Well, let's not go gentle into that good night . . ."

The Final Quarter—Rose's plane comes out of the Biloxi Fault and sights the Terminal Café . . .

ROSE: "Should be starting any moment . . ."

Rose walks into the Terminal Café.

She finds Quelch in his seat and starts to move towards him. He looks disconcerted, places his hand protectively around his box.

ROSE: "I thought you'd be here, Horace."

Rose looks in the box and sees a goldfish bowl with fish in it. She grins.

ROSE: "Attractive pets . . ."

ROSE: "Easy to maintain, are they?"

QUELCH: "Oh, they get plenty of attention, Rosie."

General Force reacts furiously to Professor Pop's interference . . .

Watched urgently by the Oldreg and the Mrs. Oldreg, General Force directs millions of Straight Arrow ships at the buckyball. They are all pointed at it, heading rapidly towards it . . .

FORCE: "They'll not thwart the Singularity! My Straight Arrows will obliterate 'em!"

The Insect seen on screen as it approaches the Grey Fees.

FORCE: "The Insect shall be unhindered in her moral devouring of a chaotic multiverse!"

MRS. O: "Clean! *Clean!* Let the great void gleam with the joys of ultimate neatness!"

OLDREG: "And the multiverse will be one vast sphere of well-regulated profit!"

MRS. O: "The ultimate *free lunch*!"

FORCE: "Now, my Arrows! Now! Crush the whole failed experiment to nothing . . ."

The Straight Arrows begin their advance.

FORCE: " . . . my final weapon'll provide a fitting end! Drown 'em in disco syrup!"

MRS. O: "Disinfect the untidy sphere and all within it!"

OLDREG: "An exemplary execution!"

FORCE: "Executed in exemplary fashion! Sweet . . . and cosmically neat!"

While within the buckyball—

A screen reveals the approaching Straight Arrows outside.

Professor Pop discards his abacus and blackboard and flings his hand to where Little Rupoldo holds two huge power cables—one coming from somewhere within the sphere, the other coming from within their tiny ship—

POP: "It's now or never, Little Rupoldo—"

The first Straight Arrows begin to pierce the buckyball—

RUPOLDO: "Too late, Prof—we've been wacoed!"

PEARL: "Split second left—hurry!"

POP: "I've had to use Laforgue's Principle, which is usually written as 'Tiens! Le multivers est a l'envers'! Okay. Here goes—now, plucky pard, now—
    REVERSE THE POLARITIES!!!!!!!!!"

The Silverskin—every aspect of the Eternal Champion—in an agony of consciousness—its skin a mirror to the multiverse . . .

Elric stands looking at the Silverskin—it resembles Spammer Gain in that it definitely has some squid characteristics . . . It's all the Eternal Champions combined—lots of faces and writhing tentacles—but the reason it's called the Silverskin is because its skin is silvery, reflective, malleable like mercury—reflecting a thousand scenes and faces (you don't have to draw all thousand at this stage, Walter . . .).

SILVERSKIN: "Help me, Elric. I am crushed by the weight of our countless identities . . ."

ELRIC: "Why should I help you—without you I'd be free."

SILVERSKIN: "Because you could not exist without me . . ."

The Silverskin's last remark causes Elric some bitter amusement.

ELRIC: "Then your death must be all the more welcome to me, sire!"

The Silverskin moves uneasily, forming, re-forming, its silvery skin reflecting, distorting, re-reflecting . . .

Elric draws Stormbringer and advances on the Silverskin.

SILVERSKIN: "We are so fragmented—our power dissipates—our memories are too many . . ."

ELRIC: "Aye, King Silverskin, consciousness can be an overrated quality . . ."

A close-up of Elric's tortured face. The tentacles begin to caress him . . .

ELRIC: "And what I do now I do because it is my doom to do it—to use all my powers and achieve the last thing in the world I desire . . ."

The polarities of the multiverse reversed . . .

What about a full-scale Kirby-type cosmic page here—maybe with the buckyball as the centre radiating—rippling out—to grow bigger and bigger and bigger as Little Rupoldo touches the ends together and gets his own aura.

RUPOLDO: "Wow! This is cool!"

. . . with endlessly unpredictable cosmic and personal consequences for all creation . . . for always . . .

At the Terminal Café, the game gets lively enough to merit, I'd say, a two-page spread.

The table erupts to near-destruction while out of it flames our main scene— the death and life of the multiverse . . . A kind of funneling effect with the Original Insect at one end and the Spammer Gain at the other—at either end and coming towards one another . . . with the Insect growing smaller and Spammer growing larger . . . at the centre are the Chaos Engineers whooping and cheering as every scale goes haywire . . .

Pop, Pearl and Rupoldo are now on the outside of an unfolding bucky-ball.

POP: "Our roles! Our poles! Our souls! Our Pearl! All saved!"

Spammer doesn't burst out of the table—she comes bursting out of the goldfish bowl beside Quelch—growing larger and larger as she does so—to the ecstatic delight of the machinoix who look up to her adoringly and cry—

MACHINOIX: ***"MOTHER!"***

SPAMMER: "Fishlings! At last, my darling fishlings!"

Inset of Spammer's beautiful fishy face—

SPAMMER: "Oh, fishlings, how you've grown!"

Quelch is shocked but Rose is triumphant! They look up to where machinoix and Spammer form the shape of a gigantic goblet . . .

QUELCH: "You mean—all I had was a bowl of red herrings? The false attractor?"

ROSE: "The true Grail hidden in the false grail . . . It's all, *mi amigo,* a question of scale . . . Did you think I'd so readily give up? Horace! Spammer herself's the sentient cup!"

Quelch is rueful.

QUELCH: "You beat me fair and square, Rose. What do you say to a celebratory glass of Poincare's Solution . . . ?"

ROSE: "It isn't quite over yet, Horace . . ."

She holds up the bowl. In her other hand, between thumb and forefinger, is the ball containing the tiny Original Insect . . .

Which she flips into the goldfish bowl . . .

(*From inside the ball*): "Foolish Force. Now we're fishfood! It's the death of our Prozac Democracy! The end of our New Order . . . *Glub.*"

A healthy-looking goldfish swallows the ball:

FISH: "Ulp! Smack! Yum."

Walter and MM are standing in the howling gale from the table grinning their heads off. They've won a move and congratulate each other.

WALTER: "We did it! We switched poles and saved the multiverse!"

MM: "But for what?"

Streaming behind goes Spammer Gain, still vaguely cup-shaped, her jubi-lant fishling machinoix all over her wonderful sinuous body . . . Off joyously into the multiverse . . .

Jack and Colinda are frowning down at their remaining cards.

COLINDA: "With Spammer redeemed and the Insect eaten, it's the full reverse . . . Looks like the game's over for us, Jack . . ."

Jack suddenly grins. He's planning something—as Spammer grows smaller and smaller in the distance he winks. . . .

JACK: "Oh, I think we still have a move or two left, Mrs. D . . ."

He reaches out of the picture towards Walter who has a card shoe waiting . . .

JACK: "Our end game decides our future—the nature of reality for the aeons ahead—Whether justice triumphs over blind appetite—Or if we're doomed to perpetual self-destruction . . ."

Walter looks directly into Jack's eyes—

WALTER: "Are you going to draw, Jack, or shall I?"

Jack reaches into the shoe and takes a card . . .

He turns the card . . .

It shows Elric in the grip of the Silverskin . . .

The albino struggled hard as his multitude of personalities reached out to absorb him . . .

Elric absolutely entangled in the Silverskin's tentacles....

SILVERSKIN: "Then if you will not help, we'll take you back—back to
our mourning womb ..."

Elric struggles to draw Stormbringer.

ELRIC: **"No, King Silverskin!"**

ELRIC: "It's my doom to die alone and calling out a question—I resist
the claims of history—I have loyalty only to the future ... to my
child and to my cause ..."

The Silverskin's many eyes are horrified ...

SILVERSKIN: "Come, sweetest of my selves—Come into my yearning
heart—come, Elric, come ..."

Elric breaks his arms free—in one hand is the sword—in the other the Horn of Fate—

ELRIC: **"NO!"**

ELRIC: "I feel the polarities reverse! This is my one moment—you shall not absorb me, Eternal Champion—"

Elric drives the Black Sword towards the centre of the Silverskin, even as its tentacles fight against him . . .

ELRIC: *"this* time—"

Elric plunges his sword into the heart of all his other myriad selves and screams with agony as he does so . . .

ELRIC: *"I shall absorb YOU!"*

Aaaaaaaaaaaaaaaaaiiiiiiiiiiiiiiiiiiiiiiiiiiii!!!!!!!!

And all those selves start to pour into the sword . . .

Until the sword glows brilliant, reflective silver—runes still flaring red— pulsing all those personalities, all that unguessable power back up into Elric—so Elric absorbs all aspects of the Eternal Champion back into himself.

Elric is now all glowing reflective silver himself—his ruby eyes glaring from his tortured face—as he absorbs King Silverskin—and lifts his horn to his lips—

ELRIC: "It's done. I am whole again with all my power! The Champion is strong enough to reduce the whole of time to a single perfect moment—*To herald in the dawn!"*

Close-up of Elric blowing the horn—

WAAAAAAAAAA-OOOOOOOOOOOO!
WAAAA-OOOOOOOOOO-aaaaaaa-aaaaaaaa-aaaaaaa-
OOOOOooooooooooooooooooooooooooooooooooooooooooooooo . . .

Enabling the mathematics of the heart to reduce the ultimate equation
to a single elegiac note—

—creating an unrepeatable moment of absolute harmony—a single
chance of redemption for the entire multiverse . . .

The big scene. Elric releases his grip on his pure white sword which rises to-
wards the apex in which a shadowy balance begins to form. In mirror image
(both imitating Craig's last scenes from Stormbringer*) the Elric of Storm-*
bringer *with the Black Sword is seen in an identical posture . . . as both*
swords plunge back into both Elrics and both are then gradually drawn up-
wards to form the Cosmic Balance itself.

—and all living creatures throughout the endless glory of existence . . .

You think you can do all that in two pages? Well, just in case . . . We're
watching all this from the table—Walter, MM, Jack, Colinda, the Rose and
Quelch . . . Elric's now part of the Balance . . . The surviving Chaos Engi-
neers are cheering. Pop and Pearl, now same size, embrace.

BUGGERLY: "Saved! Rose played for our team all along!"

MM hands the Holy Grail to Quelch. It's made out of the Spammer Gain
and all her fishlings. It steams with a rich brew of first-flush Assam tea.

MM: "The machinoix said goodbye. You ordered this . . ."

QUELCH: "At last! A decent cup of Assam . . ."

Apparently oblivious of drinking from the Grail, Quelch sips the tea appreciatively . . .

QUELCH: "Perfection itself!"

QUELCH: "Thanks, pard. You've restored an old man's faith in humanity."

The table's dead now. They're walking out of the Café. It's no longer in Biloxi but in Marrakesh, in the Square of the Dead, where our story began . . .

QUELCH: "We could be in for a few changes, eh?"

ROSE: "Nothing I won't welcome."

WALTER: "*Marrakesh?* Mike, you swore we were going back to Maryland . . ."

MM: "Don't worry, Walter, the pizza's just as good . . . and everything in the world's a plane ride away, these days . . ."

COLINDA: "You'll love it. Best root beer in the multiverse."

JACK: "Routes? They all lead here."

They're lounging at a table overlooking the Square. The awning over the café says Café Terminale. *Quelch still sips with relish from his big cup. The Rose is standing up. The helmet is now sprouting very voluptuously.*

ROSE: "Well, pards, I must be going. I have a universe to re-pot."

QUELCH: "Shall we take my schooner, Rosie?"

She looks at him, grins and winks.

ROSE: "Why not?"

We see Rose and Quelch waving farewell, tiny figures on camels . . .

ROSE: "By the way, Horace, are you any good at gardening?"

Now there's just the four of them sitting round the table. It's sunset and the palms and mountains glow around a glowing city. Another figure's approaching. At first it seems to be a story-teller from the Square. Then we realize it's Moonglum.

MOONGLUM: "Evenin', pards. I thought I'd find you all here."

Moonglum sits down at the table, fanning out a deck of cards.

MOONGLUM: "How about passing the time in a friendly game of chance?"

DUKE ELRIC
(Ridgway)

EPILOGUE—CLOSE RELATIONS

Normandy, Thursday, 18th December, 1039.

A distant figure (it's an aged Isaak) approaches a church. Outside, a very aged monk (from Part One) is ringing a bell.

Old Isaak and old monk are now inside the church. We see books and scrolls shelved in the background.

ISAAK: "Duke Elric spoke of you as a friend . . ."

MONK: "His confessor, at least. Our records show he first came here over two hundred years ago. Raving mad. He claimed to be dreaming *himself*—a dream which was to last another thousand years!" (*pause*) "Too much conscience for a demon, their abbot decided . . ."

MONK (*over flashback*): "He spoke an unknown language. But slowly they communicated. He'd sought and found that horn—but lacked the courage to return to his homeland with it. The brothers learned no more. Our drugs brought him back to health . . ."

Close-ups of the two men. Isaak looks astonished. Monk stares into the middle distance as he speaks, remembering this flashback where two other monks are tending a sickly Elric who lies on a bed in a cell, raving . . .

MONK: "In return, he served our great cause—a knight under the Emperor Charlemagne. They said he was a reincarnation of Roland . . ."

Elric, in helmet and byrnie and other accoutrements of the period, his red eyes blazing, sits a charging white horse, leading his Charlemagnian soldiers into the thick of the battle.

MONK: "We heard only stories of him . . . until he returned to claim his sword . . ."

Another close-up of Isaak and the monk, who still has the haunted look to him as he speaks.

ISAAK: "He had a sister, I heard—?"

MONK: "She wasn't his sister . . ."

ISAAK: "Then, who—?"

MONK: "It's complicated . . ."

ISAAK: "Was she not his kin?"

MONK: "Well, you know—he—she . . ."

ISAAK: "He? She? Which?"

The monk is exasperated, hardly able to blurt out in his confusion what he's trying to say (and doesn't really want to say):

MONK: "She was **him.** He was **her.** They were male and female versions of the same person . . ."

While Isaak looks on in puzzlement the priest holds his head in his hands, sweating . . .

MONK: "And they had offspring . . ."

Isaak is horrified.

ISAAK: "Where are they now? What were they like?"

Monk again looks into the middle distance, unwilling to image what he speaks about. His head is superimposed over a page where two demonic fig-ures—Elric and a woman who has to be his twin—both with blazing red eyes—charge into battle against frightened human figures while overhead fly part of the dragon swarm, the Phoorn, their shadows falling across the battle panorama which is lit by fires from a burning city . . .

MONK: "We can only imagine . . ."

AN END

ASPECTS OF FANTASY (2)

ASPECTS OF FANTASY
(1963)

In this second article in our new series, Michael Moorcock likens the early Gothic writings to drug-induced states, which had a similar effect upon both author and reader. The eighteenth century laid the foundation to many outstanding macabre tales to come.

John Carnell, *Science Fantasy* No. 62, December 1963

2. THE FLOODGATES
OF THE UNCONSCIOUS

TRANCE-INDUCING DRUGS like mescalin, LSD and opium produce in the individual spectacular visions. I have experienced similar visions *without* recourse to drugs, meditation or fasting. I have been awake and conversing rationally while at the same time everything I see has taken on a surrealistic perspective. People's faces have appeared to change; I have had a condensed or extended time sense, heightened sensibility to the point where I feel aware of the individual muscles, nerves and sinews at work, the very blood-cells racing through both my own veins and the veins of whoever has been with me; I have observed people in the minutest detail and their conversation has had profound significance far beyond its intended content.

Secondly, I have at a later stage been overwhelmed by an intense and irrational fear, have found myself running madly upstairs, stumbling, falling—quite unable to control my limbs except by an extreme effort of will. Later still I have lain in the dark surrounded by hallucinations of the utmost horror.

I'm as sane as most; it is simply that my experiences were similar to those of people under the influence of drugs. Thomas de Quincey:

> The unimaginable horror which these dreams of oriental imagery and mythological tortures impressed upon me . . . I was stared at, hooted at, grinned at, chattered at, by monkeys, by paroquets, by cockatoos. I ran into pagodas, and was fixed for centuries at the summit, or in secret rooms; I was the idol; I was the

priest; I was worshipped; I was sacrificed ... I came suddenly upon Isis and Osiris: I had done a deed, they said, which the ibis and the crocodile trembled at. Thousands of years I lived and was buried in stone coffins, with mummies and sphinxes, in narrow chambers at the heart of eternal pyramids. I was kissed, with cancerous kisses, by crocodiles, and was laid, confounded with all unutterable abortions, amongst reeds and Nilotic mud.

(Confessions of an English Opium Eater)

Aldous Huxley:

That chair—shall I ever forget it? Where the shadows fell on the canvas upholstery, stripes of a deep but glowing indigo alternated with stripes of an incandescence so intensely bright that it was hard to believe they could be made of anything but blue fire. For what seemed an immensely long time I gazed without knowing, even without wishing to know, what it was that confronted me. At any other time I would have seen a chair barred with alternate light and shade. Today the percept had swallowed up the concept. I was so completely struck by what I actually saw, that I could not be aware of anything else ... The event was this succession of azure furnace-doors separated by gulfs of unfathomable gentian. It was inexpressibly wonderful, wonderful to the point, almost, of being terrifying. And suddenly I had an inkling of what it must be like to be mad.

(The Doors of Perception)

Both these passages describe drug-induced hallucinations. You have read my experience. I have never in my life taken opium or mescalin. What produced *my* experiences?

In a word—Gothic novels.

It was the first of these experiences that convinced me that fantasy stories, in particular "tales of terror," directly relate to the unconscious mind and that, in the hands of a good writer, such a story can act as a bridge between the conscious and the unconscious, that the world of the Gothic novel and its like is not the external or supernatural world but the *world of the psyche*; for, coupled with a mood of deep concentration and introspection, it was the reading of certain passages in certain Gothic novels (for purposes of research) that induced these hallucinations. I began to get them after a day's hard work and a week of immersion in the Gothics themselves—colours became richer, perspectives changed, sounds and sights took on a deeper significance. I am perhaps more suggestible than most to these books, but the fact remains that they have on different occasions produced varying mental states quite unlike my normal state; almost uncontrollable, extremely terrifying and at the same time marvelously rewarding. Also I have made psychological tests whilst undergoing these hallucinations and find that they have little relation to sex, which leads me to change my earlier opinion that the symbolism of the terror tale was primarily sexual.

So what chords *does* the fantasy tale strike in its readers? Jung was unable to answer this definitely so I am sure I can't. Only by discussing the tales themselves can I hope to help the reader form his own opinion.

Therefore, for me, and I suspect for many other readers, the effective fantasy tale, like an hallucinogenic drug or a nightmare opens the floodgates of the unconscious, releases into the reader's conscious mind a world of experience which, though not recognizably that of the "normal" world, is as real and as relevant to our existence as the world of, say, *Saturday Night and Sunday Morning*.

One of the best Gothic novelists was Mrs. Ann Radcliffe, a respectable, retiring, middle-class lady whose books shocked her husband and became the rage of the circulating libraries in the late eighteenth and early nineteenth centuries.

Her most successful book *The Mysteries of Udolpho*[1] was published in 1794 and had, without doubt, a measurable influence on the work of many later writers, particularly Scott, the Brontës, Dickens, Balzac and Hugo.

Ann Radcliffe specialized in evocative descriptions of natural scenery and architecture, using them to build up her atmosphere of horror. The horrors themselves are not, in fact, as effective as the means she employed to prepare the reader for them. Most of her books, like most of the other Gothic novels, involved a wicked nobleman dwelling in a massive and oppressive Gothic castle, part of which was ruined. The wicked nobleman pursues and incarcerates, incarcerates and pursues the pure heroine through the labyrinthine corridors of his castle until she is finally rescued by the upright hero who is likely to be the true heir of the castle and its lands. This basic plot was, in slightly different forms, virtually the only plot of the Gothics, and the mixture was varied by its choice of supernatural events, although several spectres were always included. Ann Radcliffe was not its inventor (the formula was Fielding's and Richardson's, the setting Walpole's), but she was its greatest exponent and, because of her superior talents, lifted it beyond its melodramatic and sensational origins to form it into something which often comes close to real art. A single illustrative quote is hard to find, but here Radcliffe describes the heroine's first sight of Udolpho:

> Emily gazed with melancholy awe upon the castle . . . for, though it was now lighted up by the setting sun, the Gothic greatness of its features, and its mouldering walls of dark grey stone, rendered it a gloomy and sublime object . . . The light died away on its walls, leaving a melancholy purple tint, which spread deeper and deeper as the thin vapour crept up the mountain, while the battlements above were still tipped with splendour . . . Silent, lonely, and sublime,

---

[1] Everyman Library (2 Vols) Nos. 865–6

it seemed to stand the sovereign of the scene and to frown defiance on all who dared its solitary reign. As the twilight deepened, its features became more aweful in obscurity . . . till its clustering towers were alone seen rising over the tops of the woods . . . The extent and darkness of these tall woods awakened terrific images in her mind . . . [She] soon after reached the castle gates, where the deep tone of the portal bell . . . increased the fearful emotions that had assailed [her] . . . she anxiously surveyed the edifice; but the gloom that overspread it allowed her to distinguish little more than . . . the massy walls of the ramparts, and to know that it was vast, ancient and dreary.

A little heavy-going, perhaps, but the overall effect of *The Mysteries of Udolpho* is one of acute terror and, if deliberately read in this context, an insight into the darker depths of one's own mind. In his introduction to *The Gothic Flame* by Dr. P. Varma (Arthur Barker, 1957), Sir Herbert Read says:

The Gothic castle itself, that formidable place, ruinous yet an effective prison, phantasmagorically shifting its outline as ever new vaults extended their labyrinths, scene of solitary wanderings, cut off from light and human contact, of unformulated menace and the terror of the living dead—this hold, with all its hundred names, now looms to investigators as the symbol of a neurosis; they see it as the gigantic symbol of anxiety, the dread of oppression and of the abyss, the response to the . . . insecurity of disturbed times.

Perhaps the current revival of interest in the tale of terror is also a response to the "insecurity of disturbed times"?

*   *   *

Going on from Radcliffe and the eighteenth century and ignoring the better writers of the horror romance whom I shall deal with in later articles, we come to possibly the greatest of the nineteenth-century authors writing in the direct tradition of Mrs. Radcliffe's school—Edgar Allan Poe.

Poe was evidently far more aware of the true nature of his material than Radcliffe, possibly because his personality was less stable. He is known to have taken opium and, in many of his best tales, to have used his experiences under the drug. Since Poe, also, will be treated in more detail later, I shall deal with him fairly briefly here.

> I learned, moreover, at intervals ... another singular feature of his mental condition. He was enchained by certain superstitious impressions in regard to the dwelling which he tenanted [the House of Usher] ... in regard to an influence whose supposititious force was conveyed in terms too shadowy here to be restated—an influence which some peculiarities in the mere form and substance of his family mansion, had, by dint of long sufferance, he said, obtained over his spirit—an effect which the *physique* of the grey walls and turrets, and of the dim tarn into which they all looked down, had, at length, brought about upon the *morale* of his existence.
>
> (*The Fall of the House of Usher*)

Not one of Poe's best passages, but a good illustration of how he linked the mental states of his characters with their apparently physical environment. It was Ann Radcliffe who taught later writers how to use natural scenery and effects to mirror the mood of their characters and, though less skilled authors overdid this and have continued to overdo it, it is easy to see how the corridors of Udolpho and the House of Usher mirror the secret passages of our own minds, how the labyrinths of these tales are the labyrinths in which we find ourselves running in nightmares, how the oppressive architecture links with the sense of

helpless horror and depression which we all have at times whether
sleeping or waking, how the chasm which Udolpho overhangs or the
tarn above which the House of Usher is suspended, is rarely to be found
in the physical world, yet always to be found in dreams.

It is this gorge into which we fall, bottomless, boundless, dark, unknown and terrifying, when we sleep—the gorge of the human mind.

> We stand upon the brink of a precipice. We peer into
> the abyss—we grow sick and dizzy. Our first impulse
> is to shrink from the danger. Unaccountably, we re-
> main. By slow degrees our sickness and dizziness and
> horror become merged in a cloud of unnamable feel-
> ing. By gradations, still more imperceptible, this cloud
> assumes shape, as did the vapour from the bottle out of
> which arose the genius in the *Arabian Nights*. But out
> of this *our* cloud upon the precipice's edge, there grows
> into palpability, a shape, far more terrible than any ge-
> nius or any demon of a tale, and yet it is but a thought,
> although a fearful one, and one which chills the very
> marrow of our bones with the fierceness of the delight
> in its horror . . . And this fall—this rushing annihila-
> tion—for the very reason that it involves that one most
> ghastly and loathsome of all the most ghastly and
> loathsome images of death and suffering which have
> ever presented themselves to our imagination—for
> this very cause do we now the most vividly desire it.
>
> (*The Imp of the Perverse*)

Poe can speak for himself on that last point, but this passage does
serve to show us how Poe's approach varies from other writers of the
tale of terror, for whereas Radcliffe, and in this century Lovecraft, gave
their terrors supernatural guise, Poe was obsessed with the fears which
sprang directly from the human mind. In those unpleasantly morbid

stories like *The Fall of the House of Usher, The Pit and the Pendulum* and *Descent into the Maelstrom,* most of the horrors stem from *within* the characters, not, as in the usual horror story, from *without.* Lovecraft could describe the *Colour Out of Space* or the *Dunwich Horror,* but he described them as coming from beyond the Earth we know. The affinities between Radcliffe, Poe and Lovecraft show that their inspiration came from the same source, but only Poe was really aware of the fact that he was actually describing certain aspects of his own mind.

I am not, I must admit, so familiar with the work of Lovecraft, since I find most of his stories hard going. He appears to lack the scope of Radcliffe and Poe at their best, but those stories I have read certainly seem to illustrate the point of this article. His hints of lurking horrors on the threshold of our awareness (described, of course, in supernatural terms), his landscapes and set-pieces all show the influence of those earlier writers, as well as being in close affinity with the visions of the mescalin-eater, madman or nightmare-sufferer. His "nightmare landscapes" are, of course, just that.

Though one could find more effective passages in Lovecraft, the following description ties in with Udolpho and Usher and shows Lovecraft using a similar device:

> ... A certain huge, dark church ... stood out with especial distinctness at certain hours of the day, and at sunset the great tower and tapering steeple loomed blackly against the flaming sky. It seemed to rest on especially high ground; for the grimy façade, and the obliquely seen north side with sloping roof and the tops of great pointed windows, rose boldly above the tangle of surrounding ridgepoles and chimney-pots. Peculiarly grim and austere, it appeared to be built of stone, stained and weathered with the smoke and storms of a century or more. The style, so far as the glass could show, was the earliest experimental

form of Gothic revival . . . The longer he watched the
more his imagination worked, till at length he began
to fancy curious things.

(The Haunter of the Dark)

It was, incidentally, the revival of interest in Gothic architecture
which was responsible for the first Gothic novel—Walpole's *Castle of
Otranto.* I shall deal with this aspect later. Several people have pointed
out that the buildings which we term "Gothic" invest in people a
strange, transcendental sensibility often almost as strong as similar feelings released by drugs.

Just as the sight of Gothic architecture releases the images and fears
and fancies lurking beneath our conscious minds, so sleep acts to produce nightmares, opium to bring marvelous dreams, mescalin to alter
our view of the world, or the fantasy tale to give us an insight into our
unconscious lives. The feelings of terror and wonder which these descriptions of the "supernatural" inspire in us are created *not* by the suggestion that there is something "out there" trying to get in, but by the
knowledge that there is something "in there" trying to get out.

There is no doubt of the significance of the fantasy tale in terms of
its often unconscious description of the unconscious mind. This is why
it disturbs and terrifies—because we sense the uncontrollable forces
which are acting upon us, forces which the writer may describe as supernatural but which are, in fact, entirely natural. They are the forces
locked in our own skulls—and there is nothing we can do to exorcize
them.

THE FLANEUR DES ARCADES
DE L'OPERA

THE FLANEUR DES ARCADES DE L'OPERA
(2008)

CHAPTER ONE

In the Luxembourg Gardens

I N ALL THE many cases investigated by Sir Seaton Begg of the Home Office Metatemporal Investigative Agency, one of the most curious concerned his cooperation with his opposite number, Commissaire Lapointe of the Sûreté du Temps Perdu, involving not only the albino gentleman connected to a royal house whom we call "Monsieur Zenith," but members of an infamous terrorist gang, a long dead enemy of Begg's German cousins and the well-known adventuress, Mrs. Una Persson. As Begg's friend, the pathologist Dr. "Taffy" Sinclair, remarked, "for a while it seemed that Chaos, in all its unchained wildness, had been let loose through every region of our vast and complex multiverse, so that even now we cannot be certain whether it was contained or whether we are merely experiencing a moment of relative harmony in a howling cacophony . . ."

"I cannot tell you, my old friend, how delighted I am that you should come over at such short notice."

Lapointe, his assistant LeBec, Taffy and Begg were wandering through the pale gold autumn light of the Luxembourg Gardens. The chestnut trees were shedding dark reds and yellows, and the flower beds were full of beauty on the verge of succumbing to winter. Lapointe had thought it expedient for them to talk in the open air where there was less chance of being overheard.

"The train? Was it comfortable?"

In his light tweed sports jacket, white shirt and well pressed flannels, Lapointe had a bulky, stiff-necked, slightly professorial air, with a great wave of grey hair untidily arranged over his pale forehead. His deep, green eyes, angular features and heavy body gave him the air of a large amiable dinosaur. Begg knew his opposite number had one of the sharpest minds on the Continent. Singlehandedly Lapointe had captured the ex-police inspector turned crook: George Marsden Plummer (alias "Maigret" in France) who had once been Lapointe's chief. Lapointe had also been the one to bring "Fantômas" to book at last. Together he and Begg had tracked down "Jock Collyn," otherwise known as The Master Mummer, and been instrumental in his lingering to this day on Devil's Island.

Inspector LeBec, on the other hand, had no spectacular record but was much admired at the Quai des Orfevriers for his methodology and his coolness under pressure. Small and dark, he seemed permanently and privately amused. He wore a buttoned-up three-piece grey suit and what was evidently an English school tie.

The two Home Office men had come from London via the recently opened Subchannel Excavation whose roads and railway lines now connected the two nations, a material addition to the decades-old Entente Cordiale, an alliance which had been cemented by the signing of a European-wide Mutual Co-operation Pact, which, with the Universal Civil Rights Act, united all the Great Powers, including the Confederated Forty-seven States of America, in one mighty alliance sharing common laws and goals.

"Perfectly, thank you," said Begg, speaking excellent French. Lapointe had put the STP's private express at his disposal. The journey had taken less than an hour and a half from London to Paris. "I must say, Lapointe, that you French chaps have your priorities well in hand—rapid and comfortable transport and excellent food among them. We had a superb lunch en route."

The French detective acknowledged this compliment with a small, self-deprecating shrug.

Taffy, taller than the others, murmured his own discreet appreciation.

"I gather, Dr. Sinclair, that you are recently back from the Republic of Texas?" Lapointe courteously acknowledged the pathologist, whose expertise was internationally famous.

"Indeed." Sinclair removed his wide panama and wiped his glistening head with a large Voysey-patterned Liberty's handkerchief, which seemed an uncharacteristic part of his otherwise muted wardrobe. Save for his taste in haberdashery, no-one would have guessed that during his time at Oxford he had been a leading light in the post-PreRaphaelite revival and that women had swooned over his massive head of hair and melancholy features almost as much as they had over his poetry. Like his friend and colleague, he wore a cream-coloured linen suit, but whereas Begg's tie was a rather flamboyant bow, Sinclair's neck was adorned by his old school colours. Indeed his tie was identical to LeBec's. The two had been contemporaries at Blackfriars School and later had attended the Sorbonne before LeBec, eldest son of a somewhat infamous Aquilonian house, entered the service of the Quai D'Orsay and Sinclair, after a spell in the army, decided to follow his father into medicine and the civil service.

"You are familiar with the shopping arcades which radiate off the Place de l'Opera?" asked Lapointe once they were strolling down a broad avenue of chestnut trees towards the gardens' rue Guynemer entrance. "And you are aware, I am sure, of the reputation the area has at night, where assignations of the heart are pursued, and men and women of a certain inclination are said to come together."

"I have read something of the place," said Begg, while Taffy nodded gravely.

"These arcades are the most complex in Paris, of course, and extend into and beneath the surrounding buildings, in turn becoming a warren of corridors and suites of chambers connected to the catacombs. They have never been fully mapped. It is said that some poor devils have been lost there for eternity, cursed to wander forever beneath the city."

Begg smiled. "I am familiar with Smith's Kitchen in London, which is similarly configured. I know the stories of the arcades, yes. How fanciful they are, I have yet to judge. I know, too, that they were spared destruction by Haussmann, when he was building the boulevards of Paris for Louis Napoleon, because the emperor himself wished to preserve his own somewhat lavish pied-de-terre where he maintained the notorious Comtesse de Gavray."

"Exactly, my friend. Whose favours he was said to share with Balzac the Younger. I gather there was some scandal. Didn't Balzac denounce her as a German spy?"

"In 1876. Yes. It was the end of her career. She fled to Berlin and finished her days in penury. Strangely this present case has echoes of that one."

As he reached the little glass and wrought-iron café across from the Theatre du Marionettes, Lapointe paused. "The coffee here isn't too bad, and I see there is a table just over there where we are unlikely to be disturbed."

With the acquiescence of the others, Lapointe let them seat themselves at the dark-green metal table and signaled for a *serviteur,* who came immediately, recognizing a regular customer. A brief exchange followed. Typically, the Englishmen ordered café crème, and the Frenchmen took theirs espresso. They sat in silence for a little while, admiring the merry-go-round with its vividly painted horses rising and falling in comforting regularity, circling to the tune of a complex steam-driven fairground calliope, as excited little boys and girls waved to waiting parents. The puppet theatre was yet to open and many of the children, Begg knew, would disappear into its darkness soon enough to witness the traditional bloody escapades of Guignol which had entertained French children for the past century or more.

It delighted Begg to see that the same diversions which he had enjoyed as a boy were equally pleasing to this, the first generation of the new century. He was always grateful that his father's diplomatic work had allowed him to make a home in the French capital. For him London and Paris made a natural marriage, if not exactly of opposites, then of complementary personalities. Both had powerful public images and a thousand secrets, not all of them by any means sinister.

Commissioner Lapointe leaned forward so that his voice could only be heard by the other three men at the table. "You have no doubt already reached the conclusion, my friends, that this business concerns the ongoing problems we have in Germany. While the insurgency is generally under control, Hitler's terrorists continue to trouble the German government, and our friends in the Reichstag have asked us for help. In the main we have done our best to remain uninvolved with internal German politics. After defeating Hitler and driving him out of Poland, we were quickly able to support a new democratic government and withdraw our troops to this side of the Rhine. However—" Lapointe shrugged, slowly stirring his coffee.

"Röhm and his Freikorps?" murmured Begg.

"Precisely. They are relatively few, of course. But Röhm's insurgents continue to do considerable damage. They have attacked Wehrmacht barracks, civilian institutions and even targets outside the country. They have set off bombs in public places and continue to violate synagogues and Jewish cemeteries. While Hitler remains at large, insurgent morale remains high and their plans ambitious. Disaffected petites-bourgeoisie for the most part, who had hoped to succeed in war where they had failed in peace. Well, gentlemen, we have reason to believe they are planning an ambitious attack outside Germany's borders. This attack, we think, is aimed at creating a large number of civilian casualties, probably Jewish. And we are fairly certain that it will occur in France, probably in Paris."

"And how can we be of assistance?" asked Begg, clearly puzzled by being asked to engage in what, on the surface, appeared to be primarily an internal matter for the French government.

"In two words, my old friend—" Lapointe glanced around before dropping his voice even lower—"*Monsieur Zenith . . .*"

Now the British investigator understood. He sat back in his chair, his face suddenly grave. From his pocket he took his ancient briar and a tobacco pouch. He began to fill the pipe with dark shag. Taffy Sinclair, too, was frowning. A profound silence surrounded the four men. At last Inspector LeBec spoke. "He is known to be in Paris. Indeed, he has been here for some time. A familiar figure in the Opera Arcades. Since his pardon, he has exposed himself quite openly, yet, whenever our people attempted to speak to him, *pouf*! He is gone like smoke."

"Eventually, it became clear to us that we would be better engaged in keeping watch on him," continued Lapointe. "For some months he has continued the same habits. Every morning between eleven and one he appears in the Passage D'Iappe wearing perfect morning dress. He takes his coffee at L'Albertine. He reads his newspaper: *Le Figaro,* usually, but sometimes the *New York Herald Tribune.* He strolls. He makes a small purchase or two. He enters a bookshop and inspects a few volumes. He has even been known to visit Larnier's Waxworks. Occasionally, he buys a book, usually a classic of some kind. Then at lunchtime he either strolls towards the Quartier Latin, taking the Pont St-Michel, where he eats lunch at Lipp's or he enters one of the more shadowy branches of the arcades and—vanishes! Sometimes he can be seen again in the afternoon making his way to the Louvre, where he inspects a different exhibit each day, though he seems to favour Da Vinci's *Portrait of a Young Jew in Female Dress.* Then he returns to the arcades and, yes, he disappears again."

"He speaks to no-one?"

"Oh, he passes the time of day with any number of persons. He is politeness itself, especially where a lady is concerned. He has conversed with more than one of our own people, usually realizing immediately who they are. He is the very model of a gentlemanly *flaneur,* whiling away his hours in what some would call a desultory way. He buys his cigarettes at Sullivan's and his newspaper from the same kiosk at the south-eastern corner of the arcades. He carries a cane in ebony and silver. His gloves are always that perfect shade of lavender, matching his cravat. His coat is cut just so, his hat sits at just such an angle, and in his buttonhole always the same crimson rosebud emphasizing those blood red eyes of his. Women, of course, are fascinated by him. Yet, with a recent exception, he keeps no regular engagements with anyone, though he enjoys a little flirtation over an apéritif, perhaps. He tips well and is much liked by the staff wherever he takes refreshment. Sometimes a Lagonda limousine calls for him at the north-west entrance. We have been able to trace the car to the general area of Clichy, but all we know is that it is driven by a Japanese chauffeur and is garaged in rue Clément in the name of a Monsieur Amano. There its batteries are recharged. Everything is in order. The Lagonda has not left Paris since we have been observing it."

"And as far as you know neither has Monsieur Zenith?"

"Exactly."

"Where does he go at night?" Dr. Sinclair wanted to know.

"That's the thing, old man," said LeBec in English, "we simply can't find out!"

"It is as if he becomes invisible from the evening hours until mid-morning," added Lapointe. "Then, suddenly, he appears in the Opera Arcades, perfectly dressed and poised, as ever. Even if we had a cause to arrest him, which we have not, he would still evade us. Indeed if he had not been seen in the company of a suspected Nazi agent, we would not devote so much interest to him. He is a decorated war hero, after all, leading a Polish electric cavalry brigade during the recent conflict. But sadly his actions suggest that he is helping organize whatever Nazi plot is about to be unleashed on honest civilians. His name has come up more than once in various coded messages we have intercepted. Sometimes he is merely Monsieur Z, sometimes 'Zenith' and sometimes 'Zodiac.' All versions of his own given name, of course. There is no doubt at all that he is Count Rudolf Zoran von Bek, descendant of the infamous 'Crimson Eyes' who terrorized the people of Mirenburg and London in the course of the last century. He renounced his title as hereditary ruler of Wäldenstein. So as for Hitler's intention to restore Zenith as puppet monarch there, had his plans for the conquest of Europe been successful, it is surely nonsense!"

"He has never regretted giving up his title," mused Sir Seaton. From his mouth now issued alarming quantities of dark smoke as he fired up his old pipe. "I am still curious as to why he moved his base from London to Paris. He was even rumoured to have been seen recently in Berlin. It is as if he were fascinated by our friend Herr Hitler.

This is not the first time he and that gentleman have been linked in various incarnations across the multiverse."

"Perhaps he agrees with Hitler's ideas?" ventured Lapointe. But Begg shook his head.

"They are scarcely 'ideas.' They are the opinions of beerhall braggarts of the kind commonly found throughout the world. They emerge to fill a vacuum. They might appeal to an uneducated and unemployed labourer, a dispossessed shopkeeper or disenchanted professional soldier like Röhm—even some brainless and inbred titled fool. But Zenith is none of those things. He is both well educated and of superior intelligence. His only weakness is his thirst for danger, for the thrill which fills the veins with pounding blood and which takes one's mind off the dullness of the day-to-day." Begg knew exactly what moved his old adversary. The expression on Dr. Sinclair's face suggested that he thought the metatemporal investigator's remark might well have been a self-description. Begg continued, "He would only ally himself with such a creature if it somehow suited his own schemes. Years ago after he was rescued from secret police headquarters where he had been imprisoned and tortured for his resistance to the dictator, he gave me his solemn promise that he was renouncing his old ways and from then on would only steal from the thieves, as it were, and contribute most of his gains to excellent causes, some of which would founder completely if he didn't help. And the Polish military will tell you how he equipped that electric tank division from his own pocket!"

"So you think he is planning a job in Paris?" asked the commissioner. He allowed a small smile to flicker across his face. "After all, we are not short of the undeserving rich . . ."

"Perhaps. Or he could be diverting himself here while all the time what he is doing at night is the important thing. Eh?" From under his lowering, sardonic brow, Sir Seaton returned Lapointe's smile. "Might he be making himself so public that all our attention is drawn to his flaneurism, and we ignore his true activities?"

"What do you suggest? We need to know details of Hitler's plans soon, Sir Seaton. We must anticipate and counter whatever terror the Nazi insurgents intend to unleash."

"Naturally you must. What else can you tell me?"

"Only that the adventuress Mrs. Una Persson recently took rooms above the arcades shortly after I contacted you. For the last three days she has been seen in the gardens walking her two cats, one grey and one black Oriental shorthair. She is a known associate of Monsieur Zenith."

"Of him and others," agreed Begg, his eyes narrowing in an expression of reminiscence. "And does she have a female companion, perhaps? A Miss Cornelius?"

"Not as far as we know."

Sinclair seemed surprised. His eyes darted from Lapointe to Begg and then to LeBec, who shrugged.

"Mrs. Persson has been seen talking to Zenith," LeBec offered. "Yesterday she had lunch with him at L'Albertine. We had a lip reader eating at a nearby table. Zenith mentioned Hitler and Röhm. He might have spoken of an explosive charge in Paris. Unfortunately we did not learn where. She said that she had investigated a site where a bomb would create the most damage. So certain of those among our superiors are now convinced they are working together for the Nazi insurgents."

Lapointe interrupted rapidly. "Of course, I find that impossible to believe." He shrugged. "But I, as do we all, have certain bosses owing their jobs more to their connections than their native abilities, who insist on believing Zenith and Mrs. Persson are in league with Hitler and his underground army. It could be, perhaps, that they are working for themselves and that they have plans which Hitler's activities will facilitate. My guess is that some treasure is involved, for it is not Zenith's habit to dabble in civilian politics. At least as far as I know. Not so, of course, Mrs. Persson. Is there a way you could find out any more, Sir Seaton? Something I could take to my superiors which will put me onto the real business Zenith has in Paris? Whatever that may be."

Sir Seaton finished his café crème, smiling out at a group of little boys and girls running with fixed attention towards the pleasure of the carousel.

"I could ask him," he said.

CHAPTER TWO

A Conversation at L'Albertine

Inevitably Seaton Begg met his albino cousin close to the noon hour in the Arcades de l'Opera which branched, eight galleries, off a central court containing a paved piazza and an elaborate fountain. He appeared almost by magic, smiling courteously and lifting his hat in greeting. Impeccably well-mannered, Zenith, of course, was incapable of ignoring him.

"Bonjour, cher cousin!" The albino raised his own tall grey hat. "What a pleasure to come upon you like this! We have a great deal to talk about since our last meeting. Perhaps you would be good enough to take a cup of coffee with me at L'Albertine?"

After they dispensed with their hats and ordered, Count Zenith leaned back in his chair and moved his ebony cane in an elegant, economic gesture in the direction of a beautiful young woman, wearing a long, military-style black coat and with a helmet of raven black hair, walking two cats in the sunny gardens at the centre of the arcades. He gave no indication that he was already acquainted with the woman who was, of course, Mrs. Una Persson. "Has anyone, I wonder, ever really tried to imagine what it must be like to have the mind of a beast, even a domesticated beast, like one of those exquisite cats? I think to enter such a brain, however small, would be to go utterly mad, don't you, Sir Seaton?"

"Quite." The Englishman smiled up at a pretty waitress (for which L'Albertine in the morning was famous) and thanked her as she laid out the coffee things. "I have heard of certain experiments in which a beast's brain has been exchanged with that of a human being, but I don't believe they have ever been successful. Though," and in this he was far more direct than was his usual habit, "some say that Adolf Hitler, the deposed Chancellor of Germany, succeeded and that he did indeed go quite mad as a result. Certainly his insolent folly in attacking three great Empires at once would indicate the theory perhaps has some substance!"

Only by the slightest movement of an eyebrow did Zenith indicate his surprise at Begg's raising this subject. He said nothing for a moment before mentioning how the Russo-Polish empire was already at the point of collapse. His own Middle European seat remained part of that sphere of influence, as Begg knew, and the fact was considered a source of some distress to the albino.

"As one who showed such courage on their side during the war, you cannot think Hitler should have been encouraged to attack the 'alliance of eagles'?" Begg offered. "The other Great Powers have since made an oath to protect the Slavic empire. Perhaps you feel that we have not been more resolute in tracking down the Hitler gang? I cannot believe you share their views."

"My dear Begg, the deposed Chancellor was a barrack-room lawyer supported by a frustrated military bully, a plump bore with aristocratic pretension and a third-rate broadcasting journalist!" References to Röhm, Goering and Goebbels, whose popular radio programme was thought to have helped Hitler to power. "It was a matter of duty for anyone of taste to frustrate his ambitions. He was warned often enough by the Duma, the Assembly and your Parliament. His refusal to sign the articles of confederation was the last straw. He should have been stopped then, before he was ever allowed to marshal his land leviathans and aerial battleships. As it was, it should have taken three days, not a year, to defeat him. And now we have the current situation where he and his riff-raff remain at large, doubtless somewhere in Bavaria, and far too many of our armed forces, as well as those of Germany herself, are engaged in putting a stop to his Freikorps' activities. I understand that some fools in the French foreign service think I yearn to 'free' my ancestral lands from the Pan-Slavic yoke, but believe me I have no such dream. If I were to deceive myself that the people were free under my family's reign, I would deserve the contempt of every realist on the planet. And if some self-esteeming coxcombs on the Quai D'Orsay continue to believe I would ally myself with degenerate opportunists, I shall, in my own time, seek them out and require them to repeat their presumptions."

Begg permitted himself a small smile of acquiescence. He had needed only this statement to confirm his understanding. But what was Zenith doing here in Paris keeping such a strange, yet regular schedule? He knew that there was little chance of the albino offering him an explanation. All he had done was rule out the theory, as his French opposite number had hoped, of certain under-admired civil servants at the Quai d'Orsay. He regretted that he was not on terms of such intimacy with Mrs. Persson. Although unlikely, she could be allying herself with the Hitler gang to further her own schemes.

Of course Zenith had said nothing of any collaboration between himself and the Englishwoman, though it was probably not the first time he and she had worked together. Zenith required a great deal of money with which to maintain his lifestyle and finance his favoured causes. He employed at least six Japanese servants of uncommon loyalty and proficiency and maintained several houses in the major cities of Europe and the Côte d'Azur. Though he had received an amnesty from the European Alliance after the war, he remained wanted by the police in certain countries, especially the American Confederation, yet lived elegantly in such insouciant openness that he had only occasionally been captured.

The secret of Zenith's great success was that he understood the psychology of his opponents marginally better than they understood his. Thus his penchant for openness and his willingness to depend entirely on his own quick wits should he ever be in danger. One day, Begg hoped, that cool intelligence would be employed entirely on the side of the law. He remained convinced of Zenith's highly developed sense of honour, which meant the albino never lied to those he himself respected.

Moreover, Zenith was equally hated and feared by the criminal classes. That ebony stick of his hid a slender sword remarkable in that it was black and carved with certain peculiar scarlet markings which gave the appearance of moving whenever the blade was unsheathed.

In the old days Begg had pursued Zenith across the multiverse more than once and knew that sometimes the sword became an altogether larger weapon, sometimes carried in an instrument case of some kind. Zenith was a skilled musician, as expert in the classical cello and violin as he was with the popular guitar. Begg knew also that more than once Zenith's opponents had been found dead, drained in some terrible way not only of blood but of their very life-force. Underworld legend suggested that Zenith was a kind of vampire, drawing his considerable physical power from the souls of his enemies.

At that moment any casual customer of the salon would have seen one elegant man of the world in amiable conversation with another. An observer might have noted that both seemed to be taking an admiring interest in the tall woman walking, *à la* Colette, her two Oriental cats in the noon sunlight sparkling through the waters of the central fountain where classical marble merfolk paid homage to a Neptune whose trident was green with verdigris. The spraying water formed a blur of rainbow colour giving the woman an almost unearthly appearance as she passed by. She stood for a while staring thoughtfully into the middle distance seemingly utterly oblivious of the two men.

Begg smiled to himself, well aware that this was Mrs. Persson's characteristic way of taking stock of those she believed were watching her. It had the effect of disconcerting any observer and causing them to turn their gaze away. Even though she aroused no such response in Begg or Zenith, whom she recognized, nonetheless it seemed even to them that somehow she stepped through the shimmering wash of colour and, with her cats, disappeared.

"You are acquainted, I know, with Mrs. Persson." Begg lowered his voice. "The Quai d'Orsay, if not the Quai des Orfevriers, are convinced that she works for the German insurgency. I would be surprised if it's true. I thought her nature too romantic to let her fall in with such a gang."

"Mrs. Persson rarely confides in me." Monsieur Zenith raised one finger as a signal for the waiter to bring him a drink. "Will you join me, Begg? Is it too early for an Armagnac?"

When the detective acquiesced, Zenith raised a second finger and made a small gesture. The waiter nodded. Zenith watched with approval as the *serviteur* mixed his absinthe and placed two specially formed pieces of sugar in the saucer, while Begg received a generous measure of St-Aubyn. It was rarely his habit to drink his favourite Special Reserve before lunch, but he was unusually anxious to remain on agreeable terms with his old opponent. Zenith appeared to live chiefly on Turkish ovals and absinthe.

"Would you permit me, cousin, to ask you a rather direct question?" he inquired after a couple of appreciative sips.

"How could I refuse?" A smile crossed Zenith's handsome lips. Clearly this approach amused him, and Begg knew he desired amusement almost as much as he required action to relieve his ennui.

"I have to assume that your business in Paris has something to do with the present situation in Germany. I am also curious to know what Mrs. Persson's association with the Germans might mean."

"Any confidence Mrs. Persson chooses to share with me must remain just that." Zenith's voice sharpened a little. "Naturally the British and French are in haste to conclude their present problems with Colonel Hitler, but, while I wish them well, you must know—"

"Of course." Begg regretted his directness. He suspected he had offended his cousin whose sense of decorum was if anything somewhat exaggerated. But there was no retreat now. "I suppose I am asking your help. There is some suggestion that many innocent lives are at stake."

"My dear Begg, why should you and I care if a few bourgeois more or less are gone from central Paris by next Sunday." Monsieur Zenith finished his absinthe. He removed a large, crisp note from his slender case, laid it on the table and stood up. "And now, if you will forgive me, I have some business which cannot wait."

Begg rose, trying to frame some kind of apology or even protestation but for once was at a loss. With his usual litheness and speed,

Zenith slipped his hat from the shelf and with a perfunctory bow strolled towards the exit. Cursing himself for his uncharacteristic impatience, Begg watched his relation depart.

Only as he took up his own broad-brimmed hat did he allow a small smile to appear on his face while under his breath he offered a heartfelt "Merci beaucoup."

CHAPTER THREE

Into the Labyrinth

Commissaire Lapointe had set his men in waiting for M. Zenith, and the albino was followed once again, and once again, as his old colleague was bound to admit to Begg, they had lost him. Mrs. Persson, too, was gone. The four metatemporal detectives met that afternoon in Lapointe's rather grand offices overlooking the Seine.

"She was last seen visiting Caron's print shop in that section of the arcades known as La Galerie de l'Horloge. But she was never seen emerging. Two of our fellows entered on a pretext just as old Caron was closing for lunch. The shop is small. It has long been suspected as a place of illegal assignations concerning the Bourse and the arms trade. There is an even smaller room behind it. Neither Mrs. Persson nor the trio of men were to be found. My chaps did, however, discover a good excuse for making a further visit to Caron's. He also specializes, it appears, in a particularly unsavoury form of pornography in which Nazi insurgents are portrayed in acts of torture or worse with their victims. The photographs are almost certainly authentic. Caron made an error. He omitted to hide the photographs in his office when our men entered. So although they pretended to notice nothing, it will be possible for us to stage a raid, ostensibly by that of the regular vice department, to see what else we can discover. Would you and Dr. Sinclair care to accompany us?"

"I would be unable to resist such an invitation," said Begg. Sinclair assented by lowering his magnificent head.

"I think you are right, old friend, in your interpretation of Monsieur Zenith's communication," added Lapointe. "Not only will Hitler's plot be realized in a crowded part of Paris, it will occur before next Sunday."

"So he suggested. But whether Mrs. Persson is party to this plot, we still do not know. The sooner we can question her, I think, the better."

"Precisely!" Lapointe inspected his watch. "Come, gentlemen. A powerful car awaits us! Her batteries are charged and ready!"

So it was that the four men accompanied by two uniformed sergeants arrived at the Galerie de l'Horloge with its magnificent glass, wrought-iron roofs and ornate gas lamps, its rows of small shops on either side. They crowded into M. Caron's little establishment carrying a search warrant on the excuse that he was known to be selling forbidden material.

Begg felt almost sorry for the short, plump, grey-haired print seller, who shivered in terror at the understanding he faced possible arrest. When, however, the material, which was the excuse for the raid, was revealed, Begg's sympathy dissipated. These were almost certainly pictures taken from the infamous Stadelheim fortress where prisoners were tortured, humiliated and subjected to unmentionable sexual horrors. Caron swore that he was not responsible for the material being in his office. "It was the woman, I assure you, gentlemen. The English woman. She knows—she . . ." And the little man broke down weeping.

It did not take long to elicit from the print seller the secret of Mrs. Persson's ability to vanish. Behind a large cabinet of prints, he revealed another door with steps leading down into dank darkness which echoed as if into the infinite cosmos. "She—she insisted, messieurs. She knew my shop had once been a gate into the labyrinth. It is by no means the only one leading from the arcades. As I am sure you are aware, the labyrinth has long served as a sanctuary for those who do not wish to be apprehended for a variety of reasons. I wanted nothing to do with it, thus the cabinet pushed against the wall, but the Englishwoman—she knew what was hidden. She demanded to be shown the gate." Again he began to weep. "She knew about my—little business. She threatened to expose me. The photographs. I was greedy. I should have known not to trust such degenerates."

Commissaire Lapointe was counting the large denomination banknotes he had discovered in the old man's safe. "Degenerates who were apparently helping to make you rich, m'sieu! We also know about your arms brokering." He replaced the money in the safe and locked it, pocketing the key. "Have you told us everything? Have the passages been used by members of the German 'underground'? Is it they who gave you the photographs? In exchange for guns?"

"I don't know who they were. They appeared in this room one day, having pushed aside the cabinet. It's true they had come to know of me through my interest in perfectly legal discontinued ordnance. They supplied the photographs in return for using the door occasionally. They were foreign civilians, they assured me. They spoke poor French, but I could not recognize the accents. As for the woman, she came and went only by day. She only occasionally used my premises out of normal hours. I never saw her with anyone else. She was never below for very long. This is, I promise you, the longest she has ever been d-down there . . ." With a shudder he turned his back on the mysterious doorway.

"Well," Lapointe decided, "we shall have to wait for her, I think. Meanwhile, m'sieu, you will be charged with distributing pornography. Take him away."

After the terrified proprietor had been led off still sniveling, the metatemporal detectives replaced the door and cabinet exactly as they had discovered it and settled down to await Mrs. Persson's return. But the afternoon turned to evening, hours after the print seller would have closed his shop, and still she made no appearance.

Eventually LeBec was dispatched to Mrs. Persson's apartments and soon returned to report that they were unoccupied save for two somewhat hungry and outraged Siamese cats. "I fed them and cleaned their litter, of course, but . . ." He shrugged.

This news brought a look of concern to Begg's aquiline features. "I think I know Mrs. Persson pretty well. She would not desert her cats, especially without making arrangements to have them fed. She has not only broken her usual habits, but perhaps not willingly."

"My God, Begg! Do you mean she has been captured by whoever it was she has been seeing in the labyrinth? Murdered. By Zenith, perhaps? Could he be playing a double game?"

"Possibly, old man. Instinct tells me that if she is not found soon, she will be in no condition to help us with our enquiries."

"Maybe her paymasters have turned against her? Or Zenith has betrayed her?" Lapointe drew a deep breath of air.

"Monsieur le Commissaire, time is in all likelihood running out for Mrs. Persson, if she still lives. We could be further away than we thought from discovering which public place is under threat. And we have, if Monsieur Zenith told me what I think, only three more days at most before they strike! Come on, gentlemen! Help me shift his cabinet."

The doorway once again revealed, Begg took a small but powerful electric lantern from his overcoat pocket. With a serviceable Webley .45 revolver in his other hand, he led the way down into the echoing darkness. The two sergeants were left behind to guard the entrance.

From somewhere below came a slow, rhythmic, tuneful booming, as of some great clock. Familiar to three of the detectives, the sound caused in each man a thrill of horror. For a second Begg hesitated. Then he continued down the long flight of stone steps which revealed, by the marks in the mould which grew inches thick upon them, recent usage.

Only LeBec had never before heard the thrumming sound. "What on earth is it?" he enquired of Sinclair.

The pathologist drew his brows together, clearly wondering if he should reply. Then he spoke rapidly and quietly: "Well, firstly, old man, it is not exactly *of* our earth. It is what we, who have traveled frequently between the worlds, sometimes refer to as the Cosmic Regulator. Others know it as the Grand Balance. I have heard it more than once but have never seen it. There are many conflicting descriptions. Perhaps every person who has seen it has imposed their own image upon it. The Regulator is said to lie at the very centre of the multiverse, if the multiverse can be said to possess a centre."

"Have you ever known anyone who has seen it?" whispered LeBec, wiping cold sweat from his brow. He had only recently been transferred to the STP.

Sinclair nodded. "I believe both Begg and Lapointe have set eyes on it, but even they, articulate as they are, have never described it. It is often represented in mythological iconography as a kind of scale, with one side representing Chaos and the other Law, but no-one knows its true form, if it has one."

"Law and Chaos? Are those not Zoroastrian conceptions? The forces which war for control of the world?"

"So far no-one has ever gained power over the Balance, but should someone eventually succeed it will mean the end of time but not of consciousness. If Chaos or Law controls existence, we shall all *continue to live at the exact moment prior to the extinction of everything*. For eternity! Or so the theory goes. But there will always be madmen to challenge that conception, to believe that by controlling the Cosmic Balance they can exert their *own* desired reality upon the multiverse. Heaven help us if Hitler and his lunatics have in mind such an attempt!"

Only half comprehending this idea, LeBec firmed his shoulders and continued to follow Begg's thin ray of light down into the sonorous darkness.

Chapter Four

The Roads Between the Worlds

As they reached the bottom of the steps, they found themselves on uneven flagstones peering through a series of vaults supported by ancient pillars.

"No doubt," suggested Sinclair, "these are your famous Parisian catacombs?"

"Possibly. I am not familiar with every aspect of them." LeBec peered into the rustling darkness.

The strange, distant booming continued. Was the noise mechanical or natural? Lapointe and Begg both cocked their heads to listen. The echoes resounding through the vaults made it almost impossible to determine their source. At one moment Sinclair thought it might be water, at another, some sort of engine. But he was also of a disposition to discount his own metaphysical speculation.

The vaults seemed endless, and their darkness sucked the light from Begg's lantern, yet the detective continued to lead the way as if he had some idea where an exit might be.

"The arcades above us are a maze," remarked Lapointe, "which to some degree duplicate this second maze below."

"Remarkable," murmured Begg. "I had some idea of what to expect but did not realize we were so close to the Regulator. This is not the first time I have used such a gate myself to move between one reality and another. But I have never before felt so near the centre. What about you, Lapointe?"

"I must admit I have heard it before only as a very distant echo," replied the Frenchman. "Until now I have used mechanical means to negotiate the spaces between realities. We are issued with Roburian speedshells by the department. Naturally, old friend, I knew that you had not always taken advantage of such vehicles . . ."

"One learns," the detective muttered to himself. "One learns." His progress seemed erratic and without logic as he moved backwards and forwards, then side to side, keeping the sound constant at a certain distance, treading a trail which only he could perceive.

Suddenly a silvery light appeared ahead.

"Can it be possible that the Arcades de l'Opera lead directly to the roads between the worlds?"

Hearing this, Sinclair gave an involuntary shudder.

Above them the great arches grew taller and taller until they were impossibly high, no longer structures of human architecture but part of a natural vault which had become one with the night itself.

All four men gasped and stopped in their tracks as Begg's lantern revealed a long, twisting pathway which seemed to vanish into infinity. Above them, as well as below them, were myriad paths, crossing and recrossing. And on some could be distinguished tiny figures, not all of them human, walking back and forth along the causeways.

When Sir Seaton Begg turned to address his fellow detectives his eyes were glistening with tears.

"Gentlemen," he whispered, dousing the lantern, "I believe we have discovered the roads between the worlds!"

Their eyes soon became accustomed to the light which emanated from the moonbeam roads themselves. Paths stretched in every possible direction. The legendary trails which led to all possible planes of the multiverse.

"I have dreamed of this discovery," said Begg. "On occasion I have glimpsed these roads as I passed from one aspect of reality to another, but I never suspected I would ever discover access to them, particularly by accident. Just think: the gateway has existed in Paris since the beginning of time, their patterns perhaps unconsciously imitated by the architects who designed the city above. Our mythologies and folk-tales have hinted at this, of course, through sensational tales. Yet they hardly prepare one for the reality. Is this Zenith's and Mrs. Persson's secret, do you think?"

"And is it also Hitler's?" asked Lapointe grimly. "Are his ambitions greater than we ever expected?"

Dwarfed by the vast network of moonbeam roads, the detectives were frozen in their uncertainty. There were no maps, no evident routes to follow. They had made an extraordinary discovery!

"At least it is no longer a mystery as to how Zenith was able to evade our men. And Mrs. Persson also. How long have they known of this route?" LeBec wondered.

Begg shook his head slowly. "I believe Mrs. Persson has probably been using these roads for a very long time. Yet it is my guess that she did not come this far voluntarily."

"How on earth can you make that supposition, Begg?" enquired Lapointe.

"Her cats," said Begg. "I know she would never have left her cats unattended. She would have brought them with her, or she would have made arrangements for them to be looked after. No, gentlemen, if she was not faced with an overwhelming emergency, I believe Mrs. Persson was lured down here and then made a prisoner."

"By Zenith?"

"Possibly."

"If not by Zenith, then by whom?"

"By Hitler. Or one of his people." Begg placed his foot firmly upon the road which led away into the darkness. There seemed nothing below them but more roads on which the tiny wayfarers came and went.

"How do you know she came this way, old man?" Taffy Sinclair wished to know.

"I have only instinct, Taffy. An instinct honed, I might say, by a lifetime spent traveling between the worlds."

And steadily, still unseen, came the booming of that unearthly Balance.

CHAPTER FIVE

An Unexpected Newcomer

With the familiar world far behind them, Begg and his fellow detectives were by now crossing a long, sinuous path from which gleamed a faint silvery light.

"What surprises me," said Lapointe, "is why so few people have reported finding this entrance to the moonbeam roads."

"I suspect because it is not always open," Begg speculated. "If Mrs. Persson came this way and was abducted, perhaps she opened the gate but had no time to close it. My guess is that Hitler's men, with whom she was clearly involved in some way, stumbled on the road and bribed Caron, who had already sold them arms, with those filthy photographs. No doubt they also paid M. Caron to let them know when she next planned to use his shop. Your men said they saw others enter the shop and not emerge, eh?"

"Three of them. Isn't it possible Mrs. Persson unwittingly led them here?"

"Impossible to say, Lapointe. I am hoping that question will shortly be solved!"

"But how do you know we are even on the right road?"

Begg pointed downward. Stretching ahead of them the others now detected the faintest of glowing pale traces, like ghostly drops of blood.

"What is it?" Lapointe wanted to know.

"I believe those frauds of mystics like to call it ectoplasm," said Begg, "but I prefer to think of it as the traces left by each human soul as it passes through the world—or, in this case, between them. Only those 'old souls' like Mrs. Persson, who has moved for so long between planes and has developed a form of longevity we might call immortality, leave such clear traces." His smile was grim. "We are still on her trail."

Only when he looked back, did Taffy Sinclair see, not unexpectedly, similar phosphorescent traces running behind them. And he knew for certain who had left those.

After walking a bit further, when the booming of the Balance seemed closer, Sinclair realized they had left the moonbeam roads and were once again passing through a more earthly sequence of vaulted chambers. Still the electric lamp was in Begg's left hand. And still his right hand gripped his service revolver. Was it his imagination, the Home Office pathologist asked himself, or was there something familiar about the smell of the air? Was it pine trees? Impossible!

"Where are we?" enquired Lapointe in a whisper.

"If I am not mistaken, my old friend," answered the Englishman, "we are somewhere in the Bavarian mountains. Probably near a place called Berchtesgaden. Either that, or my nose deceives me!"

"So we were right!" LeBec exclaimed. "Mrs. Persson *is* working for the German insurgents!"

"That, Inspector LeBec," responded Begg, "remains to be determined."

Soon the ground began to slope upward, and they heard voices loud enough to drown out the chiming Balance. Unmistakably speaking German, the loudest of them had a distinct Austrian accent.

Sir Seaton doused his lamp but did not return his revolver to his pocket.

The unseen Austrian's voice rose with excitement. "Victory is in our grasp, my friends. Our army is passing through the Eagle Gate as we speak, to assemble in the Great Siegfried Cavern, where they await our signal. Those degenerate fools thought they had defeated us, reduced us to a mere rabble. But they did not reckon with our heritage, the ancient Nordic secrets locked deep within our Bavarian homeland. The Hollow Earth theory has been proven a scientific fact. You have done well, Frau Persson, leading us to this road. We should have been sad if you were to become the subject of the next set of pictures sold in Herr Caron's shop. By next Saturday the course of history will be changed for ever. We shall strike a blow against the Jewish race from which it will never recover. And if you continue to cooperate, you shall witness my becoming world leader, master of time and space. You will make a fitting consort. Together we shall rule the universe!"

They heard only a faint reply. But the Austrian, evidently Colonel

Hitler, continued his monologue unchecked. He hardly understood the nature of his own situation, so blinded was he by petty dreams of power and banal notions of his own superiority. A typical megalomaniac. Yet why on earth would a woman of Una Persson's intelligence and integrity lend herself to such evil folly?

Using the ancient columns as cover, the four crept closer. In a circle of light stood the figures of a short fat man, a squat military type with a hideously disfigured face, another with gaunt, skeletal features and a black medical boot. To one side of these stood a tall, lugubrious looking individual and another man of medium height with a short, dark "Charlie Chaplin" moustache and a lock of greasy hair falling over one eye. They were recognized immediately from their "Wanted" posters. Here was the entire über-heirarchy of the Hitler gang.

Three more revolvers were now drawn to join Begg's, and all four detectives advanced. This was their chance to capture all the leaders of the German insurgency.

Mrs. Persson, seated at ease on a chair to one side of the main group, was the first to notice them.

"Raise your hands!" Begg barked in German, motioning with his Webley. "You are all under arrest."

"Thunder and lightning!" The tall man, whom they recognized as Captain Hess, one of Hitler's closest co-conspirators, made a movement to his belt. But Lapointe crossed quickly and placed his hand on the man's arm.

Colonel Hitler glowered, his tiny blue eyes points of almost insane rage. "How did you—?"

"Cross from one plane of the multiverse to another? The same way Mrs. Persson did. Indeed, she led us to you . . ."

"But only a few of us knew the secret!" Herman Goering, the fat Nazi, looked rapidly from face to face. "Zenith swore—"

"So Zenith is in league with you!" Lapointe looked almost disappointed. "Well, he, too, will be arrested in good time."

"But I am surprised, Mrs. Persson, that you should associate yourself with such scum. Enemies of all that is civilized . . ." Begg shook his head.

Una Persson stood up. Her beautiful face was an icy mask and her eyes showed no expression. "Ah, Sir Seaton." Her voice mocked him. "So you are, like so many of your kind, the sole arbiter of what is civilized."

"Englishman, *we* are the ones who will save everything valuable in civilization!" The gaunt man with the medical boot was Herr Goebbels, the journalist. "Without Germany there would be no civilization. No music, no art, no poetry. All that is best in your own country is the creation of the Nordic soul. All that threatens you, from without and within, is also Jewish. By saving Europe from the Jews, we shall establish a new Golden Age across our Continent. Even the Slavs will welcome this renaissance and willingly join in. Soon we shall be able to manipulate the very stuff of Creation."

Unthinking, a furious Taffy Sinclair took a step closer to the crazed creature. "I find you unconvincing, Colonel Hitler. You would establish this new civilization by blowing up innocents and throwing the whole of our world into turmoil?"

The hideously scarred Captain Erich Röhm laughed in Sinclair's face. "Only through blood and iron will Europe be cleansed. I am a soldier. I know nothing but the art of battle. And even I understand how the Jews continue to corrupt political and cultural life! Martin Luther warned us. So, too, have a succession of popes and bishops. Not only do Jews refuse the true messiah, they wish to wipe all trace of Jesus Christ from the world! Once the warriors of Europe rose up to save Christendom from destruction. Now we rise again to mount our great crusade against the sons of Abraham. By working against us, gentlemen, you are making a terrible mistake. Join us! The Holy Grail itself will soon be in our hands. He who holds the Grail controls the Balance and therefore the universe itself!"

"You are as mad as I understood you to be, messieurs." Lapointe drew a set of handcuffs from his overcoat pocket and advanced towards the glowering Hitler. "Now, if you will kindly—"

A shot rang out from the shadows, and the revolver went spinning from Lapointe's grasp. Another shot and LeBec clutched his right shoulder. Blood began to seep through his fingers.

"Drop your weapons!" came a cold commanding voice. "Drop them or you shall all die immediately."

And strolling out into the circle of light came a tall, stiff-backed man dressed in perfect evening clothes and wearing a black domino obscuring the upper half of his face. In his right hand was a smoking 9mm Sabatini automatic.

Begg recognized him immediately. "So it was true," he murmured. "I have been guilty of underestimating you, mein herr. I knew that if Monsieur Zenith was not helping this gang, it had to be someone equally knowledgeable in the ways of the multiverse."

The newcomer's thin lips formed a mocking smile of triumph. "You had thought me defeated, Sir Seaton, in the matter of the Corsican Collar. Then your life was saved by my old enemy, your cousin, who calls himself Zenith. But you knew I would return to continue with my quest."

Lowering his revolver, Begg turned at once to Colonel Hitler. "Believe me, if you think to link your interests with this creature's you are mistaken. He will betray you as he has betrayed every other man, woman or spirit whom he has persuaded to act with him. You might know him by another name, but I can tell you his real identity, for he is the master of lies. He is Hieronymous Klosterheim. Some believe him a fallen angel expelled from hell itself, but I know that he was once a member of the Society of Jesus before he was expelled from that order and excommunicated by the Pope himself."

"*Klosterheim!*" Captain Goering's plump features shook with amusement. "What nonsense! This is Herr Johan Cornelius. You would have us believe that we have linked our fortunes with a figure from folklore—the infamous Gaynor the Damned!"

"As he is called in the opera," said Begg quietly, "but Wagner took certain liberties with the old legends, as before him did Milton."

Lapointe, Sinclair and the pale, wounded LeBec all looked at him as if he were mad. They knew the stories from the opera of the enemy of Parsifal, who had sought the Grail and found it, only to be cursed with eternal damnation, to wander the earth until the end of time for the crime of attempting to drink Christ's very blood.

"Drop your weapons, gentlemen, or this time I shoot your colleague in his heart and not his shoulder," was Klosterheim's icy response.

The Nazi colonel himself was now staring a little nervously at the masked man, wondering whether any bargain he might have made with him could possibly still be to his advantage.

Then Mrs. Persson stepped out of the circle and joined Klosterheim, standing close beside him, making it clear she was the fiend's ally.

"It's said that promise of the Grail's power will corrupt even the noblest of human creatures," declared Begg. "Had I realized exactly what we were up against, my friends, I would never have led you here! This will be forever on my conscience."

"Fear not, Sir Seaton," came Klosterheim's hollow, terrible voice. "You will not have to suffer for very much longer. Meanwhile I shall be obliged if you will drop your weapons at your feet."

And as their revolvers clattered down, he uttered a mirthless laugh which echoed endlessly through the vaulted chambers and chilled the blood of all sojourners who heard it.

CHAPTER SIX

The Ultimate Power

Begg felt physically sick standing with his hands raised watching the Nazi gangster gloat over his reversal. He had underestimated not only Hitler and Company but everyone he had opposed. He had been foolish to assume that he alone, save for Mrs. Persson and Monsieur Zenith, knew the secret of the moonbeam roads. He had wanted too badly to trust that pair. Cursing himself for not anticipating his old enemy Klosterheim's ambitions, he refused to believe he might have been forgiven. Almost everyone believed Klosterheim to have met his end in Mirenburg a decade or more earlier. Not that Begg himself had been there to witness the evil eternal's demise. None other than Zenith had given him the information.

From his earliest appearance as a Satanic angel expelled from hell in the myths and legends of the seventeenth century, Klosterheim had been said to die more than once. But his antipathy to Begg's family, or at least the German side of the family, the von Beks, was well known. He had survived one apparent death after another through the years, remaining alive for two reasons only: to kill all who carried the blood of his old enemy, Ulrich von Bek, and to lay his hands upon the Holy Grail and thus control, in his understanding, the very nature of reality. Yet here he was in alliance with Una Persson, Countess von Bek!

Begg had narrowly escaped terrible death at the hands of this near-immortal before, and now there seemed there was no hope of escape at all.

Klosterheim's sunken sockets hid eyes which burned within like the unquenched flames of hell. He pocketed his revolver as the triumphant Nazis trained their own weapons on the detectives. Then the masked man bent and placed his thin lips upon those of Mrs. Persson. Begg was astonished. Klosterheim had never shown warmth, let alone passion, for any creature, least of all a woman. And Mrs. Persson smiled admiringly back at the cadaverous devil with whom she had cast her lot. Colonel Hitler meanwhile glowered jealously, clearly furious that the woman had collaborated with him because Klosterheim had instructed her to do so. Noting all these connections, Begg now believed himself thoroughly outwitted. Was it possible that Zenith was also part of this unholy alliance?

"I cannot believe this of you, Mrs. Persson!" exclaimed Taffy, still shocked and clearly unable to accept this turn of events. Like his colleagues, save the wounded LeBec, his hands were now firmly tied behind his back by Herr Hess. It was just possible that a tear gleamed in his eye. "How can any decent Englishwoman possibly ally herself with such riff-raff?"

"Oh, I think you'll find it's quite commonly done, Dr. Sinclair." Mrs. Persson seemed partially drunk as she leaned against the gaunt skeleton who was not only her ally but apparently also her master, perhaps even her paramour. "We women are silly creatures, eh, thoroughly addicted to powerful men? There's a larger interest here which I'm sure you'll appreciate. Very few of us are privileged to know one of Satan's very own angels . . ."

Sinclair, his mouth set in a hard, disapproving line, was frozen in horror, completely incapable of a response.

The Nazis began to herd their captives back towards the moonbeam roads.

"We await only Count Zenith," chuckled Captain Goering, "and our plan will be complete. On Saturday, the *Hindenburg* brings the Jewish Palestinian deputation from America to Munich. They intend to discuss an obscenity with Comrade von Hugenberg, chairman of the Munich Supreme Soviet—the establishment of a new Jewish state in the Bavarian lake district! Can you imagine a worse insult to our Christian community? But it will never take place. Our man Zenith will introduce a bomb on board while the *Hindenburg* refuels overnight at the Eiffel Tower in Paris. He will take the Star of Judea as his payment. The Jews intend to use that priceless emerald as downpayment for the land they buy from the treacherous Bavarian soviet. The *Hindenburg* will blow up, and the French will be blamed for their sabotage. A wedge is thereby driven between the various allies. Jews, Frenchmen and Bavarian communists will all be implicated by the British and Americans. Chaos will ensue. Meanwhile, we will be prepared, as soon as news of the *Hindenburg*'s destruction comes through, to announce a new National Socialist Bavarian state. The Freikorps will already have passed through the Eagle Gate and be crossing the moonbeam roads into the Arcades of the Opera, a stone's throw from the Arc de Triomphe. We shall announce our victory there. Our guns will by that time command the whole of Paris. Germans will rise to our victorious standard, and this time the British and French will find it impossible to subdue us. Paris will already be hostage to our cannon!"

"But this is madness!" gasped Lapointe. "All you will succeed in doing is harming hundreds of innocent people. You *will* be defeated again. Your logic is entirely flawed, Captain Goering."

"Nonsense. You are addressing the cream of the Nazi élite!" barked Herr Goebbels. "Our plan is flawless!"

"Has Herr Klosterheim talked you into this?" asked LeBec through gritted teeth. His wound had, for the moment, stopped bleeding. He assured his friends that it was only a superficial flesh wound. Slowly the group came to a halt at the very edge of the silvery road through the multiverse.

"We have perfected this plan together with Herr Klosterheim's involvement," said Hess, his strange eyes shifting back and forth from one member of the group to the other. "By Sunday Europe will have accepted the reality of a new Germany. We are already certain that many Frenchmen as well as English aristocrats will flock to our standard!"

"Klosterheim uses you for his own purposes," said Begg quietly. "He has beguiled you, as he has beguiled so many others. He has no interest in reviving Nazi Germany or, indeed, doing anything but gaining control of the Cosmic Balance. Mrs. Persson. You know this to be true!"

"I have no reason to disbelieve him, Sir Seaton." With a giggle the adventuress turned away.

Once again they could hear the rhythmic booming as of a great drum. Some shivered at the sound, waiting at the beginning of the moonbeam roads. Motioning again with their pistols, the Nazis forced Begg and Co. to move ahead. Each second they moved closer to the noise of the great Regulator. And the vision of the multiverse grew more vivid, the roads more vivid and detailed.

The detectives gasped. Once again on every side of them, the distance was filled with glowing silvery roads, twisting in all directions, forming an extraordinary labyrinth. Unconscious of the drama being played between the Nazis and their enemies, travelers walked between a million realities.

"Where are they going, Begg?" muttered Dr. Sinclair.

Klosterheim read the bewilderment in Taffy's eyes. "Do not fear, Doctor. You will soon have the whole of eternity to contemplate this puzzle. Now, move on! There are still more wonders to greet you . . ."

LeBec groaned, feeling himself weakening. He was the only one of the prisoners not to be bound. His injured arm hung limp at his side, and he staunched the blood from his wounded shoulder with his right hand. He seemed dazed, unable to accept the actuality of these events. He looked up through the swirling, scintillating colour which filled the great ether, the shimmering lines of light cutting between them, the distant figures, the immense beauty of it all, then back at the grotesquely grinning uniformed men training their Lugers on the captured detectives.

Behind them, having removed the black diamond mask he affected, Klosterheim stood stock-still. He had wrapped his great cloak around him, as if against a chill, though the temperature was moderate. Within his head cold eyes shifted from face to face, displaying no expression, no empathy, no sense of humanity.

To Begg's certain knowledge, the former priest was virtually indestructible. Like Zenith, like Mrs. Persson herself, he was an eternal, one of those whose longevity was considerably greater than that of an ordinary human being. He was accustomed to life in the semi-infinite. Some said they sustained their long lives by dreaming a thousand years for every day of their ordinary existence and that what we witnessed of them were dream projections rather than the actual person. That most of them lived *for ever* was, in Begg's opinion, debatable. Yet those who had encountered Klosterheim over the centuries had come to believe the tale of his being one of Satan's favourite accomplices until the time when Satan himself sought reconciliation with their former lord. Then, it was said, Klosterheim had turned against Satan, too. As he perceived it, he had been betrayed by the two mightiest masters in his universe. For all his well hidden spirituality, Begg was not a man to accept superstition or supernatural explanation but he certainly entertained the truth in the stories as he stared back at Klosterheim. Begg's own face was expressionless as he considered ways and means of turning the tables on their captors.

Step by remorseless step they moved along the opaque, silvery causeway towards the sonorous booming until at last the road ended abruptly, upon the edge of the void, its silver falling away like mist. For the first time a smile crossed Klosterheim's thin, bloodless lips. And he looked down.

Begg was the first to follow his gaze.

The detective's immediate instinct was to step back. There below them, its blade pointing down into the dancing, obscuring mist, he could see the shape of a gigantic black sword fashioned to resemble a balance, with a cup depending from either arm. Within the metal of the black blade scarlet characters writhed and twisted; the gleaming bejeweled cups moved slowly as they measured the weight of the world's pain. Multicoloured strands of ectoplasm swirled from the bowls. Begg knew instinctively in his soul that once again he did indeed look upon the legendary Cosmic Balance which regulated the entire multiverse, weighing Law and Chaos, good and evil, truth and falsehood, life and death, love and hate, maintaining the equilibrium, and therefore the existence, of all created matter.

Through the great voice of the Balance Klosterheim's cold tones amplified clearly. "If the multiverse has a centre, it is here. I have sought it for many years and across many universes. And you, gentlemen, will have the privilege of seeing it briefly before you die. Indeed," and now he chuckled to himself, "you will *always* see it before you die . . ."

Lapointe interrupted. "You are a dangerous fool, M'sieu Klosterheim, if you believe you can control that symbol of eternal justice. Only God Almighty has the way of altering the scales maintaining the balance between Law and Chaos. What you see is doubtless only one manifestation of the Cosmic Balance. Can you *control* a symbol?"

"Perhaps not," answered the sweet, calm voice of Mrs. Persson. She had turned up the collar of her coat. Framed by her helmet of dark hair, her beautiful, pale, oval face shone with the reflected light of the great scale. Her indigo eyes sparkled with excitement. "But one who gives power to the symbol can sometimes control what it controls . . ."

With an expression of disgust Lapointe turned away. Hitler, Hess, Goering, Röhm and Goebbels had all crowded to the verge of the road to stare down at the great Balance. "All we need now is to set into that hilt the Star of Judea," said the Nazi colonel.

"Which you will not receive until Saturday, as I understand it," said Begg, genuinely puzzled. "Tomorrow?"

Hitler became suddenly alert. He turned brown, questioning eyes to Klosterheim.

"I brought you here where time has no end and no beginning, merely to show you why and for what you will die," declared Klosterheim. "A small offering to the Gods of Chaos who will soon be serving *my* cause."

"But what is the chief price you pay for their compliance?" Begg enquired coolly. "The souls of four mortals could hardly be enough."

"Oh, they are scarcely ordinary mortals. Their crimes have resonated across the entire multiverse. Their souls have far greater weight than yours, Sir Seaton, certainly in that respect. Yet will the Balance accept them? We still await the one who brings us the Star of Judea. The *Hindenburg* docked an hour ago and now stands ready at Eiffel's great mooring mast." Klosterheim's cold voice was amused. "With that great and ancient jewel, I make my true offering and in return shall have control of the Balance."

"How could a mere jewel—any jewel—have value here?" demanded Dr. Sinclair, his eyes half mad with what they had seen.

"The Star of Judea is of immense value to the Lords of Chaos, Taffy," murmured Begg. "They will hugely reward any being who brings it to them, and it will even *seem* to give that being control of the Cosmic Balance. Meanwhile . . ." He noted an opportunity and gestured, drawing the Nazis' attention away from his friends . . .

A revolver suddenly jerked upward in LeBec's left hand. Begg had anticipated this and had been deliberately distracting their captors, giving LeBec time to act. The Frenchman's eyes were a mixture of contempt and pain. "You poor, unimaginative brutes could not imagine one of us owning a second weapon. Throw up your hands and drop your guns, gentlemen."

The startled Germans swung round, staring into the barrel of LeBec's serviceable Hachette .38. They looked from him to Klosterheim to Mrs. Persson. Only the woman found some amusement in this reversal, yet she did not move either to comply or to resist.

At LeBec's demand, Captain Hess drew his elaborate, ornamental dagger from the scabbard at his belt and cut the ropes binding the metatemporal detectives. Reluctantly, he returned their weapons. Hess's deep-set eyes were dreamy, as if he believed himself the victim of an hallucination. Constantly his gaze returned to the great scintillating scales adjusting gently in constant balance, their movement continuing to create the deep booming, the heartbeat of the multiverse.

Klosterheim snarled. "Do you think you can defeat my plans now merely by turning the tables on my servants?" And without warning, arms outstretched, he rushed at Hess and pushed the startled Nazi to the edge of the moonbeam road. Before the detectives could reach him, he shoved again, and this time Hess's awkward arms flailed as he fought to keep his balance. He reached towards Klosterheim, yelling something unintelligible, and then fell backwards.

They all watched him drop, spinning and waving, like a scarecrow, falling, falling, down towards the Balance, passing the swaying beam until he hung frozen in the pulsing light rising from one of the cups. They heard him scream, a high-pitched and terrible noise, and when he had disappeared momentarily into the light, the cup suddenly flared scarlet.

Klosterheim stepped to the edge and watched with an air of satisfaction. "A sign of my good faith, I hope."

Colonel Hitler swore in German. "You bastard! You killed him. You killed my closest friend!"

Klosterheim shrugged. "It is perhaps disputable that he's actually dead, but my master needs blood and souls." He shrugged then. "The Grail—"

"That thing is not the Grail!" growled Röhm. "There cannot be *two* grails!"

Now Klosterheim smiled openly. "Not in *your* mythology, perhaps. But one cup holds the stuff of Chaos, the other holds the stuff of Law. That is what regulates the multiverse. Combined they become the Balance, but remain in constant conflict."

Still cursing Klosterheim, the Nazi colonel reached down and picked up his fallen Luger. In one movement he pointed and pulled the trigger, firing shot after shot into the mocking figure. Again came that cold, humourless chuckle, as Klosterheim spread his arms and looked down at his unwounded body. "I am not so easily killed, you see, Colonel Hitler. How can you take away the soul of a man who does not have one?"

Still Una Persson did not move. She seemed to be waiting for something, perhaps to watch the opposed groups destroy one another. Yet enigmatic amusement continued to glow in her indigo eyes.

Only when Röhm retrieved his own automatic pistol and pointed it at her did her expression change. Begg was sure, eternal though she might be, that she was not invulnerable.

"*Arioch! Arioch! Aid me now!*" called Klosterheim in that leaden voice which seemed to deaden the air it filled.

Chapter Seven

Old Souls

Begg knew he could not kill Klosterheim easily and that the Nazis would soon return their attention to the detectives. He raised his Webley and, taking careful aim, shot Röhm between the eyes. The captain's expression changed from anger to surprise, and then he, too, lost his footing and fell, his body spinning rapidly downwards then stopping suddenly, as if in the grip of some powerful magnetic force which held him spreadeagled and screaming silently in space above the Balance.

Another shot. This time it was Lapointe who sent Captain Goering into the void to hang in the air immediately above the cup which held the weight of Chaos.

"No!" cried Una Persson suddenly. "No! Don't kill them! Not yet! You don't know what you're doing. There is a plan—"

But Begg had no choice, for the malevolent clubfooted Goebbels screamed something about betrayal and turned his gun on her. The Webley's bullet found its target in Goebbels's heart, and another Nazi went down, whirling and shrieking and coming to a sudden halt when embraced by the light from the cup, which now boiled with smokey scarlet and black fumes.

"Sir Seaton!" cried Mrs. Persson. "No more shooting, I beg you! Don't you realize you're aiding Klosterheim. Their souls are already pledged to Chaos. *They* are the blood sacrifice they intended to make of you. One last action and he can use them to destroy everything. Everything!"

Begg was confused. He kept his Webley leveled at the remaining Nazi, the slavering, terrified Hitler who whispered in his lisping Austrian: "She's right. Nothing but harm will come from killing me."

"Then get down on your knees and lock your hands above your head," snapped Begg. Slowly, with every part of his body trembling, Hitler obeyed. Taffy Sinclair knew his old friend well enough to understand that Begg accepted that he had, inadvertently, done Klosterheim's work. The beat of the Balance had changed subtly. Now it was as if they heard a distant wildfire, like the crackling and snapping of burning timber.

Una Persson came to stand beside Begg. He stepped backward quickly as if she threatened him, but her expression was one of mixed anger and fear. "I did not believe you could follow me," she said. "Oh, Seaton, your courage is now likely to lose us the fight—even perhaps destroy the multiverse! Do you understand what this means?"

The massive, swordlike Balance, its cups swaying and groaning, continued to beat and pulse. The light around its hilt was a golden halo surrounding dull metal of a blackness greater than the void. From somewhere below Begg thought he heard the rattle of distant laughter.

Klosterheim's voice joined in the laughter. It was the bleakest, most desolate sound Sir Seaton Begg had ever experienced. He lowered his gun and looked helplessly from Mrs. Persson, to Klosterheim, to the kneeling, gibbering Hitler and to his friends.

"By Jupiter!" he whispered as realization dawned. "Oh, my good Lord! What have I done?"

The booming of the great Balance had now taken on yet another different, arrhythmic note. Under its deep, masculine throb, Begg thought he could hear the thin screams of the Nazis. The gulf surrounding the not-dead men now boiled vigorously with blood and black smoke.

"We would have mastered creation and moulded it in our desired image until the end of time," wept Hitler. Begg did not care that the sobbing man now lowered his hands and buried his face in them. "Klosterheim! That was what you promised me!"

"Like you, my friend, I have made many promises in my long career." Klosterheim's toneless voice betrayed no emotion. "And like you, Colonel Hitler, I have broken many promises. I helped you and your followers because it suited me. Now you have failed me and it no longer suits. Your actions brought my enemies to me, and we have reached this pass. Only the blood and souls of your colleagues will compensate for your clumsiness." He turned to the metatemporal detective. "My master has his initial sacrifices, thanks to you, Sir Seaton. Now he will come to my aid, as he promised . . ."

Begg could not disguise his own self-disgust. He was about to speak when a new voice, light and mocking, sounded from out of the scarlet mist behind them. He recognized the voice at once.

"Oh, do not count on Lord Arioch turning up just yet, Herr Klosterheim." The newcomer's tone held a kind of courage which could belong, Begg knew, only to one man. He looked in surprise back down the road which had brought them here. Strolling towards them, swinging his cane, for all the world as if he were still the insouciant flaneur of the Arcades de l'Opera in full evening dress, including a silk-lined cape and a silk hat, came Monsieur Zenith. "Good evening, gentlemen." He lifted his top hat. "Mrs. Persson. This is not quite the scene I imagined I would find. Where are Herr Hitler's friends?"

"I fear they have become at least a potential blood offering to whatever demon of Chaos Hieronymous Klosterheim obeys," replied Begg in chastened tones. "I believe I have made the greatest mistake of my life. Can it possibly be reversed, cousin?"

The elegant boulevardier paused and selected one of his opium cigarettes from his slender, silver case. He lit it with an equally elegant silver Dunhill. "I must be truthful with you, Sir Seaton. I am not sure.

Theoretically, if Chaos or Law achieves total ascendancy, then time stops. Like those fellows down there, we shall be frozen for ever at the moment before our deaths. Scarcely a palatable fate."

"Indeed." Begg looked around him and then at the great Balance below. "What is this gem they said you'd steal?"

"It is already stolen." Zenith smiled to himself. "That is what brought me here. I possessed it before the ship ever left Jerusalem. Their perception of time remains, as ever, very crude. The gem emits both light and vibrations and acts as a kind of compass. Madame Persson understood this, I believe? It was what we discussed before the situation grew less controllable. My objective remains the Da Vinci in the Louvre, which I expected to possess by now. They have absolutely no right to it, you know. I had not reckoned, however, on Herr Klosterheim's involvement. The rules of this game seem to be constantly changing. I underestimated its nature. Madame Persson suggested . . ."

"I regret that I misled you a little, old friend." Mrs. Persson still stood close to the expressionless Klosterheim. "Self-interest sometimes demands a fresh strategy. A new reality."

"The Nazis continue to be useful," said Klosterheim. "Whether their souls go to Chaos or their bodies serve my cause matters not. Like all women, Mrs. Persson understands where her loyalties are best placed."

"Great Heavens, man! Does life have no value to you?" Taffy Sinclair broke away from his fellow investigators and strode towards the cadaverous creature. "How on earth can you allow such infamy?"

Klosterheim's dreadful laughter echoed into the void. "You speak to one who has defied both God and Lucifer and now stands ready to challenge their mastery of reality itself. I am not the first to try. But I shall be the first to succeed."

"Such confidence is reassuring in these uncertain times." Zenith seemed amused. "I envy you, Herr Klosterheim. When do you expect my lord Arioch?"

"He will arrive imminently. He gave his word." Klosterheim turned those hollow eyes on the albino. "He shares my impatience as well as my ambition."

"Some would say he is already with us." Monsieur Zenith motioned with his swordstick. Klosterheim's eyes followed its direction as if he thought Zenith pointed out the powerful Chaos Lord, but he saw nothing but the Balance below and four bodies suspended above one of the cups, an instant from being absorbed into the cause of Entropy.

Behind Begg, Commissaire Lapointe was forcing Hitler to his feet and handcuffing him. "It is my duty, gentlemen, to get this fellow back to the authorities in Berlin. As to the rest of the matter, I fear it is far beyond my competence. So if you will permit me . . ." He began rapidly to push the whimpering insurgent colonel ahead of him, followed by his wounded assistant whose expression was one of regret and embarrassment. "Duty demands," said LeBec.

"Of course," agreed Begg, "I have no objection. Were the situation a little less complicated, I would be with you. Can you find your own way back?"

"I think so. With good fortune we will meet again in Paris very shortly."

"You may count on it, Commissionaire." Monsieur Zenith bowed and again raised his hat. "I will take the most conscientious care of your colleague."

Herr Klosterheim however was having none of this. "I cannot permit *any* of you to leave. Not now. Your souls are the price of my success." When LeBec's pistol was again aimed at his chest he let out an explosive guffaw. "Oh, fire away, my dear policeman. Have you any idea how many times I have been killed by the likes of you. Your lives are mine, just as these others belong to me. All are promised to my patron . . ."

"My dear Klosterheim," drawled Zenith, "are you truly so ignorant of the change in your situation that you believe you can threaten these good officers and stop them performing their duty? I believe the clinical term for your condition is 'denial.' You no longer possess any power to speak of." And, smiling, he pressed a silver stud in his ebony cane and swiftly withdrew the slender blade.

The sword now in Zenith's hand was actually darker than the ebony which had contained it. Along its slim length writhed bloody scarlet characters, the runes of some long-forgotten lexicon. Sinclair turned to question Begg and to his astonishment saw his colleague laughing and holding his Webley so loosely in his hand that it threatened to fall into the void.

"Aha!" exclaimed Begg, almost in delight. "Here is your sought-for demonic aid, my dear Klosterheim! What a jest! What a jest!" He stepped back as his cousin advanced holding before him the thrumming épée now crying with its own voice. Bewildered at last, Klosterheim looked from Mrs. Persson to Zenith to the sword.

"Mrs. Persson, you assured me . . ."

"I told you that the black broadsword you call Stormbringer was no longer in Monsieur Zenith's possession. I said nothing of any other blade perhaps bearing similar characteristics, which he finds convenient to carry in a more modern form under a different name." The Englishwoman grinned like a lioness who had just made a kill. "You must know, Herr Klosterheim, that just as the wielder of the sword takes many guises, so does the sword itself. And even the creature which inhabits the sword has more than one identity!"

She stepped aside as Klosterheim began to back away from the advancing albino. "I shall not be threatened, Monsieur! Arioch! Lord Arioch of the Seven Darks! Aid me, I beg thee. Arioch, thou promised me . . ."

"Lord Arioch's promises are of a practical and volatile nature, also," declared Zenith, the slender sword still pointed at Klosterheim's throat. "It surprises me that you did not consider this when laying out your equation for this particular adventure."

"But you forget, monsieur. That blade and your master feed on souls as well as blood." Klosterheim's smile was bitterly sardonic. "Nein?" With a quavering laugh, somehow even more disgusting than any of his previous expressions, he folded his arms and challenged Zenith to stab him.

If anything, the albino's smile stilled the onlookers' blood more than the other eternal's laughter. Without hesitation, Monsieur Zenith lunged forward in an elegant fencer's position, and his delicate, black blade took Klosterheim in the throat.

For a second the ex-priest continued to laugh . . . and then his eyes widened. He clutched at his neck, at the shivering blade . . . He gasped. He groaned. He staggered backwards towards the very edge of the moonbeam road and hung there, swaying, as blood bubbled from the wound Zenith had made. "Nein!" he said again, this time with fear. "Nein!"

He realized suddenly where he stood and attempted to regain his balance, but it was too late. His deep-set eyes burned with terror, lighting his cadaverous head with an unholy fire. Begg and the others were uncertain what emotion they witnessed, but they all agreed that it *was* emotion.

"How can this be?" Klosterheim spoke in the old, Hoch Deutsch German of his youth. "How—?"

"You forgot, Herr Klosterheim." With a lithe, reverse movement Zenith resheathed the black blade. "My sword is capable of conferring souls as well as stealing them." He stepped forward again, his hand light on Klosterheim's chest, as with two fingers he tipped him gently off into the void above the pulsing Balance. "And only a creature with a human soul, no matter how corrupt, can enjoy that moment of forever, poised between eternity and oblivion, which comes with the end of everything. Meanwhile, I send you to consider that thought for as long as you shall last. Which is, of course, until the end of time."

Klosterheim fell backwards screaming and joined the others whose distant bodies hung in the void, like flies in a web, conscious and frozen in the instant before their deaths.

Monsieur Zenith turned with a bow. Reaching out, he kissed Mrs. Persson's hand. "Well played, madam. Our plan was almost foiled by these good-hearted fellows." He inclined his head towards Begg and Sinclair.

"You two had planned all this?" Sinclair found himself torn between rage and relief. "All of it?"

"Most of it," declared Mrs. Persson, advancing towards the famous pathologist. "Really, Dr. Sinclair, we had no intention of deceiving you or your colleagues. Neither did I expect to be detained by them, so very likely you saved my life by arriving when you did. But from then on, I thought it the best strategy to pretend to ally myself with Klosterheim, at least until Monsieur Zenith made his somewhat belated appearance. We really did not know you would have either the powers of deduction or the sheer courage to reach this place. Then, when you did turn up, I for one was rather baffled. Everything Monsieur Zenith and myself had worked out was threatened." She drew a deep breath. "Happily, as you see—"

"Klosterheim, for all his evil, does not deserve such a fate," declared Begg gravely. "And neither do those others."

"Oh, I assure you, dear cousin, they *do indeed* deserve everything." Zenith looked down into the void to where the great Balance still swayed. "And this affair is probably not yet over, though your part is certainly done." And with a casual flick of his wrist, he threw his swordstick after the man on whom he had just conferred both life and a kind of death. He turned to guide the rest of the party back in the direction from which they had come. "Quickly. The thing that is my sword is not so easily defeated in its ambitions."

Begg hesitated, demurring as Zenith's face became a mask of urgency. "Hurry man! Hurry! If you value your soul!"

From somewhere below there now sounded a voice more terrifying than anything they had yet heard and blossoming upwards they saw a huge, bloody black cloud rising, roiling forward like a wave, which Begg knew must soon engulf them. The noise became deafening, bringing bile to their throats. With some alacrity Begg obeyed his cousin. Grabbing Dr. Sinclair's arm, he turned and ran, the Frenchmen, their prisoner, Mrs. Persson and Zenith the Albino immediately behind him.

As in a powerful earthquake, the moonbeam road quivered and trembled beneath their feet. They ran on, knowing that not only their lives but their eternal souls would be the price of any further hesitation . . .

. . . Until suddenly a deep calm settled over them and a silvery whiteness sprang up ahead, forming a kind of wall. They were once again in the catacombs they had seemingly left behind millennia before.

Monsieur Zenith straightened his silk hat. "I shall miss that cane," he said. "But I know the exact place I can buy another in the Galerie d'Baromètre. Come, Mrs. Persson, gentlemen. Shall we return to the Arcades de l'Opera? I think we have a rather extraordinary adventure to celebrate."

EPILOGUE

His shoulder thoroughly bandaged, LeBec joined the four men and one woman who shared an outside table at L'Albertine the following day. He was received with a round of muted applause and a great sense of celebration as the hero of the hour. "Without you, my dear LeBec, we should perhaps even now be enjoying the fate of our Nazi antagonists. As it is, the arrest of Colonel Hitler took the wind out of the Freikorps insurgents, who were indeed massing to enter the tunnel into Paris. The *Hindenburg* made a successful mooring at the Eiffel Tower and spent a tranquil night there. The Star of Judea was returned, and even now negotiations to found a new Jewish homeland in Bavaria are proceeding. It is fully expected that the exodus to Southern Germany will begin some time towards the end of next year!" Seaton Begg clapped his French colleague on his good shoulder and ordered him an Armagnac.

The autumn sun was rising high in a golden sky, and the great fountain in the centre of the arcade spread dark blue and green sheets of water over the verdigris, marble and tile of the statuary. There was a tranquil, leisurely quality to the day which Begg agreed he had not experienced for some time. The capture of Hitler and his men had created a general euphoria.

"Illusion though it might be, my friends," said Commissaire Lapointe softly, "it seems to me that our world is about to embark upon a new era of peace and prosperity. Call me optimistic, if you will, but I believe our defeat of the Nazi gang achieved something lasting. Do you follow my meaning, Sir Seaton?"

Begg permitted himself a small smile. "We can only hope you are right, my dear commissioner. But you are of another opinion, I think, Taffy?"

Dr. Sinclair did his best to make light of his own thoughts. "It was that balance," he said. "Something going on down there terrified me. And the manner of Klosterheim's death—well, I still have difficulty sleeping when I think about it." He glanced shyly at Monsieur Zenith who leaned back, taking a long puff on his Turkish oval.

"I am sorry you were forced to witness that, Dr. Sinclair. If I had had any other choice, of course I would not have conducted matters in that way. But Klosterheim was the force behind Hitler and his men. He has lived for a very long time. Some will tell you he counseled Martin Luther. Others say he was the angel who stood with Duke Arioch at Lucifer's right hand during the great war in heaven. Having no soul, he was almost impossible to destroy. Thus only by conferring a soul upon him could I kill him. Or, at least, I hope I killed him . . ."

"But I think what is concerning my old friend, Sinclair," interrupted LeBec, "is a very important question."

"Which is?" Zenith seemed genuinely puzzled.

"Taffy and I have both wondered about it." Begg leaned forward to address his cousin. "Our question would be—where did that soul come from? Whose did you use? You can surely see why we would be curious . . ."

"Aha!" Monsieur Zenith turned, laughing, to Mrs. Persson, who clearly knew the answer. She leaned down and petted her two Orientals, who lay, perfectly behaved, at her feet. "I think I will leave that explanation to you, Mrs. Persson."

The exquisitely beautiful adventuress reached for her glass of absinthe. "It was the last soul the sword drank on another plane than this one, n'est-ce pas? It has been many years, if I am not mistaken, since you have unsheathed that particular weapon on this particular plane, eh, Monsieur Zenith?"

"Oh, many. I suppose, my friends, I will let you into a secret I have kept for rather a long time. While I have in the course of the past two thousand years sired children and indeed founded a dynasty which is familiar to anyone who knows the history of the province of Wälden-stein and her capital Mirenburg, I am not truly of this world or indeed this universe. It is fair to say that I have, in the way some of you will know, been dreaming myself. I have another body, as solid as this one, which as I speak lies on a 'dream couch' in a city more ancient than the world it inhabits." He paused in sympathy as he observed their expressions.

"The civilization to which I belong is neither truly human nor of this universe. Its rulers are men and women capable of manipulating the forces of nature and, if you like, super-nature to serve their own ends. People sometimes call them sorcerers. They learn all manner of arcane wisdom by making use of their dream couches, sleeping sometimes for thousands of years while experiencing other lives. Upon waking, they forget most of the dreams save for the skills they employ to rule their world. I am one of those sorcerous aristocrats. The island where I dwell is called, as far as I can pronounce it in your language, Melniboné. We are not natives of its world, either, but were driven to inhabit it during a terrible upheaval which ultimately forced us to become the cruel rulers of another planet.

"The demonic archangel Arioch, upon whom Klosterheim called to aid him, is our people's patron. Both your Bible and the poet Milton mention him. On occasions he inhabits the black blade you saw me use. On other occasions the sword contains the souls of those its wielder has killed. Some parts of those souls are transferred to whoever uses the blade. Other parts go to placate Arioch. When Satan attempted, hundreds of years ago, to be reconciled with God, neither Klosterheim nor Arioch accepted it and have, across many planes of the multiverse, sought not only the destruction of God himself, but also of Satan, or whatever manifestations of his forces exist here."

"You have still not explained whose soul Klosterheim's body drank," pointed out Sinclair.

"Why, the last soul it took," said Monsieur Zenith in some surprise. "I thought that is what you understood."

"And whose was that—?"

Monsieur Zenith rose swiftly and elegantly and kissed Mrs. Persson's hand before moving towards the shelf where he had placed his silk hat and gloves. "You must forgive me, gentlemen. I have some unfinished business nearby."

Instinctively Commissionaire Lapointe was on his feet as if to apprehend him but then caught himself and sat down again quickly.

Sir Seaton Begg, with dawning comprehension, laid his hand on his old friend's arm, but Taffy Sinclair was insistent. "Whose, Monsieur Zenith? Whose?"

Zenith the Albino slipped gracefully from the table and in a moment seemed to disappear, merging with the sunlit spray of the fountain.

"But whose . . . ?" Sinclair turned a baffled glance at Mrs. Persson who had lifted her two cats into her lap and was stroking them gently. "Do you know?"

She inclined her head, raised her perfectly shaped eyebrows, and looked intimately at Sir Seaton Begg, whose nod was scarcely perceptible.

"It was his own, of course."

ELRIC:
A PERSONALITY AT WAR

ELRIC: A PERSONALITY AT WAR
(2008)

I CAME TO ELRIC relatively late in life, picking up a copy of the Fantasy Masterworks edition for the first time at the age of forty-three.

As I ploughed into "The Dreaming City" I began to feel that my first foray into the Moorcock Multiverse might not work out. Sword-wielding barbarian warriors have become something of a fantasy cliché, and the whole treatment seemed a little, well, derivative. It was only when I checked the publication date that I realized "The Dreaming City" was published in 1961, over forty-seven years ago! In other words it predates many other fantasy books that are now such established parts of the mainstream.

In time I realized that I was reading a work that had spawned so many pale imitations that some elements of Elric's world had almost become clichés. Once I realized this I was able to clear my mind and read on with a fresh palate, allowing the story to speak for itself.

In creating Elric, Moorcock did not pander to the reader's feelings. He is a hard character to like initially, but deeply fascinating nonetheless. He is a beguiling mixture of the vulnerable, heroic, and tragic, and your attachment to him grows almost imperceptibly as you turn the pages.

In a strange sense, Elric and his sword, Stormbringer, together represent a dysfunctional compound personality, unable to exist when separated but in constant conflict. In Freudian terms Elric represents a complex combination of ego and superego, and Stormbringer the id.

The id is a key element of our personality because it ensures that our basic needs are fulfilled from the moment of birth though our formative years. Sigmund Freud believed that the id operates purely on the pleasure principle. The id wants whatever feels good at that instant without consideration for morality or the potential consequences.

Acting as a metaphor for the id, Stormbringer's unquenchable desire to bury itself in the flesh of both men and women drives Elric from the outset.

Interestingly, in chapter nine of *The Psychopathology of Everyday Life* (1901), Freud comments on the significance of the sword as a metaphor for a phallus. Moorcock's narrative documents Elric's losing battle with the powerful yet destructive urges of his sword/phallus, driven on by his id. The metaphor becomes quite explicit when the girl he loves dies "screaming on the point of Stormbringer" at the end of chapter three of "The Dreaming City."

Within the first three years of life, a child interacts more and more with the family and the second part of the personality begins to develop. Freud called this the ego. The ego operates on the reality principle. The ego recognizes that other people are fragile and that sometimes being impulsive, selfish, or destructive can be destructive to them, and also to our best interests in the longer term.

Throughout the Elric saga the hero constantly struggles to meet the needs of Stormbringer (the id) in a controlled way, attempting to minimize the damage to those he cares for.

By the age of five the superego develops. The superego or conscience drives us to conform to the laws, moral and ethical restraints placed on us by our caregivers and society. If necessary this drives us to behave in ways that run counter to our desires and can even harm our self-interest in real terms.

In a healthy person, according to Freud, the ego needs to be the strongest element of the personality so that it can satisfy the needs of the id while striking compromises with the superego to reflect the practical realities of life. Not an easy job by any means. However, if the id becomes too dominant, impulses and self-gratification take over the person's life. As the stories make quite clear, Elric is not a healthy person, and he loses the battle with the demands of his id many times.

It is Elric's weak ego that wins over the reader's sympathies and gives him his odd quality of vulnerability. We all know how hard it is to resist the insistent cravings of habitual pleasures.

As I followed Elric through the six books that make up this volume there were sections which reminded me of Arthurian legend and other elements reminiscent of Norse mythology. However, what sets the Elric saga apart from action fiction of any period is the extent of the underpinning philosophical thought that evidently went into executing the war between the forces of Law and Chaos and its outcome.

In a sense two parallel wars develop and are fought throughout the saga. One is the external war between Law and Chaos and the other is the parallel internal conflict within Elric's personality.

As the system of checks and balances that stabilize the cosmos fail and the Lords of Law and Chaos clash in increasingly bitter conflict, Elric's ego is increasingly losing the strength needed to successfully mediate the conflicting demands of his superego (the drive for moral law) and his rampaging id (the drive for moral chaos), culminating in the climactic final pages of *Stormbringer*.

In the closing paragraphs, cosmic balance is preserved because external victory for the Lords of Law is immediately offset by the internal collapse of Elric's ego and defeat of his superego. This results in total breakdown and "his whole personality being drawn into the runesword."

As the story concludes, Elric is left "a sprawled husk" while his id spears onwards and upwards. I can imagine Freud smiling knowingly at this final tour de force of phallic symbolism in a seminal work by an author called *Moorcock*.

Adrian Snook

ORIGINS

*Early artwork associated with Elric's first appearances
in magazines and books*

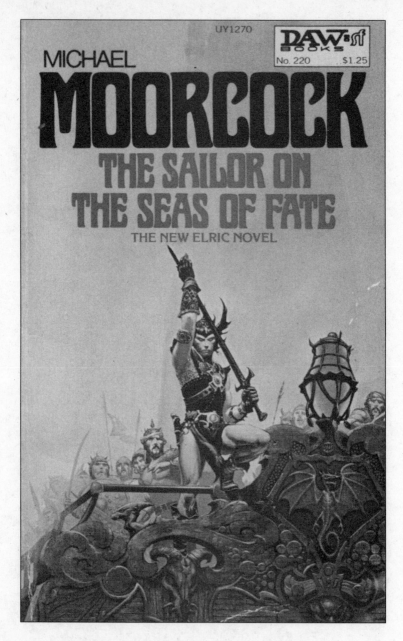

UY1270

DAW sf
BOOKS
No. 220 $1.25

MICHAEL
MOORCOCK
THE SAILOR ON THE SEAS OF FATE
THE NEW ELRIC NOVEL

Cover artwork by Michael Whelan, for *The Sailor on the Seas of Fate,* first American edition, DAW Books, 1976.

"Sailor on the Seas of Fate: Book Two: No. 3," by James Cawthorn, believed drawn circa 1979 for *Die See des Schicksals,* Heyne, Germany, and previously unpublished.

Cover artwork by Dalmazio Frau, for *The Sailor on the Seas of Fate,* first audiobook edition, AudioRealms, 2006.

Michael Moorcock's Multiverse published by DC Comics.

A page from "Duke Elric," by John Ridgway (written by Moorcock), for *Michael Moorcock's Multiverse,* DC Comics preview, 1997.

Michael Moorcock's Multiverse published by DC Comics.

Cover artwork by Walter Simonson, for *Michael Moorcock's Multiverse,* DC Comics, 1999.

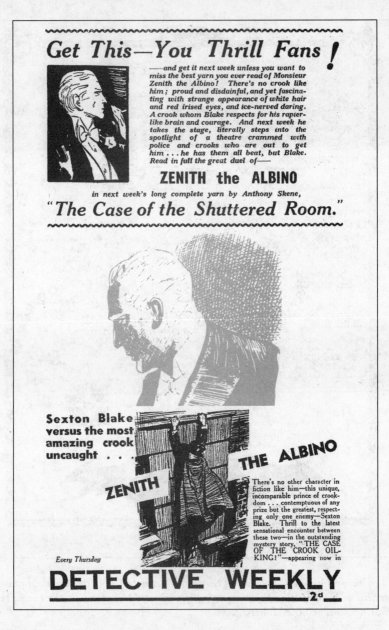

A "Zenith the Albino" advertisement collage, designed by John Coulthart, for *Monsieur Zenith the Albino,* Savoy Books, 2001.

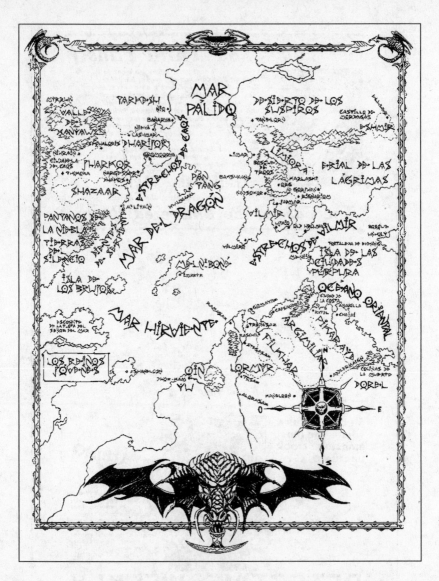

"Los Reinos Jóvenes" ("The Young Kingdoms") map by Carlos de Miguel, appeared in *Elric de Melniboné/La Fortaleza de la Perla* (*Elric of Melniboné/The Fortress of the Pearl*), Spanish edition, Edhasa, 2006.

Cover artwork by Patrick Woodroffe, for *The Sailor on the Seas of Fate,* first edition, Quartet Books, 1976.

For further information about Michael Moorcock and his work,
please send a stamped, self-addressed envelope to:

The Nomads of the Time Streams
P.O. Box 385716
Waikoloa, HI 96738

ABOUT THE AUTHOR

Michael John Moorcock is the author of a number of science fiction, fantasy, and literary novels, including the Elric novels, the Cornelius Quartet, *Gloriana, King of the City,* and many more. As editor of the controversial British science fiction magazine *New Worlds,* Moorcock fostered the development of the New Wave in the U.K. and indirectly in the U.S. He won the Nebula Award for his novella *Behold the Man.* He has also won the World Fantasy Award, the British Fantasy Award, and many others.

ABOUT THE ILLUSTRATOR

Chesley Award–winning artist JUSTIN SWEET has worked on video games, books, films, and card art for such clients as Disney, Universal Studios, Wizards of the Coast, Tor, Del Rey, and many more. He worked as a concept artist on the films *The Lion, the Witch, and the Wardobe* and *Prince Caspian*. He lives in Orange County, California, with his family.